Eduard Müller

The Dhammasangani

Edited by Edward Müller

Eduard Müller

The Dhammasangani
Edited by Edward Müller

ISBN/EAN: 9783337396718

Printed in Europe, USA, Canada, Australia, Japan

Cover: Foto ©Andreas Hilbeck / pixelio.de

More available books at **www.hansebooks.com**

Pali Text Society.

THE

DHAMMASAṄGAṆI.

EDITED BY

EDWARD MÜLLER, PH.D.

LONDON:
PUBLISHED FOR THE PALI TEXT SOCIETY.
BY HENRY FROWDE.
OXFORD UNIVERSITY PRESS WAREHOUSE, AMEN CORNER, E.C.

1885.

INTRODUCTION.

In editing the Dhammasaṅgaṇi I used a copy made for the Pâḷi Text Society by Dr. O. Frankfurter from a Burmese manuscript in the possession of the India Office, and besides a Sinhalese manuscript from the Vanavâsa Vihâra in Bentoṭa, Ceylon. Although both these manuscripts are not very correct, I believe that my text will be found comparatively free from mistakes, as the frequent repetition of words, sentences and paragraphs throughout the book enabled me to control each passage by one or several others.

In order to facilitate the use of the book, the questions have been numbered, and, besides, an alphabetical index of words has been added at the end, which contains every word with the first and one or two more passages where it occurs, but does *not* pretend to give *all* the passages. Words like dhamma, rûpa and others, which occur almost in every paragraph, have been wholly omitted.

The principal part of the Dhammasaṅgaṇi comprises the questions 1–1367, and of this part alone a summary is given in the so-called Mâtikâ at the beginning of the book. The second part, questions 1368–1599, contains a mere recapitulation of the most important paragraphs in the first part sometimes verbo tenus, as, for instance, 1014 = 1398, 1016 = 1400, 1017 = 1401, but more often with slight modifications. The terminus technicus asaṅkhatâ dhâtu 'the immaterial element,' which occurs frequently in the first part, is always replaced by nibbâna in the second; thus, for instance, in No. 1018 we have sabbañ ca rûpaṃ asaṅkhatâ ca dhâtu, while the corresponding question 1402 has rûpañ ca nibbânañ ca.

The first part begins with the question katame dhammâ kusalâ, and in this very first question a sort of programme is given containing all the subjects dealt with in the questions up to No. 57. This paragraph is thus translated by Gogerly in the "Ceylon Friend" for 1874, p. 21:—"If at any time a virtuous disposition be brought into existence in the worlds of desire, pleasing and according to wisdom, with reference to objects of corporeal form, of sounds, of odours, of flavour, of touch or of mind, or with reference to anything of any kind; at that time there is contact, sensation, perception, thought, mind, reflection, investigation, joy, happiness, mental excitement; the sense of faith, perseverance, thoughtfulness, tranquillity, wisdom, intellectuality, pleasure, and of life. There are orthodoxy in opinion, correct reasoning, holy conversation, etc., etc., or whatever other mental sensation may be produced, these are virtuous actions."

All these subjects are explained in the answers to questions 2–57. With No. 58 a new section opens. The subjects dealt with in this and the following paragraphs are:

1) The four khandhas or 'aggregates,' viz. vedanâ 'sensations,' saññâ 'perceptions,' saṅkhârâ 'confections,' viññânaṃ 'consciousness.'[1] 59–63.

[1] In other texts we always meet with five khandhâs, rûpakkhandha 'material form,' being the first; see, for instance, Dharmasaṅgraha, No. XXII., Abhidhammatthasaṅgraha VII. 8. In the Dhammasaṅgaṇi the five khandhas are mentioned for the first time at No. 1083.

2) The two âyatanas or 'objects of sense.'[1] Nos. 64-66.

3) The two dhâtus or 'principles.'[2] 67-69.

4) The three âhâras or 'nutriments.' 70-73.[3]

5) The eight indriyas or 'moral qualities.' 74-82.[4]

6) The five-fold meditation. 83-88.[5]

7) The five-fold path. 89-94.[6]

8) The seven forces. 95-102.[7]

9) The three motives. 103-106.[8]

In Nos. 121-145 the same subjects are repeated, omitting only the numbers of the khandhas, âyatanas, dhâtus, etc. At the end of No. 147 we have again a repetition of the same subjects, but with different numbers, viz. seven indriyas,

---

[1] Other texts mention twelve âyatanas, of which the manâyatanaṃ is the sixth, and the dhammâyatanaṃ the twelfth. See Dharmasaṅgraha XXIV. and Dhammasaṅgaṇi 1335.

[2] Other texts give eighteen dhâtus, of which the dhammadhâtu and manoviññâṇadhâtu are the seventeenth and eighteenth respectively. See Dharmasaṅgraha XXV., Abhidhammatthasaṅgraha VII. 8, and Dhammasaṅgaṇi 1333.

[3] Other texts give four âhâras, viz. in addition to those given here, the kabaliṅkâra âhâra; this will be found later on in No. 585, 646, 653, 816, etc. See Dharmasaṅgraha LXX., Abhidhammatthasaṅgraha VII. 4.

[4] The number of indriyas given in other texts is generally five, see Dharmasaṅgraha XLVII., Aṅguttara-Nikâya I. xxvii. 5. Abhidhammatthasaṅgraha VII. 4, however, has 22.

[5] Dharmasaṅgraha LXXII. has only four stages of meditation, but Abhidhammatthasaṅgraha VII. has seven.

[6] This comprises: sammâdiṭṭhi 'right views,' sammâsaṅkappa 'right aims,' sammâvâyâma 'perseverance in well-doing,' sammâsati 'intellectual activity,' sammâsamâdhi 'earnest meditation.' Besides these there are three more divisions of the 'noble eight-fold path,' as it is called in other texts, viz. sammâvâcâ 'right speech,' sammâkammanta 'right conduct,' sammâ-âjîva 'right livelihood'; those are not mentioned here, but form Nos. 299-301 of the Dhammasaṅgaṇi. See Dharmasaṅgraha L., and Frankfurter in the Journal of the Royal Asiatic Society, xii. 555.

[7] Other texts have only five balas, omitting hiribala and ottappabala; see Dharmasaṅgraha XLVIII. Aṅguttara-Nikâya I. xxvii. 5, omits also satibala. Abhidhammatthasaṅgraha VII. 4, has nine balas.

[8] The hetus are not mentioned in any other text except Abhidhammatthasaṅgraha VII. 4, where we find six. See Dhammasaṅgaṇi Nos. 1053-1082.

the four-fold path, six balas, two hetus, while in No. 154 we have a four-fold meditation and a five-fold path, and in 157 a four-fold meditation and a four-fold path. Later on, in No. 358 (528, 552), we have the lokuttara magga, lokuttara satipaṭṭhâna, lokuttara iddhipâda, lokuttara indriya, bala, bojjhaṅga, etc. The satta bojjhaṅgâ 'seven kinds of wisdom' are mentioned in No. 1355. See Dharmasaṅgraha XLIV., XLV., XLVIII.

The terminology in the answers of Nos. 160 and 161, Yasmiṃ samaye rûpûpapattiyâ maggaṃ bhâveti vivicc' eva kâmehi etc., and Yasmiṃ samaye rûpûpapattiyâ maggaṃ bhâveti vitakkavicârânaṃ vûpasamâ etc., seems to be a common one in Abhidhamma and other books, as we meet with it again in the Aṅguttara-Nikâya II. 2, 3, and Puggala-Paññatti, p. 59. The same may be said about the terminology in Nos. 204 ff., which is almost identical with Aṅguttara-Nikâya I. xxvii. 8, and Mahânidânasutta ap. Grimblot, Sept Suttas Pâlis, p. 261. Nos. 244–247 correspond to the passage in the Mahâparinibbânasutta, ed. Childers, p. 30, beginning: Aṭṭha kho imâni Ânanda abhibhâyatanâni katamâni aṭṭha? 'Now these, Ânanda are the eight positions of mastery. What are the eight?'[1] Nos. 248–250 correspond to the first three of the eight vimokkhas in Mahâparinibbânasutta, p. 32:[2] Rûpî rûpâni passati, 'A man possessed with the idea of forms sees forms.' Ajjhattaṃ arûpasaññî bahiddhâ rûpâni passati, 'Without the subjective idea of form, he sees forms externally.' Subhanti [eva adhimutto hoti], 'With the thought "it is well" he becomes intent.' The 4th–7th

[1] Rhys Davids' translation in Sacred Books, XI. 51 f. The expressions uddhumâtakasaññâsahagata, etc., in Nos. 263 and 264, occur again in Abhidhammatthasaṅgraha IX. 2.

[2] See Dharmasaṅgraha LIX.

vimokkha are contained in Nos. 265–268; the 8th is missing in the Dhammasaṅgaṇi.

At No. 365 begins the chapter about the akusalâ dhammâ. The answer to the introductory question is very nearly the same as that of No. 1, only with this difference, that, instead of ñânasampayuttaṃ, we have here diṭṭhigatasampayuttaṃ; further, instead of sammâdiṭṭhi, sammâsaṅkappo, sammâvâyâmo, sammâsamâdhi, we have respectively micchâdiṭṭhi, micchâsaṅkappo, micchâvâyâmo, micchâsamâdhi; instead of hiribalaṃ and ottappabalaṃ, ahirikabalam and anottappabalaṃ; instead of alobho, adoso and amoho, lobho, doso and moho, etc.

The answers to the questions from 366–397 generally correspond to those from 2–57 mutatis mutandis. No. 381 occurs also at Puggala-Paññatti II. 9, in answer to the question, Tattha katamâ diṭṭhivipatti? and No. 390 at Puggala-Paññatti II. 8, in answer to the question, Tattha katamaṃ asampajaññaṃ?

The third chapter, containing the avyâkatâ dhammâ, begins at No. 431. Here again we have a repetition of the terms phasso, vedanâ, saññâ, cetanâ, cittaṃ, upekkhâ, cittass' ekaggatâ, manindriyaṃ, upekkhindriyaṃ, jîvitindriyaṃ, to which are added, in No. 443, sukhaṃ and sukhindriyaṃ, and, in No. 455, vitakko and vicâro.

No. 584 introduces a new subject: Tattha katamaṃ sabbaṃ rûpam? to which the answer is given: Cattâro ca mahâbhûtâ catunnañ ca mahâbhûtânaṃ upâdâyarûpaṃ. This corresponds to the Abhidhammatthasaṅgraha VI. 2, where we read: Cattâri mahâbhûtâni catunnaṃ ca mahâbhûtânam upâdârûpaṃ. The sabbaṃ rûpaṃ consists of twenty-eight subdivisions, of which the first four are called bhûtarûpaṃ 'elementary matter,' and the remainder upâdâyarûpaṃ 'accidental matter.' The four mahâbhûtas are paṭhavidhâtu, âpodhâtu, tejodhâtu, vâyodhâtu (see No. 588, and Dharmasaṅgraha XXVI. and XXXIX.); and of the twenty-four upâdâs, twenty-three are given in No. 596. The list as quoted by Childers, *s.v.* Rûpa, from the Visuddhimagga, contains one more, viz. hadayavatthu, and the one given by Hardy, Manual of Buddhism, p. 414, inserts the phoṭṭhabbâyatanaṃ after the rasâyatanaṃ, but omits the kabaḷiṅkâro âhâro at the end.

The latter part of No. 584 is identical with No. 595. The following paragraphs, beginning with duvidhena rûpasaṅgaho, tividhena rûpasaṅgaho, etc., contain each the programme for a number of paragraphs in the sequel. The following list will show this:

No. 585	contains the	programme for Nos.	596—741.
No. 586	,,	,,	742—876.
No. 587	,,	,,	877—961.
No. 588	,,	,,	962—966.
No. 589	,,	,,	967.
No. 590	,,	,,	968—69.
No. 591	,,	,,	970.
No. 592	,,	,,	971—73.
No. 593	,,	,,	974—77.
No. 594	,,	,,	978—80.

More especially Nos. 596–646 give an explanation of the twenty-three constituents of the upâdârûpaṃ, 647–652 of the phoṭṭhabbâyatanaṃ (which is considered here as a constituent of the rûpaṃ no upâdâ, see above, p. ix), and of the âpodhâtu.

The chapter concerning rûpaṃ closes at No. 980, after which the discussion about the dhammas is taken up again. The question about the pleasant, unpleasant, and indifferent sensation in Nos. 984–986, occurs again in the Mahânidânasutta, ed. Grimblot, p. 257. No. 1002 brings the three saññojanas or 'fetters,' viz. sakkâyadiṭṭhi 'delusion of self,' vicikicchâ 'doubt,' and sîlabbataparâmâsa 'dependence on rites.'[1] Sakkâyadiṭṭhi may be held in twenty different ways, which is confirmed by the Saṃyutta-Nikâya, see Alwis, Nirvâna, p. 72.

Nos. 1053–1082 deal with the hetus. We have three kusalahetus or 'meritorious actions,' three akusalahetus, viz. lobho, doso, moho, and three avyâkatahetus. A parallel passage occurs in Abhidhammatthasaṅgraha III. 4, 5.

No. 1096 begins the chapter of the four âsavas or 'passions,' viz. kâmâsavo 'sensual pleasure,' bhavâsavo 'lust after life,' diṭṭhâsavo 'delusion,' avijjâsavo 'ignorance.' No. 1099 is identical with a passage of the Brahmajâlasutta ap. Grimblot, p. 36, and is also found in the Mahânidânasutta, p. 259.

Nos. 1113–1134 deal with the ten saññojanas, viz. besides the three mentioned in 980, seven more. The list given here does not quite correspond with the one drawn up by Childers, *s.v.* Saññojana, as, instead of rûparâgasaññojana, arûparâgasaññojana, uddhaccasaññojana, we have bhavarâgasaññojana, issâsaññojana, macchariyasaññojana. The last two we find mentioned in the Dharmasaṅgraha, No. LXIX., among the caturviṅçatir upakleçâḥ or 'twenty-four minor evil passions.' Both lists are given in the Abhidhammatthasaṅgraha VII. 2, the second with the addition abhidhamme, which shows that it belongs especially to the Abhidhamma books. Nos. 1121 and 1122 are identical with Puggala-Paññatti II. 3.

The next chapter, 1135–1150, is about the ganthas, then follow the oghas, yogas, and nîvaraṇas, 1152–1173. The number of the oghas and yogas is not given here, but we

---

[1] Compare also the pañca drishṭayaḥ, Dharmasaṅgraha LXVIII.

learn from Abhidhammatthasaṅgraha that there are four of each kind corresponding to the four âsavas (see above, p. xi). All these seem to be expressions belonging only to the terminology of the Abhidhamma texts, as we do not find them elsewhere.

Diṭṭhiparâmâsa is one of the pañca dṛishṭayaḥ, Dharmasaṅgraha LXVIII.

No. 1213 brings the four upâdanas: kâmupâdâna 'sensuality,' diṭṭhupâdâna 'delusion about the soul,' sîlabbatupâdâna 'ritualism,' attavâdupâdâna 'delusion of self,' and No. 1229 the ten kilesas: 'greed, hatred, pride, ignorance, heresy, doubt, idleness, vanity, impudence, recklessness.'

Question 1296, which is identical with 1599, closes the section of the Dhammasaṅgaṇi, which is repeated in an abbreviated form in the second part (Nos. 1368—1599). The questions 1297—1367 are not repeated any more afterwards.

The terms adhivacanapatha, niruttipatha, paññattipatha, in Nos. 1306, 1307, 1308, occur again in the Mahânidânasutta, ed. Grimblot, p. 255, where they are translated 'qui ouvre la voie de la dénomination, de la désignation, de l'indication.'

No. 1309 introduces a new collective term for the four khandhas already mentioned at No. 59 (see above, p. vi), viz. nâma, and No. 1310 supplies the fifth khandha, viz. rûpa.[1]

From 1313 to 1320 some of the diṭṭhis or heresies are mentioned, as the sassatadiṭṭhi, the belief that the world is everlasting, which belief, according to the Mahâvaṃsa, originated as early as the time of king Devânampiya Tissa; and its contrary, the ucchedadiṭṭhi.[2]

[1] Parallel passages from the Sammâdiṭṭhi-suttanta, Vibhaṅga and Nettipakaraṇa are quoted by Oldenberg, "Buddha," p. 450.

[2] See Rhys Davids' note, "Sacred Books," xi. 149.

Nos. 1325 and 1326 are identical with Puggala-Paññatti II. 6; Nos. 1327 and 1328 with Puggala-Paññatti II. 16. In No. 1336 we have the paṭiccasamuppâda or 'chain of causation' composed of the twelve nidânas, one of the fundamental doctrines of Buddhism, comp. Dharmasaṅgraha XLII.

The second part of No. 1343 occurs again in a passage of the Puggala-Paññatti, p. 57 of Dr. Morris's edition; 1345 and 1346 are identical with Puggala-Paññatti II. 7, 1347 with Puggala-Paññatti II. 17 (repeated IV. 24, p. 58), and a passage of the Sâmaññaphalasutta ap. Grimblot, Sept Suttas Pâlis, p. 135; 1348 again with the second part of Puggala-Paññatti II. 17, and Milindapañha, p. 366. Nos. 1349 and 1350=Puggala-Paññatti II. 8; 1361 and 1362=Puggala-Paññatti II. 9; 1363 and 1364=Puggala-Paññatti II. 19. No. 1385 mentions the cattâro âruppâ, or, as they are generally called, arûpabrahmalokas 'the four heavens peopled by formless or incorporeal brahmas.' These are, âkâsânañcâyatana, viññânañcâyatana, âkiñcaññâyatana, nevasaññânâsaññâyatana. The arûpabrahmaloka is opposed to the kâmaloka, which includes all that lies between the great hell Avîci and the heaven Paranimmitavasavatti (see No. 1281), and to the Rûpabrahmaloka (Hardy, Manual of Buddhism, p. 26). The four arûpabrahmalokas are placed in a parallel with the four jhânas in the Brahmasaṃyutta of the Saṃyuttanikâya, p. 158 (see also Burnouf's Lotus, p. 800 ff.). The term âruppa seems to be an Abhidhamma expression: we find it only once in Abhidhammatthasaṅgraha IX. 2.

I trust that this edition of the Dhammasaṅgaṇi will prove useful to all students of Buddhism, as it is one of the most important books of the Abhidhammapiṭaka. I had hoped to see Dr. Morris's edition of the whole of the Aṅguttara-Nikâya finished before completing this, as I know that he has been working at it for some time; but unfortunately this hope has not been fulfilled, and I must leave to the reader to draw a parallel between these two books, which, although belonging to different piṭakas, still show a great deal of similarity.

E. MÜLLER.

BERNE, *September*, 1886.

LIST OF ERRATA.

Page 2, l. 13 from top, *read* uppâdino.
„ 7, l. 7 from bottom, *read* khantî *instead of* kanti.
„ 13, l. 1 from top, *read* viriyabalaṃ.
„ 40, l. 9 from bottom, *read* Yasmiṃ *instead of* Tasmiṃ.
„ 55, l. 9 from bottom, *read* atthaṅgamâ nânatta° in two words.
„ 55, l. 3 from bottom, *read* katame *instead of* khatame.
„ 59, l. 12 from bottom, *read* neva saññânâsaññâyatanasahagataṃ.
„ 84, l. 17 from bottom, *read* caṇḍikkaṃ *instead of* caṇḍittaṃ.
„ 85, l. 2 from bottom, *read* apariyogâhanâ.
„ 97, l. 2 from bottom, *read* atthaṅgamâ nânatta° in two words.
„ 98, l. 4 from top, *read* arûpâvacarassa *instead of* rûp°.
„ 98, l. 2 from bottom, *read* neva saññânâsaññâyatanasahagataṃ.
„ 123, l. 7 from bottom, *read* atthaṅgamâ nânatta° in two words.
„ 125, l. 11 from bottom, *read* ajjhattikaṃ.
„ 133, l. 9 from bottom, *read* na upekkhâsahagatam.
„ 179, l. 4 and 6 from bottom, *read* dhammâyatanapariyâpannaṃ.
„ 180, l. 2 from top, *read* sampayutto *instead of* sabbayutto.
„ 180, l. 17 from top, *read* asaṅkhatâ.
„ 181, l. 5 from bottom, *read* asaṅkilitthâsaṅkilesikâ.
„ 184, l. 18 from top, *read* kusalâkusalâvyâkatâ.
„ 192, l. 8 and 10 from bottom, *read* na hetû sahetukâ.
„ 193, l. 15 from top, *read* dhammâyatanapariyâpannaṃ.
„ 201, l. 11 and 13 from top, *read* asaññojaniyâ.
„ 205, l. 11 from top, *read* yaṃ *instead of* taṃ.
„ 210, l. 16 from top, *read* yaṃ *instead of* taṃ.
„ 234, l. 18 from top: the paragraph number 1367 should stand in line 5 from the top before Saṃvego ti jâtibhayaṃ, etc.

DHAMMA-SAṄGAṆI.

Namo tassa Bhagavato Arahato Sammâsambuddhassa.

MATIKÂ.

Kusalâ dhammâ, akusalâ dhammâ, avyâkatâ dhammâ.

Sukhâya vedanâya sampayuttâ dhammâ, dukkhâya vedanâya sampayuttâ dhammâ, adukkham-asukhâya vedanâya sampayuttâ dhammâ.

Vipâkâ dhammâ, vipâkadhammadhammâ, nevavipâka-na-vipâkadhammadhammâ.

Upâdiṇṇupâdâniyâ dhammâ, anupâdiṇṇupâdâniyâ dhammâ, anupâdiṇṇa-anupâdâniyâ dhammâ.

Saṅkiliṭṭha-saṅkilesikâ dhammâ, asaṅkiliṭṭha–saṅkilesikâ dhammâ, asaṅkililiṭṭha-asaṅkilesikâ dhammâ.

Savitakka-savicârâ dhammâ, avitakka-vicâramattâ dhammâ, avitakka-avicârâ dhammâ.

Pîti-sahagatâ dhammâ, sukha-sahagatâ dhammâ, upekkhâ-sahagatâ dhammâ.

Dassanena pahâtabbâ dhammâ, bhâvanâya pahâtabbâ dhammâ, neva dassanena na bhâvanâya pahâtabbâ dhammâ.

Dassanena pahâtabba-hetukâ dhammâ, bhâvanâya pahâtabba-hetukâ dhammâ, neva dassanena na bhâvanâya pahâtabba-hetukâ dhammâ.

Âcaya-gâmino dhammâ, apacaya-gâmino dhammâ, nevâcayagâmino na apacayagâmino dhammâ.

Sekkhâ dhammâ, asekkhâ dhammâ, neva sekkhâ nâsekkhâ dhammâ.

Parittâ dhammâ, mahaggatâ dhammâ, appamâṇâ dhammâ.

Parittârammaṇâ dhammâ, mahaggatârammaṇâ dhammâ, appamâṇârammaṇâ dhammâ.

Hînâ dhammâ, majjhimâ dhammâ, paṇîtâ dhammâ.

Micchattaniyatâ dhammâ, sampattaniyatâ dhammâ, aniyatâ dhammâ.

Maggârammaṇâ dhammâ, maggahetukâ dhammâ, maggâdhipatino dhammâ.

Uppannâ dhammâ, anuppannâ dhammâ, upâdino dhammâ.

Atîtâ dhammâ, anâgatâ dhammâ, paccuppannâ dhammâ.

Atîtârammaṇâ dhammâ, anâgatârammaṇâ dhammâ, paccuppannârammaṇâ dhammâ.

Ajjhattâ dhammâ, bahiddhâ dhammâ, ajjhatta-bahiddhâ dhammâ.

Ajjhattârammaṇâ dhammâ, bahiddhârammaṇâ dhammâ, ajjhatta-bahiddhârammaṇâ dhammâ.

Sanidassana-sappaṭighâ dhammâ, anidassana-sappaṭighâ dhammâ, anidassana-appaṭighâ dhammâ.

Tikaṃ niṭṭhitaṃ.

Hetû dhammâ, na hetû dhammâ.

Sahetukâ dhammâ, ahetukâ dhammâ.

Hetu-sampayuttâ dhammâ, hetu-vippayuttâ dhammâ.

Hetû c'eva dhammâ sahetukâ ca, sahetukâ c'eva dhammâ na ca hetû.

Hetû c'eva dhammâ hetu-sampayuttâ ca, hetu-sampayuttâ c'eva dhammâ na ca hetû.

No hetû kho pana dhammâ sahetukâ pi ahetukâ pi.

Hetu-gocchakaṃ.

Sappaccayâ dhammâ, appaccayâ dhammâ.

Saṅkhatâ dhamma, asaṅkhatâ dhammâ.

Sanidassanâ dhammâ, anidassanâ dhammâ.

Sappaṭighâ dhammâ, appaṭighâ dhammâ.

Rûpino dhammâ, arûpino dhamma.

Lokiyâ dhammâ, lokuttarâ dhammâ.

Kenaci viññeyyâ dhammâ, kenaci na viññeyyâ dhammâ.

Cûḷantara-dukaṃ.

Âsavâ dhammâ, no âsavâ dhammâ.

Sâsavâ dhammâ, anâsavâ dhammâ.

Âsava-sampayuttâ dhamma, âsava-vippayuttâ dhammâ.

Âsavâ c'eva dhammâ sâsavâ ca, sâsavâ c'eva dhammâ no ca âsavâ.

Âsavâ c'eva dhammâ âsava-sampayuttâ ca, âsava-sampayuttâ c'eva dhammâ no ca âsavâ.

Âsava-vippayuttâ kho pana dhammâ sâsavâpi anâsavâpi.

Âsava-gocchakaṃ.

Saññojanâ dhammâ, no saññojanâ dhammâ.

Saññojanîyâ dhammâ, asaññojanîyâ dhammâ.

Saññojana-sampayuttâ dhammâ, saññojana-vippayuttâ dhammâ.

Saññojanâ c'eva dhammâ saññojanîyâ ca, saññojanîyâ c'eva dhammâ no ca saññojanâ.

Saññojanâ c'eva dhammâ saññojana-sampayuttâ ca, saññojana-sampayuttâ c'eva dhammâ no ca saññojanâ.

Saññojana-vippayuttâ kho pana dhammâ saññojanîyâ pi asaññojanîyâ pi.

Saññojana-gocchakaṃ.

Ganthâ dhammâ, no ganthâ dhammâ.

Ganthanîyâ dhammâ, aganthanîyâ-dhammâ.

Gantha-sampayuttâ dhammâ, gantha-vippayuttâ dhammâ.

Ganthâ c'eva dhammâ ganthanîyâ ca, ganthanîyâ c'eva dhammâ no ca ganthâ.

Ganthâ c'eva dhammâ gantha-sampayuttâ ca, gantha-sampayuttâ c'eva dhammâ no ca ganthâ.

Gantha-vippayuttâ kho pana dhammâ ganthanīyâ pi aganthanīyâ pi.

Gantha-gocchakaṃ.

Oghâ dhammâ, no oghâ dhammâ.
Oghanīyâ dhammâ, anoghanīyâ dhammâ.
Ogha-sampayuttâ dhammâ, ogha-vippayuttâ dhammâ.
Oghâ c'eva dhammâ oghanīyâ ca, oghanīyâ c'eva dhammâ no ca oghâ.
Oghâ c'eva dhammâ ogha-sampayuttâ ca, ogha-sampayuttâ c'eva dhammâ no ca oghâ.
Ogha-vippayuttâ kho pana dhammâ oghanīyâ pi anoghanīyâ pi.

Ogha-gocchakaṃ.

Yogâ dhammâ, no yogâ dhammâ.
Yoganīyâ dhammâ, ayoganīyâ dhammâ
Yoga-sampayuttâ dhammâ, yoga-vippayuttâ dhammâ.
Yogâ c'eva dhammâ yoganīyâ ca, yoganīyâ c'eva dhammâ no ca yogâ.
Yogâ c'eva dhammâ yoga-sampayuttâ ca, yoga-sampayuttâ c'eva dhammâ no ca yogâ.
Yoga-vippayuttâ kho pana dhammâ yoganīyâ pi ayoganīyâ pi.

Yoga-gocchakaṃ.

Nîvaraṇâ dhammâ, no nîvaraṇâ dhammâ.
Nîvaraṇîyâ dhammâ, anîvaraṇîyâ dhammâ
Nîvaraṇa-sampayuttâ dhammâ, nîvaraṇa-vippayuttâ dhammâ.
Nîvaraṇâ c'eva dhammâ nîvaraṇîyâ ca, nîvaraṇîyâ c'eva dhammâ no ca nîvaraṇâ.
Nîvaraṇa-vippayuttâ kho pana dhammâ nîvaraṇîyâ pi anîvaraṇîyâ pi.

Nîvaraṇa-gocchakaṃ.

Parâmâsâ dhammâ, no parâmâsâ dhammâ.

Parâmaṭṭhâ dhammâ, aparâmaṭṭhâ dhammâ.

Parâmâsa-sampayuttâ dhammâ parâmâsa - vippayuttâ dhammâ.

Parâmâsâ c'eva dhammâ parâmaṭṭhâ ca, parâmaṭṭhâ c'eva dhammâ no ca parâmâsâ.

Parâmâsa-vippayuttâ kho pana dhammâ parâmaṭṭhâ pi aparâmaṭṭhâ pi.

Parâmâsa-gocchakaṃ.

Sârammaṇâ dhammâ, anârammaṇâ dhammâ.

Cittâ dhammâ, no cittâ dhammâ.

Cetasikâ dhammâ, acetasikâ dhammâ.

Citta-sampayuttâ dhammâ, citta-vippayuttâ dhammâ.

Citta-saṃsaṭṭhâ dhammâ, citta-visaṃsaṭṭhâ dhammâ.

Citta-samuṭṭhânâ dhammâ, no citta-samuṭṭhânâ dhammâ.

Citta-sahabhuno dhammâ, no citta-sahabhuno dhammâ.

Cittânuparivattino dhammâ, no cittânuparivattino dhammâ.

Citta-saṃsaṭṭha-samuṭṭhânâ dhammâ, no citta-saṃsaṭṭha-samuṭṭhânâ dhammâ.

Citta-saṃsaṭṭha-samuṭṭhâna-sahabhuno dhammâ, no citta-saṃsaṭṭha-samuṭṭhâna-sahabhuno dhammâ.

Citta-saṃsaṭṭha-samuṭṭhânânuparivattino dhammâ, no citta-saṃsaṭṭha-samuṭṭhânânuparivattino dhammâ.

Ajjhattikâ dhammâ, bâhirâ dhammâ.

Upâdâ dhammâ, no upâdâ dhammâ.

Upâdiṇṇâ dhammâ, anupâdiṇṇâ dhammâ.

Mahantara-dukaṃ.

Upâdânâ dhammâ, no upâdânâ dhammâ.

Upâdânīyâ dhammâ, anupâdânīyâ dhammâ.

Upâdâna-sampayuttâ dhammâ, upâdâna-vippayuttâ dhammâ

Upâdânâ c'eva dhammâ upâdânīyâ ca, upâdânīyâ c'eva dhammâ no ca upâdânâ.

Upâdânâ c'eva dhammâ upâdâna-sampayuttâ ca, upâdâna-sampayuttâ c'eva dhammâ no ca upâdânâ.

Upâdâna-vippayuttâ kho pana dhammâ upâdâniyâ pi anupâdâniyâ pi.

Upâdâna-gocchakaṃ.

Kilesâ dhammâ, no kilesâ dhammâ.
Saṅkilesikâ dhammâ, asaṅkilesika dhammâ.
Saṅkiliṭṭhâ dhammâ, asaṅkiliṭṭhâ dhammâ.
Kilesa-sampayuttâ dhammâ, kilesa-vippayuttâ dhammâ.
Kilesâ c'eva dhammâ saṅkilesikâ ca, saṅkilesikâ c'eva dhammâ no ca kilesâ.
Kilesâ c'eva dhammâ saṅkiliṭṭhâ ca, saṅkiliṭṭhâ c'eva dhammâ no ca kilesâ.
Kilesâ c'eva dhammâ kilesa-sampayuttâ ca, kilesa-sampayuttâ c'eva dhammâ no ca kilesâ.
Kilesa-vippayuttâ kho pana dhammâ saṅkilesikâ pi asaṅkilesikâ pi.

Kilesa-gocchakaṃ.

Dassanena pahâtabbâ dhammâ, na dassanena pahâtabbâ dhammâ.
Bhâvanâya pahâtabbâ dhammâ, na bhâvanâya pahâtabbâ dhammâ.
Dassanena pahâtabba-hetukâ dhammâ, na dassanena pahâtabba-hetukâ dhammâ.
Bhâvanâya pahâtabba-hetukâ dhammâ, na bhâvanâya pahâtabba-hetukâ dhammâ.
Savitakkâ dhammâ, avitakkâ dhammâ.
Savicârâ dhammâ, avicârâ dhammâ.
Sappîtikâ dhammâ, appîtikâ dhammâ.
Pîti-sahagatâ dhammâ, na pîti-sahagatâ dhammâ.
Sukha-sahagatâ dhammâ, na sukha-sahagatâ dhammâ.
Upekkhâ-sahagatâ dhammâ, na upekkhâ-sahagatâ dhammâ.
Kâmâvacarâ dhammâ, na kâmâvacarâ dhammâ.
Rûpâvacarâ dhammâ, na rûpâvacarâ dhammâ.
Arûpâvacarâ dhammâ, na arûpâvacarâ dhammâ.
Pariyâpannâ dhammâ, apariyâpannâ dhammâ.
Niyyânikâ dhammâ, aniyyânikâ dhammâ.

Niyatâ dhammâ, aniyatâ dhammâ.
Sa-uttarâ dhammâ, anuttarâ dhammâ.
Saraṇâ dhammâ, asaraṇâ dhammâ.

Piṭṭhi-dukaṃ.

Abhidhamma-mâtikâ.

Vijjâbhâgino dhammâ, avijjâbhâgino dhammâ.
Vijjûpamâ dhammâ, vajirûpamâ dhammâ.
Bâlâ dhammâ, paṇḍitâ dhammâ.
Kaṇhâ dhammâ, sukkâ dhammâ.
Tapanîyâ dhammâ, atapanîyâ dhammâ.
Adhivacanâ dhammâ, adhivacanapathâ dhammâ.
Nirutti dhammâ, niruttipathâ dhammâ.
Paññatti dhammâ, paññattipathâ dhammâ.
Nâmañ ca rûpañ ca.
Avijjâ ca bhavataṇhâ ca.
Bhavadiṭṭhi ca vibhavadiṭṭhi ca.
Sassatadiṭṭhi ca ucchedadiṭṭhi ca.
Antavâdiṭṭhi ca anantavâdiṭṭhi ca.
Pubbantânudiṭṭhi ca aparantânudiṭṭhi ca.
Ahirikañ ca anottappañ ca.
Hiri ca ottappañ ca.
Dovacassatâ ca pâpamittatâ ca.
Sovacassatâ ca kalyâṇamittatâ ca.
Âpatti-kusalatâ ca âpatti-vuṭṭhâna-kusalatâ ca.
Samâpatti-kusalatâ ca samâpatti-vuṭṭhâna-kusalatâ ca.
Dhâtu-kusalatâ ca manasikâra-kusalatâ ca.
Âyatana-kusalatâ ca paṭiccasamuppâda-kusalatâ ca.
Ṭhâna-kusalatâ ca aṭṭhâna-kusalatâ ca.
Ajjavo ca maddavo ca.
Kanti ca soraccañ ca.
Sâkhalyañ ca paṭisanthâro ca.
Indriyesu agutta-dvâratâ ca bhojane amattaññutâ ca.
Indriyesu gutta-dvâratâ ca, bhojane mattaññutâ ca.
Muṭṭhasaccañ ca, asampajaññañ ca.
Sati ca sampajaññañ ca.
Paṭisaṅkhâna-balañ ca bhâvanâ-balañ ca.

Samatho ca vipassanâ ca.
Samatha-nimittañ ca paggâha-nimittañ ca.
Paggâho ca avikkhepo ca.
Sîlavipatti ca diṭṭhivipatti ca.
Sîlasampadâ ca diṭṭhisampadâ ca.
Sîlavisuddhi ca diṭṭhivisuddhi ca.
Diṭṭhi-visuddhi kho pana yathâ-diṭṭhissa ca padhânaṃ.
Saṃvego ca saṃvejanîyesu ṭhânesu saṃviggassa ca yoniso padhânaṃ.
Asantuṭṭhitâ ca kusalesu dhammesu, appaṭivânitâ ca padhânasmiṃ.
Vijjâ ca vimutti ca.
Khaye ñâṇaṃ anuppâde ñâṇan ti.

Suttanta- mâtikâ.

MÂTIKÂ NIṬṬHITÂ.

1. Katame dhammâ kusalâ?

Yasmiṃ samaye kâmâvacaraṃ kusalaṃ cittam uppannaṃ hoti, somanassasahagataṃ ñâṇasampayuttaṃ rûpârammaṇaṃ vâ saddârammaṇaṃ vâ gandhârammaṇaṃ vâ rasârammaṇaṃ vâ phoṭṭhabbârammaṇaṃ vâ dhammârammaṇaṃ vâ yaṃ yaṃ vâ panârabbha, tasmiṃ samaye phasso hoti, vedanâ hoti, saññâ hoti, cetanâ hoti, cittaṃ hoti, vitakko hoti, vicâro hoti, pîti hoti, sukhaṃ hoti, cittass' ekaggatâ hoti, saddhindriyaṃ hoti, viriyindriyaṃ hoti, satindriyaṃ hoti, samâdhindriyaṃ hoti, paññindriyaṃ hoti, manindriyaṃ hoti, somanassindriyaṃ hoti, jîvitindriyaṃ hoti, sammâdiṭṭhi hoti, sammâsaṅkappo hoti, sammâvâyâmo hoti, sammâsati hoti, sammâsamâdhi hoti, saddhâbalaṃ hoti, viriyabalaṃ hoti, satibalaṃ hoti, samâdhibalaṃ hoti, paññâbalaṃ hoti, hiribalaṃ hoti, ottappabalaṃ hoti, alobho hoti, adoso hoti, amoho hoti, anabhijjhâ hoti, avyâpâdo hoti, sammâdiṭṭhi hoti, hiri hoti, ottappam hoti, kâyapassaddhi hoti, cittapassaddhi hoti, kâyalahutâ hoti, cittalahutâ hoti, kâyamudutâ hoti, cittamudutâ hoti, kâyakammaññatâ hoti, cittakammaññatâ hoti, kâyapâguññatâ hoti, cittapâguññatâ hoti, kâyujjukatâ hoti, cittujjukatâ hoti, sati hoti, sampajaññaṃ hoti, samatho hoti, vipassanâ hoti, paggâho hoti, avikkhepo hoti, ye vâ pana tasmiṃ samaye añño pi atthi paṭicca samuppannâ arûpino dhammâ—ime dhammâ kusalâ.

2.[1] Katamo tasmiṃ samaye phasso hoti?

Yo tasmiṃ samaye phasso phusanâ samphusanâ samphusitattaṃ—ayaṃ tasmiṃ samaye phasso hoti.

3. Katamâ tasmiṃ samaye vedanâ hoti?

Yaṃ tasmiṃ samaye tajjâ manoviññâṇadhâtu[2] samphassajaṃ cetasikaṃ sâtaṃ cetasikaṃ sukhaṃ cetosamphassajaṃ

---

[1] All the following questions are repeated below, 282 and foll., but the answers occasionally differ.
[2] See 63, 66.

sâtaṃ sukhaṃ vedayitaṃ cetosamphassajâ sâtâ sukhâ vedanâ —ayaṃ tasmiṃ samaye vedanâ hoti.

4. Katamâ tasmiṃ samaye saññâ hoti?

Yâ tasmiṃ samaye tajjâ manoviññâṇadhâtu samphassajâ saññâ sañjânanâ sañjânitattaṃ—ayaṃ tasmiṃ samaye saññâ hoti.

5. Katamâ tasmiṃ samaye cetanâ hoti?

Yâ tasmiṃ samaye tajjâ manoviññâṇadhâtu samphassajâ cetanâ saṃcetanâ saṃcetayitattaṃ—ayaṃ tasmiṃ samaye cetanâ hoti.

6. Katamaṃ tasmiṃ samaye cittaṃ hoti?

Yaṃ tasmiṃ samaye cittaṃ mano mânasaṃ hadayaṃ paṇḍaraṃ mano manâyatanaṃ manindriyaṃ viññâṇaṃ viññâṇakkhandho tajjâ manoviññâṇadhâtu—idaṃ tasmiṃ samaye cittaṃ hoti.

7. Katamo tasmiṃ samaye vitakko hoti?

Yo tasmiṃ samaye takko vitakko saṅkappo appanâ-vyappanâ cetaso abhiniropanâ sammâsaṅkappo—ayaṃ tasmiṃ samaye vitakko hoti.

8. Katamo tasmiṃ samaye vicâro hoti?

Yo tasmiṃ samaye câro vicâro anuvicâro upavicâro cittassa anusandhanatâ anupekkhanatâ—ayaṃ tasmiṃ samaye vicâro hoti.

9. Katamâ tasmiṃ samaye pîti hoti?

Yâ tasmiṃ samaye pîti pâmojjaṃ âmodanâ pamodanâ hâso pahâso vitti odagyaṃ attamanatâ cittassa—ayaṃ tasmiṃ samaye pîti hoti.

10. Katamaṃ tasmiṃ samaye sukhaṃ hoti?

Yaṃ tasmiṃ samaye cetasikaṃ sâtaṃ cetasikaṃ sukhaṃ cetosamphassajaṃ sâtaṃ sukhaṃ vedayitaṃ cetosamphassajâ sâtâ sukhâ vedanâ—idaṃ tasmiṃ samaye sukhaṃ hoti.

11. Katamâ tasmiṃ samaye cittass' ekaggatâ hoti?

Yâ tasmiṃ samaye cittassa ṭhiti saṇṭhiti avaṭṭhiti avisâhâro avikkhepo avisâhaṭamânasatâ samatho samâdhindriyaṃ samâdhibalaṃ sammâsamâdhi—ayaṃ tasmiṃ samaye cittass' ekaggatâ hoti.

12. Katamaṃ tasmim samaye saddhindriyaṃ hoti?

Yâ tasmiṃ samaye saddhâ saddahanâ okappanâ abhippasâdo saddhâ saddhindriyaṃ saddhâbalaṃ — idaṃ tasmiṃ samaye saddhindriyaṃ hoti.

13. Katamaṃ tasmiṃ samaye viriyindriyaṃ hoti?

Yo tasmiṃ samaye cetasiko viriyârambho nikkamo parakkamo uyyâmo vâyâmo ussâho ussoḷhi thâmo dhiti asithilaparakkamatâ anikkhittachandatâ anikkhittadhuratâ dhurasampaggâho viriyaṃ viriyindriyaṃ viriyabalaṃ sammâvâyâmo—idaṃ tasmiṃ samaye viriyindriyaṃ hoti.

14. Katamaṃ tasmiṃ samaye satindriyaṃ hoti?

Yâ tasmiṃ samaye sati anussati paṭissati sati saraṇatâ dhâraṇatâ apilâpanatâ asammussanatâ sati satindriyaṃ satibalaṃ sammâsati—idaṃ tasmiṃ samaye satindriyaṃ hoti.

15. Katamaṃ tasmiṃ samaye samâdhindriyaṃ hoti?

Yâ tasmiṃ samaye cittassa ṭhiti saṇṭhiti avaṭṭhiti avisâhâro avikkhepo avisâhaṭamânasatâ samatho samâdhindriyaṃ samâdhibalaṃ sammâsamâdhi—idaṃ tasmiṃ samaye samâdhindriyaṃ hoti.

16. Katamaṃ tasmiṃ samaye paññindriyaṃ hoti?

Yâ tasmiṃ samaye paññâ pajânanâ vicayo pavicayo dhammavicayo sallakkhaṇâ upalakkhaṇâ paccupalakkhaṇâ paṇḍiccaṃ kosallaṃ nepuññaṃ vebhavyâ cintâ upaparikkhâ bhûrî medhâ pariṇâyikâ vipassanâ sampajaññaṃ patodo paññâ paññindriyaṃ paññâbalaṃ paññâsatthaṃ paññâpâsâdo paññâ-âloko paññâ-obhâso paññâpajjoto paññâratanaṃ amoho dhammavicayo sammâdiṭṭhi—idaṃ tasmiṃ samaye paññindriyaṃ hoti.

17. Katamaṃ tasmiṃ samaye manindriyaṃ hoti?

Yaṃ tasmiṃ samaye cittaṃ mano mânasaṃ hadayaṃ paṇḍaraṃ mano manâyatanaṃ manindriyaṃ viññâṇaṃ viññâṇakkhandho tajjâ manoviññâṇadhâtu. idaṃ tasmiṃ samaye manindriyaṃ hoti.

18. Katamaṃ tasmiṃ samaye somanassindriyaṃ hoti?

Yaṃ tasmiṃ samaye cetasikaṃ sâtaṃ cetasikaṃ sukhaṃ cetosamphassajaṃ sâtaṃ sukhaṃ vedayitaṃ cetosamphassajâ sâtâ sukhâ vedanâ—idaṃ tasmiṃ samaye somanassindriyaṃ hoti.

19. Katamaṃ tasmiṃ samaye jîvitindriyaṃ hoti?

Yo tesaṃ arûpînaṃ dhammânaṃ âyu ṭhiti yapanâ yâpanâ

iriyanâ vattanâ pâlanâ jîvitaṃ jîvitindriyaṃ hoti—idaṃ tasmiṃ samaye jîvitindriyaṃ hoti.

20. Katamâ tasmiṃ samaye sammâdiṭṭhi hoti?

Yâ tasmiṃ samaye paññâ pajânanâ vicayo pavicayo dhammavicayo sallakkhaṇâ upalakkhaṇâ paccupalakkhaṇâ paṇḍiccaṃ kosallaṃ nepuññaṃ vebhavyâ cintâ upaparikkhâ bhûrî medhâ pariṇâyikâ vipassanâ sampajaññaṃ patodo paññâ paññindriyaṃ paññâbalaṃ paññâsatthaṃ paññâ-pâsâdo paññâ-âloko paññâ-obhâso paññâ-pajjoto paññâratanaṃ amoho dhammavicayo sammâdiṭṭhi—ayaṃ tasmim samaye sammâdiṭṭhi hoti.

21. Katamo tasmiṃ samaye sammâsaṅkappo hoti?

Yo tasmiṃ samaye takko vitakko saṅkappo appanâ vyappanâ cetaso abhiniropanâ sammâsaṅkappo—ayaṃ tasmiṃ samaye sammâsaṅkappo hoti.

22. Katamo tasmiṃ samaye sammâvâyâmo hoti?

Yo tasmiṃ samaye cetasiko viriyârambho nikkamo parakkamo uyyâmo vâyâmo ussâho ussoḷhi thâmo dhiti asithilaparakkamatâ anikkhittachandatâ anikkhittadhuratâ dhurasampaggâho viriyaṃ viriyindriyaṃ viriyabalaṃ sammâvâyâmo—ayaṃ tasmiṃ samaye sammâvâyâmo hoti.

23. Katamâ tasmiṃ samaye sammâsati hoti?

Yâ tasmiṃ samaye sati anussati paṭissati sati saraṇatâ dhâraṇatâ apilâpanatâ asammussanatâ sati satindriyaṃ satibalaṃ sammâsati—ayaṃ tasmiṃ samaye sammâsati hoti.

24. Katamo tasmiṃ samaye sammâsamâdhi hoti?

Yâ tasmiṃ samaye cittassa ṭhiti saṇṭhiti avaṭṭhiti avisâhâro avikkhepo avisâhaṭamânasatâ samatho samâdhindriyaṃ samâdhibalaṃ sammâsamâdhi—ayaṃ tasmiṃ samaye sammâsamâdhi hoti.

25. Katamaṃ tasmiṃ samaye saddhâbalaṃ hoti?

Yâ tasmiṃ samaye saddhâ saddahanâ okappanâ abhippasâdo saddhâ saddhindriyaṃ saddhâbalaṃ—idaṃ tasmiṃ samaye saddhâbalaṃ hoti.

26. Katamaṃ tasmiṃ samaye viriyabalaṃ hoti?

Yo tasmiṃ samaye cetasiko viriyârambho nikkamo parakkamo uyyâmo vâyâmo ussâho ussoḷhi thâmo dhiti asithilaparakkamatâ anikkhittachandatâ anikkhittadhuratâ dhurasampaggâho viriyaṃ viriyindriyaṃ viriyabalalaṃ sammâvâyâmo —idaṃ tasmiṃ samaye viriyabalaṃ hoti.

27. Katamaṃ tasmiṃ samaye satibalaṃ hoti?

Yâ tasmiṃ samaye sati anussati paṭissati sati saraṇatâ dhâraṇatâ apilâpanatâ asammussanatâ sati satindriyaṃ satibalaṃ sammâsati—idaṃ tasmiṃ samaye satibalaṃ hoti.

28. Katamaṃ tasmiṃ samaye samâdhibalaṃ hoti?

Yâ tasmiṃ samaye cittassa ṭhiti saṇṭhiti avaṭṭhiti avisâhâro avikkhepo avisâhaṭamânasâtâ samatho samâdhindriyaṃ samâdhibalaṃ sammâsamâdhi—idaṃ tasmiṃ samaye samâdhibalaṃ hoti.

29. Katamaṃ tasmiṃ samaye paññâbalaṃ hoti?

Yâ tasmiṃ samaye paññâ pajânanâ vicayo pavicayo dhammavicayo sallakkhaṇâ upalakkhaṇâ paccupalakkhaṇâ paṇḍiccaṃ kosallaṃ nepuññaṃ vebhavyâ cintâ upaparikkhâ bhûrî medhâ pariṇâyikâ vipassanâ sampajaññaṃ patodo paññâ paññindriyaṃ paññâbalaṃ paññâsatthaṃ paññâpâsâdo paññââloko paññâ-obhâso paññâ-pajjoto paññâratanaṃ amoho dhammavicayo sammâdiṭṭhi—idaṃ tasmiṃ samaye paññâbalaṃ hoti.

30. Katamaṃ tasmiṃ samaye hiribalaṃ hoti?

Yaṃ tasmiṃ samaye hiriyati hiriyitabbena hiriyati pâpakânaṃ akusalânaṃ dhammânaṃ samâpattiyâ—idaṃ tasmiṃ samaye hiribalaṃ hoti.

31. Katamaṃ tasmiṃ samaye ottappabalaṃ hoti?

Yaṃ tasmiṃ samaye ottappati ottappitabbena ottappati pâpakânaṃ akusalânaṃ dhammânaṃ samâpattiyâ—idaṃ tasmiṃ samaye ottappabalaṃ hoti.

32. Katamo tasmiṃ samaye alobho hoti?

Yo tasmiṃ samaye alobho alubbhanâ alubbhitattaṃ asârâgo asârajjanâ asârajjitattaṃ anabhijjhâ alobho kusalamûlaṃ—ayaṃ tasmiṃ samaye alobho hoti.

33. Katamo tasmiṃ samaye adoso hoti?

Yo tasmiṃ samaye adoso adussanâ adussitattaṃ avyâpâdo avyâpajjo adoso kusalamûlaṃ—ayaṃ tasmiṃ samaye adoso hoti.

34. Katamo tasmiṃ samaye amoho hoti?

Yâ tasmaṃ samaye paññâ pajânanâ vicayo pavicayo

dhammavicayo sallakkhaṇâ upalakkhaṇâ paccupalakkhaṇâ paṇḍiccaṃ kosallaṃ nepuññaṃ vebhavyâ cintâ upaparikkhâ bhûrî medhâ pariṇâyikâ vipassanâ sampajaññaṃ patodo paññâ paññindriyaṃ paññâbalaṃ paññâsatthaṃ paññâpâsâdo paññâ-âloko paññâ-obhâso paññâpajjoto paññâratanaṃ amoho dhammavicayo sammâdiṭṭhi amoho kusalamûlaṃ—ayaṃ tasmiṃ samaye amoho hoti.

35. Katamâ tasmiṃ samaye anabhijjhâ hoti?

Yo tasmiṃ samaye alobho alubbhanâ alubbhitattaṃ asârâgo asârajjanâ asârajjitattaṃ anabhijjhâ alobho kusalamûlaṃ ayaṃ tasmiṃ samaye anabhijjhâ hoti.

36. Katamo tasmiṃ samaye avyâpâdo hoti?

Yo tasmiṃ samaye adoso adussanâ adussitattaṃ avyâpâdo avyâpajjo adoso kusalamûlaṃ—ayaṃ tasmiṃ samaye abyâpâdo hoti.

37. Katamâ tasmiṃ samaye sammâdiṭṭhi hoti?

Yâ tasmiṃ samaye paññâ pajânanâ vicayo pavicayo dhammavicayo sallakkhaṇâ upalakkhaṇâ paccupalakkhaṇâ paṇḍiccaṃ kosallaṃ nepuññaṃ vebhavyâ cintâ upaparikkhâ bhûrî medhâ pariṇâyikâ vipassanâ sampajaññaṃ patodo paññâ paññindriyaṃ paññâbalaṃ paññâsatthaṃ paññâpâsâdo paññâ-âloko paññâ-obhâso paññâpajjoto paññâratanaṃ amoho dhammavicayo sammâdiṭṭhi—ayaṃ tasmiṃ samaye sammâdiṭṭhi hoti.

38. Katamâ tasmiṃ samaye hiri hoti?

Yaṃ tasmiṃ samaye hiriyati hiriyitabbena hiriyati pâpakânaṃ akusalânaṃ dhammânaṃ samâpattiyâ—ayaṃ tasmiṃ samaye hiri hoti.

39. Katamaṃ tasmiṃ samaye ottappaṃ hoti?

Yaṃ tasmiṃ samaye ottappati ottappitabbena ottappati pâpakânaṃ akusalânaṃ dhammânaṃ samâpattiyâ—idaṃ tasmiṃ samaye ottappaṃ hoti.

40. Katamâ tasmiṃ samaye kâyapassaddhi hoti?

Yâ tasmiṃ samaye vedanâkkhandhassa saññâkkhandhassa saṅkhârakkhandhassa passaddhi paṭipassaddhi passambhanâ paṭipassambhanâ paṭipassambhitattaṃ—ayaṃ tasmiṃ samaye kâyapassaddhi hoti.

41. Katamâ tasmiṃ samaye cittapassaddhi hoti?

Yâ tasmiṃ samaye viññâṇakkhandhassa passaddhi paṭipassaddhi passambhanâ paṭipassambhanâ paṭipassambhitattaṃ —ayaṃ tasmiṃ samaye cittapassaddhi hoti.

42. Katamâ tasmiṃ samaye kâyalahutâ hoti?

Yâ tasmiṃ samaye vedanâkkhandhassa saññâkkhandhassa saṅkhârakkhandhassa lahutâ lahupariṇâmatâ adandhaṇatâ avitthanatâ—ayaṃ tasmim samaye kâyalahutâ hoti.

43. Katamâ tasmiṃ samaye cittalahutâ hoti?

Yâ tasmiṃ samaye viññâṇakkhandhassa lahutâ lahupariṇâmatâ adandhanatâ avitthanatâ—ayaṃ tasmiṃ samaye cittalahutâ hoti.

44. Katamâ tasmiṃ samaye kâyamudutâ hoti?

Yâ tasmiṃ samaye vedanâkkhandhassa saññâkkhandhassa saṅkhârakkhandhassa mudutâ maddavatâ akakkhalatâ akaṭhinatâ—ayaṃ tasmiṃ samaye kâyamudutâ hoti.

45. Katamâ tasmiṃ samaye cittamudutâ hoti?

Yâ tasmiṃ samaye viññâṇakkhandhassa mudutâ maddavatâ akakkhaḷatâ akaṭhinatâ—ayaṃ tasmiṃ samaye cittamudutâ hoti.

46. Katamâ tasmiṃ samaye kâyakammaññatâ hoti?

Yâ tasmiṃ samaye vedanâkkhandhassa saññâkkhandhassa saṅkhârakkhandhassa kammaññatâ kammaññattaṃ kammaññabhâvo — ayaṃ tasmiṃ samaye kâyakammaññatâ hoti.

47. Katamâ tasmiṃ samaye cittakammaññatâ hoti?

Yâ tasmiṃ samaye viññâṇakkhandhassa kammaññatâ kammaññattaṃ kammaññabhâvo — ayaṃ tasmiṃ samaye cittakammaññatâ hoti.

48. Katamâ tasmiṃ samaye kâyapâguññatâ hoti?

Yâ tasmiṃ samaye vedanâkkhandhassa saññâkkhandhassa saṅkhârakkhandhassa paguṇatâ paguṇattaṃ paguṇabhâvo—ayaṃ tasmiṃ samaye kâyapâguññatâ hoti.

49. Katamâ tasmiṃ samaye citta-pâguññatâ hoti?

Yâ tasmiṃ samaye viññâṇakkhandhassa paguṇatâ paguṇattaṃ paguṇabhâvo—ayaṃ tasmiṃ samaye cittapâguññatâ hoti.

50. Katamâ tasmiṃ samaye kâyujjukatâ hoti?

Yâ tasmiṃ samaye vedanâkkhandhassa saññâkkhandhassa

saṅkhârakkhandhassa ujutâ ujukatâ ajimhatâ avaṅkatâ akuṭilatâ—ayaṃ tasmiṃ samaye kâyujjukatâ hoti.

51. Katamâ tasmiṃ samaye cittujjukatâ hoti?

Yâ tasmiṃ samaye viññâṇakkhandhassa ujutâ ujjukatâ ajimhatâ avaṅkatâ akuṭilatâ—ayaṃ tasmiṃ samaye cittujjukatâ hoti.

52. Kâtamâ tasmiṃ samaye sati hoti?

Yâ tasmiṃ samaye sati anussati paṭissati sati saraṇatâ dhâraṇatâ apilâpanatâ asammussanatâ sati satindriyaṅ satibalaṃ sammâsati—ayaṃ tasmiṃ samaye sati hoti.

53. Katamaṃ tasmim samaye sampajaññaṃ hoti?

Yâ tasmiṃ samaye paññâ pajânanâ vicayo pavicayo dhammavicayo sallakkhaṇâ upalakkhanâ paccupalakkhanâ paṇḍiccaṃ kosallaṃ nepuññaṃ vebhavyâ cintâ upaparikkhâ bhûrî medhâ pariṇâyikâ vipassanâ sampajaññaṃ patodo paññâ paññindriyaṃ paññâbalaṃ paññâsatthaṃ paññâpâsâdo paññâ-âloko paññâ-obhâso paññâpajjoto paññâratanaṃ amoho dhammavicayo sammâdiṭṭhi — idaṃ tasmiṃ samaye sampajaññaṃ hoti.

54. Katamo tasmiṃ samaye samatho hoti?

Yâ tasmiṃ samaye cittassa ṭhiti saṇṭhiti avaṭṭhiti avisâhâro avikkhepo avisâhaṭamânasatâ samatho samâdhindriyaṃ samâdhibalaṃ sammâsamâdhi—ayaṃ tasmiṃ samaye samatho hoti.

55. Katamâ tasmiṃ samaye vipassanâ hoti?

Yâ tasmiṃ samaye paññâ pajânanâ vicayo pavicayo dhammavicayo sallakkhaṇâ upalakkhaṇâ paccupalakkhaṇâ paṇḍiccaṃ kosallaṃ nepuññaṃ vebhavyâ cintâ upaparikkhâ bhûrî medhâ pariṇâyikâ vipassanâ sampajaññaṃ patodo paññâ paññindriyaṃ paññâbalaṃ paññâsatthaṃ paññâpâsâdo paññâ-âloko paññâ-obhaso paññâpajjoto paññâratanaṃ amoho dhammavicayo sammâdiṭṭhi—ayaṃ tasmiṃ samaye vipassanâ hoti.

56. Katamo tasmiṃ samaye paggâho hoti?

Yo tasmiṃ samaye cetasiko viriyârambho nikkamo parakkamo uyyâmo vâyâmo ussâho ussoḷhi thâmo dhiti asithila-parakkamatâ anikkhitta-chandatâ anikkhittadhuratâ dhurasampaggâho viriyaṃ viriyindriyaṃ viriyabalaṃ sammâvâyâmo—ayaṃ tasmiṃ samaye paggâho hoti.

57. Katamo tasmiṃ samaye avikkhepo hoti? Yâ tasmiṃ samaye cittassa ṭhiti saṇṭhiti avaṭṭhiti avisâhâro avikkhepo avisâhaṭamânasatâ samatho samâdhindriyaṃ samâdhibalaṃ sammâsamâdhi—ayaṃ tasmiṃ samaye avikkhepo hoti. Ye vâ pana tasmiṃ samaye aññe pi atthi paṭiccasamuppannâ arûpino dhammâ ime dhammâ kusalâ.

Pada-bhâjaniyaṃ niṭṭhitaṃ.

PAṬHAMA-BHĀṆAVĀRAṂ.

58. Tasmiṃ kho pana samaye cattâro khandhâ honti, dvâyatanâni honti, dve dhâtuyo honti, tayo âhârâ honti, aṭṭhindriyâni honti, pañcaṅgikaṃ jhânaṃ hoti, pañcaṅgiko maggo hoti, satta balâni honti, tayo hetû honti, eko phasso hoti, ekâ vedanâ hoti, ekâ saññâ hoti, ekâ cetanâ hoti, ekaṃ cittaṃ hoti, eko vedanâkkhandho hoti, eko saññâkkhando hoti, eko saṅkhârakkhandho hoti, eko viññâṇakkhandho hoti, ekaṃ manâyatanaṃ hoti, ekaṃ manindriyaṃ hoti, ekâ mano-viññâṇadhâtu hoti, ekaṃ dhammâyatanaṃ hoti, ekâ dhammadhâtu hoti, ye vâ pana tasmiṃ samaye aññe pi atthi paṭiccasamuppannâ arûpino dhammâ—ime dhammâ kusalâ.

59. Katame tasmiṃ samaye cattâro khandhâ honti? Vedanâkkhandho saññâkkhandho saṅkhârakkhandho viññâṇakkhandho.

60. Katamo tasmiṃ samaye vedanâkkhandho hoti? Yaṃ tasmiṃ samaye cetasikaṃ sâtaṃ cetasikaṃ sukhaṃ cetosamphassajaṃ sâtaṃ sukhaṃ vedayitaṃ cetosamphassajâ sâtâ sukhâ vedanâ—ayaṃ tasmiṃ samaye vedanâkkhandho hoti.

61. Katamo tasmiṃ samaye saññâkkhandho hoti? Yâ tasmiṃ samaye saññâ sañjânanâ sañjânitattaṃ—ayaṃ tasmiṃ samaye saññâkkhandho hoti.

62.[1] Katamo tasmiṃ samaye saṅkhârakkhandho hoti? Phasso cetanâ vitakko vicâro pîti cittass' ekaggatâ sad-

[1] Compare 312 and 401.

dhindriyaṃ viriyindriyaṃ satindriyaṃ samâdhindriyaṃ paññindriyaṃ jîvitindriyaṃ sammâdiṭṭhi sammâsaṅkappo sammâvâyâmo sammâsati sammâsamâdhi saddhâbalaṃ viriyabalaṃ satibalaṃ samâdhibalaṃ paññâbalaṃ hiribalaṃ ottappabalaṃ alobho adoso amoho anabhijjhâ avyâpâdo sammâdiṭṭhi hiri ottappaṃ kâyapassaddhi cittapassaddhi kâyalahutâ cittalahutâ kâyamudutâ cittamudutâ kâyakammaññatâ cittakammaññatâ kâyapâguññatâ cittapâguññatâ kâyujjukatâ cittujjukatâ sati sampajaññaṃ samatho vipassanâ paggâho avikkhepo ye vâ pana tasmiṃ samaye aññe pi atthi paṭiccasamuppannâ arûpino dhammâ ṭhapetvâ vedanâkkhandhaṃ ṭhapetvâ saññâkkhandhaṃ ṭhapetvâ viññâṇakkhandaṃ ayaṃ tasmiṃ samaye saṅkhârakkhandho hoti.

63. Katamo tasmiṃ samaye viññâṇakkhandho koti?

Yaṃ tasmiṃ samaye cittaṃ mano mânasaṃ hadayaṃ paṇḍaraṃ mano manâyatanaṃ manindriyaṃ viññâṇaṃ viññânakkhandho tajjâ manoviññâṇadhâtu—ayaṃ tasmiṃ samaye viññâṇakkhandho hoti.

Ime tasmiṃ samaye cattâro khandhâ honti.

64. Katamâni tasmiṃ samaye dvâyatanâni honti?

Manâyatanaṃ, dhammâyatanaṃ.

65. Katamaṃ tasmiṃ samaye manâyatanaṃ hoti?

Yaṃ tasmiṃ samaye cittaṃ mano mânasaṃ hadayaṃ paṇḍaraṃ mano manâyatanaṃ manindriyaṃ viññâṇaṃ viññâṇakkhandho tajjâ manoviññâṇadhâtu—idaṃ tasmiṃ samaye manâyatanaṃ hoti.

66. Katamaṃ tasmiṃ samaye dhammâyatanaṃ hoti?

Vedanâkkhandho saññâkkhandho saṅkhârakkhandho—idam tasmiṃ samaye dhammâyatanaṃ hoti.

Imâni tasmiṃ samaye dvâyatanâni honti.

67. Katamâ tasmiṃ samaye dve dhâtuyo honti?

Manoviññâṇadhâtu, dhammadhâtu.

68. Katamâ tasmiṃ samaye manoviññâṇadhâtu hoti.

Yaṃ tasmiṃ samaye cittaṃ mano mânasaṃ hadayaṃ paṇḍaraṃ mano manâyatanaṃ manindriyaṃ viññâṇaṃ viññâṇakkhandho tajjâ manoviññâṇadhâtu—ayaṃ tasmiṃ samaye manoviññânadhâtu hoti.

69. Katamâ tasmiṃ samaye dhammadhâtu hoti?

Vedanâkkhandho saññâkkhandho saṅkhârakkhandho ayaṃ tasmiṃ samaye dhammadhâtu hoti.

Imâ tasmiṃ samaye dve dhâtuyo honti.

70. Katame tasmiṃ samaye tayo âhârâ honti?

Phassâhâro, manosañcetanâhâro, viññâṇâhâro.

71. Katamo tasmiṃ samaye phassâhâro hoti?

Yo tasmiṃ samaye phasso phusanâ samphusanâ samphusitattaṃ—ayaṃ tasmiṃ samaye phassâhâro hoti.

72. Katamo tasmiṃ samaye manosañcetanâhâro hoti?

Yâ tasmiṃ samaye cetanâ sañcetanâ saṃcetayitattaṃ—ayaṃ tasmiṃ samaye manosañcetanâhâro hoti.

73. Katamo tasmiṃ samaye viññâṇâhâro hoti?

Yaṃ tasmiṃ samaye cittaṃ mano mânasaṃ hadayaṃ paṇḍaraṃ mano manâyatanaṃ manindriyaṃ viññâṇaṃ viññâṇakkhandho tajjâ manoviññâṇadhâtu—ayaṃ tasmiṃ samaye viññâṇâhâro hoti.

Ime tasmiṃ samaye tayo âhârâ honti.

74. Katamâni tasmiṃ samaye aṭṭhindriyâni honti?

Saddhindriyaṃ, viriyindriyaṃ, satindriyaṃ, samâdhindriyaṃ, paññindriyaṃ, manindriyaṃ, somanassindriyaṃ, jîvitindriyaṃ.

75. Katamaṃ tasmiṃ samaye saddhindriyaṃ hoti?

Yâ tasmiṃ samaye saddhâ saddahanâ okappanâ abhippasâdo saddhâ saddhindriyaṃ saddhâbalaṃ — idaṃ tasmiṃ samaye saddhindriyaṃ hoti.

76. Katamaṃ tasmiṃ samaye viriyindriyaṃ hoti?

Yo tasmiṃ samaye cetasiko viriyârambho nikkamo parakkamo uyyâmo vâyâmo ussâho ussoḷhi thâmo dhiti asithila-parakkamatâ anikkhitta-chandatâ anikkhitta-dhuratâ dhurasampaggâho viriyaṃ viriyindriyaṃ viriyabalaṃ sammâvâyamo—idaṃ tasmiṃ samaye viriyindriyaṃ hoti.

77. Katamaṃ tasmiṃ samaye satindriyaṃ hoti?

Yâ tasmiṃ samaye sati anussati paṭissati sati saraṇatâ dhâraṇatâ apilâpanatâ asaṃmussanatâ sati satindriyaṃ satibalaṃ sammâsati—idaṃ tasmiṃ samaye satindriyaṃ hoti.

78. Katamaṃ tasmim samaye samâdhindriyaṃ hoti?

Yâ tasmiṃ samaye cittassa ṭhiti saṇṭhiti avaṭṭhiti avisâhâro avikkhepo avisâhaṭamânasatâ samatho samâdhindriyaṃ samâdhibalaṃ sammâsamâdhi—idaṃ tasmiṃ samaye samâdhindriyaṃ hoti.

79. Katamaṃ tasmiṃ samaye paññindriyaṃ hoti?

Yâ tasmiṃ samaye paññâ pajânanâ vicayo pavicayo dhammavicayo sallakkhaṇâ upalakkhaṇâ paccupalakkhaṇâ paṇḍiccaṃ kosallaṃ nepuññaṃ vebhavyâ cintâ upaparikkhâ bhûrî medhâ pariṇâyikâ vipassanâ sampajaññaṃ patodo paññâ paññindriyaṃ paññâbalaṃ paññâsatthaṃ paññâpâsâdo paññâ-âloko paññâ-obhâso paññâpajjoto paññâratanaṃ amoho dhammavicayo sammâdiṭṭhi—idaṃ tasmiṃ samaye paññindriyaṃ hoti.

80. Katamaṃ tasmiṃ samaye manindriyaṃ hoti?

Yaṃ tasmiṃ samaye cittaṃ mano mânasaṃ hadayaṃ paṇḍaraṃ mano manâyatanaṃ manindriyaṃ viññâṇaṃ viññâṇakkhandho tajjâ manoviññâṇadhâtu—idaṃ tasmiṃ samaye manindriyaṃ hoti.

81. Katamam tasmiṃ samaye somanassindriyaṃ hoti?

Yaṃ tasmiṃ samaye cetasikaṃ sâtaṃ cetasikaṃ sukhaṃ cetosamphassajaṃ sâtaṃ sukhaṃ vedayitaṃ cetosamphassajâ sâtâ sukhâ vedanâ—idaṃ tasmiṃ samaye somanassindriyaṃ hoti.

82. Katamaṃ tasmiṃ samaye jîvitindriyaṃ hoti?

Yo tesaṃ arûpînaṃ dhammânaṃ âyu ṭhiti yapanâ yâpanâ iriyanâ vattanâ pâlanâ jîvitaṃ jîvitindriyaṃ—idaṃ tasmiṃ samaye jîvitindriyaṃ hoti.

Imâni tasmiṃ samaye aṭṭhindriyâni honti.

---

83. Katamaṃ tasmiṃ samaye pañcaṅgikaṃ jhânaṃ hoti?

Vitakko, vicâro, pîti, sukhaṃ, cittass' ekaggatâ.

84. Katamo tasmiṃ samaye vitakko hoti?

Yo tasmiṃ samaye takko vitakko saṅkappo appanâ vyappanâ cetaso abhiniropanâ sammâsaṅkappo—ayaṃ tasmiṃ samaye vitakko hoti.

85. Katamo tasmiṃ samaye vicâro hoti?

Yo tasmiṃ samaye câro vicâro anuvicâro upavicâro cittassa anusandhanatâ anupekkhanatâ—ayaṃ tasmiṃ samaye vicâro hoti.

86. Katamâ tasmiṃ samaye pîti hoti?

Yâ tasmiṃ samaye pîti pâmojjaṃ âmodanâ pamodanâ hâso pahâso vitti odagyaṃ attamanatâ cittassa—ayaṃ tasmiṃ pîti hoti.

87. Katamaṃ tasmiṃ samaye sukhaṃ hoti?

Yaṃ tasmiṃ samaye cetasikaṃ sâtaṃ cetasikaṃ sukhaṃ cetosamphassajaṃ sâtaṃ sukhaṃ vedayitaṃ cetosamphassajâ sâtâ sukhâ vedanâ—idaṃ tasmiṃ samaye sukhaṃ hoti.

88. Katamâ tasmiṃ samaye cittass' ekaggatâ hoti?

Yâ tasmiṃ samaye cittassa ṭhiti saṇṭhiti avaṭṭhiti avisâhâro avikkhepo avisâhaṭamânasatâ samatho samâdhindriyaṃ samâdhibalaṃ sammâsamâdhi—ayaṃ tasmiṃ samaye cittass' ekaggatâ hoti.

Idaṃ tasmiṃ samaye pañcaṅgikaṃ jhânaṃ hoti.

---

89. Katamo tasmiṃ samaye pañcaṅgiko maggo hoti?

Sammâdiṭṭhi, sammâsaṅkappo, sammâvâyâmo, sammâsati, sammâsamâdhi.

90. Katamâ tasmiṃ samaye sammâdiṭṭhi hoti?

Yâ tasmiṃ samaye paññâ pajânanâ vicayo pavicayo dhammavicayo sallakkhaṇâ upalakkhaṇâ paccupalakkhaṇâ paṇḍiccaṃ kosallaṃ nepuññaṃ vebhavyâ cintâ upaparikkhâ bhûrî medhâ pariṇâyikâ vipassanâ sampajaññaṃ patodo paññâ paññindriyaṃ paññâbalaṃ paññâsatthaṃ paññâpâsâdo paññâ-âloko paññâ-obhâso paññâpajjoto paññâratanaṃ amoho dhammavicayo sammâdiṭṭhi—ayaṃ tasmiṃ samaye sammâdiṭṭhi hoti.

91. Katamo tasmiṃ samaye sammâsaṅkappo hoti?

Yo tasmiṃ samaye takko vitakko saṅkappo appanâ vyappanâ cetaso abhiniropanâ sammâsaṅkappo—ayaṃ tasmiṃ samaye sammâsaṅkappo hoti.

92. Katamo tasmiṃ samaye sammâvâyâmo hoti?

Yo tasmiṃ samaye cetasiko viriyârambho nikkamo parakkamo uyyâmo vâyâmo ussâho ussoḷhi thâmo dhîti asithilaparakkamatâ anikkhittachandatâ anikkhittadhuratâ dhurasampaggaho viriyaṃ viriyindriyaṃ viriyabalaṃ sammâvâyâmo—ayaṃ tasmiṃ samaye sammâvâyâmo hot.

93. Katamâ tasmiṃ samaye sammâsati hoti?

Yâ tasmiṃ samaye sati anussati paṭissati sati saraṇatâ dhâraṇatâ apilâpanatâ asammussanatâ sati satindriyaṃ satibalaṃ sammâsati—ayaṃ tasmiṃ samaye sammâsati hoti.

94. Katamo tasmiṃ samaye sammâsamâdhi hoti?

Yâ tasmiṃ samaye cittassa ṭhiti saṇṭhiti avaṭṭhiti avisâhâro avikkhepo avisâhaṭamânasatâ samatho samâdhindriyaṃ samâdhibalaṃ sammâsamâdhi—ayaṃ tasmiṃ samaye sammâsamâdhi hoti.

Ayaṃ tasmiṃ samaye pañcaṅgiko maggo hoti.

---

95. Katamâni tasmiṃ samaye satta balâni honti?

Saddhâbalaṃ, viriyabalaṃ, satibalaṃ, samâdhibalaṃ, paññâbalaṃ hiribalaṃ, ottappabalaṃ.

96. Katamaṃ tasmiṃ samaye saddhâbalaṃ hoti?

Yâ tasmiṃ samaye saddhâ saddahanâ okappanâ abhippasâdo saddhâ saddhindriyaṃ saddhâbalaṃ—idaṃ tasmiṃ samaye saddhâbalaṃ hoti.

97. Katamaṃ tasmiṃ samaye viriyabalaṃ hoti?

Yo tasmiṃ samaye cetasiko viriyârambho nikkamo parakkamo uyyâmo vâyâmo ussâho ussoḷhi thâmo dhiti asithilaparakkamatâ anikkhittachandatâ anikkhittadhuratâ dhurasampaggâho viriyaṃ viriyindriyaṃ viriyabalaṃ sammâvâyâmo.

Idaṃ tasmiṃ samaye viriyabalaṃ hoti.

98. Katamaṃ tasmiṃ samaye satibalaṃ hoti?

Yâ tasmiṃ samaye sati anussati paṭissati sati saraṇatâ dhâraṇatâ apilâpanatâ asammussanatâ sati satindriyaṃ satibalaṃ sammâsati—idaṃ tasmiṃ samaye satibalaṃ hoti.

99. Katamaṃ tasmiṃ samaye samâdhibalaṃ hoti?

Yâ tasmiṃ samaye cittassa ṭhiti saṇṭhiti avaṭṭhiti avisâhâro avikkhepo avisâhaṭamânasaṭâ samatho samâdhindriyaṃ samâdhibalaṃ sammâsamâdhi—idaṃ tasmiṃ samaye samâdhibalaṃ hoti.

100. Katamaṃ tasmiṃ samaye paññâbalaṃ hoti?

Yâ tasmiṃ samaye paññâ pajânanâ vicayo pavicayo dhammavicayo sallakkhaṇâ upalakkhaṇâ paccupalakkhaṇâ paṇḍiccaṃ kosallaṃ nepuññaṃ vebhavyâ cintâ upaparikkhâ bhûrî medhâ pariṇâyikâ vipassanâ sampajaññaṃ patodo paññâ paññindriyaṃ paññâbalaṃ paññâsatthaṃ paññâpâsâdo paññâ-âloko paññâ-obhâso paññâpajjoto paññâratanaṃ amoho dhammavicayo sammâdiṭṭhi—idaṃ tasmiṃ samaye paññâbalaṃ hoti.

101. Katamaṃ tasmiṃ samaye hiribalaṃ hoti?

Yaṃ tasmiṃ samaye hiriyati hiriyitabbena hiriyati pâpakânaṃ akusalânaṃ dhammânaṃ samâpattiyâ—idaṃ tasmiṃ samaye hiribalaṃ hoti.

102. Katamaṃ tasmiṃ samaye ottappabalaṃ hoti?

Yaṃ tasmiṃ samaye ottappati ottappitabbena ottappati pâpakânaṃ akusalânaṃ dhammânaṃ samâpattiyâ — idaṃ tasmiṃ samaye ottappabalaṃ hoti.

Imâni tasmiṃ samaye satta balâni honti.

---

103. Katame tasmiṃ samaye tayo hetû honti?

Alobho, adoso amoho.

104. Katamo tasmiṃ samaye alobho hoti?

Yo tasmiṃ samaye alobho alubbhanâ alubbhitattaṃ asârâgo asârajjanâ asârajjitattaṃ anabhijjhâ alobho kusalamûlaṃ—ayaṃ tasmiṃ samaye alobho hoti.

105. Katamo tasmiṃ samaye adoso hoti?

Yo tasmiṃ samaye adoso adussanâ adussitattaṃ avyâpâdo avyâpajjo adoso kusalamûlaṃ—ayaṃ tasmiṃ samaye adoso hoti.

106. Katamo tasmiṃ samaye amoho hoti?

Yâ tasmiṃ samaye paññâ pajânanâ . . . pe (34) . . . amoho dhammavicayo sammâdiṭṭhi—ayaṃ tasmiṃ samaye amoho hoti.

Ime tasmiṃ samaye tayo hetû honti.

---

107. Katamo tasmiṃ samaye eko phasso hoti?

Yo tasmiṃ samaye phasso phusanâ samphusanâ samphusitattaṃ—ayaṃ tasmiṃ samaye eko phasso hoti.

108. Katamâ tasmiṃ samaye ekâ vedanâ hoti?

Yaṃ tasmiṃ samaye cetasikaṃ sâtaṃ cetasikaṃ sukhaṃ cetosamphassajaṃ sâtaṃ sukhaṃ vedayitaṃ cetosamphassajâ sâtâ sukhâ vedanâ—ayaṃ tasmiṃ samaye ekâ vedanâ hoti.

109. Katamâ tasmiṃ samaye ekâ saññâ hoti?

Yâ tasmiṃ samaye saññâ sañjânanâ sañjânitattaṃ—ayaṃ tasmiṃ samaye ekâ saññâ hoti.

110. Katamâ tasmiṃ samaye ekâ cetanâ hoti?

Yâ tasmiṃ samaye cetanâ sañcetanâ cetayitattaṃ—ayaṃ tasmiṃ samaye ekâ cetanâ hoti.

111. Katamaṃ tasmiṃ samaye ekaṃ cittaṃ hoti?

Yaṃ tasmiṃ samaye cittaṃ mano mânasaṃ hadayaṃ paṇḍaraṃ mano manâyatanaṃ manindriyaṃ viññâṇaṃ viññâṇakkhandho tajjâ manoviññâṇadhâtu—idaṃ tasmiṃ samaye ekaṃ cittaṃ hoti.

112. Katamo tasmiṃ samaye eko vedanâkkhandho hoti?

Yaṃ tasmiṃ samaye cetasikaṃ sâtaṃ cetasikaṃ sukhaṃ cetosamphassajaṃ sâtaṃ sukhaṃ vedayitaṃ cetosamphassajâ sâtâ sukhâ vedanâ—ayaṃ tasmiṃ samaye eko vedanâkkhandho hoti.

113. Katamo tasmiṃ samaye eko saññâkkhandho hoti?

Yâ tasmiṃ samaye saññâ sañjânanâ sañjânitattaṃ—ayaṃ tasmiṃ samaye eko saññâkkhandho hoti.

114. Katamo tasmiṃ samaye eko saṅkhârakkhandho hoti?

Phasso vedanâ vitakko vicâro pîti cittass' ekaggatâ saddhindriyaṃ viriyindriyaṃ satindriyaṃ samâdhindriyaṃ paññindriyaṃ jîvitindriyaṃ sammâdiṭṭhi sammâsaṅkappo sammâvâyâmo sammâsati sammâsamâdhi saddhâbalaṃ viriyabalaṃ satibalaṃ samâdhibalaṃ paññâbalaṃ hiribalaṃ ottappabalaṃ alobho adoso amoho anabhijjhâ avyâpâdo sammâdiṭṭhi hiri ottappaṃ kâyapassaddhi cittapassaddhi kâyalahutâ cittalahutâ kâyamudutâ cittamudutâ kâyakammaññatâ cittakammaññatâ kâyapâguññatâ cittapâguññatâ kâyujjukatâ cittujjukatâ sati sampajaññaṃ samatho vipassanâ paggâho avikkhepo—ye vâ pana tasmiṃ samaye aññe pi atthi paṭiccasamuppannâ arûpino dhammâ, ṭhapetvâ vedanâkkhandhaṃ ṭhapetvâ saññâkkhandhaṃ ṭhapetvâ viññâṇakkhandhaṃ—ayaṃ tasmiṃ samaye eko saṅkhârakkhandho hoti.

115. Katamo tasmiṃ samaye eko viññâṇakkhandho hoti?

Yaṃ tasmiṃ samaye cittaṃ mano mânasaṃ hadayaṃ paṇḍaraṃ mano manâyatanaṃ manindriyaṃ viññâṇaṃ viññâṇakkhandho tajjâ manoviññâṇadhâtu—ayaṃ tasmiṃ samaye eko viññâṇakkhandho hoti.

116. Katamaṃ tasmiṃ samaye ekaṃ manâyatanaṃ hoti? Yaṃ tasmiṃ samaye cittaṃ mano mânasaṃ hadayaṃ paṇḍaraṃ mano manâyatanaṃ manindriyaṃ viññaṇaṃ viññâṇakkhandho tajjâ manoviññâṇadhâtu—idaṃ tasmiṃ samaye ekaṃ manâyatanaṃ hoti.

117. Katamaṃ tasmiṃ samaye ekaṃ manindriyaṃ hoti? Yaṃ tasmiṃ samaye cittaṃ mano mânasaṃ hadayaṃ paṇḍaraṃ mano manâyatanaṃ manindriyaṃ viññâṇaṃ viññâṇakkhandho tajjâ manoviññâṇadhâtu—idaṃ tasmiṃ samaye ekaṃ manindriyaṃ hoti.

118. Katamâ tasmiṃ samaye ekâ manoviññâṇadhâtu hoti? Yaṃ tasmiṃ samaye cittaṃ mano mânasaṃ hadayaṃ paṇḍaraṃ mano manâyatanaṃ manindriyaṃ viññâṇaṃ viññâṇakkhandho tajjâ manoviññâṇadhâtu—ayaṃ tasmiṃ samaye ekâ manoviññâṇadhâtu hoti.

119. Katamaṃ tasmiṃ samaye ekaṃ dhammâyatanaṃ hoti? Vedanâkkhandho saññâkkhandho saṅkhârakkhandho — idaṃ tasmiṃ samaye ekaṃ dhammâyatanaṃ hoti.

120. Katamâ tasmiṃ samaye ekâ dhammadhâtu hoti? Vedanâkkhandho saññâkkhandho saṅkhârakkhandho — ayaṃ tasmiṃ samaye ekâ dhammadhâtu hoti.

Ye vâ pana tasmiṃ samaye aññe pi atthi paṭiccasamuppannâ arûpino dhammâ—ime dhammâ kusalâ.

Koṭṭhâsavâraṃ.

121. Tasmiṃ kho pana samaye dhammâ honti, khandhâ honti, âyatanâni honti, dhâtuyo honti, âhârâ honti, indriyâni honti, jhânaṃ hoti, maggo hoti, balâni honti, hetû honti, phasso hoti, vedanâ hoti, saññâ hoti, cetanâ hoti, cittaṃ hoti, vedanâkkhandho hoti, saññâkkhandho hoti, saṅkhârakkhandho hoti, viññâṇakkhandho hoti, manâyatanaṃ hoti, manindriyaṃ hoti, manoviññâṇadhâtu hoti, dhammâyatanaṃ hoti, dhammadhâtu hoti, ye vâ pana tasmiṃ samaye aññe pi atthi paṭiccasamuppannâ arûpino dhammâ—ime dhammâ kusalâ.

122. Katame tasmiṃ samaye dhammâ honti? Vedanâkkhandho, saññâkkhandho, saṅkhârakkhandho, viññâṇakkhandho—ime tasmiṃ samaye dhammâ honti.

123. Katame tasmiṃ samaye khandhâ honti?

Vedanâkkhandho, saññâkkhandho, saṅkhârakkhandho, viññâṇakkhandho—ime tasmiṃ samaye khandhâ honti.

124. Katamâni tasmiṃ samaye âyatanâni honti?

Manâyatanaṃ dhammâyatanaṃ — imâni tasmiṃ samaye âyatanâni honti.

125. Katamâ tasmiṃ samaye dhâtuyo honti?

Manoviññâṇadhâtu dhammadhâtu, imâ tasmiṃ samaye dhâtuyo honti.

126. Katame tasmiṃ samaye âhârâ honti?

Phassâhâro manosañcetanâhâro viññâṇâhâro—ime tasmiṃ samaye âhârâ honti.

127. Katamâni tasmiṃ samaye indriyâni honti?

Saddhindriyaṃ, viriyindriyaṃ, satindriyaṃ, samâdhindriyaṃ paññindriyaṃ, manindriyaṃ, somanassindriyaṃ, jîvitindriyaṃ—imâni tasmiṃ samaye indriyâni honti.

128. Katamaṃ tasmiṃ samaye jhânaṃ hoti?

Vitakko vicâro pîti sukhaṃ cittass' ekaggatâ—idaṃ tasmiṃ samaye jhânaṃ hoti.

129. Katamo tasmiṃ samaye maggo hoti?

Sammâdiṭṭhi sammâsaṅkappo sammâvâyâmo sammâsati sammâsamâdhi—ayaṃ tasmiṃ samaye maggo hoti.

130. Katamâni tasmiṃ samaye balâni honti?

Saddhâbalaṃ, viriyabalaṃ, satibalaṃ, samâdhibalaṃ, paññâbalaṃ, hiribalaṃ, ottappabalaṃ—imâni tasmiṃ samaye balâni honti.

131. Katame tasmiṃ samaye hetû honti?

Alobho adoso amoho—ime tasmiṃ samaye hetû honti.

132–145. The questions repeated with . . . pe (107–120) . . . phasso vedanâ saññâ cetanâ cittaṃ vedanâkkhandho saññâkkhandho saṅkhârakkhando viññâṇakkhandho manâyatanaṃ manindriyaṃ viññâṇadhâtu dhammâyatanaṃ dhammadhâtu ye vâ pana tasmiṃ samaye aññe pi atthi paṭiccasamuppannâ arûpino dhammâ—ime dhammâ kusalâ.

Suññatavâro. Paṭhamacittaṃ.

146.[1] Katame dhammâ kusalâ?

---

[1] Compare 411 and following.

Yasmiṃ samaye kâmâvacaraṃ kusalaṃ cittaṃ uppannaṃ hoti, somanassasahagataṃ ñâṇasampayuttaṃ sasaṅkhârena rûpârammaṇaṃ vâ . . . pe (147) . . . dhammârammaṇaṃ vâ, yaṃ yaṃ vâ pan' ârabbha tasmiṃ samaye phasso hoti . . . pe (147) . . . avikkhepo hoti . . . pe (147) . . . ime dhammâ kusalâ.

Dutiyaṃ.

147. Katame dhammâ kusalâ ?

Yasmiṃ samaye kâmâvacaraṃ kusalaṃ cittaṃ uppannaṃ hoti, somanassasahagataṃ ñâṇavippayuttaṃ rûpârammaṇaṃ vâ saddârammaṇaṃ vâ gandhârammaṇaṃ vâ rasârammaṇaṃ vâ phoṭṭhabbârammaṇaṃ vâ dhammârammaṇaṃ vâ, yaṃ yaṃ vâ pan'ârabbha tasmiṃ samaye phasso hoti, vedanâ hoti, saññâ hoti, cetanâ hoti, cittaṃ hoti, vitakko hoti, vicâro hoti, pîti hoti, sukhaṃ hoti, cittass' ekaggatâ hoti, saddhindriyaṃ hoti, viriyindriyaṃ hoti, satindriyaṃ hoti, samâdhindriyaṃ hoti, manindriyaṃ hoti, somanassindriyaṃ hoti, jîvitindriyam hoti, sammâdiṭṭhi hoti, sammâsaṅkappo hoti, sammâvâyâmo hoti, sammâsati hoti, sammâsamâdhi hoti, saddhâbalaṃ hoti, viriyabalaṃ hoti, satibalaṃ hoti, samâdhibalaṃ hoti, hiribalaṃ hoti, ottappabalaṃ hoti, alobho hoti, adoso hoti, anabhijjhâ hoti, avyâpâdo hoti, hiri hoti, ottappaṃ hoti, kâyapassadhi hoti, cittapassaddhi hoti, kâyalahutâ hoti, cittalahutâ hoti, kâyamudutâ hoti, cittamudutâ hoti, kâyakammaññatâ hoti, cittakammaññatâ hoti, kâyapâguññatâ hoti, cittapâguññatâ hoti, kâyujjukatâ hoti, cittujjukatâ hoti, sati hoti, samatho hoti, paggâho hoti, avikkhepo hoti, yo vâ pana tasmiṃ samaye añño pi atthi paṭiccasamuppannâ arûpino dhammâ—ime dhammâ kusalâ. Tasmiṃ kho pana samaye cattâro khandhâ honti; dvâyatanâni honti, dve dhâtuyo honti, tayo âhârâ honti, sattindriyâni honti, pañcaṅgikaṃ jhânaṃ hoti, caturaṅgiko maggo hoti, cha balâni honti, dve hetû honti, eko phasso hoti . . . pe (58) . . . ekaṃ dhammâyatanaṃ hoti, ekâ dhammadhâtu hoti, yo vâ pana tasmiṃ samaye añño pi atthi paṭiccasamuppannâ arûpino dhammâ—ime dhammâ kusalâ.

Tatiyaṃ.

148. Katamo tasmiṃ samaye saṅkhârakkhandho hoti? Phasso . . . pe (62) . . . saṅkhârakkhandho hoti . . . pe . . . ime dhammâ kusalâ.

149. Katame dhammâ kusalâ? Yasmiṃ samaye kâmâvacaraṃ kusalaṃ . . . pe (147) . . . avikkhepo hoti . . . pe (147) . . . ime dhammâ kusalâ.

Catutthaṃ.

150. Katame dhammâ kusalâ. Yasmiṃ samaye kâmâvacaraṃ . . . pe (156) . . . avikkhepo hoti . . . pe . . . ime dhammâ kusalâ.

151. Katamo tasmiṃ samaye phasso hoti? Yo tasmiṃ samaye phasso phusanâ samphusanâ samphusitattaṃ—ayaṃ tasmiṃ samaye phasso hoti.

152. Katamâ tasmiṃ samaye vedanâ hoti? Yaṃ tasmiṃ samaye tajjâ manoviññâṇadhâtu samphassajaṃ cetasikaṃ neva sâtaṃ nâsâtaṃ cetosaṃphassajaṃ adukkhamasukhaṃ vedayitaṃ cetosamphassajâ adukkhamasukhâ vedanâ—ayaṃ tasmiṃ samaye vedanâ hoti . . . pe . . .

153. Katamâ tasmiṃ samaye upekkhâ hoti? Yaṃ tasmiṃ samaye cetasikaṃ neva sâtaṃ nâsâtaṃ cetosamphassajaṃ adukkhamasukhaṃ vedayitaṃ cetosamphassajâ adukkhamasukhâ vedanâ—ayaṃ tasmiṃ samaye upekkhâ hoti . . . pe . . .

154. Katamaṃ tasmiṃ samaye upekkhindriyaṃ hoti? Yaṃ tasmiṃ samaye cetasikaṃ . . . pe (153) . . . vedanâ idaṃ tasmiṃ samaye upekkhindriyaṃ hoti . . . pe . . . ye vâ pana tasmiṃ samaye aññe pi atthi paṭiccasamuppannâ arûpino dhammâ—ime dhammâ kusalâ.

Tasmiṃ kho pana samaye cattâro khandhâ honti dvâyatanâni honti, dve dhâtuyo honti, tayo âhârâ honti, aṭṭhindriyâni honti, caturaṅgikaṃ jhânaṃ hoti, pañcaṅgiko maggo hoti, satta balâni honti, tayo hetû honti, eko phasso hoti . . . pe (58) . . . ekaṃ dhammâyatanaṃ hoti, ekâ dhammadhâtu hoti, ye vâ pana tasmiṃ samaye aññe pi atthi paṭiccasamuppannâ arûpino dhammâ—ime dhammâ kusalâ . . . pe . . . (59–61)

155. Katamo tasmiṃ samaye saṅkhârakkhandho hoti? Phasso . . . pe (62) . . . saṅkhârakkhandho hoti.

Imo dhammâ kusalâ.

Pañcamaṃ.

156. Katame dhammâ kusalâ? Yasmiṃ samaye kâmâvacaraṃ kusalaṃ cittaṃ uppannaṃ hoti upekkhâsahagataṃ ñâṇasampayuttaṃ sasaṅkhâreṇa rûpârammaṇaṃ vâ . . . pe . . . dhammârammaṇaṃ vâ, yaṃ yaṃ vâ pan' ârabbha tasmiṃ samaye phasso hoti . . . pe . . . avikkhepo hoti . . . ime dhammâ kusalâ.

Chaṭṭhaṃ.

157. Katame dhammâ kusalâ? Yasmiṃ samaye kâmâvacaraṃ kusalaṃ cittaṃ uppannaṃ hoti upekkhâsahagataṃ ñâṇavippayuttaṃ rûpârammaṇaṃ vâ saddârammaṇaṃ vâ gandhârammaṇaṃ vâ rasârammaṇaṃ vâ phoṭṭhabbârammaṇaṃ vâ dhammârammaṇaṃ vâ, yaṃ yaṃ vâ panârabbha, tasmiṃ samaye phasso hoti, vedanâ hoti, saññâ hoti, cetanâ hoti, cittaṃ hoti, vitakko hoti, vicâro hoti, upekkhâ hoti, cittass' ekaggatâ hoti, saddhindriyaṃ hoti, viriyindriyaṃ hoti, satindriyaṃ hoti, samâdhindriyaṃ hoti, ñâṇindriyaṃ hoti, upekkhindriyaṃ hoti, jîvitindriyaṃ hoti, ← sammâsaṅkappo hoti, sammâvâyâmo hoti, sammâsati hoti, sammâsamâdhi hoti, saddhâbalaṃ hoti, viriyabalaṃ hoti, satibalaṃ hoti, samâdhibalaṃ hoti, hiribalaṃ hoti, ottappabalaṃ hoti, alobho hoti, adoso hoti, anabhijjhâ hoti, avyâpâdo hoti, hiri hoti, ottappaṃ hoti, kâyapassaddhi hoti, cittapassaddhi hoti, kâyalahutâ hoti, cittalahutâ hoti, kâyamudutâ hoti, cittamudutâ hoti, kâyakammaññatâ hoti, cittakammaññatâ hoti, kâyapâguññatâ hoti, cittapâguññatâ hoti, kâyujjukatâ hoti, cittujjukatâ hoti, sati hoti, sampajaññaṃ hoti, samatho hoti, paggâho hoti, avikkhepo hoti; ye vâ pana tasmiṃ samaye añño pi atthi paṭiccasamuppannâ arûpino dhammâ—ime dhammâ kusalâ. Tasmiṃ kho pana samaye cattâro khandhâ honti, dvâyatanâni honti, dve dhâtuyo honti, tayo âhârâ

honti, sattindriyâni honti, caturaṅgikaṃ jhânaṃ hoti, caturaṅgiko maggo hoti, cha balâni honti, dve hetû honti, eko phasso hoti . . . pe (58) . . . ekaṃ dhammâyatanaṃ hoti, ekâ dhammadhâtu hoti—ye vâ pana tasmiṃ samaye añño pi atthi paṭiccasamuppannâ arûpino dhammâ — ime dhammâ kusalâ . . . pe . . . (59–61)

158. Katamo tasmiṃ samaye saṅkhârakkhandho hoti?

Phasso cetanâ vitakko vicâro cittass' ekaggatâ saddhindriyaṃ viriyindriyaṃ satindriyaṃ samâdhindriyaṃ jîvitindriyaṃ sammâsaṅkappo, sammâvâyâmo, sammâsati, sammâsamâdhi, saddhâbalaṃ, viriyabalaṃ, satibalaṃ, samâdhibalaṃ, hiribalaṃ ottappabalaṃ, alobho, adoso, anabhijjhâ, avyâpâdo, hiri, ottappaṃ, kâyapassaddhi, cittapassaddhi, kâyalahutâ, cittalahutâ, kâyamudutâ, cittamudutâ, kâyakammaññatâ, cittakammaññatâ, kâyapâguññatâ, cittapâguññatâ, kâyujjukatâ, cittujjukatâ, sati, samatho, paggâho, avikkhepo, ye vâ pana tasmiṃ samaye añño pi atthi paṭiccasamuppannâ arûpino dhammâ, ṭhapetvâ vedanâkkhandhaṃ, ṭhapetvâ saññâkkhandhaṃ, ṭhapetvâ viññâṇakkhandhaṃ; ayaṃ tasmiṃ samaye saṅkhârakkhandho hoti, ye vâ pana tasmiṃ samaye añño pi atthi paṭiccasamuppannâ arûpino dhammâ — ime dhammâ kusalâ.

Sattamaṃ.

159. Katame dhammâ kusalâ?

Yasmiṃ samaye kâmâvacaraṃ kusalaṃ cittaṃ uppannaṃ hoti, upekkhâsahagataṃ ñâṇavippayuttaṃ sasaṅkhârena rûpârammaṇaṃ vâ . . . pe (147) . . . dhammârammaṇaṃ vâ, yaṃ yaṃ vâ panârabbha tasmiṃ samaye phasso hoti . . . pe (147) . . . avikkhepo hoti . . . pe (147) . . . ime dhammâ kusalâ.

Aṭṭhamaṃ.

Kâmâvacara-aṭṭhamahâcittâni.

DUTIYAṂ BHÂṆAVÂRAṂ.

160. Katame dhammâ kusalâ?

Yasmiṃ samaye rûpûpapattiyâ maggaṃ bhâveti vivicc' eva kâmehi vivicca akusalehi dhammehi savitakkaṃ savicâraṃ vivekajaṃ pîtisukhaṃ paṭhamaṃ jhânaṃ upasampajja viharati pathavîkasiṇaṃ tasmiṃ samaye phasso hoti . . . pe (147) . . . avikkhepo hoti—ye vâ pana tasmim samaye añño pi atthi paṭiccasamuppannâ arûpino dhammâ—ime dhammâ kusalâ.

161. Katamo dhammâ kusalâ?

Yasmiṃ samaye rûpûpapattiyâ maggaṃ bhâveti vitakkavicârânaṃ vûpasamâ ajjhattaṃ sampasâdanaṃ cetaso ekodibhavaṃ avitakkaṃ avicâraṃ samâdhijaṃ pîtisukhaṃ dutiyaṃ jhânaṃ upasampajja viharati pathavîkasiṇaṃ, tasmiṃ samaye phasso hoti, vedanâ hoti, saññâ hoti, cetanâ hoti, cittaṃ hoti, pîti hoti, sukhaṃ hoti, citass' ekaggatâ hoti, saddhindriyaṃ hoti, viriyindriyaṃ hoti, satindriyaṃ hoti, samâdhindriyaṃ hoti, paññindriyaṃ hoti, manindriyaṃ hoti, somanassindriyaṃ hoti, jîvitindriyaṃ hoti, sammâdiṭṭhi hoti, sammâvâyâmo hoti . . . pe (157) . . . paggâho hoti, avikkhepo hoti —ye vâ pana tasmiṃ samaye aññe pi atthi paṭiccasamuppannâ arûpino dhammâ—ime dhammâ kusalâ.

Tasmiṃ kho pana samaye cattâro khandhâ honti dvâyatanâni honti dve dhâtuyo honti tayo âhârâ honti aṭṭhindriyâni honti tivaṅgikaṃ jhânaṃ hoti caturaṅgiko maggo hoti satta balâni honti tayo hetû honti eko phasso hoti . . . pe . . . ekaṃ dhammâyatanaṃ hoti, ekâ dhammadhâtu hoti, ye vâ pana tasmiṃ samaye aññe pi atthi paṭiccasamuppannâ arûpino dhammâ—ime dhammâ kusalâ . . . pe.

162. Katamo tasmiṃ samaye saṅkhârakkhandho hoti?

Phasso cetanâ pîti cittas' ekaggatâ saddhindriyaṃ viriyindriyaṃ satindriyaṃ samâdhindriyaṃ paññindriyaṃ jîvitindriyaṃ sammâdiṭṭhi sammâvâyâmo . . . pe (158) . . . paggâho avikkhepo ye vâ pana tasmiṃ samaye añño pi atthi paṭiccasamuppannâ arûpino dhammâ, ṭhapetvâ vedanâkkhandhaṃ ṭhapetvâ saññâkkhandhaṃ ṭhapetvâ viññâṇakkhandhaṃ—ayaṃ tasmiṃ samaye saṅkhârakkhandho hoti . . . pe . . . ime dhammâ kusalâ.

163. Katamo dhammâ kusalâ?

Yasmiṃ samaye rûpûpapattiyâ maggaṃ bhâveti pîtiyâ ca virâgâ upekkhako ca viharati sato ca sampajâno sukhañ ca kâyena paṭisaṃvedeti yaṃ taṃ ariyâ âcikkhanti upekkhako satimâ sukhavihârîti tatiyaṃ jhânaṃ upasampajja viharati pathavîkasiṇaṃ—tasmiṃ samaye phasso hoti vedanâ hoti saññâ hoti cetanâ hoti cittaṃ hoti sukhaṃ hoti cittass' ekaggatâ hoti saddhindriyaṃ hoti viriyindriyaṃ hoti samâdhindriyam hoti paññindriyaṃ hoti manindriyaṃ hoti somanassindriyaṃ hoti jîvitindriyaṃ hoti sammâdiṭṭhi hoti sammâsati hoti sammâvâyâmo hoti . . . pe (157) . . . paggâho hoti avikkhepo hoti ye vâ pana tasmiṃ samaye aññe pi atthi paṭiccasamuppannâ arûpino dhammâ—ime dhammâ kusalâ . . . pe . . . Tasmiṃ kho pana samaye cattâro khandhâ honti dvâyatanâni honti dve dhâtuyo honti tayo âhârâ honti aṭṭhindriyâni honti duvaṅgikaṃ jhânaṃ hoti caturaṅgiko maggo hoti satta balâni honti tayo hetû honti eko phasso hoti . . . pe . . . ekaṃ dhammâyatanaṃ hoti ekâ dhammadhâtu hoti—ye vâ pana tasmiṃ samaye aññe pi atthi paṭiccasamuppannâ arûpino dhammâ—ime dhammâ kusalâ . . . pe . . .

164. Katamo tasmiṃ samaye saṅkhârakkhandho hoti?

Phasso cetanâ cittass' ekaggatâ saddhindriyaṃ viriyindriyaṃ satindriyaṃ samâdhindriyaṃ paññindriyaṃ jîvitindriyaṃ sammâdiṭṭhi sammâvâyâmo . . . pe (148) . . . paggâho avikkhepo, ye vâ pana tasmiṃ samaye aññe pi atthi paṭiccasamuppannâ arûpino dhammâ ṭhapetvâ vedanâkkhandhaṃ ṭhapetvâ saññâkkhandhaṃ ṭhapetvâ viññâṇakkhandhaṃ—ayaṃ tasmiṃ samaye saṅkhârakkhandho hoti—ye vâ pana tasmiṃ samaye aññe pi atthi paṭiccasamuppannâ arûpino dhammâ—ime dhammâ kusalâ.

165. Katame dhammâ kusalâ?

Yasmiṃ samaye rûpûpapattiyâ maggaṃ bhâveti sukhassa ca pahânâ dukkhassa ca pahânâ pubb' eva somanassadomanassânaṃ atthaṅgamâ adukkhamasukhaṃ upekkhâ satipârisuddhiṃ catutthaṃ jhânaṃ upasampajja viharati paṭhavîkasiṇaṃ, tasmiṃ samaye phasso hoti vedanâ hoti saññâ hoti cetanâ hoti cittaṃ hoti upekkhâ hoti cittass' ekaggatâ hoti saddhindriyaṃ hoti viriyindriyaṃ hoti satindriyaṃ hoti samâdhindriyaṃ hoti paññindriyaṃ hoti manindriyaṃ hoti upekkhindriyaṃ hoti jîvitindriyaṃ hoti sammâdiṭṭhi hoti sammâvâyâmo hoti . . . pe (157) . . . paggâho hoti avikkhepo hoti—ye vâ pana tasmiṃ samaye aññe pi atthi paṭiccasamuppannâ arûpino dhammâ—ime dhammâ kusalâ . . . pe . . . tasmiṃ kho pana samaye cattâro khandhâ honti dvâyatanâni honti dve dhâtuyo honti tayo âhârâ honti aṭṭhindriyâni honti duvaṅgikaṃ jhânaṃ hoti caturaṅgiko maggo hoti satta balâni honti tayo hetû honti eko phasso hoti . . . pe (58) . . . ekaṃ dhammâyatanaṃ hoti ekâ dhammadhâtu hoti ye vâ pana tasmiṃ samaye aññe pi atthi paṭiccasamuppannâ arûpino dhammâ—ime dhammâ kusalâ . . . pe . . . (59-61)

166. Katamo tasmiṃ samaye saṅkhârakkhandho hoti?

Phasso cetanâ cittassekaggatâ saddhindriyaṃ viriyindriyaṃ samâdhindriyaṃ paññindriyaṃ jîvitindriyaṃ sammâdiṭṭhi sammâvâyâmo . . . pe . . . paggâho avikkhepo ye vâ pana tasmiṃ samaye aññe pi atthi paṭiccasamuppannâ arûpino dhammâ ṭhapetvâ vedanâkkhandhaṃ ṭhapetvâ saññâkkhandhaṃ ṭhapetvâ viññâṇakkhandhaṃ—ayaṃ tasmiṃ samaye saṅkhârakkhandho hoti . . . pe . . . ime dhammâ kusalâ.

Catukkanayo.

167. Katame dhammâ kusalâ?

Yasmiṃ samaye rûpûpapattiyâ maggaṃ bhâveti vivicceva kâmehi . . . pe . . . paṭhamaṃ jhânaṃ upasampajja viharati pathavîkasiṇaṃ tasmiṃ samaye phasso hoti . . . pe . . . avikkhepo hoti . . . pe . . . ime dhammâ kusalâ.

168. Katame dhammâ kusalâ?

Yasmiṃ samaye rûpûpapattiyâ maggaṃ bhâveti avitakkaṃ vicâramattaṃ samâdhijaṃ pîtisukhaṃ dutiyaṃ jhânaṃ upasampajja viharati pathavîkasiṇaṃ tasmiṃ samaye phasso hoti vedanâ hoti saññâ hoti cetanâ hoti cittaṃ hoti vicâro hoti pîti hoti sukhaṃ hoti cittass' ekaggatâ hoti saddhindriyaṃ hoti viriyindriyaṃ hoti satindriyaṃ hoti samâdhindriyaṃ hoti paññindriyaṃ hoti manindriyaṃ hoti somanassindriyaṃ hoti jîvitindriyaṃ hoti sammâdiṭṭhi hoti sammâvâyâmo hoti . . . pe . . . paggâho hoti avikkhepo hoti ye vâ pana tasmiṃ samaye aññe pi atthi paṭiccasamuppannâ arûpino dhammâ—

ime dhammâ kusalâ . . . pe . . . Tasmiṃ kho pana samaye cattâro khandhâ honti dvâyatanâni honti dve dhâtuyo honti tayo âhârâ honti aṭṭhindriyâni honti caturaṅgikaṃ jhânaṃ hoti caturaṅgiko maggo hoti satta balâni honti tayo hetû honti eko phasso hoti . . . pe . . . ekaṃ dhammâyatanaṃ hoti ekâ dhammadhâtu hoti—ye vâ pana tasmiṃ samaye aññe pi atthi paṭiccasamuppannâ arûpino dhammâ—ime dhammâ kusalâ . . . pe . . . (59–61)

169. Katamo tasmiṃ samaye saṅkhârakkhandho hoti?

Phasso cetanâ vicâro pîti cittass' ekaggatâ saddhindriyaṃ viriyindriyaṃ satindriyaṃ samâdhindriyaṃ paññindriyaṃ jîvitindriyaṃ sammâdiṭṭhi sammâvâyâmo . . . pe . . . paggâho avikkhepo ye vâ pana tasmiṃ samaye aññe pi atthi paṭiccasamuppannâ arûpino dhammâ ṭhapetvâ vedanâkkhandhaṃ ṭhâpetvâ saññâkkhandhaṃ ṭhapetvâ viññânakkhandhaṃ ayaṃ tasmiṃ samaye saṅkhârakkhandho hoti . . . pe . . . ime dhammâ kusalâ.

170. Katame dhammâ kusalâ?

Yasmiṃ samaye rûpûpapattiyâ maggaṃ bhâveti vitakkavicârânaṃ vûpasamâ . . . pe . . . tatiyaṃ jhânaṃ upasampajja viharati pathavîkasiṇaṃ tasmiṃ samaye phasso hoti vedanâ hoti saññâ hoti cetanâ hoti cittaṃ hoti pîti hoti sukhaṃ hoti cittass' ekaggatâ hoti saddhindriyaṃ hoti viriyindriyaṃ hoti satindriyaṃ hoti samâdhindriyaṃ hoti paññindriyaṃ hoti manindriyaṃ hoti somanassindriyaṃ hoti jîvitindriyaṃ hoti sammâdiṭṭhi hoti sammâvâyâmo hoti . . . pe . . . paggâho hoti avikkhepo hoti ye vâ pana tasmiṃ samaye aññe pi atthi paṭiccasamuppannâ arûpino dhammâ—ime dhammâ kusalâ . . . pe . . . (157)

Tasmiṃ kho pana samaye cattâro khandhâ honti dvâyatanâni honti dve dhâtuyo honti tayo âhârâ honti aṭṭhindriyâni honti tivaṅgikaṃ jhânaṃ hoti caturaṅgiko maggo hoti satta balâni honti tayo hetû honti eko phasso hoti . . . pe . . . ekaṃ dhammâyatanaṃ hoti, ekâ dhammadhâtu hoti ye vâ pana tasmiṃ samaye aññe pi atthi paṭiccasamuppannâ arûpino dhammâ—ime dhammâ kusalâ . . . pe . . . (59–61)

171. Katamo tasmiṃ samaye saṅkhârakkhandho hoti?

Phasso cetanâ pîti[sukhaṃ] cittass' ekaggatâ saddhindriyaṃ viriyindriyaṃ satindriyaṃ samâdhindriyaṃ paññindriyaṃ jîvitindriyaṃ sammâdiṭṭhi sammâvâyâmo . . . pe . . . paggâho avikkhepo ye vâ pana tasmiṃ samaye aññe pi atthi paṭiccasamuppannâ arûpino dhammâ, ṭhapetvâ vedanâkkhandhaṃ ṭhapetvâ saññâkkhandhaṃ, ṭhapetvâ viññâṇakkhandhaṃ ayaṃ tasmiṃ samaye saṅkhârakkhandho hoti . . . pe . . . ime dhammâ kusalâ.

172. Katame dhammâ kusalâ?

Yasmiṃ samaye rûpûpapattiyâ maggaṃ bhâveti pîtiyâ ca virâgâ . . . pe . . . catutthaṃ jhânaṃ upasampajja viharati paṭhavîkasiṇaṃ tasmiṃ samaye phasso hoti vedanâ hoti saññâ hoti cetanâ hoti cittaṃ hoti sukhaṃ hoti cittass' ekaggatâ hoti saddhindriyaṃ hoti viriyindriyaṃ hoti satindriyaṃ hoti samâdhindriyaṃ hoti paññindriyaṃ hoti manindriyaṃ hoti somanass' indriyaṃ hoti jîvitindriyaṃ hoti sammâdiṭṭhi hoti sammâvâyâmo hoti . . . pe . . . paggâho hoti avikkhepo hoti ye vâ pana tasmiṃ samaye aññe pi atthi paṭiccasamuppannâ arûpino dhammâ—ime dhammâ kusalâ . . . pe . . . tasmiṃ kho pana samaye cattâro khandhâ honti dvâyatanâni honti dve dhâtuyo honti tayo âhârâ honti aṭṭhindriyâni honti duvaṅgikaṃ jhânaṃ hoti caturaṅgiko maggo hoti satta balâni honti tayo hetû honti eko phasso hoti . . . pe . . . ekaṃ dhammâyatanaṃ hoti ekâ dhammadhâtu hoti ye vâ pana tasmiṃ samaye aññe pi atthi paṭiccasamuppannâ arûpino dhammâ—ime dhammâ kusalâ . . . pe . . . (59-61)

173. Katamo tasmiṃ samaye saṅkhârakhhandho hoti?

Phasso cetanâ citass' ekaggatâ saddhindriyaṃ viriyindriyaṃ satindriyaṃ samâdhindriyaṃ paññindriyaṃ jîvitindriyaṃ sammâdaṭṭhi sammâvâyâmo . . . pe . . . paggâho avikkhepo ye vâ pana tasmiṃ samaye aññe pi atthi paṭiccasamuppannâ arûpino dhammâ ṭhapetvâ vedanâkkhandhaṃ, ṭhapetvâ saññâkkhandhaṃ ṭhapetvâ viññâṇakkhandhaṃ—ayaṃ tasmiṃ samaye saṅkhârakkhandho hoti . . . pe . . . ime dhammâ kusalâ.

174. Katame dhammâ kusalâ?

Yasmiṃ samaye rûpûpapattiyâ maggaṃ bhâveti sukhassa ca pahânâ . . . pe . . . pañcamaṃ jhânaṃ upasampajja viharati pathavîkasiṇam tasmiṃ samaye phasso hoti vedanâ hoti saññâ hoti cetanâ hoti cittaṃ hoti upekkhâ hoti cittass' ekaggatâ hoti saddhindriyaṃ hoti viriyindriyaṃ hoti satindriyaṃ hoti samâdhindriyaṃ hoti paññindriyaṃ hoti manindriyaṃ hoti upekkhindriyaṃ hoti jîvitindriyaṃ hoti sammâdiṭṭhi hoti sammâvâyâmo hoti . . . pe . . . paggâho hoti avikkhepo hoti ye vâ pana tasmiṃ samaye aññe pi atthi paṭiccasamuppannâ arûpino dhammâ—ime dhammâ kusalâ . . . pe . . . (157) tasmiṃ kho pana samaye cattâro khandhâ honti dvâyatanâni honti dve dhâtuyo honti tayo âhârâ honti aṭṭhindriyâni honti duvaṅgikaṃ jhânaṃ hoti caturaṅgiko maggo hoti satta balâni honti tayo hetu honti eko phasso hoti . . . pe . . . (58) ekaṃ dhammâyatanaṃ hoti ekâ dhammadhâtu hoti, ye vâ pana tasmiṃ samaye aññe pi atthi paṭiccasamuppannâ arûpino dhammâ — ime dhammâ kusalâ . . . pe . . . (59–61)

175. Katamo tasmiṃ samaye saṅkhârakkhandho hoti?

Phasso cetanâ cittass' ekaggatâ saddhindriyaṃ viriyindriyaṃ satindriyaṃ samâdhindriyaṃ paññindriyaṃ jîvitindriyaṃ sammâdiṭṭhi sammâvâyâmo . . . pe . . . paggâho avikkhepo ye vâ pana tasmiṃ samaye aññe pi atthi paṭiccasamuppannâ arûpino dhammâ ṭhapetvâ vedanâkkhandhaṃ ṭhapetvâ saññâkkhandaṃ ṭhapetvâ viññâṇakkhandhaṃ ayaṃ tasmiṃ samaye saṅkhârakkhandho hoti . . . pe . . . ime dhammâ kusalâ.

Pañcakanayo.

176. Katame dhammâ kusalâ?

Yasmiṃ samaye rûpûpapattiyâ maggaṃ bhâveti vivicceva kâmehi . . . pe . . . paṭhamaṃ jhânaṃ upasampajja viharati dukkhâpaṭipadaṃ dandhâbhiññaṃ pathavîkasiṇaṃ—tasmiṃ samaye phasso hoti . . . pe . . . avikkhepo koti . . . pe . . . ime dhammâ kusalâ.

177. Katame dhammâ kusalâ?

Yasmiṃ samaye rûpûpapattiyâ maggaṃ bhâveti vivicceva kâmehi . . . pe . . . paṭhamaṃ jhânaṃ upasampajja viharati dukkhâpaṭipadaṃ khippâbhiññaṃ pathavîkasiṇaṃ tasmiṃ samaye phasso hoti . . . pe . . . avikkhepo hoti . . . pe . . . ime dhammâ kusalâ.

178. Katame dhammâ kusalâ?

Yasmiṃ samaye rûpûpapattiyâ maggaṃ bhâveti vivicceva kâmehi . . . pe . . . paṭhamaṃ jhânaṃ upasampajja viharati sukhâpaṭipadaṃ dandhâbhiññaṃ pathavîkasiṇaṃ tasmiṃ samaye phasso hoti . . . pe . . . avikkhepo hoti . . . pe . . . ime dhammâ kusalâ.

179. Katame dhammâ kusalâ?

Yasmiṃ samaye rûpûpapattiyâ maggaṃ bhâveti vivicceva kâmehi . . . pe . . . paṭhamaṃ jhânaṃ upasampajja viharati sukhâpaṭipadaṃ khippâbhiññaṃ pathavîkasinaṃ tasmiṃ samaye phasso hoti . . . pe . . . avikkhepo hoti . . . ime dhammâ kusalâ.

180. Katame dhammâ kusalâ?

Yasmiṃ samaye rûpûpapattiyâ maggaṃ bhâveti vitakkavicârânaṃ vûpasamâ . . . pe . . . dutiyaṃ jhânaṃ . . . pe . . . tatiyaṃ jhânaṃ . . . pe . . . catutthaṃ jhânaṃ . . . pe . . . paṭhamaṃ jhânaṃ . . . pe . . . pañcamaṃ jhânaṃ upasampajja viharati dukkhâpaṭipadaṃ dandhâbhiññaṃ pathavîkasiṇaṃ . . . pe . . . dukkhâpaṭipadaṃ khippâbhiññaṃ pathavîkasiṇaṃ . . . pe . . . sukhâpaṭipadaṃ dandhâbhiññaṃ pathavîkasinaṃ . . . pe . . . sukhâpaṭipadaṃ khippâbhiññaṃ pathavîkasiṇaṃ—tasmiṃ samaye phasso hoti . . . pe . . . avikkhepo hoti . . . pe . . . ime dhammâ kusalâ.

Catasso paṭipadâ.

181. Katame dhammâ kusalâ?

Yasmiṃ samaye rûpûpapattiyâ maggaṃ bhâveti vivicceva kâmehi . . . pe . . . paṭhamaṃ jhânaṃ upasampajja viharati parittaṃ parittârammaṇaṃ pathavîkasiṇaṃ, tasmiṃ samaye phasso hoti . . . pe . . . avikkhepo hoti . . . pe . . . ime dhammâ kusalâ.

182. Katame dhammâ kusalâ?

Yasmiṃ samaye rûpûpapattiyâ maggaṃ bhâveti vivicceva kâmehi . . . pe . . . paṭhamaṃ jhânaṃ upasampajja viharati parittaṃ appamâṇârammaṇaṃ pathavîkasiṇaṃ—tasmiṃ samaye phasso hoti . . . pe . . . avikkhepo hoti . . . pe . . . ime dhammâ kusalâ.

183. Katame dhammâ kusalâ?

Yasmiṃ samaye rûpûpapattiyâ maggaṃ bhâveti vivicceva kâmehi . . . pe . . . paṭhamaṃ jhânaṃ upasampajja viharati appamâṇaṃ parittârammaṇaṃ pathavîkasiṇaṃ—tasmiṃ samaye phasso hoti . . . pe . . . avikkhepo hoti . . . pe . . . ime dhammâ kusalâ.

184. Katame dhammâ kusalâ?

Yasmiṃ samaye rûpûpapattiyâ maggaṃ bhâveti vivicceva kâmehi . . . pe . . . paṭhamaṃ jhânaṃ upasampajja viharati appamâṇaṃ appamâṇârammaṇaṃ pathavîkasinaṃ tasmiṃ samaye phasso hoti . . . pe . . . avikkhepo hoti . . . pe . . . ime dhammâ kusalâ.

185. Katame dhammâ kusalâ?

Yasmim samaye rûpûpapattiyâ maggaṃ bhâveti vitakkavicârânaṃ vûpasamâ . . . pe . . . dutiyaṃ jhânaṃ . . . pe . . . tatiyaṃ jhânaṃ . . . pe . . . catutthaṃ jhânaṃ . . . pe . . . paṭhamaṃ jhânaṃ upasampajja viharati parittaṃ parittârammaṇaṃ pathavîkasiṇaṃ . . . pe . . . parittaṃ appamânârammaṇaṃ pathavîkasiṇaṃ . . . pe . . . appamâṇaṃ parittârammaṇaṃ pathavîkasiṇaṃ . . . pe . . . appamâṇaṃ appamâṇârammaṇaṃ pathavîkasiṇam, tasmiṃ samaye phasso hoti . . . pe . . . avikkhepo hoti—ime dhammâ kusalâ.

Cattâri ârammaṇâni.

186. Katame dhammâ kusalâ?

Yasmiṃ samaye rûpûpapattiyâ maggaṃ bhâveti vivicceva kâmehi . . . pe . . . paṭhamaṃ jhânaṃ upasampajja viharati dukkhâpaṭipadam dandhâbhiññaṃ parittaṃ parittârammaṇaṃ pathavîkasiṇaṃ tasmiṃ samaye phasso hoti . . . pe . . . avikkhepo hoti—ime dhammâ kusalâ.

187. Katame dhammâ kusalâ?

Yasmiṃ samaye rûpûpapattiyâ maggaṃ bhâveti vivicceva kâmehi . . . pe . . . paṭhamaṃ jhânaṃ upasampajja viharati dukkhâpaṭipadaṃ dandhâbhiññam parittaṃ appamânârammaṇaṃ pathavîkasiṇaṃ, tasmiṃ samaye phasso hoti . . . pe . . . avikkhepo hoti . . . pe . . . ime dhammâ kusalâ.

188. Katame dhammâ kusalâ?

Yasmiṃ samaye rûpûpapattiyâ maggaṃ bhâveti vivicceva kâmehi . . . pe . . . paṭhamaṃ jhâṇaṃ upasampajja viharati dukkhâpaṭipadaṃ dandhâbhiññaṃ appamâṇaṃ parittârammaṇaṃ pathavîkasiṇaṃ—tasmiṃ samaye phasso hoti . . . pe . . . avikkhepo hoti . . . pe . . . ime dhammâ kusalâ.

189. Katame dhammâ kusalâ?

Yasmiṃ samaye rûpûpapattiyâ maggaṃ bhâveti vivicceva kâmehi . . . pe . . . paṭhamaṃ jhânaṃ upasampajja viharati dukkhâpaṭipadaṃ dandhâbhiññaṃ appamâṇaṃ appamâṇârammaṇaṃ paṭhavîkasiṇaṃ tasmiṃ samaye phasso hoti . . . pe . . . avikkhepo hoti . . . pe . . . ime dhammâ kusalâ.

190. Katame dhammâ kusalâ?

Yasmiṃ samaye rûpûpapattiyâ maggaṃ bhâveti vivicceva kâmehi . . . pe . . . paṭhamaṃ jhânaṃ upasampajja viharati dukkhâpaṭipadaṃ khippâbhiññaṃ parittaṃ parittârammaṇaṃ paṭhavîkasiṇaṃ tasmiṃ samaye phasso hoti . . . pe . . . avikkhepo hoti . . . pe . . . ime dhammâ kusalâ.

191. Katame dhammâ kusalâ?

Yasmiṃ samaye rûpûpapattiyâ maggaṃ bhâveti vivicceva kâmehi . . . pe . . . paṭhamaṃ jhânaṃ upasampajja viharati dukkhâpaṭipadaṃ khippâbhiññaṃ parittaṃ appamâṇârammaṇaṃ paṭhavîkasiṇaṃ, tasmiṃ samaye phasso hoti . . . pe . . . avikkhepo hoti . . . pe . . . ime dhammâ kusalâ.

192. Katame dhammâ kusalâ?

Yasmiṃ samaye rûpûpapattiyâ maggaṃ bhâveti vivicceva kamehi . . . pe . . . paṭhamaṃ jhânaṃ upasampajja viharati dukkhâpaṭipadaṃ khippâbhiññaṃ appamâṇam parittârammaṇaṃ paṭhavîkasiṇaṃ tasmiṃ samaye phasso hoti . . . pe . . . avikkhepo hoti . . . pe . . . ime dhammâ kusalâ.

193. Katame dhammâ kusalâ?

Yasmiṃ samaye rûpûpapattiyâ maggaṃ bhâveti vivicceva kâmehi . . . pe . . . paṭhamaṃ jhânaṃ upasampajja viharati dukkhâpaṭipadaṃ khippâbhiññaṃ appamâṇaṃ appamâṇârammaṇaṃ paṭhavîkasiṇaṃ, tasmiṃ samaye phasso hoti . . . pe . . . avikkhepo hoti . . . pe . . . ime dhammâ kusalâ.

194. Katame dhammâ kusalâ?

Yasmiṃ samaye rûpûpapattiyâ maggaṃ bhâveti vivicceva kâmehi . . . pe . . . paṭhamaṃ jhânaṃ upasampajja viharati sukhâpaṭipadaṃ dandhâbhiññaṃ parittârammaṇaṃ pathavîkasiṇaṃ—tasmiṃ samaye phasso hoti . . . pe . . . avikkhepo hoti . . . pe . . . ime dhammâ kusalâ.

195. Katame dhammâ kusalâ?

Yasmiṃ samaye rûpûpapattiyâ maggaṃ bhâveti vivicceva kâmehi . . . pe . . . paṭhamaṃ jhânaṃ upasampajja viharati sukhâpaṭipadaṃ dandhâbhiññaṃ parittaṃ appamâṇârammaṇaṃ pathavîkasiṇaṃ tasmiṃ samaye phasso hoti . . . pe . . . avikkhepo hoti . . . pe . . . ime dhammâ kusalâ

196. Katame dhammâ kusalâ?

Yasmiṃ samaye rûpûpapattiyâ maggaṃ bhâveti vivicceva kâmehi . . . pe . . . paṭhamaṃ jhânaṃ upasampajja viharati sukhâpaṭipadaṃ dandhâbhiññaṃ appamâṇaṃ parittârammaṇaṃ pathavîkasiṇaṃ tasmiṃ samaye phasso hoti . . . pe . . . avikkhepo hoti . . . pe . . . ime dhammâ kusalâ.

197. Katame dhammâ kusalâ?

Yasmiṃ samaye rûpûpapattiyâ maggaṃ bhâveti vivicceva kâmehi . . . pe . . . paṭhamaṃ jhânaṃ upasampajja viharati sukhâpaṭipadaṃ dandhâbhiññaṃ appamâṇaṃ appamâṇârammaṇaṃ pathavîkasiṇaṃ tasmiṃ samaye phasso hoti . . . pe . . . avikkhepo hoti . . . pe . . . ime dhammâ kusalâ.

198. Katame dhammâ kusalâ?

Tasmiṃ samaye rûpûpapattiyâ maggaṃ bhâveti vivicceva kâmehi . . . pe . . . paṭhamaṃ jhânaṃ upasampajja viharati sukhâpaṭipadaṃ khippâbhiññaṃ parittaṃ parittârammaṇaṃ pathavîkasiṇaṃ tasmiṃ samaye phasso hoti . . . pe . . . avikkhepo hoti . . . pe . . . ime dhammâ kusalâ.

199. Katame dhammâ kusalâ?

Yasmiṃ samaye rûpûpapattiyâ maggaṃ bhâveti vivicceva kâmehi . . . pe . . . paṭhamaṃ jhânaṃ upasampajja viharati sukhâpaṭipadaṃ khippâbhiññaṃ parittaṃ appamâṇârammaṇaṃ pathavîkasiṇaṃ tasmiṃ samaye phasso hoti . . . pe . . . avikkhepo hoti . . . pe . . . ime dhammâ kusalâ.

200. Katame dhammâ kusalâ?

Yasmiṃ samaye rûpûpapattiyâ maggaṃ bhâveti vivicceva kâmehi . . . pe . . . paṭhamaṃ jhânaṃ upasampajja viharati sukhâpaṭipadaṃ khippâbhiññaṃ appamâṇaṃ parittârammaṇaṃ pathavîkasiṇaṃ tasmiṃ samaye phasso hoti . . . pe . . . avikkhepo hoti . . . pe . . . ime dhammâ kusalâ.

201. Katame dhammâ kusalâ?

Yasmiṃ samaye rûpûpapattiyâ maggaṃ bhâveti vivicceva kâmehi . . . pe . . . paṭhamaṃ jhânaṃ upasampajja viharati sukhâpaṭipadaṃ khippâbhiññaṃ appamâṇaṃ appamâṇârammaṇaṃ pathavîkasiṇaṃ tasmiṃ samaye phasso hoti . . . pe . . . avikkhepo hoti . . . pe . . . ime dhammâ kusalâ.

202. Katame dhammâ kusalâ?

Yasmiṃ samaye rûpûpapattiyâ maggaṃ bhâveti vitakkavicârânaṃ vûpasamâ . . . pe . . . dutiyaṃ jhânaṃ . . . pe . . . tatiyaṃ jhânaṃ . . . pe . . . catutthaṃ jhânaṃ . . . pe . . . paṭhamaṃ jhânaṃ . . . pe . . . pañcamaṃ jhânaṃ upasampajja viharati dukkhâpaṭipadaṃ dandhâbhiññaṃ parittaṃ parittârammaṇaṃ pathavîkasiṇaṃ . . . pe . . . dukkhâpaṭipadaṃ dandhâbhiññaṃ parittaṃ appamâṇârammaṇaṃ pathavîkasiṇaṃ . . . pe . . . dukkhâpaṭipadaṃ dandhâbhiññaṃ appamâṇaṃ parittârammaṇaṃ pathavîkasiṇaṃ . . . pe . . . dukkhâpaṭipadaṃ dandhâbhiññaṃ appamâṇaṃ appamâṇârammaṇaṃ pathavîkasiṇaṃ . . . pe . . . dukkhâpaṭipadaṃ khippâbhiññaṃ parittaṃ parittârammaṇaṃ pathavîkasiṇaṃ . . . pe . . . dukkhâpaṭipadaṃ khippâbhiññaṃ parittaṃ appamâṇârammaṇaṃ pathavîkasiṇaṃ . . . pe . . . dukkhâpaṭipadaṃ khippâbhiññaṃ appamâṇaṃ parittârammaṇaṃ pathavîkasiṇaṃ . . . pe . . . dukkhâpaṭipadaṃ khippâbhiññaṃ appamâṇaṃ appamâṇârammaṇaṃ pathavîkasiṇaṃ . . . pe . . . sukhâpaṭipadaṃ dandhâbhiññaṃ parittaṃ parittârammaṇaṃ pathavîkasiṇaṃ . . . pe . . . sukhâpaṭipadaṃ dandhâbhiññaṃ parittaṃ appamâṇârammaṇaṃ pathavîkasiṇaṃ . . . pe . . . sukhâpaṭipadaṃ dandhâbhiññaṃ appamâṇaṃ parittârammaṇaṃ pathavîkasiṇaṃ . . . pe . . .

sukhâpaṭipadaṃ dandhâbhiññaṃ appamâṇaṃ appamâṇârammaṇaṃ pathavîkasiṇaṃ . . . pe . . . sukhâpaṭipadaṃ khippâbhiññaṃ parittaṃ parittârammaṇaṃ pathavîkasiṇaṃ . . . pe . . . sukhâpaṭipadaṃ khippâbhiññaṃ parittaṃ appamâṇârammaṇaṃ pathavîkasiṇaṃ . . . pe . . . sukhâpaṭipadaṃ khippâbhiññaṃ appamâṇaṃ parittârammaṇaṃ paṭhavîkasiṇaṃ . . . pe . . . sukhâpaṭipadaṃ khippâbhiññaṃ appamâṇaṃ appamâṇârammaṇaṃ pathavîkasiṇaṃ—tasmiṃ samaye phasso hoti . . . pe . . . avikkhepo hoti . . . pe . . . ime dhammâ kusalâ.

Soḷasakkhattukaṃ.

203. Katame dhammâ kusalâ ?

Yasmiṃ samaye rûpûpapattiyâ maggaṃ bhâveti vivicceva kâmehi . . . pe . . . paṭhamaṃ jhânaṃ upasampajja viharati âpokasiṇaṃ . . . pe . . . tejokasiṇaṃ . . . pe . . . vâyokasiṇaṃ . . . pe . . . nîlakasiṇaṃ . . . pe . . . pîtakasiṇaṃ . . . pe . . . lohitakasiṇaṃ . . . pe . . . odâtakasiṇaṃ—tasmiṃ samaye phasso hoti . . . pe . . . avikkhepo hoti—ime dhammâ kusalâ.

Aṭṭhakasiṇaṃ soḷasakkhattukaṃ.

204. Katame dhammâ kusalâ ?

Yasmiṃ samaye rûpûpapattiyâ maggaṃ bhâveti ajjhattam arûpasaññî bahiddhâ rûpâni passati parittâni tâni abhibhuyya jânâmi passâmîti vivicceva kâmehi . . . pe . . . paṭhamaṃ jhânaṃ upasampajja viharati—tasmiṃ samaye phasso hoti . . . pe . . . avikkhepo hoti . . . pe . . . ime dhammâ kusalâ.

205. Katame dhammâ kusalâ ?

Yasmiṃ samaye rûpûpapattiyâ maggaṃ bhâveti ajjhattaṃ arûpasaññi bahiddhâ rûpâni passati parittâni tâni abhibhuyya jânâmi passâmîti vitakkavicârânaṃ vûpasamâ . . . pe . . . dutiyaṃ jhânaṃ . . . pe . . . tatiyaṃ jhânaṃ . . . pe catutthaṃ jhânaṃ . . . pe . . . paṭhamaṃ jhânaṃ . . . pe pañcamaṃ jhânaṃ upasampajja viharati—tasmiṃ samaye phasso hoti . . . pe . . . avikkhepo hoti . . . pe . . . ime dhammâ kusalâ.

206. Katame dhammâ kusalâ?

Yasmiṃ samaye rûpûpapattiyâ maggaṃ bhâveti ajjhattaṃ arûpasaññî bahiddhâ rûpâni passati parittâni tâni abhibhuyya jânâmi passâmîti vivicceva kâmehi . . . pe . . . paṭhamaṃ jhânaṃ upasampajja viharati dukkhâpaṭipadaṃ dandhâbhiññaṃ tasmiṃ samaye phasso hoti . . . pe . . . avikkhepo hoti . . . pe . . . ime dhammâ kusalâ.

207. Katame dhammâ kusalâ?

Yasmiṃ samaye rûpûpapattiyâ maggaṃ bhâveti ajjhattaṃ arûpasaññî bahiddhâ rûpâni passati parittâni tâni abhibhuyya jânâmi passâmîti vivicceva kâmehi . . . pe . . . paṭhamaṃ jhânaṃ upasampajja viharati dukkhâpaṭipadaṃ khippâbhiññaṃ tasmiṃ samaye phasso hoti . . . pe . . . avikkhepo hoti . . . pe . . . ime dhammâ kusalâ.

208. Katame dhammâ kusalâ?

Yasmiṃ samaye rûpûpapattiyâ maggaṃ bhâveti, ajjhattaṃ arûpasaññî bahiddhâ rûpâni passati parittâni tâni abhibhuyya jânâmi passâmîti vivicceva kâmehi . . . pe . . . paṭhamaṃ jhânaṃ upasampajja viharati sukhâpaṭipadaṃ dandhâbhiññaṃ—tasmiṃ samaye phasso hoti . . . pe . . . avikkhepo hoti—ime dhammâ kusalâ.

209. Katame dhammâ kusalâ?

Yasmiṃ samaye rûpûpapattiyâ maggaṃ bhâveti ajjhattaṃ arûpasaññî bahiddhâ rûpâni passati parittâni tâni abhibhuyya jânâmi passâmîti vivicceva kâmehi . . . pe . . . paṭhamaṃ jhânaṃ upasampajja viharati sukhâpaṭipadaṃ khippâbhiññaṃ tasmiṃ samaye phasso hoti . . . pe . . . avikkhepo hoti . . . pe . . . ime dhammâ kusalâ.

210. Katame dhammâ kusala?

Yasmiṃ samaye rûpûpapattiyâ maggaṃ bhâveti ajjhattaṃ arûpasaññî bahiddhâ rûpâni passati parittâni tâni abhibhuyya jânâmi passâmîti vitakkavicârânaṃ vûpasamâ . . . pe . . . dutiyaṃ jhânaṃ . . . pe . . . tatiyaṃ jhânaṃ . . . pe . . . catutthaṃ jhânaṃ . . . pe . . . paṭhamaṃ jhânaṃ . . . pe pañcamaṃ jhânaṃ upasampajja viharati dukkhâpaṭipadaṃ dandhâbhiññaṃ . . . pe . . . dukkhâpaṭipadaṃ khippabhiññaṃ . . . pe . . . sukhâpaṭipadaṃ dandhâbhiññaṃ . . . pe . . . sukhâpaṭipadaṃ khippâbhiññaṃ tasmiṃ samaye phasso hoti . . . pe . . . avikkhepo hoti . . . pe , . . ime dhammâ kusalâ.

Catasso paṭipadâ.

211. Katame dhammâ kusalâ?
Yasmiṃ samaye rûpûpapattiyâ maggaṃ bhâveti ajjhattaṃ arûpasaññî bahiddhâ rûpâni passati parittâni tâni abhibhuyya jânâmi passâmîti vivicceva kâmehi . . . pe . . . paṭhamaṃ jhânaṃ upasampajja viharati parittaṃ parittârammaṇaṃ tasmiṃ samaye phasso hoti . . . pe . . . avikkhepo hoti . . . pe . . . ime dhammâ kusalâ.

212. Katame dhammâ kusalâ?
Yasmiṃ samaye rûpûpapattiyâ maggaṃ bhâveti ajjhattaṃ arûpasaññî bahiddhâ rûpâni passati parittâni tâni abhibhuyya jânâmi passâmîti vivicceva kâmehi . . . pe . . . paṭhamaṃ jhânaṃ upasampajja viharati appamâṇaṃ parittârammaṇaṃ—tasmiṃ samaye phasso hoti . . . pe . . . avikkhepo hoti . . . pe . . . ime dhammâ kusalâ.

213. Katame dhammâ kusalâ?
Yasmiṃ samaye rûpûpapattiyâ maggaṃ bhâveti ajjhattaṃ arûpasaññî bahiddhâ rûpâni passati parittâni, tâni abhibhuyya jânâmi passâmîti vitakkavicârânaṃ vûpasamâ . . . pe . . . dutiyaṃ jhânaṃ . . . pe . . . tatiyaṃ jhânam . . . pe . . . catutthaṃ jhânaṃ . . . pe . . . paṭhamaṃ jhânaṃ . . . pe . . . pañcamaṃ jhânaṃ upasampajja viharati parittaṃ parittârammaṇaṃ . . . pe . . . appamâṇaṃ parittârammaṇaṃ tasmiṃ samaye phasso hoti . . . pe . . . ime dhammâ kusalâ.

Dve ârammaṇâni.

214. Katame dhammâ kusalâ?
Yasmiṃ samaye rûpûpapattiyâ maggaṃ bhâveti ajjhattaṃ arûpasaññî bahiddhâ rûpâni passati parittâni tâni abhibhuyya jânâmi passâmîti vivicceva kâmehi . . . pe . . . paṭhamaṃ jhânaṃ upasampajja viharati dukkhâpaṭipadaṃ dandhâbhiññaṃ parittaṃ parittârammanaṃ tasmiṃ samaye

phasso hoti . . . pe . . . avikkkepo hoti . . . pe . . . ime dhammâ kusalâ.

215. Katame dhammâ kusalâ?

Yasmiṃ samaye rûpûpapattiyâ maggaṃ bhâveti ajjhattaṃ arûpasaññî bahiddhâ rûpâni passati parittâni, tâni abhibhuyya jânâmi passâmîti viviceeva kâmehi . . . pe . . . paṭhamaṃ jhânaṃ upasampajja viharati dukkhâpaṭipadaṃ dandhâbhiññaṃ appamâṇaṃ parittârammaṇaṃ — tasmiṃ samaye phasso hoti . . . pe . . . avikkhepo hoti . . . pe . . . ime dhammâ kusalâ.

216. Katame dhammâ kusalâ?

Yasmiṃ samaye rûpûpapattiyâ maggaṃ bhâveti ajjhattaṃ arûpasaññî bahiddhâ rûpâni passati parittâni, tâni abhibhuyya jânâmi passâmîti viviceeva kâmehi . . . pe . . . paṭhamaṃ jhânaṃ upasampajja viharati dukkhâpaṭipadaṃ khippâbhiññaṃ parittaṃ parittârammaṇaṃ—tasmiṃ samaye phasso hoti . . . pe . . . avikkhepo hoti . . . pe . . . ime dhammâ kusalâ.

217. Katame dhammâ kusalâ?

Yasmiṃ samaye rûpûpapattiyâ maggaṃ bhâveti ajjhattaṃ arûpasaññî bahiddhâ rûpâni passati parittâni tâni abhibhuyya jânâmi passâmîti viviceeva kâmehi . . . pe . . . paṭhamaṃ jhânaṃ upasampajja viharati dukkhâpaṭipadaṃ khippâbhiññaṃ appamâṇaṃ parittârammaṇaṃ: tasmiṃ samaye phasso hoti . . . pe . . . avikkhepo hoti . . . pe . . . ime dhammâ kusalâ.

218. Katame dhammâ kusalâ?

Yasmiṃ samaye rûpûpapattiyâ maggaṃ bhâveti ajjhattaṃ arûpasaññî bahiddhâ rûpâni passati parittâni; tâni abhibhuyya jânâmi passâmîti viviceeva kâmehi . . . pe . . . paṭhamaṃ jhânaṃ upasampajja viharati sukhâpaṭipadaṃ dandhâbhiññaṃ parittaṃ parittârammaṇaṃ: tasmiṃ samaye phasso hoti . . . pe . . . avikkhepo hoti . . . pe . . . ime dhammâ kusalâ.

219. Katame dhammâ kusalâ?

Yasmiṃ samaye rûpûpapattiyâ maggaṃ bhâveti ajjhattaṃ arûpasaññî bahiddhâ rûpâni passati parittâni tâni abhibhuyya jânâmi passâmîti viviceeva kâmehi . . . pe . . .

paṭhamaṃ jhânaṃ upasampajja viharati, sukhâpaṭipadaṃ dandhâbhiññaṃ appamâṇaṃ parittârammaṇaṃ tasmiṃ samaye phasso hoti . . . pe . . . avikkhepo hoti . . . pe . . . ime dhammâ kusalâ.

220. Katame dhammâ kusalâ ?

Yasmiṃ samaye rûpûpapattiyâ maggaṃ bhâveti ajjhattaṃ arûpasaññî bahiddhâ rûpâni passati parittâni tâni abhibhuyya jânâmi passâmîti vivicceva kâmehi . . . pe . . . paṭhamaṃ jhânaṃ upasampajja viharati sukhâpaṭipadaṃ khippâbhiññaṃ parittaṃ parittârammaṇaṃ tasmiṃ samaye phasso hoti . . . pe . . . avikkhepo hoti—ime dhammâ kusalâ.

221. Katame dhammâ kusalâ ?

Yasmiṃ samaye rûpûpapattiyâ maggaṃ bhâveti ajjhattaṃ arûpasaññî bahiddhâ rûpâni passati parittâni tâni abhibhuyya jânâmi passâmîti vivicceva kâmehi . . . pe . . . paṭhamaṃ jhânaṃ upasampajja viharati sukhâpaṭipadaṃ khippâbhiññaṃ appamâṇaṃ parittârammaṇaṃ: tasmiṃ samaye phasso hoti . . . pe . . . avikkhepo hoti—ime dhammâ kusalâ.

222. Katame dhammâ kusalâ ?

Yasmiṃ samaye rûpûpapattiyâ maggaṃ bhâveti ajjhattaṃ arûpasaññî bahiddhâ rûpâni passati parittâni tâni abhibhuyya jânâmi passâmîti vitakkavicârânaṃ vûpasamâ . . . pe . . . dutiyaṃ jhânaṃ . . . pe . . . tatiyaṃ jhânaṃ . . . pe . . . catutthaṃ jhânaṃ . . . pe . . . paṭhamaṃ jhânaṃ . . . pe . . . pañcamaṃ jhânaṃ upasampajja viharati dukkhâpaṭipadaṃ dandhâbhiññaṃ parittaṃ parittârammaṇaṃ . . . pe . . . dukkhâpaṭipadaṃ dandhâbhiññaṃ appamâṇaṃ parittârammaṃaṃ . . . pe . . . dukkhâpaṭipadaṃ khippâbhiññaṃ parittaṃ parittârammaṇaṃ . . . pe . . . dukkhâpaṭipadaṃ khippâbhiññaṃ appamâṇaṃ parittârammaṇaṃ . . . pe . . . sukhâpaṭipadaṃ dandhâbhiññaṃ parittaṃ parittârammaṇaṃ . . . pe . . . sukhâpaṭipadaṃ dandhâbhiññaṃ appamâṇaṃ parittârammaṇaṃ . . . pe . . . sukhâpaṭipadaṃ khippâbhiññaṃ parittaṃ parittârammaṇaṃ . . . pe . . . sukhâpaṭipadaṃ khippâbhiññaṃ appamâṇaṃ parittârammaṇaṃ—tasmiṃ samaye phasso hoti . . . pe . . . avikkhepo hoti . . . pe . . . ime dhammâ kusalâ.

Aṭṭhakkhattuṃ.

223. Katame dhammâ kusalâ?

Yasmiṃ samaye rûpûpapattiyâ maggaṃ bhâveti ajjhattaṃ arûpasaññî bahiddhâ rûpâni passati parittâni suvaṇṇadubbaṇṇâni tâni abhibhuyya jânâmi passâmîti vivicceva kâmehi . . . pe . . . paṭhamaṃ jhânaṃ upasampajja viharati tasmiṃ samaye phasso hoti . . . pe . . . avikkhepo hoti . . . pe . . . ime dhammâ kusalâ.

224. Katame dhammâ kusalâ?

Yasmiṃ samaye rûpûpapattiyâ maggaṃ bhâveti ajjhattaṃ arûpasaññî bahiddhâ rûpâni passati parittâni suvaṇṇadubbaṇṇâni tâni abhibhuyya jânâmi passâmîti vitakkavicârânaṃ vûpasamâ . . . pe . . . dutiyaṃ jhânaṃ . . . pe . . . tatiyaṃ jhânaṃ . . . pe . . . catutthaṃ jhânaṃ . . . pe paṭhamaṃ jhânaṃ . . . pe . . . pañcamaṃ jhânaṃ upasampajja viharati: tasmiṃ samaye phasso hoti . . . pe . . . avikkhepo hoti . . . pe . . . ime dhammâ kusalâ.

Idaṃ pi aṭṭhakkhattuṃ.

225. Katame dhammâ kusalâ?

Yasmiṃ samaye rûpûpapattiyâ maggaṃ bhâveti ajjhattaṃ arûpasaññî bahiddhâ rûpâni passati appamâṇâni: tâni abhibhuyya jânâmi passâmîti vivicceva kâmehi . . . pe . . . paṭhamaṃ jhânaṃ upasampajja viharati — tasmiṃ samaye phasso hoti . . . pe . . . avikkhepo hoti . . . pe . . . ime dhammâ kusalâ.

226. Katame dhammâ kusalâ?

Yasmiṃ samaye rûpûpapattiyâ maggaṃ bhâveti ajjhattaṃ arûpasaññî bahiddhâ rûpâni passati appamâṇâni: tâni abhibhuyya jânâmi passâmîti vitakkavicârânaṃ vûpasamâ . . . pe . . . dutiyaṃ jhânaṃ . . . pe . . . tatiyaṃ jhânaṃ . . . pe . . . catutthaṃ jhânaṃ . . . pe . . . paṭhamaṃ jhânaṃ . . . pe . . . pañcamaṃ jhânaṃ upasampajja viharati: tasmiṃ samaye phasso hoti . . . pe . . . avikkhepo hoti . . . pe . . . ime dhammâ kusalâ.

227. Katame dhammâ kusalâ?

Yasmiṃ samaye rûpûpapattiyâ maggaṃ bhâveti ajjhattaṃ arûpasaññî bahiddhâ rûpâni passati appamâṇâni: tâni abhibhuyya jânâmi passâmîti vivicceva kâmehi . . . pe . . . paṭhamaṃ jhânaṃ upasampajja viharati dukkhâpaṭipadaṃ dandhâbhiññaṃ: tasmiṃ samaye phasso hoti . . . pe . . . avikkhepo hoti . . . pe . . . ime dhammâ kusalâ.

228. Katame dhammâ kusalâ ?

Yasmiṃ samaye rûpûpapattiyâ maggaṃ bhâveti ajjhattaṃ arûpasaññî bahiddhâ rûpâni passati appamâṇâni: tâni abhibhuyya jânâmi passâmîti vivicceva kâmehi . . . pe . . . paṭhamaṃ jhânaṃ upasampajja viharati dukkhâpaṭipadaṃ khippâbhiññaṃ tasmiṃ samaye phasso hoti . . . pe . . . avikkhepo hoti . . . pe . . . ime dhammâ kusalâ.

229. Katame dhammâ kusalâ ?

Yasmiṃ samaye rûpûpapattiyâ maggaṃ bhâveti ajjhattaṃ arûpasaññî bahiddhâ rûpâni passati appamâṇâni tâni abhibhuyya jânâmi passâmîti vivicceva kâmehi . . . pe . . . paṭhamaṃ jhânaṃ upasampajja viharati—sukhâpaṭipadaṃ dandhâbhiññaṃ tasmiṃ samaye phasso hoti . . . pe . . . avikkhepo hoti . . . pe . . ime dhammâ kusalâ.

230. Katame dhammâ kusalâ ?

Yasmiṃ samaye rûpûpapattiyâ maggaṃ bhâveti ajjhattaṃ arûpasaññî bahiddhâ rûpâni passati appamâṇâni tâni abhibhuyya jânâmi passâmîti vivicceva kâmehi . . . pe . . . paṭhamaṃ jhânaṃ upasampajja viharati—sukhâpaṭipadaṃ khippâbhiññaṃ tasmiṃ samaye phasso hoti . . . pe . . . avikkhepo hoti . . . pe . . . ime dhammâ kusalâ.

231. Katame dhammâ kusalâ ?

Yasmiṃ samaye rûpûpapattiyâ maggaṃ bhâveti ajjhattaṃ arûpasaññî bahiddhâ rûpâni passati appamâṇâni: tâni abhibhuyya jânâmi passâmîti vitakkavicârânaṃ vûpasamâ . . . pe . . . dutiyaṃ jhânaṃ . . . pe . . . tatiyaṃ jhânaṃ . . . pe . . . catutthaṃ jhânaṃ . . . pe . . . paṭhamaṃ jhânaṃ . . . pe . . . pañcamaṃ jhânaṃ upasampajja viharati dukkhâpaṭipadaṃ dandhâbhiññaṃ . . . pe . . . dukkhâpaṭipadaṃ khippâbhiññaṃ . . . pe . . . sukhâpaṭipadaṃ dandhâbhiññaṃ . . . pe . . . sukhâpaṭipadaṃ khippâbhiññaṃ—tasmiṃ samaye phasso hoti . . . pe . . . avikkhepo hoti . . . pe . . . ime dhammâ kusalâ.

Catasso paṭipadâ.

232. Katame dhammâ kusalâ?

Yasmiṃ samaye rûpûpapattiyâ maggaṃ bhâveti ajjhattaṃ arûpasaññî bahiddhâ rûpâni passati appamâṇâni: tâni abhibhuyya jânâmi passâmîti vivicceva kâmehi . . . pe . . . paṭhamaṃ jhânaṃ upasampajja viharati parittaṃ appamâṇârammaṇaṃ: tasmiṃ samaye phasso hoti . . . pe . . . avikkhepo hoti . . . pe . . . ime dhammâ kusalâ.

233. Katame dhammâ kusalâ?

Yasmiṃ samaye rûpûpapattiyâ maggaṃ bhâveti ajjhattaṃ arûpasaññî bahiddhâ rûpâni passati appamâṇâni: tâni abhibhuyya jânâmi passâmîti vivicceva kâmehi . . . pe . . . paṭhamaṃ jhânaṃ upasampajja viharati appamàṇaṃ appamâṇârammaṇaṃ tasmiṃ samaye phasso hoti . . . pe . . . avikkhepo hoti . . . pe . . . ime dhammâ kusalâ.

234. Katame dhammâ kusalâ?

Yasmiṃ samaye rûpûpapattiyâ maggaṃ bhâveti ajjhattaṃ arûpasaññî bahiddhâ rûpâni passati appamâṇâni: tâni abhibhuyya jânâmi passâmîti vitakkavicârânaṃ vûpasamâ . . . pe . . . dutiyaṃ jhânaṃ . . . pe . . . tatiyaṃ jhânaṃ . . . pe . . . catutthaṃ jhânaṃ . . . pe . . . paṭhamaṃ jhânaṃ . . . pe . . . pañcamaṃ jhânaṃ upasampajja viharati parittaṃ appamâṇârammaṇaṃ . . . pe . . . appamâṇaṃ appamâṇârammaṇaṃ tasmiṃ samaye phasso hoti . . . pe . . . avikkhepo hoti . . . pe . . . ime dhammâ kusalâ.

Dve ârammaṇâni.

235. Katame dhammâ kusalâ?

Yasmiṃ samaye rûpûpapattiyâ maggaṃ bhâveti ajjhattaṃ arûpasaññî bahiddhâ rûpâni passati appamâṇâni tâni abhibhuyya jânâmi passâmîti vivicceva kâmehi . . . pe . . . paṭhamaṃ jhânaṃ upasampajja viharati dukkhâpaṭipadaṃ dandhâbhiññaṃ parittaṃ appamâṇârammaṇaṃ tasmiṃ samaye phasso hoti . . . pe . . . avikkhepo hoti . . . pe ime dhammâ kusalâ.

236. Katame dhammâ kusalâ?

Yasmiṃ samaye rûpûpapattiyâ maggaṃ bhâveti ajjhattaṃ arûpasaññî bahiddhâ rûpâni passati appamâṇâni: tâni abhibhuyya jânâmi passâmîti vivicceva kâmehi . . . pe . . . paṭhamaṃ jhânaṃ upasampajja viharati dukkhâpaṭipadaṃ dandhâbhiññaṃ appamâṇaṃ appamâṇârammaṇaṃ : tasmiṃ samaye phasso hoti . . . pe . . . avikkhepo hoti . . . pe . . . ime dhammâ kusalâ.

237. Katame dhammâ kusalâ?

Yasmiṃ samaye rûpûpapattiyâ maggaṃ bhâveti ajjhattaṃ arûpasaññî bahiddhâ rûpâni passati appamânâni : tâni abhibhuyya jânâmi passâmîti vivicceva kâmehi . . . pe . . . paṭhamaṃ jhânaṃ upasampajja viharati dukkhâpaṭipadaṃ khippâbhiññaṃ parittaṃ appamâṇârammaṇaṃ : tasmiṃ samaye phasso hoti . . . pe . . . avikkhepo hoti . . . pe . . . ime dhammâ kusalâ.

238. Katame dhammâ kusalâ?

Yasmiṃ samaye rûpûpapattiyâ maggaṃ bhâveti ajjhattaṃ arûpasaññî bahiddhâ rûpâni passati appamâṇâni : tâni abhibhuyya jânâmi passâmîti vivicceva kâmehi . . . pe . . . paṭhamaṃ jhânaṃ upasampajja viharati dukkhâpaṭipadaṃ khippâbhiññaṃ appamâṇaṃ appamâṇârammaṇaṃ : tasmiṃ samaye phasso hoti . . . pe . . . avikkhepo hoti . . . pe . . . ime dhammâ kusalâ.

239. Katame dhammâ kusalâ?

Yasmiṃ samaye rûpûpapattiyâ maggaṃ bhâveti ajjhattaṃ arûpasaññî bahiddhâ rûpâni passati appamâṇâni : tâni abhibhuyya jânâmi passâmîti vivicceva kâmehi . . . pe . . . paṭhamaṃ jhânaṃ upasampajja viharati sukhâpaṭipadaṃ dandhâbhiññaṃ parittaṃ appamâṇârammaṇaṃ — tasmiṃ samaye phasso hoti . . . pe . . . avikkhepo hoti . . . pe . . . ime dhammâ kusalâ.

240. Katame dhammâ kusalâ?

Yasmiṃ samaye rûpûpapattiyâ maggaṃ bhâveti ajjhattaṃ arûpasaññî bahiddhâ rûpâni passati appamâṇâni : tâni abhibhuyya jânâmi passâmîti vivicceva kâmehi . . . pe . . . paṭhamaṃ jhânaṃ upasampajja viharati sukhâpaṭipadaṃ dandhâbhiññaṃ appamâṇaṃ appamâṇârammaṇaṃ : tasmiṃ samaye phasso hoti . . . pe . . . avikkhepo hoti . . . pe . . . ime dhammâ kusalâ.

241. Katame dhammâ kusalâ?

Yasmiṃ samaye rûpûpapattiyâ maggaṃ bhâveti ajjhattaṃ arûpasaññî bahiddhâ rûpâni passati appamâṇâni: tâni abhibhuyya jânâmi passâmîti vivicceva kâmehi . . . pe . . . paṭhamaṃ jhânaṃ upasampajja viharati sukhâpaṭipadaṃ khippâbhiññaṃ parittaṃ appamâṇârammaṇaṃ: tasmiṃ samaye phasso hoti . . . pe . . . avikkhepo hoti . . . pe . . . ime dhammâ kusalâ.

242. Katame dhammâ kusalâ?

Yasmiṃ samaye rûpûpapattiyâ maggaṃ bhâveti ajjhattaṃ arûpasaññî bahiddhâ rûpâni passati appamâṇâni: tâni abhibhuyya jânâmi passâmîti vivicceva kâmehi . . . pe . . . paṭhamaṃ jhânaṃ upasampajja viharati sukhâpaṭipadaṃ khippâbhiññaṃ appamâṇaṃ appamâṇârammaṇaṃ: tasmiṃ samaye phasso hoti . . . pe . . . avikkhepo hoti . . . ime dhammâ kusalâ.

243. Katame dhammâ kusalâ?

Yasmiṃ samaye rûpûpapattiyâ maggaṃ bhâveti ajjhattaṃ arûpasaññî bahiddhâ rûpâni passati appamâṇâni tâni abhibhuyya jânâmi passâmîti vitakkavicârânaṃ vûpasamâ . . . pe . . . dutiyaṃ jhânaṃ . . . pe . . . tatiyaṃ jhânaṃ . . . pe . . . catutthaṃ jhânaṃ . . . pe . . . paṭhamaṃ jhânaṃ . . . pe . . . pañcamaṃ jhânaṃ upasampajja viharati dukkhâpaṭipadam dandhâbhiññaṃ parittaṃ appamâṇârammaṇaṃ . . . pe . . . dukkhâpaṭipadaṃ dandhâbhiññaṃ appamâṇaṃ appamâṇârammaṇaṃ . . . pe . . . dukkhâpaṭipadaṃ khippâbhiññaṃ parittaṃ appamâṇârammaṇaṃ . . . pe . . . dukkhâpaṭipadaṃ khippâbhiññaṃ appamâṇaṃ appamâṇârammaṇaṃ . . . pe . . . sukhâpaṭipadaṃ dandhâbhiññaṃ parittaṃ appamâṇârammaṇaṃ . . . pe . . . sukhâpaṭipadaṃ dandhâbhiññaṃ appamâṇaṃ appamâṇârammaṇaṃ . . . pe sukhâpaṭipadaṃ khippâbhiññaṃ parittam appamâṇârammaṇaṃ . . . pe . . . sukhâpaṭipadaṃ khippâbhiññaṃ appamâṇaṃ appamâṇârammaṇaṃ—tasmiṃ samaye phasso hoti . . . pe . . . avikkhepo hoti . . . pe . . . ime dhammâ kusalâ.

Aparaṃ pi aṭṭhakkhattukam.

244. Katame dhammâ kusalâ?

Yasmiṃ samaye rûpûpapattiyâ maggaṃ bhâveti ajjhattaṃ arûpasaññî bahiddhâ rûpâni passati appamâṇâni suvaṇṇadubbaṇṇâni: tâni abhibhuyya jânâmi passâmîti vivicceva kâmehi . . . pe . . . paṭhamaṃ jhânaṃ upasampajja viharati: tasmiṃ samaye phasso hoti . . . pe . . . avikkhepo hoti . . . pe . . . ime dhammâ kusalâ.

245. Katame dhammâ kusalâ?

Yasmiṃ samaye rûpûpapattiyâ maggaṃ bhâveti ajjhattaṃ arûpasaññî bahiddhâ rûpâni passati appamâṇâni suvaṇṇadubbaṇṇâni tâni abhibhuyya jânâmi passâmîti vitakkavicârânaṃ vûpasamâ . . . pe . . . dutiyaṃ jhânaṃ . . . pe . . . tatiyaṃ jhânaṃ . . . pe . . . catutthaṃ jhânaṃ . . . pe paṭhamaṃ jhânaṃ . . . pe . . . pañcamaṃ jhânaṃ upasampajja viharati: tasmiṃ samaye phasso hoti . . . pe . . . avikkhepo hoti . . . pe . . . ime dhammâ kusalâ.

idam pi aṭṭhakkhattukaṃ.

246. Katame dhammâ kusalâ?

Yasmiṃ samaye rûpûpapattiyâ maggaṃ bhâveti ajjhattaṃ arûpasaññi bahiddhâ rûpâni passati nîlâni nîlavaṇṇâni nîlanidassanâni nîlanibhâsâni tâni abhibhuyya jânâmi passâmîti vivicceva kâmehi . . . pe . . . paṭhamaṃ jhânaṃ upasampajja viharati: tasmiṃ samaye phasso hoti . . . pe . . . avikkhepo hoti . . . pe . . . ime dhammâ kusalâ.

247. Katame dhammâ kusalâ?

Yasmiṃ samaye rûpûpapattiyâ maggaṃ bhâveti ajjhattaṃ arûpasaññî bahiddhâ rûpâni passati pîtâni pîtavaṇṇâni pîtanidassanâni pîtanibhâsâni . . . pe . . . lohitakâni lohitakavaṇṇâni lokitakanidassanâni lohitakanibhâsâni . . . pe . . . odâtâni odâtavaṇṇâni odâtanidassanâni odâtanibhâsâni tâni abhibhuyya jânâmi passâmîti vivicceva kâmehi . . . pe . . . paṭhamaṃ jhânaṃ upasampajja viharati: tasmiṃ samaye phasso hoti . . . pe . . . avikkhepo hoti . . . pe . . . ime dhammâ kusalâ.

Imâni pi abhibhâyatanâni soḷasakkhattukâni.

248. Katame dhammâ kusalâ?

Yasmiṃ samaye rûpûpapattiyâ maggaṃ bhâveti rûpî rûpâni passati vivicceva kâmehi . . . pe . . . paṭhamaṃ jhânaṃ upasampajja viharati: tasmiṃ samaye phasso hoti . . . pe . . . avikkhepo hoti . . . pe . . . ime dhammâ kusalâ.

249. Katame dhammâ kusalâ?

Yasmiṃ samaye rûpûpapattiyâ maggaṃ bhâveti ajjhattaṃ arûpasaññî bahiddhâ rûpâni passati vivicceva kâmehi . . . pe . . . paṭhamaṃ jhânaṃ upasampajja viharati: tasmim samaye phasso hoti . . . pe . . . avikkhepo hoti . . . pe . . . ime dhammâ kusalâ.

250. Katame dhammâ kusalâ?

Yasmiṃ samaye rûpûpapattiyâ maggaṃ bhâveti subhanti vivicceva kâmehi . . . pe . . . paṭhamaṃ jhânaṃ upasampajja viharati: tasmiṃ samaye phasso hoti . . . pe . . . avikkhepo hoti . . . pe . . . ime dhammâ kusalâ.

Imâni pi tîṇi vimokkhâni soḷasakkhattukâni.

251. Katame dhammâ kusalâ?

Yasmiṃ samaye rûpûpapattiyâ maggaṃ bhâveti vivicceva kâmehi . . . pe . . . paṭhamaṃ jhânaṃ upasampajja viharati mettâsahagataṃ: tasmiṃ samaye phasso hoti . . . pe . . . avikkhepo hoti . . . pe . . . ime dhammâ kusalâ.

252. Katame dhammâ kusalâ?

Yasmiṃ samaye rûpûpapattiyâ maggaṃ bhâveti vitakkavicârânaṃ vûpasamâ . . . pe . . . dutiyaṃ jhânaṃ upasampajja viharati mettâsahagataṃ: tasmiṃ samaye phasso hoti . . . pe . . . avikkhepo hoti . . . pe . . . ime dhammâ kusalâ.

253. Katame dhammâ kusalâ?

Yasmiṃ samaye rûpûpapattiyâ maggaṃ bhâveti pîtiyâ ca virâgâ . . . pe . . . tatiyaṃ jhânaṃ upasampajja viharati mettâsahagataṃ: tasmim samaye phasso hoti . . . pe . . . avikkhepo hoti . . . pe . . . ime dhammâ kusalâ.

254. Katame dhammâ kusalâ?

Yasmiṃ samaye rûpûpapattiyâ maggaṃ bhâveti vivicceva kâmehi . . . pe . . . paṭhamaṃ jhânaṃ upasampajja viharati mettâsahagataṃ: tasmiṃ samaye phasso hoti . . . pe . . . avikkhepo hoti . . . pe . . . ime dhammâ kusalâ.

255. Katame dhammâ kusalâ?

Yasmiṃ samaye rûpûpapattiyâ maggaṃ bhâveti avitakkavicâramattaṃ samâdhijaṃ pîtisukhaṃ dutiyaṃ jhânaṃ upasampajja viharati mettâsahagataṃ: tasmiṃ samaye phasso hoti . . . pe . . . avikkhepo hoti . . . pe . . . ime dhammâ kusalâ.

256. Katame dhammâ kusalâ?

Yasmiṃ samaye rûpûpapattiyâ maggaṃ bhâveti vitakkavicârânaṃ vûpasamâ . . . pe . . . tatiyaṃ jhânaṃ upasampajja viharati mettâsahagataṃ: tasmiṃ samaye phasso hoti . . . pe . . . avikkhepo hoti . . . pe . . . ime dhammâ kusalâ.

257. Katame dhammâ kusalâ?

Yasmiṃ samaye rûpûpapattiyâ maggaṃ bhâveti pîtiyâ ca virâgâ . . . pe . . . catutthaṃ jhânaṃ upasampajja viharati mettâsahagataṃ: tasmiṃ samaye phasso hoti . . . pe . . . avikkhepo hoti . . . pe . . . ime dhammâ kusalâ.

258. Katame dhammâ kusalâ?

Yasmiṃ samaye rûpûpapattiyâ maggaṃ bhâveti vivicceva kâmehi . . . pe . . . paṭhamaṃ jhânaṃ upasampajja viharati karuṇâsahagataṃ: tasmiṃ samaye phasso hoti . . . pe . . . avikkhepo hoti . . . pe . . . ime dhammâ kusalâ.

259. Katame dhammâ kusalâ?

Yasmiṃ samaye rûpûpapattiyâ maggaṃ bhâveti vitakkavicârânaṃ vûpasamâ . . . pe . . . dutiyaṃ jhânaṃ . . . pe . . . tatiyaṃ jhânaṃ . . . pe . . . pathamaṃ jhânaṃ . . . pe . . . catutthaṃ jhânaṃ upasampajja viharati karuṇâsahagataṃ tasmiṃ samaye phasso hoti . . . pe . . . avikkhepo hoti . . . pe . . . ime dhammâ kusalâ.

260. Katame dhammâ kusalâ?

Yasmiṃ samaye rûpûpapattiyâ maggaṃ bhâveti vivicceva kâmehi . . . pe . . . paṭhamaṃ jhânaṃ upasampajja viharati muditâsahagataṃ tasmiṃ samaye phasso hoti . . . pe . . . avikkhepo hoti . . . pe . . . ime dhammâ kusalâ.

261. Katame dhammâ kusalâ?

Yasmiṃ samaye rûpûpapattiyâ maggaṃ bhâveti vitakkavicârânaṃ vûpasamâ . . . pe . . . dutiyaṃ jhânaṃ . . . pe . . . tatiyaṃ jhânaṃ . . . pe . . . paṭhamaṃ jhânaṃ . . . pe . . . catutthaṃ jhânaṃ upasampajja viharati muditâsahagataṃ tasmiṃ samaye phasso hoti . . . pe . . . avikkhepo hoti . . . pe . . . ime dhammâ kusalâ.

262. Katame dhammâ kusalâ.

Yasmiṃ samaye rûpûpapattiyâ maggaṃ bhâveti sukhassa ca pahânâ . . . pe . . . catutthaṃ jhânaṃ upasampajja viharati upekkhâsahagataṃ: tasmiṃ samaye phasso hoti . . . pe . . . avikkhepo hoti . . . ime dhammâ kusalâ.

Cattâri brahmavihârajhânâni soḷasakkhattukâni.

263. Katame dhammâ kusalâ?

Yasmiṃ samaye rûpûpapattiyâ maggaṃ bhâveti vivicceva kâmehi . . . pe . . . paṭhamaṃ jhânaṃ upasampajja viharati uddhumâtakasaññâsahagataṃ: tasmiṃ samaye phasso hoti . . . pe . . . avikkhepo hoti . . . pe . . . ime dhammâ kusalâ.

264. Katame dhammâ kusalâ?

Yasmiṃ samaye rûpûpapattiyâ maggaṃ bhâveti vivicceva kâmehi . . . pe . . . paṭhamaṃ jhânaṃ upasampajja viharati vinîlakasaññâsahagataṃ . . . pe . . . vipubbakasaññâsahagataṃ . . . pe . . . vichiddakasaññâsahagataṃ . . . pe . . . vikkhâyitakasaññâsahagataṃ . . . pe . . . vikkhittakasaññâsahagataṃ . . . pe . . . hatavikkhittakasaññâsahagataṃ . . . pe . . . lohitakasaññâsahagataṃ . . . pe . . . puḷavakasaññâsahagataṃ . . . pe . . . aṭṭhikasaññâsahagataṃ . . . pe . . . tasmiṃ samaye phasso hoti . . . pe . . . avikkhepo hoti . . . pe . . . ime dhammâ kusalâ.

Asubhajhânaṃ soḷasakkhattukaṃ.

Rûpâvacarakusalaṃ.

265. Katame dhammâ kusalâ?

Yasmiṃ samaye arûpûpapattiyâ maggaṃ bhâveti sabbaso rûpasaññâṇaṃ samatikkamâ paṭighasaññâṇaṃ atthaṅgamânânattasaññânaṃ amanasikârâ âkâsânañcâyatanasaññâsahagataṃ sukhassa ca pahânâ . . . pe . . . catutthaṃ jhânaṃ upasampajja viharati upekkhâsahagataṃ tasmiṃ samaye phasso hoti . . . pe . . . avikkhepo hoti . . . pe . . . ime dhammâ kusalâ.

266. Khatame dhammâ kusalâ?

Yasmiṃ samaye arûpûpapattiyâ maggaṃ bhâveti sabbaso âkâsânañcâyatanaṃ samatikkamâ viññâṇañcâyatanasaññâsahagataṃ sukhassa ca pahânâ . . . pe . . . catutthaṃ jhânaṃ upasampajja viharati upekkhâsahagataṃ: tasmiṃ samaye phasso hoti . . . pe . . . avikkhepo hoti . . . pe . . . ime dhammâ kusalâ.

267. Katame dhammâ kusalâ?

Yasmiṃ samaye arûpûpapattiyâ maggaṃ bhâveti sabbaso viññâṇañcâyatanaṃ samatikkamâ âkiñcaññâyatanasaññâsahagataṃ sukhassa ca pahânâ . . . pe . . . catutthaṃ jhânaṃ upasampajja viharati upekkhâsahagataṃ tasmiṃ samaye phasso hoti . . . pe . . . avikkhepo hoti . . . pe . . . ime dhammâ kusalâ?

268. Katame dhammâ kusalâ?

Yasmiṃ samaye arûpûpapattiyâ maggaṃ bhâveti sabbaso âkiñcaññâyatanaṃ samatikkamâ nevasaññânâsaññâyatanasaññâsahagataṃ sukhassa ca pahânâ . . . pe . . . catutthaṃ jhânaṃ upasampajja viharati upekkhâsahagataṃ tasmiṃ samaye phasso hoti . . . pe . . . avikkhepo hoti . . . pe . . . ime dhammâ kusalâ.

Cattâri arûpajjhânâni soḷasakkhattukâni.

269. Katame dhammâ kusalâ?

Yasmiṃ samaye kâmâvacaraṃ kusalaṃ cittaṃ uppannaṃ hoti somanassasahagataṃ ñâṇasampayuttaṃ hînaṃ . . . pe majjhimaṃ . . . pe . . . paṇîtaṃ . . . pe . . . chandâdhipateyyaṃ . . . pe . . . viriyâdhipateyyaṃ . . . pe . . . cittâdhipateyyaṃ . . . pe . . . vimaṃsâdhipateyyaṃ . . . pe . . . chandâdhipateyyam hînaṃ . . . pe . . . majjhimaṃ . . . pe . . . paṇîtaṃ . . . pe . . . viriyâdhipateyyaṃ hînaṃ . . . pe . . . majjhimaṃ . . . pe . . . paṇîtaṃ . . . pe . . . cittâdhipateyyaṃ hînaṃ . . . pe . . . majjhimaṃ . . . pe . . . paṇîtaṃ . . . pe . . . vimaṃsâdhipateyyaṃ hînaṃ . . . pe . . . majjhimaṃ . . . pe . . . paṇîtaṃ tasmiṃ samaye phasso hoti . . . pe . . . avikkhepo hoti . . . pe . . . ime dhammâ kusalâ.

270. Katame dhammâ kusalâ?

Yasmiṃ samaye kâmâvacaraṃ kusalaṃ cittaṃ uppannaṃ hoti somanassasahagataṃ ñâṇasampayuttaṃ sasaṅkhâreṇa

. . . pe . . . somanassasahagataṃ ñâṇavippayuttaṃ . . . pe . . . somanassasahagataṃ ñâṇavippayuttaṃ sasaṅkhârena . . . pe . . . upekkhâsahagataṃ ñâṇasampayuttaṃ . . . pe . . . upekkhâsahagataṃ ñâṇasampayuttaṃ sasaṅkhârena . . . pe . . . upekkhâsahagataṃ ñâṇavippayuttaṃ . . . pe . . . upekkhâsahagataṃ ñâṇavippayuttaṃ sasaṅkhârena hînaṃ . . . pe . . . majjhimaṃ . . . pe . . . paṇîtaṃ . . . pe . . . chandâdhipateyyaṃ . . . pe . . . viriyâdhipateyyaṃ . . . . pe . . . cittâdhipateyyaṃ . . . pe . . . chandâdhipateyyaṃ hînaṃ . . . pe . . . majjhimaṃ . . . pe . . . paṇîtaṃ . . . pe . . . viriyâdhipateyyaṃ hînaṃ . . . pe majjhimaṃ . . . pe . . . paṇîtaṃ . . . pe . . . cittâdhipateyyaṃ hînaṃ . . . pe . . . majjhimaṃ . . . pe . . . paṇîtaṃ: tasmiṃ samaye phasso hoti . . . pe . . . avikkhepo hoti . . . pe . . . ime dhammâ kusalâ.

Kâmâvacarakusalaṃ.

271. Katame dhammâ kusalâ?

Yasmiṃ samaye rûpûpapattiyâ maggaṃ bhâveti vivicceva kâmehi . . . pe . . . paṭhamaṃ jhânaṃ upasampajja viharati pathavîkasiṇaṃ hînaṃ . . . pe . . . majjhimaṃ . . . pe . . . pe . . . paṇîtaṃ . . . pe . . . chandâdhipateyyaṃ . . . pe . . . viriyâdhipateyyaṃ . . . pe . . . cittâdhipateyyaṃ . . . pe . . . vimaṃsâdhipateyyaṃ . . . chandâdhipateyyaṃ hînaṃ . . . pe . . . majjhimaṃ . . . pe . . . paṇîtaṃ. . . . pe . . . viriyâdhipateyyaṃ hînaṃ . . . pe . . . majjhimaṃ . . . pe . . . paṇîtaṃ . . . pe . . . cittâdhipateyyaṃ hînaṃ . . . pe . . . majjhimaṃ . . . pe . . . paṇîtaṃ . . . pe . . . . vimaṃsâdhipateyyaṃ hînaṃ . . . pe . . . majjhimaṃ . . . pe . . . panîtaṃ . . . pe . . . tasmiṃ samaye phasso hoti . . . pe . . . avikkhepo hoti . . . pe . . . ime dhammâ kusalâ.

272. Katame dhammâ kusalâ.

Yasmiṃ samaye rûpûpapattiyâ maggaṃ bhâveti vitakkavicârânaṃ vûpasamâ . . . pe . . . dutiyaṃ jhânaṃ . . . pe . . . tatiyaṃ jhânaṃ . . . pe . . . catutthaṃ jhânaṃ . . . pe . . . paṭhamaṃ jhânaṃ . . . pe . . . pañcamaṃ jhânaṃ upasampajja viharati paṭhavîkasiṇaṃ hînaṃ . . . pe . . . majjhimaṃ . . . pe . . . paṇîtaṃ . . . pe . . . chandâdhipateyyaṃ . . . pe . . . viriyâdhipateyyaṃ . . . pe . . . cittâdhipateyyaṃ . . . pe . . . vimaṃsâdhipateyyaṃ . . . pe . . . chandâdhipateyyaṃ hînaṃ . . . pe . . . majjhimaṃ . . . pe . . . paṇîtaṃ . . . pe . . . viriyâdhipateyyaṃ hînaṃ . . . pe . . . majjhimaṃ . . . pe . . . paṇîtaṃ . . . pe . . . cittâdhipateyyaṃ hînaṃ . . . pe . . . majjhimaṃ . . . pe . . . paṇîtaṃ . . . pe . . . vimaṃsâdhipateyyaṃ hînaṃ . . . pe . . . majjhimaṃ . . . pe . . . paṇîtaṃ tasmiṃ samaye phasso hoti . . . pe . . . avikkhepo hoti . . . pe . . . ime dhammâ kusalâ.

Rûpâvacara-kusalaṃ.

273. Katame dhammâ kusalâ?

Yasmiṃ samaye arûpûpapattiyâ maggaṃ bhâveti sabbaso rûpasaññânaṃ samatikkamâ paṭighasaññânaṃ atthaṅgamâ-nânattasaññânaṃ amanasikârâ âkâsânañcâyatanasaññâsahagataṃ sukhassa ca pahânâ . . . pe . . . catutthaṃ jhânaṃ upasampajja viharati hînaṃ . . . pe . . . majjhimaṃ . . . pe . . . paṇîtaṃ . . . pe . . . chandâdhipateyyaṃ . . . pe . . . viriyâdhipateyyaṃ . . . pe . . . cittâdhipateyyaṃ . . . pe . . . vimaṃsâdhipateyyaṃ . . . pe . . . chandâdhipateyyaṃ hînaṃ . . . pe . . . majjhimaṃ . . . pe . . . panîtaṃ . . . pe . . . viriyâdhipateyyaṃ hînaṃ . . . pe . . . majjhimaṃ . . . pe . . . panîtaṃ . . . pe . . . cittâdhipateyyaṃ hînaṃ . . . pe . . . majjhimaṃ . . . pe . . . panîtaṃ . . . pe . . . vimaṃsâdhipateyyaṃ hînaṃ . . . pe . . . majjhimaṃ . . . pe . . . paṇîtaṃ tasmiṃ samaye phasso hoti . . . pe . . . avikkhepo hoti . . . pe . . . ime dhammâ kusalâ.

274. Katame dhammâ kusalâ.

Yasmiṃ samaye arûpûpapattiyâ maggaṃ bhâveti sabbaso âkâsânañcâyatanaṃ samatikkamâ viññâṇañcâyatanasaññâsahagataṃ sukhassa ca pahânâ . . . pe . . . catutthaṃ jhânaṃ upasampajja viharati hînaṃ . . . pe . . . majjhimaṃ . . . pe . . . paṇîtaṃ . . . pe . . . chandâdhipateyyaṃ . . . pe . . . viriyâdhipateyyaṃ . . . pe . . . cittâdhipateyyaṃ . . . pe . . . vimaṃsâdhipateyyaṃ . . . pe . . . chandâdhipateyyaṃ hînaṃ . . . pe . . . majjhimaṃ . . . pe . . . paṇîtaṃ . . . pe . . . viriyâdhipateyyaṃ hînaṃ . . . pe . . . majjhimaṃ . . . pe . . . paṇîtaṃ . . . pe . . . cittâdhipateyyaṃ hînaṃ . . . pe . . . majjhimaṃ . . . pe . . . paṇîtaṃ . . . pe . . . vimaṃsâdhipateyyaṃ hînaṃ . . . pe . . . majjhimaṃ . . . pe . . . paṇîtaṃ : tasmiṃ samaye phasso hoti . . . pe . . . avikkhepo hoti . . . pe . . . ime dhammâ kusalâ.

275. Katame dhammâ kusalâ ?

Yasmiṃ samaye arûpûpapattiyâ maggaṃ bhâveti sabbaso viññâṇañcâyatanaṃ samatikkamâ âkiñcaññâyatanasaññâsahagataṃ sukhassa ca pahânâ . . . pe . . . catutthaṃ jhânaṃ upasampajja viharati hînaṃ . . . pe . . . majjhimaṃ . . . pe . . . paṇîtaṃ . . . pe . . . chandâdhipateyyaṃ . . . pe . . . viriyâdhipateyyaṃ . . . pe . . . cittâdhipateyyaṃ . . . pe . . . vimaṃsâdhipateyyaṃ . . . pe . . . chandâdhipateyyaṃ hînaṃ . . . pe . . . majjhimaṃ . . . pe . . . paṇîtaṃ . . . pe . . . viriyâdhipateyyaṃ hînaṃ . . . pe . . . majjhimaṃ . . . pe . . . paṇîtaṃ . . . pe . . . cittâdhipateyyaṃ hînaṃ . . . pe . . . vimaṃsâdhipateyyaṃ hînaṃ . . . pe . . . majjhimaṃ . . . pe . . . paṇîtaṃ tasmiṃ samaye phasso hoti . . . pe . . . avikkhepo hoti . . . pe . . . ime dhammâ kusalâ.

276. Katame dhammâ kusalâ ?

Yasmiṃ samaye arûpûpapattiyâ maggaṃ bhâveti sabbaso âkiñcaññâyatanaṃ samatikkamâ nevasaññânâsaññâyatana saññâsahagataṃ sukhassa ca pahânâ . . . pe . . . catutthaṃ jhânaṃ upasampajja viharati hînaṃ . . . pe . . . majjhimaṃ . . . pe . . . paṇîtaṃ . . . pe . . . chandâdhipateyyaṃ . . . pe . . . viriyâdhipateyyaṃ . . . pe . . . cittâdhipateyyaṃ . . . pe . . . vimaṃsâdhipateyyaṃ . . . pe . . . chandâdhipateyyaṃ hînaṃ . . . pe . . . majjhimaṃ . . . pe . . . paṇîtaṃ . . . pe . . . viriyâdhipateyyaṃ hînaṃ . . . pe . . . majjhimaṃ . . . pe . . . paṇîtaṃ . . . pe . . . cittâdhipateyyaṃ hînaṃ . . . pe . . . majjhimaṃ . . . pe . . . paṇîtaṃ . . . pe . . . vimaṃsâdhipacyyaṃ hînaṃ . . . pe . . . majjhimaṃ . . . pe . . . paṇîtaṃ tasmiṃ samaye phasso hoti . . . pe . . . avikkhepo hoti . . . pe . . . ime dhammâ kusalâ.

Arûpâvacarakusalaṃ.

277. Katame dhammâ kusalâ?

Yasmiṃ samaye lokuttaraṃ jhânaṃ bhâveti niyyânikaṃ apacayagâmiṃ diṭṭhigatânaṃ pahânâya paṭhamâya bhummiyâ-pattiyâ vivicceva kâmehi . . . pe . . . paṭhamaṃ jhânaṃ upasampajja viharati dukkhâpaṭipadaṃ dandhâbhiññaṃ: tasmiṃ samaye phasso hoti vedanâ hoti saññâ hoti cetanâ hoti cittaṃ hoti vitakko hoti vicâro hoti pîti hoti sukhaṃ hoti cittass ekaggatâ hoti saddhindriyaṃ hoti viriyindriyaṃ hoti satindriyaṃ hoti samâdhindriyaṃ hoti paññindriyaṃ hoti manindriyaṃ hoti somanassindriyaṃ hoti jîvitindriyaṃ hoti anaññâtaññassâmîtindriyaṃ hoti, sammâdiṭṭhi hoti sammâsaṅkappo hoti sammâvâcâ hoti sammâkammanto hoti sammââjîvo hoti sammâvâyâmo hoti sammâsati hoti sammâsamâdhi hoti saddhâbalaṃ hoti viriyabalaṃ hoti satibalaṃ hoti samâdhibalaṃ hoti paññâbalaṃ hoti hiribalaṃ hoti ottappabalaṃ hoti alobho hoti adoso hoti amoho hoti anabhijjhâ hoti avyâpâdo hoti sammâdiṭṭhi hoti hiri hoti ottappaṃ hoti kâyapassaddhi hoti cittapassaddhi hoti kâyalahutâ hoti cittalahutâ hoti kâyamudutâ hoti cittamudutâ hoti kâyakammaññatâ hoti cittakammaññatâ hoti kâyapâguññatâ hoti cittapâguññatâ hoti kâyujjukatâ hoti cittujjukatâ hoti sati hoti sampajaññaṃ hoti samatho hoti vipassanâ hoti paggâho hoti avikkhepo hoti: ye vâ pana tasmiṃ samaye aññe pi atthi paṭiccasamuppannâ arûpino dhammâ—ime dhammâ kusalâ.

278.[1] Katamo tasmiṃ samaye phasso hoti?

Yo tasmiṃ samayo phasso phusanâ samphusanâ samphusitattaṃ—ayaṃ tasmiṃ samaye phasso hoti.

279. Katamâ tasmiṃ samaye vedanâ hoti?

Yaṃ tasmiṃ samaye tajjâ manoviññâṇadhâtu samphassa-

---

[1] Questions 282–302 are the same as questions 2–21, but 300 is a fresh one inserted; 303–305 are new; 306–341 are the same as 22–57. The answers differ slightly throughout. Some of the same questions recur, 370–400 and 407–411, and 446 foll.

jaṃ cetasikaṃ sâtaṃ cetasikaṃ sukhaṃ cetosamphassajaṃ sâtaṃ sukhaṃ vedayitaṃ cetosamphassajâ sâtâ sukhâ vedanâ —ayaṃ tasmiṃ samaye vedanâ hoti.

280. Katamâ tasmiṃ samaye saññâ hoti?

Yâ tasmiṃ samaye tajjâ manoviññâṇadhâtu samphassajâ saññâ sañjânanâ sañjânitattaṃ—ayaṃ tasmiṃ samaye saññâ hoti.

281. Katamâ tasmiṃ samaye cetanâ hoti?

Yâ tasmiṃ samaye tajjâ manoviññâṇadhâtu samphassajâ cetanâ sañcetanâ cetayitattaṃ—ayaṃ tasmiṃ samaye cetanâ hoti.

282. Katamaṃ tasmiṃ samaye cittaṃ hoti?

Yaṃ tasmiṃ samaye cittaṃ mano mânasaṃ hadayaṃ paṇḍaraṃ mano manâyatanaṃ manindriyaṃ viññâṇaṃ viññâṇakkhandho tajjâ manoviññâṇadhâtu—idaṃ tasmiṃ samaye cittaṃ hoti.

283. Katamo tasmiṃ samaye vitakko hoti?

Yo tasmiṃ samaye takko vitakko saṅkappo appanâ vyappanâ cetaso abhiniropanâ sammâsaṅkappo maggaṅgaṃ maggapariyâpannaṃ—ayaṃ tasmiṃ samaye vitakko hoti.

284. Katamo tasmiṃ samaye vicâro hoti?

Yo tasmiṃ samaye câro vicâro anuvicâro upavicâro cittassa anusandhanatâ anupekkhanatâ—ayaṃ tasmiṃ samaye vicâro hoti.

285. Katamâ tasmiṃ samaye pîti hoti?

Yâ tasmiṃ samaye pîti pâmojjaṃ âmodanâ pamodanâ hâso pahâso vitti odagyaṃ attamanatâ cittassa pîtisambojjhaṅgo—ayaṃ tasmiṃ samaye pîti hoti.

286. Katamaṃ tasmiṃ samaye sukhaṃ hoti?

Yaṃ tasmiṃ samaye cetasikaṃ sâtaṃ cetasikaṃ sukhaṃ cetosamphassajaṃ sâtaṃ sukhaṃ vedayitaṃ cetosamphassajâ sâtâ sukhâ vedanâ—idaṃ tasmiṃ samaye sukhaṃ hoti.

287. Katamâ tasmiṃ samaye cittass ekaggatâ hoti?

Yâ tasmiṃ samaye cittassa ṭhiti saṇṭhiti avaṭṭhiti avisâhâro avikkhepo avisâhaṭamânasatâ samatho samâdhindriyaṃ samâdhibalaṃ sammâsamâdhi samâdhisambojjhaṅgo maggaṅgaṃ maggapariyâpannaṃ: ayaṃ tasmiṃ samaye cittassekaggatâ hoti.

288. Katamaṃ tasmiṃ samaye saddhindriyaṃ hoti? Yâ tasmiṃ samaye saddhâ saddahanâ okappanâ abhippasâdo saddhâ saddhindriyaṃ saddhâbalaṃ — idaṃ tasmiṃ samaye saddhindriyaṃ hoti.

289. Katamaṃ tasmiṃ samaye viriyindriyaṃ hoti? Yo tasmiṃ samaye cetasiko viriyârambho nikkamo parakkamo uyyâmo vâyâmo ussâho ussoḷhi thâmo dhiti asithilaparakkamatâ anikkhittachandatâ anikkhittadhuratâ dhurasampaggâho viriyaṃ viriyindriyaṃ viriyabalam sammâvâyâmo viriyasambojjhaṅgo maggaṅgaṃ maggapariyâpannaṃ—idaṃ tasmiṃ samaye viriyindriyaṃ hoti.

290. Katamaṃ tasmiṃ samaye satindriyaṃ hoti? Yâ tasmiṃ samaye sati anussati paṭissati saraṇatâ dhâraṇatâ apilâpanatâ asammussanatâ sati satindriyaṃ satibalaṃ sammâsati satisambojjhaṅgo maggaṅgaṃ maggapariyâpannaṃ—idaṃ tasmiṃ samaye satindriyaṃ hoti.

291. Katamaṃ tasmiṃ samaye samâdhindriyaṃ hoti? Yâ tasmiṃ samaye cittassa ṭhiti saṇṭhiti avaṭhiti avisâhâro avikkhepo avisâhaṭamânasatâ samatho samâdhindriyaṃ samâdhibalaṃ sammâsamâdhi samâdhisambojjhaṅgo maggaṅgaṃ maggapariyâpannaṃ—idaṃ tasmiṃ samaye samâdhindriyaṃ hoti.

292. Katamaṃ tasmiṃ samaye paññindriyaṃ hoti? Yâ tasmiṃ samaye paññâ pajânanâ vicayo pavicayo dhammavicayo sallakkhaṇâ upalakkhaṇâ paccupalakkhaṇâ paṇḍiccaṃ kosallaṃ nepuññaṃ vebhavyâ cintâ upaparikkhâ bhûrî medhâ pariṇâyikâ vipassanâ sampajaññaṃ patodo paññâ paññindriyaṃ paññâbalaṃ paññâsatthaṃ paññâpâsâdo paññâ-âloko paññâ-obhâso paññâpajjoto paññâratanaṃ amoho dhammavicayo sammâdiṭṭhi dhammavicayasambojjhaṅgo maggaṅgaṃ maggapariyâpannaṃ — idaṃ tasmiṃ samaye paññindriyaṃ hoti.

293. Katamaṃ tasmiṃ samaye manindriyaṃ hoti? Yaṃ tasmiṃ samaye cittaṃ mano mânasaṃ hadayaṃ paṇḍaraṃ mano manâyatanaṃ manindriyaṃ viññâṇaṃ viññâṇakkhandho tajjâ manoviññâṇadhâtu — idaṃ tasmiṃ samaye manindriyaṃ hoti.

294. Katamaṃ tasmiṃ samaye somanassindriyam hoti?

Yaṃ tasmiṃ samaye cetasikaṃ sâtaṃ cetasikaṃ sukhaṃ cetosamphassajaṃ sâtaṃ sukhaṃ vedayitaṃ cetosamphassajâ sâtâ sukhâ vedanâ—idaṃ tasmiṃ samaye somanassindriyaṃ hoti.

295. Katamaṃ tasmiṃ samaye jîvitindriyaṃ hoti?

Yo tesaṃ arûpînaṃ dhammânaṃ âyu ṭhiti yapanâ yâpanâ iriyanâ vattanâ pâlanâ jîvitaṃ jîvitindriyaṃ—idaṃ tasmiṃ samaye jîvitindriyaṃ hoti.

296. Katamaṃ tasmiṃ samaye anaññâtaññassâmîtindriyaṃ hoti?

Yâ tesaṃ dhammânaṃ aññâtânaṃ adiṭṭhânaṃ apattânaṃ aviditânaṃ asacchikatânaṃ sacchikiriyâya paññâ pajânanâ vicayo pavicayo dhammavicayo sallakkhaṇâ upalakkhaṇâ paccupalakkhanâ paṇḍiccaṃ kosallaṃ nepuññaṃ vebhavyâ cintâ upaparikkhâ bhûrî medhâ pariṇâyikâ vipassanâ sampajaññaṃ patodo paññâ paññindriyaṃ paññâbalaṃ paññâsatthaṃ pâññâpâsâdo paññâ-âloko paññâ-obhâso paññâpajjoto paññâratanaṃ amoho dhammavicayo sammâdiṭṭhi dhammavicayasambojjhaṅgo maggaṅgaṃ maggapariyâpannaṃ—idaṃ tasmiṃ samaye anaññâtaññassâmîtindriyaṃ hoti.

297. Katamâ tasmiṃ samaye sammâdiṭṭhi hoti?

Yâ tasmiṃ samaye paññâ pajânanâ vicayo pavicayo dhammavicayo sallakkhaṇâ upalakkhaṇâ paccupalakkhaṇâ paṇḍiccaṃ kosallaṃ nepuññaṃ vebhavyâ cintâ upaparikkhâ bhûrî medhâ pariṇâyikâ vipassanâ sampajaññaṃ patodo paññâ paññindriyaṃ paññâbalaṃ paññâsatthaṃ paññâpâsâdo paññâ-âloko paññâ-obhâso paññâpajjoto paññâratanaṃ amoho dhammavicayo sammâdiṭṭhi dhammavicayasambojjhaṅgo maggaṅgaṃ maggapariyâpannaṃ—ayaṃ tasmiṃ samaye sammâdiṭṭhi hoti.

298. Katamo tasmiṃ samaye sammâsankappo hoti?

Yo tasmiṃ samaye takko vitakko saṅkappo appanâ vyappanâ cetaso abhiniropanâ sammâsaṅkappo maggaṅgaṃ maggapariyâpannaṃ—ayaṃ tasmiṃ samaye sammâsaṅkappo hoti.

299. Katamâ tasmiṃ samaye sammâvâcâ hoti?

Yâ tasmiṃ samaye catûhi vacîduccaritehi ârati virati paṭivirati veramaṇî akiriyâ akaraṇaṃ anajjhâpatti velâ anatikkamo setughâto sammâvâcâ maggaṅgaṃ maggapariyâpannaṃ—ayaṃ tasmiṃ samaye sammâvâcâ hoti.

300. Katamo tasmiṃ samaye sammâkammanto hoti?

Yâ tasmiṃ samaye tîhi kâyaduccaritehi ârati virati paṭivirati veramaṇî akiriyâ akaraṇaṃ anajjhâpatti velâ anatikkamo setughâto sammâkammanto maggaṅgaṃ maggapariyâpannaṃ—ayaṃ tasmiṃ samaye sammâkammanto hoti.

301. Katamo tasmiṃ samaye sammâ-âjîvo hoti?

Yâ tasmiṃ samaye micchâjîvâ ârati virati paṭivirati veramaṇî akiriyâ akaraṇaṃ anajjhâpatti velâ anatikkamo setughâto sammâ-âjîvo maggaṅgaṃ maggapariyâpannaṃ—ayaṃ tasmiṃ samaye sammâ-âjîvo hoti.

302. Katamo tasmiṃ samaye sammâvâyâmo hoti?

Yo tasmiṃ samaye cetasiko viriyârambho nikkamo parakkamo uyyâmo vâyâmo ussâho ussoḷhi thâmo dhiti asithilaparakkamatâ anikkhittachandatâ anikkhittadhuratâ dhurasampaggâho viriyaṃ viriyindriyaṃ viriyabalaṃ sammâvâyamo viriyasambojjhaṅgo maggaṅgaṃ maggapariyâpannaṃ—ayaṃ tasmiṃ samaye sammâvâyâmo hoti.

303. Katamâ tasmiṃ samaye sammâsati hoti?

Yâ tasmiṃ samaye sati anussati paṭissati sati saraṇatâ dhâraṇatâ apilâpanatâ asammussanatâ sati satindriyaṃ satibalaṃ sammâsati satisambojjhaṅgo maggaṅgaṃ maggapariyâpannaṃ—ayaṃ tasmiṃ samaye sammâsati hoti.

304. Katamo tasmiṃ samaye sammâsamâdhi hoti?

Yâ tasmiṃ samaye cittassa ṭhiti saṇṭhiti avaṭṭhiti avisâhâro avikkhepo avisâhaṭamânasatâ samatho samâdhindriyaṃ samâdhibalaṃ sammâsamâdhisambojjhaṅgo maggaṅgaṃ maggapariyâpannaṃ—ayaṃ tasmiṃ samaye sammâsamâdhi hoti.

305. Katamaṃ tasmiṃ samaye saddhâbalaṃ hoti?

Yâ tasmiṃ samaye saddhâ saddahanâ okappanâ abhippasâdo saddhâ saddhindriyaṃ saddhâbalaṃ—idaṃ tasmiṃ samaye saddhâbalaṃ hoti.

306. Katamaṃ tasmiṃ samaye viriyabalaṃ hoti?

Yo tasmiṃ samaye cetasiko viriyârambho nikkamo parakkamo uyyâmo vâyâmo ussâho ussoḷhi thâmo dhiti asithilaparakkamatâ anikkhittachandatâ anikkhittadhuratâ dhurasampaggâho viriyaṃ viriyindriyaṃ viriyabalaṃ sammâvâyâmo viriyasambojjhaṅgo maggaṅgaṃ maggapariyâpannaṃ—idaṃ tasmiṃ samaye viriyabalaṃ hoti.

307. Katamaṃ tasmiṃ samaye satibalaṃ hoti?

Yâ tasmiṃ samaye sati anussati paṭissati sati saraṇatâ dhâraṇatâ apilâpanatâ asammussanatâ sati satindriyaṃ satibalaṃ sammâsati satisambojjhaṅgo maggaṅgaṃ maggapariyâpannaṃ—idaṃ tasmiṃ samaye satibalaṃ hoti.

308. Katamaṃ tasmiṃ samaye samâdhibalaṃ hoti?

Yâ tasmiṃ samaye cittassa ṭhiti saṇṭhiti avaṭṭhiti avisâhâro avikkhepo avisâhaṭamânasatâ samatho samâdhindriyaṃ samâdhibalaṃ sammâsamâdhi samâdhisambojjhaṅgo maggaṅgaṃ maggapariyâpannaṃ—idaṃ tasmiṃ samaye samâdhibalaṃ hoti.

309. Katamaṃ tasmiṃ samaye paññâbalaṃ hoti?

Yâ tasmiṃ samaye paññâ pajânanâ vicayo pavicayo dhammavicayo sallakkhaṇâ upalakkhaṇâ paccupalakkhaṇâ paṇḍiccaṃ kosallaṃ nepuññaṃ vebhavyâ cintâ upaparikkhâ bhûrî medhâ pariṇâyikâ vipassanâ sampajaññaṃ patodo paññâ paññindriyaṃ paññâbalaṃ paññâsatthaṃ paññâpâsâdo paññâ-âloko paññâ-obhâso paññâpajjoto paññâratanaṃ amoho dhammavicayo sammâdiṭṭhi dhammavicayasambojjhaṅgo maggaṅgaṃ maggapariyâpannaṃ—idaṃ tasmiṃ samaye paññâbalaṃ hoti.

310. Katamaṃ tasmiṃ samaye hiribalaṃ hoti?

Yaṃ tasmiṃ samaye hiriyati hiriyitabbena, hiriyati pâpakânaṃ akusalânaṃ dhammânaṃ samâpattiyâ—idaṃ tasmiṃ samaye hiribalaṃ hoti.

311. Katamaṃ tasmiṃ samaye ottappabalaṃ hoti?

Yaṃ tasmiṃ samaye ottappati ottappitabbena, ottappati pâpakânaṃ akusalânaṃ dhammânaṃ samâpattiyâ—idaṃ tasmiṃ samaye ottappabalaṃ hoti.

312. Katamo tasmiṃ samaye alobho hoti?

Yo tasmiṃ samaye alobho alubbhanâ alubbhitattaṃ asârâgo asârajjanâ asârajjitattaṃ anabhijjhâ alobho kusalamûlaṃ—ayaṃ tasmiṃ samaye alobho hoti.

313. Katamo tasmiṃ samaye adoso hoti?

Yo tasmiṃ samaye adoso adussanâ adussitattaṃ avyâpâdo avyâpajjo adoso kusalamûlaṃ—ayaṃ tasmiṃ samaye adoso hoti.

314. Katamo tasmiṃ samaye amoho hoti?

Yâ tasmiṃ samaye paññâ pajânanâ vicayo . . . pe . . .

dhammavicayasambojjhaṅgo maggaṅgaṃ maggapariyâpannaṃ—ayaṃ tasmiṃ samaye amoho hoti.

315. Katamâ tasmiṃ samaye anabhijjhâ hoti?

Yo tasmiṃ samaye alobho alubbhanâ alubbhitattaṃ asârâgo asârajjanâ asârajjitattaṃ anabhijjhâ alobho kusalamûlaṃ—ayaṃ tasmiṃ samaye anabhijjhâ hoti.

316. Katamo tasmiṃ samaye avyâpâdo hoti.

Yo tasmiṃ samaye adoso adussanâ adussitattaṃ avyâpâdo avyâpajjo adoso kusalamûlaṃ—ayaṃ tasmiṃ samaye avyâpâdo hoti.

317. Katamâ tasmiṃ samaye sammâdiṭṭhi hoti?

Yâ tasmiṃ samaye paññâ pajânanâ vicayo . . . pe . . . dhammavicayo sambojjhaṅgo maggaṅgaṃ maggapariyâpannaṃ—ayaṃ tasmiṃ samaye sammâdiṭṭhi hoti.

318. Katamâ tasmiṃ samaye hiri hoti?

Yaṃ tasmiṃ samaye hiriyati hiriyitabbena hiriyati pâpakânaṃ akusalânaṃ dhammânaṃ samâpattiyâ—ayaṃ tasmiṃ samaye hiri hoti.

319. Katamaṃ tasmiṃ samaye ottappaṃ hoti?

Yaṃ tasmiṃ samaye ottappati ottappitabbena ottappati pâpakânaṃ akusalânaṃ dhammânaṃ samâpattiyâ—idaṃ tasmiṃ samaye ottappaṃ hoti.

320. Katamâ tasmiṃ samaye kâyapassaddhi hoti?

Yâ tasmiṃ samaye vedanâkkhandhassa saññâkkhandhassa saṅkhârakkhandhassa passaddhi paṭipassaddhi passambhanâ paṭipassambhanâ paṭipassambhitattaṃ passaddhisambojjhaṅgo—ayaṃ tasmiṃ samaye kâyapassaddhi hoti.

321. Katamâ tasmiṃ samaye cittapassaddhi hoti?

Yâ tasmiṃ samaye viññâṇakkhandhassa passaddhi paṭipassaddhi passambhanâ paṭipassambhanâ paṭipassambhitattaṃ passaddhisambojjhaṅgo—ayaṃ tasmiṃ samaye cittapassaddhi hoti.

322. Katamâ tasmiṃ samaye kâyalahutâ hoti?

Yâ tasmiṃ samaye vedanâkkhandhassa saññâkkhandhassa saṅkhârakkhandhassa lahutâ lahupariṇâmatâ adandhanatâ avitthanatâ—ayaṃ tasmiṃ samaye kâyalahutâ hoti.

323. Katamâ tasmiṃ samaye cittalahutâ hoti?

Yâ tasmiṃ samaye viññâṇakkhandhassa lahutâ lahupariṇâmatâ adandhanatâ avitthanatâ—ayaṃ tasmiṃ samaye citta-lahutâ hoti.

324. Katamâ tasmiṃ samaye kâyamudutâ hoti.

Yâ tasmiṃ samaye vedanâkkhandhassa saññâkkhandhassa saṅkhârakkhandhassa mudutâ maddavatâ akakkhaḷatâ akathinatâ—ayaṃ tasmiṃ samaye kâyamudutâ hoti.

325. Katamâ tasmiṃ samaye cittamudutâ hoti.

Yâ tasmiṃ samaye viññâṇakkhandhassa mudutâ maddavatâ akakkhaḷatâ akathinatâ—ayaṃ tasmiṃ samaye cittamudutâ hoti.

326. Katamâ tasmiṃ samaye kâyakammaññatâ hoti?

Yâ tasmiṃ samaye vedanâkkhandhassa saññâkkhandhassa saṅkhârakkhandhassa kammaññatâ kammaññattaṃ kammaññabhâvo—ayaṃ tasmiṃ samaye kâyakammaññatâ hoti.

327. Katamâ tasmiṃ samaye cittakammaññatâ hoti?

Yâ tasmiṃ samaye viññâṇakkhandhassa kammaññatâ kammaññattaṃ kammaññabhâvo—ayaṃ tasmiṃ samaye cittakammaññatâ hoti.

328. Katamâ tasmiṃ samaye kâyapâguññatâ hoti?

Yâ tasmiṃ samaye vedanâkkhandhassa saññâkkhandhassa saṅkhârakkhandhassa paguṇatâ paguṇattaṃ paguṇabhâvo—ayaṃ tasmiṃ samaye kâyapâguññatâ hoti.

329. Katamâ tasmiṃ samaye cittapâguññatâ hoti?

Yâ tasmiṃ samaye viññâṇakkhandhassa paguṇatâ paguṇattaṃ paguṇabhâvo—ayaṃ tasmiṃ samaye cittapâguññatâ hoti.

330. Katamâ tasmiṃ samaye kâyujjukatâ hoti?

Yâ tasmiṃ samaye vedanâkkhandhassa saññâkkhandhassa saṅkhârakkhandhassa ujutâ ujjukatâ ajimhatâ avaṅkatâ akuṭilatâ—ayaṃ tasmiṃ samaye kâyujjukatâ hoti.

331. Katamâ tasmiṃ samaye cittujjukatâ hoti?

Yâ tasmiṃ samaye viññâṇakkhandhassa ujutâ ujjukatâ ajimhatâ avaṅkatâ akuṭilatâ—ayaṃ tasmiṃ samaye cittujjukatâ hoti.

332. Katamâ tasmiṃ samaye sati hoti?

Yâ tasmiṃ samaye sati anussati paṭissati sati saraṇatâ dhâraṇatâ apilâpanatâ asammussanatâ sati satindriyaṃ satibalaṃ sammâsatisambojjhaṅgo maggaṅgaṃ maggapariyâpannaṃ—ayaṃ tasmiṃ samaye sati hoti.

333. Katamaṃ tasmiṃ samaye sampajaññaṃ hoti?

Yâ tasmiṃ samaye paññâ pajânanâ . . . pe . . . dhammavicayasambojjhaṅgo maggaṅgaṃ maggapariyâpannaṃ—idaṃ tasmiṃ samaye sampajaññaṃ hoti.

334. Katamo tasmiṃ samaye samatho hoti?

Yâ tasmiṃ samaye cittassa ṭhiti . . . pe . . . samâdhisambojjhaṅgo maggaṅgaṃ maggapariyâpannaṃ—ayaṃ tasmiṃ samaye samatho hoti.

335. Katamâ tasmiṃ samaye vipassanâ hoti?

Yâ tasmiṃ samaye paññâ pajânanâ . . . pe . . . dhammavicayasambojjhaṅgo maggaṅgaṃ maggapariyâpannaṃ—ayaṃ tasmiṃ samaye vipassanâ hoti.

336. Katamo tasmiṃ samaye paggâho hoti?

Yo tasmiṃ samaye cetasiko viriyârambho . . . pe . . . viriyasambojjhaṅgo maggaṅgaṃ maggapariyâpannaṃ—ayaṃ tasmiṃ samaye paggâho hoti.

337. Katamo tasmiṃ samaye avikkhepo hoti?

Yâ tasmiṃ samaye cittassa ṭhiti . . . pe . . . samâdhisambojjhaṅgo maggaṅgaṃ maggapariyâpannaṃ—ayaṃ tasmiṃ samaye avikkhepo hoti, ye vâ pana tasmiṃ samaye aññe pi atthi paṭiccasamuppannâ arûpino dhammâ—ime dhammâ kusalâ. Tasmiṃ kho pana samaye cattâro khandhâ honti dvâyatanâni honti, dve dhâtuyo honti, tayo âhârâ honti, navindriyâni honti, pañcaṅgikaṃ jhânaṃ hoti, aṭṭhaṅgiko maggo hoti, satta balâni honti, tayo hetû honti, eko phasso hoti, ekâ vedanâ hoti, ekâ saññâ hoti, ekâ cetanâ hoti, ekaṃ cittaṃ hoti, eko vedanâkkhandho hoti, eko saññâkkhandho hoti, eko saṅkhârakkhandho hoti, eko viññâṇakkhandho hoti, ekaṃ manâyatanaṃ hoti, ekaṃ manindriyaṃ hoti, ekâ manoviññâṇadhâtu hoti, ekaṃ dhammâyatanaṃ hoti, ekâ dhammadhâtu hoti—ye vâ pana tasmiṃ samaye aññe pi atthi paṭiccasamuppannâ arûpino dhammâ—ime dhammâ kusalâ . . . pe . . .

338.[1] Katamo tasmiṃ samaye saṅkhârakkhandho hoti?

Phasso vedanâ vitakko vicâro pîti cittassekaggatâ saddhindriyaṃ viriyindriyaṃ satindriyaṃ samâdhindriyaṃ paññin-

---

[1] Compare 62.

driyaṃ jîvitindriyaṃ anaññâtaññassâmîtindriyaṃ sammâdiṭṭhi sammâsaṅkappo sammâvâcâ sammâkammanto, sammâ-âjîvo, sammâvâyâmo, sammâsati, sammâsamâdhi, saddhâbalaṃ, viriyabalaṃ, satibalaṃ, samâdhibalaṃ, paññâbalaṃ, hiribalaṃ, ottappabalaṃ, alobho, adoso, amoho, anabhijjhâ, avyâpâdo, sammâdiṭṭhi hiri ottappaṃ kâyapassaddhi cittapassaddhi kâyalahutâ cittalahutâ kâyamudutâ, cittamudutâ, kâyakammaññatâ, cittakammaññatâ, kâyapâguññatâ, cittapâguññatâ, kâyujjukatâ cittujjukatâ, sati, sampajaññaṃ, samatho, vipassanâ, paggâho avikkhepo—ye vâ pana tasmiṃ samaye aññe pi atthi paṭiccasamuppannâ arûpino dhammâ, ṭhapetvâ vedanâkkhandhaṃ, ṭhapetvâ saññâkkhandhaṃ, ṭhapetvâ viññâṇakkhandhaṃ—ayaṃ tasmiṃ samaye saṅkhârakkhandho hoti . . . pe . . . ime dhammâ kusalâ.

339. Katame dhammâ kusalâ?

Yasmiṃ samaye lokuttaraṃ jhânaṃ bhâveti niyyânikaṃ apacayagâmiṃ diṭṭhigatânaṃ pahânâya paṭhamâya bhummiyâpattiyâ vivicceva kâmehi . . . pe . . . paṭhamaṃ jhânaṃ upasampajja viharati dukkhâpaṭipadaṃ dandhâbhiññam: tasmiṃ samaye phasso hoti . . . pe . . . avikkhepo hoti . . . pe . . . ime dhammâ kusalâ?

340. Katame dhammâ kusalâ?

Yasmiṃ samaye lokuttaraṃ jhânaṃ bhâveti niyyânikaṃ apacayagâmiṃ diṭṭhigatânaṃ pahânâya paṭhamâya bhummiyâpattiyâ vivicceva kâmehi . . . pe . . . paṭhamaṃ jhânaṃ upasampajja viharati dukkhâpaṭipadaṃ khippâbhiññaṃ: tasmiṃ samaye phasso hoti . . pe . . . avikkhepo hoti . . . pe . . . ime dhammâ kusalâ.

341. Katame dhammâ kusalâ?

Yasmiṃ samaye lokuttaraṃ . . . pe . . . viharati sukhâpaṭipadaṃ dandhâbhiññaṃ—tasmiṃ samaye phasso hoti . . . pe . . . avikkhepo hoti . . . pe . . . ime dhammâ kusalâ.

342. Katame dhammâ kusalâ?

Yasmiṃ samaye lokuttaraṃ . . . pe . . . viharati sukhâpaṭipadaṃ khippâbhiññaṃ tasmiṃ samaye phasso hoti . . . pe . . . avikkhepo hoti . . . pe . . . ime dhammâ kusalâ.

343. Katame dhammâ kusalâ?

Yasmiṃ samaye lokuttaraṃ . . . pe . . . pattiyâ vitakkavicârânaṃ vûpasamâ . . . pe . . . dutiyaṃ jhânaṃ . . . pe . . . tatiyaṃ jhânaṃ . . . pe . . . catutthaṃ jhânaṃ . . . pe . . . paṭhamaṃ jhânaṃ . . . pe . . . pañcamaṃ jhânaṃ upasampajja viharati dukkhâpaṭipadaṃ dandhâbhiññaṃ . . . pe . . . dukkhâpaṭipadaṃ khippâbhiññaṃ . . . pe . . . sukhâpaṭipadaṃ dandhâbhiññaṃ . . . pe . . . sukhâpaṭipadaṃ khippâbhiññaṃ . . . pe . . . tasmiṃ samaye phasso hoti . . . pe . . . avikkhepo hoti . . . pe . . . ime dhammâ kusalâ.

Suddhikapaṭipadâ.

344. Katame dhammâ kusalâ?

Yasmiṃ samaye lokuttaraṃ jhânaṃ bhâveti niyyânikaṃ apacayagâmiṃ diṭṭhigatânaṃ pahânâya paṭhamâya bhummiyâpattiyâ vivicceva kâmehi . . . pe . . . paṭhamaṃ jhânaṃ upasampajja viharati suññataṃ: tasmiṃ samaye phasso hoti . . . pe . . . avikkhepo hoti . . . pe . . . ime dhammâ kusalâ.

345. Katame dhammâ kusalâ?

Yasmiṃ samaye lokuttaraṃ jhânaṃ . . . pe . . . pattiyâ vitakkavicârânaṃ vûpasamâ . . . pe . . . dutiyaṃ jhânaṃ . . . pe . . . tatiyaṃ jhânaṃ . . . pe . . . catutthaṃ jhânaṃ . . . pe . . . paṭhamaṃ jhânaṃ . . . pe . . . pañcamaṃ jhânaṃ upasampajja viharati suññataṃ: tasmiṃ samaye phasso hoti . . . pe . . . avikkhepo hoti . . . pe . . . ime dhammâ kusalâ.

Suññataṃ.

346. Katame dhammâ kusalâ?

Yasmiṃ samaye lokuttaraṃ . . . pe . . . pattiyâ vivicceva kâmehi . . . pe . . . paṭhamaṃ jhânaṃ upasampajja viharati dukkhâpaṭipadaṃ dandhâbhiññaṃ suññataṃ: tasmiṃ samaye phasso hoti . . . pe . . . avikkhepo hoti . . . pe . . ime dhammâ kusalâ.

347. Katame dhammâ kusalâ?

Yasmiṃ samaye lokuttaraṃ jhânaṃ bhâveti niyyânikaṃ

apacayagâmiṃ diṭṭhigatânaṃ pahânâya paṭhamâya bhummiyâpattiyâ viviccova kâmehi . . . pe . . . paṭhamaṃ jhânaṃ upasampajja viharati dukkhâpaṭipadaṃ khippâbhiññaṃ suññataṃ : tasmiṃ samaye phasso hoti . . . pe . . . avikkhepo hoti . . . pe . . . ime dhammâ kusalâ.

348. Katame dhammâ kusalâ ?

Yasmiṃ samaye lokuttaraṃ jhânaṃ . . . pe . . . kâmehi . . . pe . . . paṭhamaṃ jhânaṃ upasampajja viharati sukhâpaṭipadaṃ dandhâbhiññaṃ suññataṃ: tasmiṃ samaye phasso hoti . . . pe . . . avikkhepo hoti . . . pe . . . ime dhammâ kusalâ.

349. Katame dhammâ kusalâ ?

Yasmiṃ samaye lokuttaraṃ . . . pe . . . kâmehi . . . pe . . . paṭhamaṃ jhânaṃ upasampajja viharati sukhâpaṭipadaṃ khippâbhiññaṃ suññataṃ : tasmiṃ samaye phasso hoti . . . pe . . . avikkhepo hoti . . . pe . . . ime dhammâ kusalâ.

350. Katame dhammâ kusalâ ?

Yasmiṃ samaye lokuttaraṃ . . . pe . . . pattiyâ vitakkavicârânaṃ vûpasamâ . . . pe . . . dutiyaṃ jhânaṃ . . . pe . . . tatiyaṃ jhânaṃ . . . pe . . . catutthaṃ jhânaṃ . . . pe . . . paṭhamaṃ jhânaṃ . . . pe . . . pañcamaṃ jhânaṃ upasampajja viharati dukkhâpaṭipadaṃ dandhâbhiññaṃ suññataṃ . . . pe . . . dukkhâpaṭipadaṃ khippâbhiññaṃ suññataṃ . . . pe . . . sukhâpaṭipadaṃ dandhâbhiññaṃ suññataṃ . . . pe . . . sukhâpaṭipadaṃ khippâbhiññaṃ suññataṃ : tasmiṃ samaye phasso hoti . . . pe . . . avikkhepo hoti . . . pe . . . ime dhammâ kusalâ.

Suññatamûlakapaṭipadâ.

351. Katame dhammâ kusalâ ?

Yasmiṃ samaye lokuttaraṃ . . . pe . . . pattiyâ vivicceva kâmehi . . . pe . . . paṭhamaṃ jhânaṃ upasampajja viharati appaṇihitaṃ : tasmiṃ samaye phasso hoti . . . pe . . . avikkhepo hoti . . . pe . . . ime dhammâ kusalâ.

352. Katame dhammâ kusalâ ?

Yasmiṃ samaye lokuttaraṃ . . . pe . . . pattiyâ vitakkavicârânaṃ vûpasamâ . . . pe . . . dutiyaṃ jhânaṃ . . .

pe . . . catuttham jhânam . . . pe . . . paṭhamam jhânam . . . pe . . . pañcamam jhânam upasampajja viharati appaṇihitam—tasmim samaye phasso hoti . . . pe . . . avikkhepo hoti . . . pe . . . ime dhammâ kusalâ.

Appaṇihitam.

353. Katame dhammâ kusalâ?

Yasmim samaye lokuttaram . . . pe . . . pattiyâ vivicceva kâmehi . . . pe . . . paṭhamam jhânam upasampajja viharati dukkhâpaṭipadam dandhâbhiññam appaṇihitam : tasmim samaye phasso hoti . . . pe . . . avikkhepo hoti . . . pe . . . ime dhammâ kusalâ.

354. Katame dhammâ kusalâ?

Yasmim samaye lokuttaram . . . pe . . . pattiyâ vivicceva kâmehi . . . pe . . . paṭhamam jhânam upasampajja viharati dukkhâpaṭipadam khippâbhiññam appaṇihitam : tasmim samaye phasso hoti . . . po . . . avikkhepo hoti . . . pe . . . ime dhammâ kusalâ.

355. Katame dhammâ kusalâ?

Yasmim samaye lokuttaram . . . pe . . . pattiyâ vivicceva kâmehi . . . pe . . . paṭhamam jhânam upasampajja viharati sukhâpaṭipadam dandhâbhiññam appaṇihitam: tasmim samaye phasso hoti . . . pe . . . avikkhepo hoti . . . pe . . . ime dhammâ kusalâ.

356. Katame dhammâ kusalâ?

Yasmim samaye lokuttaram . . . pe . . . pattiyâ vivicceva kàmehi. . . pe . . . paṭhamam jhânam upasampajja viharati sukhâpaṭipadam khippâbhiññam appaṇihitam : tasmim samaye phasso hoti . . . pe . . . avikkhepo hoti . . . pe . . . ime dhammâ kusalâ.

357. Katame dhammâ kusalâ?

Yasmim samaye lokuttaram . . . pe . . . pattiyâ vitakkavicârânam vûpasamâ . . . pe . . . dutiyam jhânam . . . pe . . . tatiyam jhânam . . . pe . . . catuttham jhânam . . . pe . . . paṭhamam jhânam . . . pe . . . pañcamam jhânam upasampajja viharati dukkhâpaṭipadam dandhâbhiññam appaṇihitam . . . pe . . . dukkhâpaṭipadam khippâbhiññaṃ appaṇihitaṃ . . . pe . . . sukhâpaṭipadaṃ dandhâbhiññaṃ appaṇihitaṃ . . . pe . . . sukhâpaṭipadaṃ khippâbhiññaṃ appaṇihitaṃ: tasmiṃ samaye phasso hoti . . . pe . . . avikkhepo hoti . . . pe . . . ime dhammâ kusalâ.

Appaṇihitamûlakapaṭipadaṃ.

358. Katame dhammâ kusalâ?

Yasmiṃ samaye lokuttaraṃ maggaṃ bhâveti . . . pe . . . lokuttaraṃ satipaṭṭhânaṃ bhâveti . . . pe . . . lokuttaraṃ sammappadhânaṃ bhâveti . . . pe . . . lokuttaraṃ iddhipâdaṃ bhâveti . . . pe . . . lokuttaraṃ indriyaṃ bhâveti . . . pe . . . lokuttaraṃ balaṃ bhâveti . . . pe . . . lokuttaraṃ bojjhaṅgaṃ bhâveti . . . pe . . . lokuttaraṃ saccaṃ bhâveti . . . pe . . . lokuttaraṃ samathaṃ bhâveti . . . pe . . . lokuttaraṃ dhammaṃ bhâveti . . . pe . . . lokuttaraṃ khandhaṃ bhâveti . . . pe . . . lokuttaraṃ âyatanaṃ bhâveti . . . pe . . . lokuttaraṃ dhâtuṃ bhâveti . . . lokuttaraṃ âhâraṃ bhâveti . . . pe . . . lokuttaraṃ phassaṃ bhâveti . . . pe . . . lokuttaraṃ vedanaṃ bhâveti . . . pe . . . lokuttaraṃ saññaṃ bhâveti . . . pe . . . lokuttaraṃ cetanaṃ bhâveti . . . pe . . . lokuttaraṃ cittaṃ bhâveti niyyânikaṃ apacayagâmiṃ diṭṭhigatânaṃ pahânâya paṭhamâya bhummiyâpattiyâ vivicceva kâmehi . . . pe . . . paṭhamaṃ jhânaṃ upasampajja viharati dukkhâpaṭipadaṃ dandhâbhiññaṃ—tasmiṃ samaye phasso hoti . . . pe . . . avikkhepo hoti . . . pe . . . ime dhammâ kusalâ.

Vîsati mahânayâ.

359. Katame dhammâ kusalâ?

Yasmiṃ samaye lokuttaraṃ jhânaṃ bhâveti . . . pe . . . pattiyâ viviccева kâmehi . . . pe . . . paṭhamaṃ jhânaṃ upasampajja viharati dukkhâpaṭipadaṃ dandhâbhiññaṃ chandâdhipateyyaṃ viriyâdhipateyyaṃ cittâdhipateyyaṃ vimaṃsâdhipateyyaṃ: tasmiṃ samaye phasso hoti . . . pe . . . avikkhepo hoti . . . pe . . . ime dhammâ kusalâ.

360. Katame dhammâ kusalâ?

Yasmiṃ samaye lokuttaraṃ . . . pe . . . pattiyâ vitakka-vicârânaṃ vûpasamâ . . . pe . . . dutiyaṃ jhânaṃ . . . pe . . . tatiyaṃ jhânaṃ . . . pe . . . catutthaṃ jhânaṃ . . . pe . . . paṭhamaṃ jhânaṃ . . . pe . . . pañcamaṃ jhânaṃ upasampajja viharati dukkhâpaṭipadaṃ dandhâbhiññaṃ chandâdhipateyyaṃ . . . pe . . . vimaṃsâdhipateyyaṃ: tasmiṃ samaye phasso hoti . . . pe . . . avikkhepo hoti . . . pe . . . ime dhammâ kusalâ.

361. Katame dhammâ kusalâ?

Yasmiṃ samaye lokuttaraṃ maggaṃ bhâveti . . . pe . . . lokuttaraṃ cittaṃ bhâveti niyyânikaṃ apacayagâmiṃ diṭṭhigatânaṃ pahânâya paṭhamâya bhummiyâpattiyâ vivicceva kâmehi . . . pe . . . paṭhamaṃ jhânaṃ upasampajja viharati dukkhâpaṭipadaṃ dandhâbhiññaṃ chandâdhipateyyaṃ . . . pe . . . vimaṃsâdhipateyyaṃ: tasmiṃ samaye phasso hoti . . . pe . . . avikkhepo hoti . . . pe . . . ime dhammâ kusalâ.

Adhipati.

Paṭhamo maggo.

362. Katame dhammâ kusalâ?

Yasmiṃ samaye lokuttaraṃ jhânaṃ bhâveti niyyânikaṃ apacayagâmiṃ kâmarâgavyâpâdânaṃ patanûbhâvâya dutiyâya bhummiyâpattiyâ vivicceva kâmehi. . . . pe . . . paṭhamaṃ jhânaṃ upasampajja viharati dukkhâpaṭipadaṃ dandhâbhiññaṃ: tasmiṃ samaye phasso hoti . . . pe . . . aññindriyaṃ hoti . . . pe . . . avikkhepo hoti . . . pe . . . ime dhammâ kusalâ.

Dutiyo maggo.

363. Katame dhammâ kusalâ?

Yasmiṃ samaye lokuttaraṃ jhânaṃ bhâveti niyyânikaṃ apacayagâmiṃ kâmarâgavyâpâdânaṃ anavasesappahânâya tatiyâya bhummiyâpattiyâ vivicceva kâmehi . . . pe . . . paṭhamaṃ jhânaṃ upasampajja viharati dukkhâpaṭipadaṃ dandhâbhiññaṃ : tasmiṃ samaye phasso hoti . . . pe . . . aññindriyaṃ hoti . . . pe . . . avikkhepo hoti . . . pe . . . ime dhammâ kusalâ.

Tatiyo maggo.

364. Katame dhammâ kusalâ?

Yasmiṃ samaye lokuttaraṃ jhânaṃ bhâveti niyyânikaṃ apacayagâmiṃ rûparâga-arûparâgamâna-uddhacca-avijjâya anavasesappahânâya catutthâya bhummiyâpattiyâ vivicceva kâmehi . . . pe . . . paṭhamaṃ jhânaṃ upasampajja viharati dukkhâpaṭipadaṃ dandhâbhiññaṃ : tasmiṃ samaye phasso hoti . . . pe . . . aññindriyaṃ hoti . . . pe . . . avikkhepo hoti . . . pe . . . ime dhammâ kusalâ.

Katamaṃ tasmiṃ samaye aññindriyaṃ hoti.

Yâ tesaṃ dhammânaṃ ñâtânaṃ diṭṭhânaṃ pattânaṃ viditânaṃ sacchikatânaṃ sacchikiriyâya paññâ pajânanâ vicayo pavicayo dhammavicayo . . . pe . . . dhammavicayasammâdiṭṭhi dhammavicayasambojjhaṅgo maggaṅgaṃ maggapariyâpannaṃ—idaṃ tasmiṃ samaye aññindriyaṃ hoti . . . pe . . . avikkhepo hoti . . . pe . . . ye vâ pana tasmiṃ samaye aññe pi atthi paṭiccasamuppannâ arûpino dhammâ—ime dhammâ kusalâ.

Catuttho maggo.

LOKUTTARAṂ CITTAṂ.

365. Katame dhammâ akusalâ?

Yasmiṃ samaye akusalaṃ cittaṃ uppannaṃ hoti somanassasahagataṃ diṭṭhigatasampayuttaṃ rûpârammaṇaṃ vâ saddârammaṇaṃ vâ gandhârammaṇaṃ vâ phoṭṭhabbârammaṇaṃ vâ dhammârammaṇaṃ vâ yaṃ yaṃ vâ panârabbha : tasmiṃ samaye phasso hoti, vedanâ hoti, saññâ hoti, cetanâ hoti, cittaṃ hoti, vitakko hoti, vicâro hoti, pîti hoti, sukhaṃ hoti, cittassekaggatâ hoti, viriyindriyaṃ hoti, samâdhindriyaṃ hoti, manindriyaṃ hoti, somanassindriyaṃ hoti, jîvitindriyaṃ hoti, micchâdiṭṭhi hoti, micchâsaṅkappo hoti, micchâvâyâmo hoti, micchâsamâdhi hoti, viriyabalaṃ hoti, samâdhibalaṃ hoti, ahirikabalaṃ hoti, anottappabalaṃ hoti, lobho hoti, moho hoti, abhijjhâ hoti, micchâdiṭṭhi hoti, ahirikaṃ hoti, anottappaṃ hoti, samatho hoti, vipassanâ hoti, paggâho hoti, avikkhepo hoti, ye vâ pana tasmiṃ samaye aññe pi atthi paṭiccasamuppannâ arûpino dhammâ—ime dhammâ kusalâ.

366.[1] Katamo tasmiṃ samaye phasso hoti?

Yo tasmiṃ samaye phasso phusanâ samphusanâ samphusitattaṃ—ayaṃ tasmiṃ samaye phasso hoti.

367. Katamâ tasmiṃ samaye vedanâ hoti?

Yaṃ tasmiṃ samaye tajjâ manoviññâṇadhâtu samphassajaṃ cetasikaṃ sâtaṃ cetasikaṃ sukhaṃ cetosamphassajaṃ sâtaṃ sukhaṃ vedayitaṃ cetosamphassajâ sâtâ sukhâ vedanâ : ayaṃ tasmiṃ samaye vedanâ hoti.

368. Katamâ tasmiṃ samaye saññâ hoti?

Yâ tasmiṃ samaye tajjâ manoviññâṇadhâtu samphassajâ saññâ sañjânanâ sañjânitattaṃ : ayaṃ tasmiṃ samaye saññâ hoti.

369. Katamâ tasmiṃ samaye cetanâ hoti?

Yâ tasmiṃ samaye tajjâ manoviññâṇadhâtu samphassajâ cetanâ sañcetanâ cetayitattaṃ : ayaṃ tasmiṃ samaye cetanâ hoti.

370. Katamaṃ tasmiṃ samaye cittaṃ hoti?

Yaṃ tasmiṃ samaye cittaṃ mano mânasaṃ hadayaṃ paṇḍaraṃ mano manâyatanaṃ manindriyaṃ viññâṇaṃ viññâṇakkhandho tajjâ manoviññâṇadhâtu : idaṃ tasmiṃ samaye cittaṃ hoti.

371. Katamo tasmiṃ samaye vitakko hoti?

Yo tasmiṃ samaye takko vitakko saṅkappo appanâ vyappanâ cetaso abhiniropanâ micchâsaṅkappo—ayaṃ tasmiṃ samaye vitakko hoti.

372. Katamo tasmiṃ samaye vicâro hoti?

Yo tasmiṃ samaye câro vicâro anuvicâro upavicâro cittassa

---

[1] The questions following are the same as 2 foll. and 282 foll., but the answers sometimes differ.

anusandhanatâ anupekkhanatâ : ayaṃ tasmiṃ samaye vicâro hoti.

373. Katamâ tasmiṃ samaye pîti hoti?

Yâ tasmiṃ samaye pîti pâmojjaṃ âmodanâ pamodanâ hâso pahâso vitti odagyaṃ attamanatâ cittassa—ayaṃ tasmiṃ samaye pîti hoti.

374. Katamaṃ tasmiṃ samaye sukhaṃ hoti?

Yaṃ tasmiṃ samaye cetasikaṃ sâtaṃ cetasikaṃ sukhaṃ cetosamphassajaṃ sâtaṃ sukhaṃ vedayitaṃ cetosamphassajâ sâtâ sukhâ vedanâ—idaṃ tasmiṃ samaye sukhaṃ hoti.

375. Katamâ tasmiṃ samaye cittass' ekaggatâ hoti?

Yâ tasmiṃ samaye cittassa ṭhiti saṇṭhiti avaṭṭhiti avisâhâro avikkhepo avisâhaṭamânasatâ samatho samâdhindriyaṃ samâdhibalaṃ micchâsamâdhi — ayaṃ tasmiṃ samaye cittass' ekaggatâ hoti.

376. Katamaṃ tasmiṃ samaye viriyindriyaṃ hoti?

Yo tasmiṃ samaye cetasiko viriyârambho nikkamo parakkamo uyyâmo vâyâmo ussâho ussoḷhi thâmo dhiti asithilaparakkamatâ anikkhittachandatâ anikkhittadhuratâ dhurasampaggâho viriyaṃ viriyindriyaṃ viriyabalaṃ micchâvâyâmo —idaṃ tasmiṃ samaye viriyindriyaṃ hoti.

377. Katamaṃ tasmiṃ samaye samâdhindriyaṃ hoti?

Yâ tasmiṃ samaye cittassa ṭhiti saṇṭhiti avaṭṭhiti avisâhâro avikkhepo avisâhaṭamânasatâ samatho samâdhindriyaṃ samâdhibalaṃ micchâsamâdhi—idaṃ tasmiṃ samaye samâdhindriyaṃ hoti.

378. Katamaṃ tasmiṃ samaye manindriyaṃ hoti?

Yaṃ tasmiṃ samaye cittaṃ mano mânasaṃ hadayaṃ paṇḍaraṃ mano manâyatanaṃ manindriyaṃ viññâṇaṃ viññâṇakkhandho tajjâ manoviññâṇadhâtu : idaṃ tasmiṃ samaye manindriyaṃ hoti.

379. Katamaṃ tasmiṃ samaye somanassindriyaṃ hoti?

Yaṃ tasmiṃ samaye cetasikaṃ sâtaṃ cetasikaṃ sukhaṃ cetosamphassajaṃ sâtaṃ sukhaṃ vedayitaṃ cetosamphassajâ sâtâ sukhâ vedanâ—idaṃ tasmiṃ samaye somanassindriyaṃ hoti.

380. Katamaṃ tasmiṃ samaye jîvitindriyaṃ hoti?

Yo tesaṃ arûpînaṃ dhammânaṃ âyu ṭhiti yapanâ yâpanâ

iriyanâ vattanâ pâlanâ jîvitaṃ jîvitindriyaṃ—idaṃ tasmiṃ samaye jîvitindriyaṃ hoti.

381. Katamâ tasmiṃ samaye micchâdiṭṭhi hoti?

Yâ tasmiṃ samaye diṭṭhi diṭṭhigataṃ diṭṭhigahaṇaṃ diṭṭhikantâro diṭṭhivisûkâyikaṃ diṭṭhivipphanditaṃ diṭṭhisaññojanaṃ gâho patiggâho abhiniveso parâmâso kummaggo micchâpatho micchattaṃ titthâyatanaṃ vipariyesagâho—ayaṃ tasmiṃ samaye micchâdiṭṭhi hoti.

382. Katamo tasmiṃ samaye micchâsaṅkappo hoti?

Yo tasmiṃ samaye takko vitakko saṅkappo appanâ vyappanâ cetaso abhiniropanâ micchâsaṅkappo—ayaṃ tasmiṃ samaye micchâsaṅkappo hoti.

383. Katamo tasmiṃ samaye micchâvâyâmo hoti?

Yo tasmiṃ samaye cetasiko viriyârambho nikkamo parakkamo uyyâmo vâyâmo ussâho ussoḷhi thâmo dhiti asithilaparakkamatâ anikkhittachandatâ anikkhittadhuratâ dhurasampaggâho viriyaṃ viriyindriyaṃ viriyabalaṃ micchâvâyâmo: ayaṃ tasmiṃ samaye micchâvâyâmo hoti.

384. Katamo tasmiṃ samaye micchâsamâdhi hoti?

Yâ tasmiṃ samaye cittassa ṭhiti saṇṭhiti avaṭṭhiti avisâhâro avikkhepo avisâhaṭamânasatâ samatho samâdhindriyaṃ samâdhibalaṃ micchâsamâdhi: ayaṃ tasmiṃ samaye micchâsamâdhi hoti.

385. Katamaṃ tasmiṃ samaye viriyabalaṃ hoti?

Yo tasmiṃ samaye cetasiko . . . pe . . . micccchâvâyâmo—idaṃ tasmiṃ samaye viriyabalaṃ hoti.

386. Katamaṃ tasmiṃ samaye samâdhibalaṃ hoti?

Yâ tasmiṃ samaye cittassa ṭhiti . . . pe . . . micchâsamâdhi—idaṃ tasmiṃ samaye samâdhibalaṃ hoti.

387. Katamaṃ tasmiṃ samaye ahirikabalaṃ hoti?

Yaṃ tasmiṃ samaye na hiriyati hiriyitabbena, na hiriyati pâpakânaṃ akusalânaṃ dhammânaṃ samâpattiyâ—idaṃ tasmiṃ samaye ahirikabalaṃ hoti.

388. Katamaṃ tasmiṃ samaye anottappabalaṃ hoti?

Yaṃ tasmiṃ samaye na ottappati ottappitabbena ottappati pâpakânaṃ akusalânaṃ dhammânaṃ samâpattiyâ—idaṃ idaṃ tasmiṃ samaye anottappabalaṃ hoti.

389. Katamo tasmiṃ samaye lobho hoti?

Yo tasmiṃ samaye lobho lubbhanâ lubbhitattaṃ sârâgo sârajjanâ sârajjitattaṃ abhijjhâ lobho akusalamûlaṃ—ayaṃ tasmiṃ samaye lobho hoti.

390. Katamo tasmiṃ samaye moho hoti?

Yaṃ tasmiṃ samaye aññâṇaṃ adassanaṃ anabhisamayo ananubodho asambodho appaṭivedho asaṃgâhanâ apariyogâhanâ asamapekkhanâ apaccavekkhanâ apaccakkhakammaṃ dummejjhaṃ balyaṃ asampajaññaṃ moho pamoho sammoho avijjâ avijjogho avijjâyogo avijjânusayo avijjâpariyuṭṭhânaṃ avijjâlaṅgî moho akusalamûlaṃ—ayaṃ tasmiṃ samaye moho hoti.

391. Katamâ tasmiṃ samaye abhijjhâ hoti?

Yo tasmiṃ samaye lobho . . . pe . . . abhijjhâ lobho akusalamûlaṃ—ayaṃ tasmiṃ samaye abhijjhâ hoti.

392. Katamâ tasmiṃ samaye micchâdiṭṭhi hoti?

Yâ tasmiṃ samaye diṭṭhi diṭṭhigataṃ . . . pe . . . vipariyesagâho—ayaṃ tasmiṃ samaye micchâdiṭṭhi hoti.

393. Katamaṃ tasmiṃ samaye ahirikaṃ hoti?

Yaṃ tasmiṃ samaye na hiriyati . . . pe . . . samâpattiyâ—idaṃ tasmiṃ samaye ahirikaṃ hoti.

394. Katamaṃ tasmiṃ samaye anottappaṃ hoti?

Yaṃ tasmiṃ samaye na ottappati . . . pe . . . samâpattiyâ—idaṃ tasmiṃ samaye anottappaṃ hoti.

395. Katamo tasmiṃ samaye samatho hoti?

Yâ tasmiṃ samaye cittassa ṭhiti . . . pe . . . micchâsamâdhi—ayaṃ tasmiṃ samaye samatho hoti.

396. Katamo tasmiṃ samaye paggâho hoti?

Yo tasmiṃ samaye cetasiko viriyârambho . . . pe . . . micchâvâyâmo—ayaṃ tasmiṃ samaye paggâho hoti.

397. Katamo tasmiṃ samaye avikkhepo hoti.

Yâ tasmiṃ samaye cittassa ṭhiti . . . pe . . . micchâsamâdhi—ayaṃ tasmiṃ samaye avikkhepo hoti.

Ye vâ pana tasmiṃ samaye añño pi atthi paṭiccasamuppannâ arûpino dhammâ—ime dhammâ akusalâ. Tasmiṃ kho pana samaye cattâro khandhâ honti, dvâyatanâni honti, dve dhâtuyo honti, tayo âhârâ honti, pañcindriyâni honti, pañcaṅgikaṃ jhânaṃ hoti, caturaṅgiko maggo hoti, cattâri balâni honti, dve hetû honti, eko phasso hoti . . . pe . . . ekaṃ dhammâyatanaṃ hoti, ekâ dhammadhâtu hoti—ye vâ pana tasmiṃ samaye aññe pi atthi paṭiccasamuppannâ arûpino dhammâ—ime dhammâ akusalâ.

398.[1] Katamo tasmiṃ samaye saṅkhârakkhandho hoti?

Phasso cetanâ vitakko vicâro pîti cittassekaggatâ viriyindriyaṃ samâdhindriyaṃ jîvitindriyaṃ micchâdiṭṭhi micchâsaṅkappo micchâvâyâmo micchâsamâdhi viriyabalaṃ samâdhibalaṃ ahirikabalaṃ anottappabalaṃ lobho moho abhijjhâ micchâdiṭṭhi ahirikaṃ anottappaṃ samatho paggâho avikkhepo—ye vâ pana tasmiṃ samaye aññe pi atthi paṭiccasamuppannâ arûpino dhammâ ṭhapetvâ vedanâkkhandhaṃ ṭhapetvâ saññâkkhandhaṃ ṭhapetvâ viññâṇakkhandhaṃ—ayaṃ tasmiṃ samaye saṅkhârakkhandho hoti . . . pe . . . ime dhammâ akusalâ.

399. Katame dhammâ akusalâ?

Yasmiṃ samaye akusalacittaṃ uppannaṃ hoti somanassasahagataṃ diṭṭhigatasampayuttaṃ sasaṅkhârena rûpârammaṇaṃ vâ . . . pe . . . dhammârammaṇaṃ vâ yaṃ yaṃ vâ panârabbha: tasmiṃ samaye phasso hoti . . . pe . . . avikkhepo hoti . . . pe . . . ime dhammâ akusalâ.

400. Katame dhammâ akusalâ?

Yasmiṃ samaye akusalacittaṃ . . . pe . . . diṭṭhigatavippayuttaṃ rûpârammaṇaṃ vâ saddârammaṇaṃ vâ gandhârammaṇaṃ vâ rasârammaṇaṃ vâ phoṭṭhabbârammaṇaṃ vâ dhammârammaṇaṃ vâ yaṃ yaṃ vâ panârabbha: tasmiṃ samaye phasso hoti vedanâ hoti saññâ hoti cetanâ hoti cittaṃ hoti vitakko hoti vicâro hoti pîti hoti sukhaṃ hoti cittassekaggatâ hoti viriyindriyaṃ hoti samâdhindriyaṃ hoti manindriyaṃ hoti [somanassindriyaṃ hoti] jîvitindriyaṃ hoti micchâsaṅkappo hoti micchâvâyâmo hoti micchâsamâdhi hoti viriyabalam hoti samâdhibalaṃ hoti ahirikabalaṃ hoti anottappabalaṃ hoti lobho hoti moho hoti abhijjhâ hoti ahirikaṃ hoti anottappaṃ hoti samatho hoti paggâho hoti avikkhepo hoti—ye vâ pana tasmiṃ samaye aññe pi atthi paṭiccasamuppannâ arûpino dhammâ—ime dhammâ akusalâ. Tasmiṃ kho pana

[1] Compare 62 and 342.

samaye cattâro khandhâ honti . . . pe . . . tivaṅgiko maggo hoti . . . pe . . . eko phasso hoti . . . pe . . . ekaṃ dhammâyatanaṃ hoti ekâ dhammadhâtu hoti: ye vâ pana tasmiṃ samaye aññe pi atthi paṭiccasamuppannâ arûpino dhammâ—ime dhammâ akusalâ.

401. Katamo tasmiṃ samaye saṅkhârakkhandho hoti?

Phasso . . . pe (398) . . . ime dhammâ akusalâ.

(Omitting micchâdiṭṭhi.)

402. Katame dhammâ akusalâ?

Yasmiṃ samaye akusalaṃ cittaṃ uppannaṃ hoti somanassasahagataṃ diṭṭhigatavippayuttaṃ sasaṅkhârena rûpârammaṇaṃ vâ . . . pe . . . dhammârammaṇaṃ vâ yaṃ yaṃ vâ panârabbha—tasmiṃ samaye phasso hoti . . . pe . . . avikkhepo hoti . . . pe . . . ime dhammâ akusalâ.

403. Katame dhammâ akusalâ?

Yasmiṃ samaye akusalacittaṃ uppannaṃ hoti upekkhâsahagataṃ diṭṭhigatasampayuttaṃ rûpârammaṇaṃ vâ saddârammaṇaṃ vâ gandhârammaṇaṃ vâ rasârammaṇaṃ vâ phoṭṭhabbârammaṇaṃ vâ dhammârammaṇaṃ vâ yaṃ yaṃ vâ panârabbha: tasmiṃ samaye phasso hoti vedanâ hoti saññâ hoti cetanâ hoti cittaṃ hoti vitakko hoti vicâro hoti upekkhâ hoti cittassekaggatâ hoti viriyindriyaṃ hoti samâdhindriyaṃ hoti manindriyaṃ hoti upekkhindriyaṃ hoti jîvitindriyaṃ hoti micchâdiṭṭhi hoti micchâsaṅkappo hoti micchâvâyâmo hoti micchâsamâdhi hoti viriyabalaṃ hoti samâdhibalaṃ hoti ahirikabalaṃ hoti anottappabalaṃ hoti lobho hoti moho hoti abhijjhâ hoti micchâdiṭṭhi hoti ahirikaṃ hoti anottappaṃ hoti samatho hoti paggâho hoti avikkhepo hoti—ye vâ pana tasmiṃ samaye aññe pi atthi paṭiccasamuppannâ arûpino dhammâ—ime dhammâ akusalâ.

404. Katamo tasmiṃ samaye phasso hoti?

Yo tasmiṃ samaye phasso phusanâ samphusanâ samphusitattaṃ—ayaṃ tasmiṃ samaye phasso hoti.

405. Katamâ tasmiṃ samaye vedanâ hoti?

Yaṃ tasmiṃ samaye tajjâ manoviññâṇadhâtu samphassajaṃ cetasikaṃ neva sâtaṃ nâsâtaṃ cetosamphassajaṃ adukkhaṃ asukhaṃ vedayitaṃ cetosamphassajâ adukkhamasukhâ vedanâ —ayaṃ tasmiṃ samaye vedanâ hoti.

406. Katamâ tasmiṃ samaye upekkhâ hoti?

Yaṃ tasmiṃ samaye cetasikaṃ neva sâtaṃ nâsâtaṃ cetosamphassajaṃ adukkhamasukhaṃ vedayitaṃ cetosamphassajâ adukkhamasukhâ vedanâ—ayaṃ tasmiṃ samaye upekkhâ hoti.

407. Katamaṃ tasmiṃ samaye upekkhindriyaṃ hoti?

Yaṃ tasmiṃ samaye cetasikaṃ . . . pe . . . vedanâ—idaṃ tasmiṃ samaye upekkhindriyaṃ hoti . . . pe . . . ye vâ pana tasmiṃ samaye aññe pi atthi paṭiccasamuppannâ arûpino dhammâ—ime dhammâ akusalâ. Tasmiṃ kho pana samaye cattâro khandhâ honti . . . pe . . . caturaṅgikaṃ jhânaṃ hoti, caturaṅgiko maggo hoti . . . pe . . . arûpino dhammâ—ime dhammâ akusalâ.

408. Katamo tasmiṃ samaye saṅkhârakkhandho hoti?

Phasso . . . pe . . . omitting pîti . . . pe (398) . . . ṭhapetvâ viññâṇakkhandhaṃ—ayaṃ tasmiṃ samaye saṅkhârakkhandho hoti . . . pe . . . ime dhammâ akusalâ.

409.[1] Katame dhammâ akusalâ?

Yasmiṃ samaye akusalaṃ cittaṃ uppannaṃ hoti upekkhâsahagataṃ diṭṭhigatasampayuttaṃ sasaṅkhârena rûpârammaṇaṃ vâ . . . pe (403) . . . dhammârammaṇaṃ vâ yaṃ yaṃ vâ panârabbha—tasmiṃ samaye phasso hoti . . . pe (403) . . . avikkhepo hoti . . . pe (403) . . . ime dhammâ akusalâ.

410. Katame dhammâ akusalâ?

Yasmiṃ samaye akusalaṃ cittaṃ uppannaṃ hoti upekkhâsahagataṃ diṭṭhigatavippayuttaṃ rûpârammaṇaṃ vâ saddârammaṇaṃ vâ gandhârammaṇaṃ vâ rasârammaṇaṃ vâ phoṭṭhabbârammaṇaṃ vâ dhammârammaṇaṃ vâ yaṃ yaṃ vâ panârabbha: tasmiṃ samaye phasso hoti, vedanâ hoti, saññâ hoti, cetanâ hoti, cittaṃ hoti, vitakko hoti, vicâro hoti, upekkhâ hoti, cittass' ekaggatâ hoti, viriyindriyaṃ hoti, samâdhindriyaṃ hoti, manindriyaṃ hoti, upekkhindriyaṃ

---

[1] Compare 147 and following.

hoti, jîvitindriyaṃ hoti, micchâsaṅkappo hoti, micchâvâyâmo hoti, micchâsamâdhi hoti, viriyabalaṃ hoti, samâdhibalaṃ hoti, ahirikabalaṃ hoti, anottappabalaṃ hoti, lobho hoti, moho hoti, abhijjhâ hoti, ahirikaṃ hoti, anottappaṃ hoti, samatho hoti, paggâho hoti, avikkhepo hoti ye vâ pana tasmiṃ samaye aññe pi atthi paṭiccasamuppannâ arûpino dhammâ—ime dhammâ akusalâ. Tasmiṃ kho pana samaye cattâro khandhâ honti dvâyatanâni honti dve dhâtuyo honti, tayo âhârâ honti pañcindriyâni honti caturaṅgikaṃ jhânaṃ hoti tivaṅgiko maggo hoti cattâri balâni honti dve hetû honti eko phasso hoti . . . pe . . . ekaṃ dhammâyatanaṃ hoti ekâ dhammadhâtu hoti ye vâ pana tasmiṃ samaye aññe pi atthi paṭiccasamuppannâ arûpino dhammâ—ime dhammâ akusalâ.

411. Katamo tasmiṃ samaye saṅkhârakkhandho hoti?

Phasso cetanâ . . . pe . . . [omitting pîti and micchâdiṭṭhi] ṭhapetvâ viññâṇakkhandaṃ—ayaṃ tasmiṃ samaye saṅkhârakkhandho hoti . . . pe . . . ime dhammâ akusalâ.

412. Katame dhammâ akusalâ?

Yasmiṃ samaye akusalaṃ cittaṃ uppannaṃ hoti upekkhâsahagataṃ diṭṭhigatavippayuttaṃ sasaṅkhârena rûpârammaṇaṃ vâ . . . pe . . . dhammârammaṇaṃ vâ yaṃ yaṃ vâ panârabbha: tasmiṃ samaye phasso hoti . . . pe . . . avikkhepo hoti . . . pe . . . ime dhammâ akusalâ.

413. Katame dhammâ akusalâ?

Yasmiṃ samaye akusalaṃ cittaṃ uppannaṃ hoti domanassasahagataṃ paṭighasampayuttaṃ rûpârammaṇaṃ vâ saddârammaṇaṃ vâ gandhârammaṇaṃ vâ rasârammaṇaṃ vâ phoṭṭhabbârammaṇaṃ vâ dhammârammaṇaṃ vâ—yaṃ yaṃ vâ panârabbha tasmiṃ samaye phasso hoti, vedanâ hoti, saññâ hoti, cetanâ hoti, cittaṃ hoti, vitakko hoti, vicâro hoti, dukkhaṃ hoti, cittass' ekaggatâ hoti, viriyindriyaṃ hoti, samâdhindriyam hoti, manindriyaṃ hoti, domanassindriyaṃ hoti, jîvitindriyaṃ hoti, micchâsaṅkappo hoti, micchâvâyâmo hoti, micchâsamâdhi hoti, viriyabalaṃ hoti, samâdhibalaṃ hoti, ahirikabalaṃ hoti, anottappabalaṃ hoti, doso hoti, moho hoti, vyâpâdo hoti, ahirikaṃ hoti, anottappaṃ hoti, samatho hoti, paggâho hoti, avikkhepo hoti, ye vâ pana tasmiṃ samaye aññe pi atthi paticcasamuppannâ arûpino dhammâ—ime dhammâ akusalâ.

414. Katamo tasmiṃ samaye phasso hoti?

Yo tasmiṃ samaye phasso phusanâ samphusanâ samphusitattam—ayaṃ tasmiṃ samaye phasso hoti.

415. Katamâ tasmiṃ samaye vedanâ hoti?

Yaṃ tasmiṃ samaye tajjâ manoviññâṇadhâtu samphassajaṃ cetasikaṃ asâtaṃ cetasikaṃ dukkhaṃ cetosamphassajaṃ asâtaṃ dukkhaṃ vedayitaṃ cetosamphassajâ asâtâ dukkhâ vedanâ—ayaṃ tasmiṃ samaye vedanâ hoti.

416. Katamaṃ tasmiṃ samaye dukkhaṃ hoti?

Yaṃ tasmiṃ samaye cetasikaṃ asâtaṃ cetasikam dukkhaṃ cetosamphassajaṃ asâtaṃ dukkhaṃ vedayitaṃ cetosamphassajâ asâtâ dukkhâ vedanâ—idaṃ tasmiṃ samaye dukkhaṃ hoti.

417. Katamaṃ tasmiṃ samaye domanassindriyaṃ hoti?

Yaṃ tasmiṃ samaye cetasikaṃ asâtaṃ cetasikaṃ dukkhaṃ cetosamphassajaṃ asâtaṃ dukkhaṃ vedayitaṃ cetosamphassajâ asâtâ dukkhâ vedanâ—idaṃ tasmiṃ samaye domanassindriyaṃ hoti.

418. Katamo tasmiṃ samaye doso hoti?

Yo tasmiṃ samaye doso dussanâ dussitattaṃ vyâpatti vyâpajjanâ virodho paṭivirodho caṇḍittaṃ asuropo anattamanatâ cittassa—ayaṃ tasmiṃ samaye doso hoti.

419. Katamo tasmiṃ samaye vyâpâdo hoti?

Yo tasmiṃ samaye doso . . . pe . . . cittassa, ayaṃ tasmiṃ samaye vyâpâdo hoti . . . pe . . . ye vâ pana tasmiṃ samaye aññe pi atthi paṭiccasamuppannâ arûpino dhammâ—ime dhammâ akusalâ.

Tasmiṃ kho pana samaye cattâro khandhâ honti dvâyatanâni honti, dve dhâtuyo honti, tayo âhârâ honti, pañcindriyâni honti, caturaṅgikaṃ jhânaṃ hoti, tivaṅgiko maggo hoti cattâri balâni honti, dve hetû honti, eko phasso hoti . . . pe . . . ekam dhammâyatanaṃ hoti, ekâ dhammadhâtu hoti—ye vâ pana tasmiṃ samaye aññe pi atthi paticcasamuppannâ arûpino dhammâ—ime dhammâ akusalâ.

420. Katamo tasmiṃ samaye saṅkhârakkhandho hoti?

Phasso, cetanâ, vitakko, vicâro, cittass' ekaggatâ, viriyindriyaṃ, samâdhindriyaṃ, jîvitindriyaṃ, micchâsaṅkappo, micchâvâyâmo, micchâsamâdhi, viriyabalaṃ, samâdhibalam, ahirikabalaṃ anottappabalaṃ, doso, moho, vyâpâdo, ahirikaṃ, anottappaṃ, samatho, paggâho, avikkhepo, ye vâ pana tasmiṃ samaye aññe pi atthi paṭiccasamuppannâ arûpino dhammâ—ṭhapetvâ vedanâkkhandhaṃ, ṭhapetvâ saññâkkhandhaṃ, ṭhapetvâ viññâṇakkhandhaṃ—ayaṃ tasmiṃ samaye saṅkhârakkhandho hoti . . . pe . . . ime dhammâ akusalâ.

421. Katame dhammâ akusalâ ?

Yasmiṃ samaye akusalaṃ cittaṃ uppannaṃ hoti domanassasahagataṃ paṭighasampayuttaṃ sasaṅkhârena rûpârammaṇaṃ vâ . . . pe . . . dhammârammaṇaṃ vâ . . . pe . . . yaṃ yaṃ vâ panârabbha : tasmiṃ samaye phasso hoti . . . pe . . . avikkhepo hoti . . . pe . . . ime dhammâ akusalâ.

422. Katame dhammâ akusalâ ?

Yasmiṃ samaye akusalaṃ cittaṃ uppannaṃ hoti upekkhâsahagataṃ vicikicchâsampayuttaṃ rûpârammaṇaṃ vâ, saddârammaṇaṃ vâ, gandhârammaṇaṃ vâ, rasârammaṇaṃ vâ, phoṭṭhabbârammaṇaṃ vâ, dhammârammaṇaṃ vâ yaṃ yaṃ vâ panârabbha : tasmiṃ samaye phasso hoti, vedanâ hoti, saññâ hoti, cetanâ hoti, cittaṃ hoti, vitakko hoti, vicâro hoti, upekkhâ hoti, cittass' ekaggatâ hoti, viriyindriyaṃ hoti, manindriyaṃ hoti, upekkhindriyaṃ hoti, jîvitindriyaṃ hoti, micchâsaṅkappo hoti, micchâvâyâmo hoti, viriyabalaṃ hoti, akirikabalaṃ hoti, anottappabalaṃ hoti, vicikicchâ hoti, moho hoti, ahirikaṃ hoti, anottappaṃ hoti, paggâho hoti ; ye vâ pana tasmiṃ samaye aññe pi atthi paṭiccasamuppannâ arûpino dhammâ—ime dhammâ akusalâ.

423. Katamo tasmiṃ samaye phasso hoti ?

Yo tasmiṃ samaye phasso phusanâ . . . pe . . . ayaṃ tasmiṃ samaye phasso hoti . . . pe . . .

424. Katamâ tasmiṃ samaye cittass' ekaggatâ hoti ?

Yâ tasmiṃ samaye cittassa ṭhiti . . . pe . . . ayaṃ tasmiṃ samaye cittass' ekaggatâ hoti . . . pe . . .

425. Katamâ tasmiṃ samaye vicikicchâ hoti ?

Yâ tasmiṃ samaye kaṅkhâ kaṅkhâyanâ kaṅkhâyitattaṃ vimati vicikicchâ dveḷhakaṃ dvedhâpatho saṃsayo anekaṃsagâho âsappanâ parisappanâ apariyogâhanâ thambhitattaṃ cittassa mano vilekho—ayaṃ tasmiṃ samaye vicikicchâ hoti

. . . pe . . . ye vâ pana tasmiṃ samaye aññe pi atthi paṭiccasamuppannâ arûpino dhammâ—ime dhammâ akusalâ. Tasmiṃ kho pana samaye cattâro khandhâ honti, dvâyatanâni honti, dve dhâtuyo honti, tayo âhârâ honti, cattâri indriyâni honti, caturaṅgikaṃ jhânaṃ hoti, duvaṅgiko maggo hoti, tîni balâni honti, eko hetu hoti, eko phasso hoti . . . pe . . . ekaṃ dhammâyatanaṃ hoti, ekâ dhammadhâtu hoti, ye vâ pana tasmiṃ samaye aññe pi atthi paṭiccasamuppannâ arûpino dhammâ—ime dhammâ akusalâ.

426. Katamo tasmiṃ samaye saṅkhârakkhandho hoti?

Phasso cetanâ vitakko vicâro cittassekaggatâ viriyindriyaṃ jîvitindriyaṃ micchâsaṅkappo micchâvâyâmo viriyabalaṃ ahirikabalaṃ anottappabalaṃ vicikicchâ moho ahirikaṃ anottappaṃ paggâho—ye vâ pana tasmiṃ samaye aññe pi atthi paṭiccasamuppannâ arûpino dhammâ—ṭhapetvâ vedanâkkhandhaṃ ṭhapetvâ saññâkkhandhaṃ ṭhapetvâ viññâṇakkhandhaṃ—ayaṃ tasmiṃ samaye saṅkhârakkhandho hoti . . . pe . . . ime dhammâ akusalâ.

427. Katame dhammâ akusalâ?

Yasmiṃ samaye akusalaṃ cittaṃ uppannaṃ hoti upekkhâsahagataṃ uddhaccasampayuttaṃ rûpârammaṇaṃ vâ . . . pe . . . yam yam vâ panârabbha—tasmiṃ samaye phasso hoti, vedanâ hoti, saññâ hoti, cetanâ hoti, cittaṃ hoti, vitakko hoti, vicâro hoti, upekkhâ hoti, cittass' ekaggatâ hoti, viriyindriyaṃ hoti, samâdhindriyaṃ hoti, manindriyam hoti, upekkhindriyaṃ hoti, jîvitindriyaṃ hoti, micchâsaṅkappo hoti, micchâvâyâmo hoti, micchâsamâdhi hoti, viriyabalaṃ hoti, samâdhibalaṃ hoti, ahirikabalaṃ hoti, anottappabalaṃ hoti, uddhaccaṃ hoti, moho hoti, ahirikaṃ hoti, anottappaṃ hoti, samatho hoti, paggâho hoti, ye vâ pana tasmiṃ samaye aññe pi atthi paṭiccasamuppannâ arûpino dhammâ—ime dhammâ akusalâ.

428. Katamo tasmiṃ samaye phasso hoti?

Yo tasmiṃ samaye phasso phusanâ samphusanâ samphusitattaṃ—ayaṃ tasmiṃ samaye phasso hoti.

429. Katamaṃ tasmiṃ samaye uddhaccaṃ hoti?

Yaṃ tasmiṃ samaye cittassa uddhaccaṃ avûpasamo cetaso vikkhepo bhantattaṃ cittassa: idaṃ tasmiṃ samaye uddhaccaṃ hoti . . . pe . . . ye vâ pana tasmiṃ samaye aññe pi atthi paṭiccasamuppannâ arûpino dhammâ: ime dhammâ akusalâ. Tasmiṃ kho pana samaye cattâro khandhâ honti, dvâyatanâni hoti, dve dhâtuyo honti, tayo âhârâ honti, pañcindriyâni honti, caturaṅgikaṃ jhânaṃ hoti, tivaṅgiko maggo hoti, cattâri balâni honti, eko hetu hoti, eko phasso hoti . . . pe . . . ekaṃ dhammâyatanaṃ hoti, ekâ dhammadhâtu hoti: ye vâ pana tasmiṃ samaye aññe pi atthi paṭiccasamuppannâ arûpino dhammâ—ime dhammâ akusalâ.

430. Katamo tasmiṃ samaye saṅkhârakkhandho hoti?

Phasso cetanâ vitakko vicâro cittass' ekaggatâ viriyindriyaṃ samâdhiindriyaṃ jîvitindriyaṃ micchâsaṅkappo micchâvâyâmo micchâsamâdhi viriyabalaṃ samâdhibalaṃ ahirikabalaṃ anottappabalaṃ uddhaccaṃ moho ahirikaṃ anottappaṃ samatho paggâho avikkhepo ye vâ pana tasmiṃ samaye aññe pi atthi paṭiccasamuppannâ arûpino dhammâ ṭhapetvâ vedanâkkhandhaṃ ṭhapetvâ saññâkkhandhaṃ ṭhapetvâ viññâṇakkhandhaṃ—ayaṃ tasmiṃ samaye saṅkhârakkhandho hoti . . . pe . . . ime dhammâ akusalâ.

Dvâdasa akusalacittâni.

431. Katame dhammâ avyâkatâ.

Yasmiṃ samaye kâmâvacarassa kusalassa kammassa katattâ upacitattâ vipâkaṃ cakkhuviññâṇaṃ uppannaṃ hoti upekkhâsahagataṃ rûpârammaṇaṃ: tasmiṃ samaye phasso hoti vedanâ hoti saññâ hoti cetanâ hoti cittaṃ hoti upekkhâ hoti cittass' ekaggatâ hoti manindriyaṃ hoti upekkhindriyaṃ hoti jîvitindriyaṃ hoti: ye vâ pana tasmiṃ samaye aññe pi atthi paṭiccasamuppannâ arûpino dhammâ—ime dhammâ avyâkatâ.

432. Katamo tasmiṃ samaye phasso hoti?

Yo tasmiṃ samaye phasso phusanâ samphusanâ samphusitattaṃ—ayaṃ tasmiṃ samaye phasso hoti.

433. Katamâ tasmiṃ samaye vedanâ hoti?

Yâ tasmiṃ samaye tajjâ cakkhuviññâṇadhâtu samphassajaṃ cetasikaṃ neva sâtaṃ nâsâtaṃ cetosamphassajaṃ adukkhamasukhaṃ vedayitaṃ cetosamphassajâ adukkhamasukhâ vedanâ—ayaṃ tasmiṃ samaye vedanâ hoti.

434. Katamâ tasmiṃ samaye saññâ hoti? Yâ tasmiṃ samaye tajjâ cakkhuviññâṇadhâtu samphassajâ saññâ sañjânanâ sañjânitattaṃ—ayaṃ tasmiṃ samaye saññâ hoti.

435. Katamâ tasmiṃ samaye cetanâ hoti? Yâ tasmiṃ samaye tajjâ cakkhuviññâṇadhâtu samphassajâ cetanâ sañcetanâ cetayitattaṃ—ayaṃ tasmiṃ samaye cetanâ hoti.

436. Katamaṃ tasmiṃ samaye cittaṃ hoti? Yaṃ tasmiṃ samaye cittaṃ mano mânasaṃ hadayaṃ paṇḍaraṃ mano manâyatanaṃ manindriyaṃ viññâṇaṃ viññâṇakkhandho tajjâ cakkhuviññâṇadhâtu—idaṃ tasmiṃ samaye cittaṃ hoti.

437. Katamâ tasmiṃ samaye upekkhâ hoti? Yaṃ tasmiṃ samaye cetasikaṃ neva sâtaṃ nâsâtaṃ cetosamphassajaṃ adukkhamasukhaṃ vedayitaṃ cetosamphassajâ adukkhamasukhâ vedanâ—ayaṃ tasmiṃ samaye upekkhâ hoti.

438. Katamâ tasmiṃ samaye cittassekaggatâ hoti? Yâ tasmiṃ samaye cittassa ṭhiti . . . pe . . . ayaṃ tasmiṃ samaye cittassekaggatâ hoti.

439. Katamaṃ tasmiṃ samaye manindriyaṃ hoti? Yaṃ tasmiṃ samaye cittaṃ mano mânasaṃ hadayaṃ paṇḍaraṃ mano manâyatanaṃ manindriyaṃ viññâṇaṃ viññâṇakkhandho tajjâ cakkhuviññâṇadhâtu—idaṃ tasmiṃ samaye manindriyaṃ hoti.

440. Katamaṃ tasmiṃ samaye upekkhindriyaṃ hoti? Yaṃ tasmiṃ samaye cetasikaṃ . . . pe . . . vedanâ—idaṃ tasmiṃ samaye upekkhindriyaṃ hoti.

441. Katamaṃ tasmiṃ samaye jîvitindriyaṃ hoti? Yo tesaṃ arûpînaṃ dhammânaṃ âyu ṭhiti yapanâ yâpanâ iriyanâ vattanâ pâlanâ jîvitaṃ jîvitindriyaṃ—idaṃ tasmiṃ samaye jîvitindriyaṃ hoti. Ye vâ pana tasmiṃ samaye aññe pi atthi paṭiccasamuppannâ arûpino dhammâ—ime dhammâ avyâkatâ. Tasmiṃ kho pana samaye cattâro khandhâ honti, dvâyatanâni honti, dve dhâtuyo honti, tayo âhârâ honti, tîṇindriyâni honti, eko phasso hoti . . . pe . . . ekâ cakkhuviññâṇadhâtu hoti, ekaṃ dhammâyatanaṃ hoti,

ekâ dhammadhâtu hoti, yo vâ pana tasmiṃ samaye aññe pi atthi paṭiccasamuppannâ arûpino dhammâ—ime dhammâ avyâkatâ . . . pe . . .

442. Katamo tasmiṃ samaye saṅkhârakkhandho hoti?

Phasso cetanâ cittassekaggatâ jîvitindriyaṃ: yo vâ pana tasmiṃ samaye aññe pi atthi paṭiccasamuppannâ arûpino dhammâ ṭhapetvâ vedanâkkhandhaṃ, ṭhapetvâ saññâkkhandhaṃ ṭhapetvâ viññânakkhandhaṃ — ayaṃ tasmiṃ samaye saṅkhârakkhandho hoti . . . pe . . . ime dhammâ avyâkatâ.

443. Katame dhammâ avyâkatâ.

Yasmiṃ samaye kâmâvacarassa kusalassa kammassa katattâ upacitattâ vipâkaṃ sotaviññâṇaṃ uppannaṃ hoti, upekkhâsahagataṃ saddârammaṇaṃ . . . pe . . . ghâṇaviññâṇaṃ uppannaṃ hoti upekkhâsahagataṃ gandhârammaṇaṃ . . . pe . . . jivhâviññâṇaṃ uppannaṃ hoti upekkhâsahagataṃ rasârammaṇaṃ . . . pe . . . kâyaviññâṇaṃ uppannaṃ hoti sukhasahagataṃ phoṭṭhabbârammaṇaṃ: tasmiṃ samaye phasso hoti, saññâ hoti, cetanâ hoti, cittaṃ hoti, sukhaṃ hoti, cittassekaggatâ hoti, manindriyaṃ hoti, sukhindriyaṃ hoti, jîvitindriyaṃ hoti, ye vâ pana tasmiṃ samaye aññe pi atthi paṭiccasamuppannâ arûpino dhammâ—ime dhammâ avyâkatâ.

444. Katamo tasmiṃ samaye phasso hoti?

Yo tasmiṃ samaye phasso phusanâ samphusanâ samphusitattaṃ—ayaṃ tasmiṃ samaye phasso hoti.

445. Katamâ tasmiṃ samaye vedanâ hoti?

Yaṃ tasmiṃ samaye tajjâ kâyaviññâṇadhâtu samphassajaṃ kâyikaṃ sâtaṃ kâyikaṃ sukhaṃ kâyasamphassajaṃ sâtaṃ sukhaṃ vedayitaṃ kâyasamphassajâ sâtâ sukhâ vedanâ—ayaṃ tasmiṃ samaye vedanâ hoti.

446. Katamâ tasmiṃ samaye saññâ hoti?

Yâ tasmiṃ samaye tajjâ kâyaviññâṇadhâtu samphassajâ saññâ sañjânanâ sañjânitattaṃ—ayaṃ tasmiṃ samaye saññâ hoti.

447. Katamâ tasmiṃ samaye cetanâ hoti?

Yâ tasmiṃ samaye tajjâ kâyaviññâṇadhatu samphassajâ cetanâ sañcetanâ cetayitattaṃ—ayaṃ tasmiṃ samaye cetanâ hoti.

448. Katamaṃ tasmiṃ samaye cittaṃ hoti?

Yaṃ tasmiṃ samaye cittaṃ mano mânasaṃ hadayaṃ paṇḍaraṃ mano manâyatanaṃ manindriyaṃ viññâṇaṃ viññâṇakkhandho tajjâ kâyaviññâṇadhâtu—idaṃ tasmiṃ samaye cittaṃ hoti.

449. Katamaṃ tasmiṃ samaye sukhaṃ hoti?

Yaṃ tasmiṃ samaye kâyikaṃ sâtaṃ kâyikaṃ sukhaṃ kâyasamphassajam sâtaṃ sukhaṃ vedayitaṃ kâyasamphassajâ sâtâ sukhâ vedanâ—idaṃ tasmiṃ samaye sukhaṃ hoti.

450. Katamâ tasmiṃ samaye cittassekaggatâ hoti?

Yaṃ tasmiṃ samaye cittassa ṭhiti . . . pe . . . ayaṃ tasmiṃ samaye cittassekaggatâ hoti.

451. Katamaṃ tasmiṃ samaye manindriyaṃ hoti?

Yaṃ tasmiṃ samaye cittaṃ . . . pe . . . viññâṇadhâtu—idaṃ tasmiṃ samaye manindriyaṃ hoti.

452. Katamaṃ tasmiṃ samaye sukhindriyaṃ hoti?

Yaṃ tasmiṃ samaye kâyikaṃ sâtaṃ . . . pe . . . sukhâ vedanâ—idaṃ tasmiṃ samaye sukhindriyaṃ hoti.

453. Katamaṃ tasmiṃ samaye jîvitindriyaṃ hoti?

Yo tesaṃ arûpînaṃ dhammânaṃ âyu ṭhiti yapanâ yâpanâ iriyanâ vattanâ pâlanâ jîvitaṃ jîvitindriyaṃ—idaṃ tasmiṃ samaye jîvitindriyaṃ hoti—ye vâ pana tasmiṃ samaye aññe pi atthi paṭiccasamuppannâ arûpino dhammâ—ime dhammâ avyâkatâ.

Tasmiṃ kho pana samaye cattâro khandhâ honti, dvâyatanâni honti, dve dhâtuyo honti, tayo âhârâ honti, tîṇindriyâni honti, eko phasso hoti . . . pe . . . ekâ kâyaviññâṇadhâtu hoti, ekaṃ dhammâyatanaṃ hoti, ekâ dhammadhâtu hoti—ye vâ pana tasmiṃ samaye aññe pi atthi paṭiccasamuppannâ arûpino dhammâ—ime dhammâ avyâkatâ . . . pe . . .

454. Katamo tasmiṃ samaye saṅkhârakkhandho hoti?

Phasso cetanâ cittassekaggatâ jîvitindriyaṃ—ye vâ pana tasmiṃ samaye aññe pi atthi paṭiccasamuppannâ arûpino dhammâ — ṭhapetvâ vedanâkkhandhaṃ ṭhapetvâ saññâkkhandhaṃ ṭhapetvâ viññâṇakkhandhaṃ: ayaṃ tasmiṃ samaye saṅkhârakkhandho hoti . . . pe . . . ime dhammâ avyâkatâ.

Kusalavipâkâni pañcaviññâṇâni.

455. Katame dhammâ avyâkatâ?

Yasmiṃ samaye kâmâvacarassa kusalassa kammassa katattâ upacitattâ vipâkâ manodhâtu uppannâ hoti upekkhâsahagatâ rûpârammaṇâ vâ . . . pe . . . phoṭṭhabbârammaṇâ vâ yaṃ yaṃ vâ panârabbha—tasmiṃ samaye phasso hoti, vedanâ hoti, saññâ hoti, cetanâ hoti, cittaṃ hoti, vitakko hoti, vicâro hoti, upekkhâ hoti, cittassekaggatâ hoti, manindriyaṃ hoti, upekkhindriyaṃ hoti, jîvitindriyaṃ hoti; ye vâ pana tasmiṃ samaye añño pi atthi paṭiccasamuppannâ arûpino dhammâ—ime dhammâ avyâkatâ.

456. Katamo tasmiṃ samaye phasso hoti?

Yo tasmiṃ samaye phasso phusanâ samphusanâ samphusitattaṃ—ayaṃ tasmiṃ samaye phasso hoti.

457. Katamâ tasmiṃ samaye vedanâ hoti?

Yaṃ tasmiṃ samaye tajjâ manodhâtu samphassajaṃ cetasikaṃ neva sâtaṃ nâsâtaṃ cetosamphassajaṃ adukkhamasukhaṃ vedayitaṃ cetosamphassajâ adukkhamasukhâ vedanâ—ayaṃ tasmiṃ samaye vedanâ hoti.

458. Katamâ tasmiṃ samaye saññâ hoti?

Yâ tasmiṃ samaye tajjâ manodhâtu samphassajâ saññâ sañjânanâ sañjânitattaṃ—ayaṃ tasmiṃ samaye saññâ hoti.

459. Katamâ tasmiṃ samaye cetanâ hoti?

Yâ tasmiṃ samaye tajjâ manodhâtu samphassajâ cetanâ sañcetanâ cetayitattaṃ—ayaṃ tasmiṃ samaye cetanâ hoti.

460. Katamaṃ tasmiṃ samaye cittaṃ hoti?

Yaṃ tasmiṃ samaye cittaṃ mano mânasaṃ hadayaṃ paṇḍaraṃ mano manâyatanaṃ manindriyaṃ viññâṇaṃ viññâṇakkhandho tajjâ manodhâtu—idaṃ tasmiṃ samaye cittaṃ hoti.

461. Katamo tasmiṃ samaye vitakko hoti.

Yo tasmiṃ samaye takko vitakko saṅkappo appanâ vyappanâ cetaso abhiniropanâ—ayaṃ tasmiṃ samaye vitakko hoti.

462. Katamo tasmiṃ samaye vicâro hoti?

Yo tasmiṃ samaye câro vicâro anuvicâro upavicâro cittassa anusandhanatâ anupekkhanatâ—ayaṃ tasmiṃ samaye vicâro hoti.

463. Katamâ tasmiṃ samaye upekkhâ hoti?

Yaṃ tasmiṃ samaye cetasikaṃ neva sâtaṃ nâsâtaṃ cetosamphassajaṃ adukkhamasukhaṃ vedayitaṃ cetosamphassajâ adukkhamasukhâ vedanâ—ayaṃ tasmiṃ samaye upekkhâ hoti.

464. Katamâ tasmiṃ samaye cittass' ekaggatâ hoti?

Yâ tasmiṃ samaye cittassa ṭhiti . . . pe (11) . . . ayaṃ tasmiṃ samaye cittass' ekaggatâ hoti.

465. Katamaṃ tasmiṃ samaye manindriyaṃ hoti?

Yaṃ tasmiṃ samaye cittaṃ mano . . . pe (17) . . . tajjâ manodhâtu—idaṃ tasmiṃ samaye manindriyaṃ hoti.

466. Katamaṃ tasmiṃ samaye upekkhindriyaṃ hoti?

Yaṃ tasmiṃ samaye cetasikaṃ neva sâtaṃ . . . pe (465) . . . adukkhamasukhâ vedanâ — idaṃ tasmiṃ samaye upekkhindriyaṃ hoti.

467. Katamaṃ tasmiṃ samaye jîvitindriyaṃ hoti?

Yo tesaṃ arûpînaṃ dhammânaṃ . . . pe (19) jîvitindriyaṃ—idaṃ tasmiṃ samaye jîvitindriyaṃ hoti—ye vâ pana tasmiṃ samaye aññe pi atthi paṭiccasamuppannâ arûpino dhammâ—ime dhammâ avyâkatâ. Tasmiṃ kho pana samaye cattâro khandhâ honti, dvâyatanâni honti, dve dhâtuyo honti, tayo âhârâ honti, tîṇindriyâni honti, eko phasso hoti . . . pe (58) . . . ekâ manodhâtu hoti, ekaṃ dhammâyatanaṃ hoti, ekâ dhammadhâtu hoti—ye vâ pana tasmiṃ samaye aññe pi atthi paṭiccasamuppannâ arûpino dhammâ—ime dhammâ avyâkatâ . . . pe . . .

468. Katamo tasmiṃ samaye saṅkhârakkhandho hoti?

Phasso cetanâ vitakko vicâro cittass' ekaggatâ jîvitindriyaṃ ye vâ pana tasmiṃ samaye aññe pi atthi paṭiccasamuppannâ arûpino dhammâ—ṭhapetvâ vedanâkkhandhaṃ ṭhapetvâ saññâkkhandhaṃ ṭhapetvâ viññâṇakkhandhaṃ—ayaṃ tasmiṃ samaye saṅkhârakkhandho hoti—ime dhammâ avyâkatâ.

Kusalavipâkâ manodhâtu.

469. Katame dhammâ avyâkatâ?

Yasmiṃ samaye kâmâvacarassa kusalassa kammassa katattâ upacitattâ vipâkâ manoviññânadhâtu uppannâ hoti somanussasahagatâ rûpârammaṇâ vâ . . . pe (147) . . . dhammârammaṇâ vâ yaṃ yaṃ vâ panârabbha—tasmiṃ samaye phasso hoti, vedanâ hoti, saññâ hoti, cetanâ hoti, cittaṃ hoti, vitakko hoti, vicâro hoti, pîti hoti, sukhaṃ hoti, cittass' ekaggatâ hoti, manindriyaṃ hoti, somanassindriyaṃ hoti, jîvitindriyaṃ hoti, ye vâ pana tasmiṃ samaye aññe pi atthi paṭiccasamuppannâ arûpino dhammâ—ime dhammâ avyâkatâ.

470. Katamo tasmiṃ samaye phasso hoti?

Yo tasmiṃ samaye phasso phusanâ samphusanâ samphusitattaṃ—ayaṃ tasmiṃ samaye phasso hoti.

471. Katamâ tasmiṃ samaye vedanâ hoti?

Yâ tasmiṃ samaye tajjâ manoviññâṇadhâtu samphassajaṃ cetasikaṃ sâtaṃ cetasikaṃ sukhaṃ cetosamphassajaṃ sâtaṃ sukhaṃ vedayitaṃ cetosamphassajâ sâtâ sukhâ vedanâ—ayaṃ tasmiṃ samaye vedanâ hoti.

472. Katamâ tasmiṃ samaye saññâ hoti?

Yâ tasmiṃ samaye tajjâ manoviññâṇadhâtu samphassajâ saññâ sañjânanâ sañjânitattaṃ—ayaṃ tasmiṃ samaye saññâ hoti.

473. Katamâ tasmiṃ samaye cetanâ hoti?

Yâ tasmiṃ samaye tajjâ manoviññâṇadhâtu samphassajâ cetanâ sañcetanâ cetayitattaṃ—ayaṃ tasmiṃ samaye cetanâ hoti.

474. Katamaṃ tasmiṃ samaye cittaṃ hoti?

Yaṃ tasmiṃ samaye cittaṃ mano mânasaṃ hadayaṃ paṇḍaraṃ mano manâyatanaṃ manindriyaṃ viññâṇaṃ viññâṇakkhando tajjâ manoviññâṇadhâtu—idaṃ tasmiṃ samaye cittaṃ hoti.

475. Katamo tasmiṃ samaye vitakko hoti?

Yo tasmiṃ samaye takko vitakko saṅkappo appanâ vyappanâ cetaso abhiniropanâ—ayaṃ tasmiṃ samaye takko hoti.

476. Katamo tasmiṃ samaye vicâro hoti?

Yo tasmiṃ samaye câro vicâro anuvicâro upavicâro cittassa anusandhanatâ anupekkhanatâ—ayaṃ tasmiṃ samaye vicâro hoti.

477. Katamâ tasmiṃ samaye pîti hoti?

Yâ tasmiṃ samaye pîti pâmojjaṃ âmodanâ pamodanâ hâso pahâso vitti odagyaṃ attamanatâ cittassa—ayaṃ tasmiṃ samaye pîti hoti.

478. Katamaṃ tasmiṃ samaye sukhaṃ hoti?

Yaṃ tasmiṃ samaye cetasikaṃ sâtaṃ cetasikaṃ sukhaṃ cetosamphassajaṃ sâtaṃ sukhaṃ vedayitaṃ cetosamphassajâ sâtâ sukhâ vedanâ: idaṃ tasmiṃ samaye sukhaṃ hoti.

479. Katamâ tasmiṃ samaye cittass' ekaggatâ hoti?

Yâ tasmiṃ samaye cittassa ṭhiti . . . pe (11) . . . ayaṃ tasmiṃ samaye cittass' ekaggatâ hoti.

480. Katamaṃ tasmiṃ samaye manindriyaṃ hoti?

Yaṃ tasmiṃ samaye cittaṃ mano mânasaṃ . . . pe (17) . . . viññâṇadhâtu idaṃ tasmiṃ samaye manindriyaṃ hoti.

481. Katamaṃ tasmiṃ samaye somanassindriyaṃ hoti?

Yaṃ tasmiṃ samaye cetasikaṃ sâtaṃ cetasikaṃ sukhaṃ cetosamphassajaṃ sâtaṃ sukhaṃ vedayitaṃ cetosamphassajâ sâtâ sukhâ vedanâ—idaṃ tasmiṃ samaye somanassindriyaṃ hoti.

482. Katamaṃ tasmiṃ samaye jîvitindriyaṃ hoti?

Yo tasmiṃ samaye arûpînaṃ dhammânaṃ âyu ṭhiti yapanâ . . . pe . . . jîvitindriyaṃ idaṃ tasmiṃ samaye jîvitindriyaṃ hoti: ye vâ pana tasmiṃ samaye aññe pi atthi paṭiccasamuppannâ arûpino dhammâ—ime dhammâ avyâkatâ.

Tasmiṃ kho pana samaye cattâro khandhâ honti dvâyatanâni honti dve dhâtuyo honti, tayo âhârâ honti, tîṇindriyâni honti, eko phasso hoti . . . pe (58) . . . ekâ manoviññâṇadhâtu hoti, ekaṃ dhammâyatanaṃ hoti, ekâ dhammadhâtu hoti, ye vâ pana tasmiṃ samaye aññe pi atthi paṭiccasamuppannâ arûpino dhammâ—ime dhammâ avyâkatâ.

483. Katamo tasmiṃ samaye saṅkhârakkhandho hoti?

Phasso cetanâ vitakko vicâro pîti cittass' ekaggatâ jîvitindriyaṃ, ye vâ pana tasmiṃ samaye aññe pi atthi paṭiccasamuppannâ arûpino dhammâ ṭhapetvâ vedanâkkhandhaṃ ṭhapetvâ saññâkkhandhaṃ ṭhapetvâ viññâṇakkhandhaṃ—ayaṃ tasmiṃ samaye saṅkhârakkhandho hoti . . . pe . . . ime dhammâ avyâkatâ.

Kusalavipâkâ somanassasahagatâ manoviññâṇadhâtu.

484. Katame dhammâ avyâkatâ?

Yasmiṃ samaye kâmâvacarassa kusalassa kammassa

katattâ upacitattâ vipâkâ manoviññâṇadhâtu uppannâ hoti upekkhâsahagatâ rûpârammaṇâ vâ . . . pe . . . dhammârammaṇâ vâ yaṃ yaṃ vâ panârabbha: tasmiṃ samaye phasso hoti, vedanâ hoti, saññâ hoti, cetanâ hoti, cittaṃ hoti, vitakko hoti, vicâro hoti, upekkhâ hoti, cittass' ekaggatâ hoti, manindriyaṃ hoti, upekkhindriyaṃ hoti, jîvitindriyaṃ hoti: ye vâ pana tasmiṃ samaye aññe pi atthi paṭiccasamuppannâ arûpino dhammâ—ime dhammâ avyâkatâ.

485. Katamo tasmiṃ samaye phasso hoti?

Yo tasmiṃ samaye phasso phusanâ samphusanâ samphusitattaṃ—ayaṃ tasmiṃ samaye phasso hoti.

486. Katamâ tasmiṃ samaye vedanâ hoti?

Yaṃ tasmiṃ samaye tajjâ manoviññâṇadhâtu . . . pe . . . adukkhamasukhâ vedanâ—ayaṃ tasmiṃ samaye vedanâ hoti.

487. Katamâ tasmiṃ samaye saññâ hoti?

Yâ tasmiṃ samaye tajjâ manoviññâṇadhâtu . . . pe . . . sañjânitattaṃ—ayaṃ tasmiṃ samaye saññâ hoti.

488. Katamâ tasmiṃ samaye cetanâ hoti?

Yâ tasmiṃ samaye tajjâ manoviññâṇadhâtu . . . pe . . . cetayitattaṃ—ayaṃ tasmiṃ samaye cetanâ hoti.

489. Katamaṃ tasmiṃ samaye cittaṃ hoti?

Yaṃ tasmiṃ samaye cittaṃ mano mânasaṃ hadayaṃ . . . pe . . . viññâṇadhâtu—idaṃ tasmiṃ samaye cittaṃ hoti.

490. Katamo tasmiṃ samaye vitakko hoti?

Yo tasmiṃ samaye takko . . . pe . . . abhiniropanâ—ayaṃ tasmiṃ samaye vitakko hoti.

491. Katamo tasmiṃ samaye vicâro hoti?

Yâ tasmiṃ samaye câro . . . pe . . . anupekkhanatâ—ayaṃ tasmiṃ samaye vicâro hoti.

492. Katamâ tasmiṃ samaye upekkhâ hoti?

Yaṃ tasmiṃ samaye cetasikaṃ neva sâtaṃ . . . pe . . . adukkhamasukhâ vedanâ—ayaṃ tasmiṃ samaye upekkhâ hoti.

493. Katamâ tasmiṃ samaye cittass' ekaggatâ hoti?

Yâ tasmiṃ samaye cittassa ṭhiti . . . pe . . . ayaṃ tasmiṃ samaye cittass' ekaggatâ hoti.

494. Katamaṃ tasmiṃ samaye manindriyaṃ hoti?

Yaṃ tasmiṃ samaye cittaṃ mano mânasaṃ . . . pe . . . viññâṇadhâtu—idaṃ tasmiṃ samaye manindriyaṃ hoti.

495. Katamaṃ tasmiṃ samaye upekkhindriyaṃ hoti?

Yâ tasmiṃ samaye cetasikaṃ neva sâtaṃ . . . pe . . . adukkhamasukhâ vedanâ—idaṃ tasmim samaye upekkhindriyaṃ hoti.

496. Katamaṃ tasmiṃ samaye jîvitindriyaṃ hoti?

Yo tesaṃ arûpînaṃ dhammânaṃ âyu ṭhiti yapanâ . . . pe . . . jîvitindriyaṃ—idaṃ tasmiṃ samaye jîvitindriyaṃ hoti—ye vâ pana tasmiṃ samaye aññe pi atthi paṭiccasamuppannâ arûpino dhammâ—ime dhammâ avyâkatâ.

Tasmiṃ kho pana samaye cattâro khandhâ honti, dvâyatanâni honti, dve dhâtuyo honti, tayo âhârâ honti, tîṇindriyâni honti, eko phasso hoti . . . pe . . . ekâ manoviññâṇadhâtu hoti ekaṃ dhammâyatanaṃ hoti ekâ dhammadhâtu hoti—ye vâ pana tasmiṃ samaye aññe pi atthi paṭiccasamuppannâ arûpino dhammâ—ime dhammâ avyâkatâ.

497. Katamo tasmiṃ samaye saṅkhârakkhandho hoti?

Phasso cetanâ vitakko vicâro cittass' ekaggatâ jîvitindriyaṃ ye vâ pana tasmiṃ samaye aññe pi atthi paṭiccasamuppannâ arûpino dhammâ, ṭhapetvâ vedanâkkhandhaṃ ṭhapetvâ saññâkkhandhaṃ ṭhapetvâ viññâṇakkhandhaṃ—ayaṃ tasmiṃ samaye saṅkhârakkhandho hoti . . . pe . . . ime dhammâ avyâkatâ.

Kusalavipâkâ upekkhâsahagatâ manoviññâṇadhâtu.

498. Katame dhammâ avyâkatâ.

Yasmiṃ samaye kâmâvacarassa kusalassa kammassa katattâ upacitattâ vipâkâ manoviññâṇadhâtu uppannâ hoti somanassasahagatâ ñâṇasampayuttâ . . . pe . . . somanassasahagatâ ñâṇasampayuttâ sasaṅkhârena . . . pe . . . somanassasahagatâ ñâṇavippayuttâ . . . pe . . . somanassasahagatâ ñâṇavippayuttâ sasaṅkhârena . . . pe . . . upekkhâsahagatâ ñâṇasampayuttâ . . . pe . . . upekkhâsahagatâ ñâṇasampayuttâ sasaṅkhârena . . . pe . . . upekkhâsahagatâ ñâṇavippayuttâ . . . pe . . . upekkhâsahagatâ ñâṇavippayuttâ sasaṅkhârena rûpârammaṇâ vâ . . . pe . . . dhammârammaṇâ vâ—yaṃ yaṃ vâpanârabbha—tasmiṃ samaye phasso hoti . . . pe . . . avikkhepo hoti . . . pe . . . ime dhammâ avyâkatâ.

Alobho avyâkatamûlaṃ . . . pe . . . adoso avyâkatamûlaṃ . . . pe . . . ime dhammâ avyâkatâ.

Aṭṭha mahâvipâkâ.

499. Katame dhammâ avyâkatâ?

Yasmiṃ samaye rûpûpapattiyâ maggaṃ bhâveti vivicceva kâmehi . . . pe . . . paṭhamaṃ jhânaṃ upasampajja viharati pathavîkasinaṃ tasmiṃ samaye phasso hoti . . . pe . . . avikkhepo hoti . . . pe . . . ime dhammâ kusalâ—tass' eva rûpâvacarassa kusalassa kammassa katattâ upacitattâ vipâkaṃ vivicceva kâmehi . . . pe . . . paṭhamaṃ jhânaṃ upasampajja viharati pathavîkasinaṃ—tasmiṃ samaye phasso hoti . . . pe . . . avikkhepo hoti . . . pe . . . ime dhammâ avyâkatâ.

500. Katame dhammâ avyâkatâ?

Yasmiṃ samaye rûpûpapattiyâ maggaṃ bhâveti vitakkavicârânaṃ vûpasamâ . . . pe . . . dutiyaṃ jhânaṃ . . . pe tatiyaṃ jhânaṃ . . . pe . . . catutthaṃ jhânaṃ . . . pe . . . paṭhamaṃ jhânaṃ . . . pe . . . pañcamaṃ jhânaṃ upasampajja viharati pathavîkasinaṃ—tasmiṃ samaye phasso hoti . . . pe . . . avikkhepo hoti . . . pe . . . ime dhammâ kusalâ: tass' eva rûpâvacarassa kusalassa kammassa katattâ upacitattâ vipâkaṃ sukhassa ca pahânâ . . . pe . . . pañcamaṃ jhânaṃ upasampajja viharati pathavîkasinaṃ—tasmiṃ samaye phasso hoti . . . pe . . . avikkhepo hoti . . . pe . . . ime dhammâ avyâkatâ.

Rûpâvacaravipâkâ.

501. Katame dhammâ avyâkatâ?

Yasmiṃ samaye arûpûpapattiyâ maggaṃ bhâveti sabbaso rûpasaññânaṃ samatikkamâ paṭighasaññânaṃ atthaṅgamânânattasaññânaṃ amanasikârâ âkâsânañcâyatanasahagataṃ sukhassa ca pahânâ . . . pe . . . catuttham jhânam upasampajja viharati: tasmiṃ samaye phasso hoti . . . pe . . . avikkhepo hoti . . . pe . . . ime dhammâ kusalâ . . . pe . . . tass' eva rûpâvacarassa kusalassa kammassa katattâ upacitattâ vipâkâ sabbaso rûpasaññânaṃ samatikkamâ paṭighasaññânaṃ atthaṅgamânânattasaññânaṃ amanasikârâ âkâsânañcâyatanasaññâsahagataṃ sukhassa ca pahânâ . . . pe . . . catutthaṃ jhânaṃ upasampajja viharati—tasmiṃ samaye phasso hoti . . . pe . . . avikkhepo hoti . . . pe . . . ime dhammâ avyâkatâ.

502. Katame dhammâ avyâkatâ?

Yasmiṃ samaye arûpûpapattiyâ maggaṃ bhâveti sabbaso âkâsânañcâyatanaṃ samatikkamâ viññâṇañcâyatanasaññâsahagataṃ sukhassa ca pahânâ . . . pe . . . catutthaṃ jhânaṃ upasampajja viharati—tasmiṃ samaye phasso hoti . . . pe . . . avikkhepo hoti . . . pe . . . ime dhammâ kusalâ . . . pe . . . tass' eva arûpâvacarassa kusalassa kammassa katattâ upacitattâ vipâkaṃ sabbaso âkâsânañcâyatanaṃ samatikkamâ viññâṇañcâyatanasaññâsahagataṃ sukhassa ca pahânâ . . . pe . . . catutthaṃ jhânaṃ upasampajja viharati tasmiṃ samaye phasso hoti . . . pe . . . avikkhepo hoti . . . pe . . . ime dhammâ avyâkatâ.

503. Katame dhammâ avyâkatâ?

Yasmiṃ samaye arûpûpapattiyâ maggaṃ bhâveti sabbaso viññâṇañcâyatanaṃ samatikkamâ âkiñcaññâyatanasaññâsahagataṃ sukhassa ca pahânâ . . . pe . . . catutthaṃ jhânaṃ upasampajja viharati: tasmiṃ samaye phasso hoti . . . pe . . . avikkhepo hoti . . . pe . . . ime dhammâ kusalâ: tass' eva arûpâvacarassa kusalassa kammassa katattâ upacitattâ vipâkaṃ sabbaso viññâṇañcâyatanaṃ samatikkamâ âkiñcaññâyatanasaññâsahagataṃ sukhassa ca pahânâ . . . pe . . . catutthaṃ jhânaṃ upasampajja viharati—tasmiṃ samaye phasso hoti . . . pe . . . avikkhepo hoti . . . pe . . . ime dhammâ avyâkatâ.

504. Katame dhammâ avyâkatâ?

Yasmiṃ samaye arûpûpapattiyâ maggaṃ bhâveti sabbaso âkiñcaññâyatanaṃ samatikkamâ neva saññâyatanasahagataṃ sukhassa ca pahânâ . . . pe . . . catutthaṃ jhânaṃ upasampajja viharati: tasmiṃ samaye phasso hoti . . . pe . . . avikkhepo hoti . . . pe . . . ime dhammâ kusalâ: tass' eva arûpâvacarassa kusalassa kammassa katattâ upacitattâ vipâkaṃ sabbaso âkiñcaññayatanaṃ samatikkamâ—neva saññânâsaññâyatanasahagataṃ sukhassa ca pahânâ . . . pe . . . catutthaṃ jhânaṃ upasampajja viharati—tasmiṃ samaye phasso hoti . . . pe . . . avikkhepo hoti . . . pe . . . ime dhammâ avyâkatâ.

Arûpâvacaravipâkâ.

505. Katame dhammâ avyâkatâ?

Yasmiṃ samaye lokuttaraṃ jhânaṃ bhâveti niyyânikaṃ apacayagâmiṃ diṭṭhigatânaṃ pahânâya paṭhamâya bhummiyâpattiyâ vivicceva kâmehi . . . pe . . . paṭhamaṃ jhânaṃ upasampajja viharati dukkhâpaṭipadaṃ dandhâbhiññaṃ—tasmiṃ samaye phasso hoti . . . pe . . . avikkhepo hoti . . . pe . . . ime dhammâ kusalâ: tass' eva lokuttarassa kusalassa jhânassa katattâ bhâvitattâ vipâkaṃ vivicceva kâmehi . . . pe . . . paṭhamaṃ jhânaṃ upasampajja viharati dukkhâpaṭidaṃ dandhâbhiññaṃ suññataṃ—tasmiṃ samaye phasso hoti . . . pe . . . aññindriyaṃ hoti . . . pe . . . avikkhepo hoti . . . pe . . . ime dhammâ avyâkatâ.

506. Katame dhammâ avyâkatâ?

Yasmiṃ samaye lokuttaraṃ jhânaṃ bhâveti niyyânikaṃ apacayagâmiṃ diṭṭhigatânaṃ pahânâya paṭhamâya bhummiyâpattiyâ vivicceva kâmehi . . . pe . . . paṭhamaṃ jhânaṃ upasampajja viharati dukkhâpaṭipadaṃ dandhâbhiññaṃ—tasmiṃ samaye phasso hoti . . . pe . . . avikkhepo hoti . . . pe . . . ime dhammâ kusalâ: tass' eva lokuttarassa kusalassa jhânassa katattâ bhâvitattâ vipâkaṃ vivicceva kâmehi . . . pe . . . paṭhamaṃ jhânaṃ upasampajja viharati dukkhâpaṭipadaṃ dandhâbhiññaṃ animittaṃ—tasmiṃ samaye phasso hoti . . . pe . . . aññindriyaṃ hoti . . . pe . . . avikkhepo hoti . . . pe . . . ime dhammâ avyâkatâ.

507. Katame dhammâ avyâkatâ.

Yasmiṃ samaye lokuttaraṃ jhânaṃ bhâveti niyyânikaṃ apacayagâmiṃ diṭṭhigatânaṃ pahânâya paṭhamâya bhummiyâpattiyâ vivicceva kâmehi . . . pe . . . paṭhamaṃ jhânaṃ upasampajja viharati dukkhâpaṭipadaṃ dandhâbhiññaṃ: tasmiṃ samaye phasso hoti . . . pe . . . paññindriyaṃ hoti . . . pe . . . avikkhepo hoti . . . pe . . . ime dhammâ kusalâ: tass' eva lokuttarassa kusalassa jhânassa katattâ bhâvitattâ vipâkaṃ vivicceva kâmehi . . . pe . . . paṭhamaṃ jhânaṃ upasampajja viharati dukkhâpaṭipadaṃ dandhâbhiññaṃ appaṇihitaṃ tasmiṃ samaye phasso hoti . . . pe . . . aññindriyaṃ hoti . . . pe . . . avikkhepo hoti . . . pe . . . ime dhammâ avyâkatâ.

508. Katame dhammâ avyâkatâ?

Yasmiṃ samaye lokuttaraṃ jhânaṃ bhâveti niyyânikaṃ apacayagâmiṃ diṭṭhigatânaṃ pahânâya paṭhamâya bhummiyâpattiyâ vitakkavicârânaṃ vûpasamâ . . . pe . . . dutiyaṃ jhânaṃ . . . pe . . . tatiyaṃ jhânaṃ . . . pe . . . catutthaṃ jhânaṃ . . . pe . . . paṭhamaṃ jhânaṃ . . . pe pañcamaṃ jhânaṃ upasampajja viharati dukkhâpaṭipadaṃ dandhâbhiññaṃ ti kusalaṃ . . . pe . . . dukkhâpaṭipadaṃ dandhâbhiññaṃ suññatan ti vipâko . . . pe . . . dukkhâpaṭipadaṃ dandhâbhiññan ti kusalaṃ . . . pe . . . dukkhâpaṭipadaṃ dandhâbhiññaṃ animittan ti vipâko . . . pe . . . dukkhâpaṭipadaṃ dandhâbhiññan ti kusalaṃ . . . pe . . . dukkhâpaṭipadaṃ dandhâbhiññaṃ appaṇihitan ti vipâko—tasmiṃ samaye phasso hoti . . . pe . . . avikkhepo hoti . . . pe . . . ime dhammâ avyâkatâ.

509. Katame dhammâ avyâkatâ?

Yasmiṃ samaye lokuttaraṃ jhânaṃ bhâveti niyyânikaṃ apacayagâmiṃ diṭṭhigatânaṃ pahânâya paṭhamâya bhummiyâpattiyâ vivicceva kâmehi . . . pe . . . paṭhamaṃ jhânaṃ upasampajja viharati dukkhâpaṭipadaṃ khippâbhiññaṃ . . . pe . . . sukhâpaṭipadaṃ dandhâbhiññaṃ . . . pe . . . sukhâpaṭipadaṃ khippâbhiññaṃ . . . pe . . . dutiyaṃ jhânaṃ . . . pe . . . tatiyaṃ jhânaṃ . . . pe . . . catutthaṃ jhânaṃ . . . pe . . . paṭhamaṃ jhânaṃ . . . pe . . . pañcamaṃ jhânaṃ upasampajja viharati sukhâpaṭipadaṃ khippâbhiññan ti kusalaṃ . . . pe . . . sukhâpaṭipadaṃ khippâbhiññaṃ suññatan ti vipâko . . . pe . . . sukhâpaṭipadaṃ khippâbhiññan ti kusalaṃ . . . pe . . . sukhâpaṭipadaṃ khippâbhiññaṃ animittan ti vipâko . . . pe . . . sukhâpaṭipadaṃ khippâbhiññan ti kusalaṃ . . . pe . . . sukhâpaṭipadaṃ khippâbhiññaṃ appaṇihitan ti vipâko—tasmiṃ samaye phasso hoti . . . pe . . . avikkhepo hoti . . . pe . . . ime dhammâ avyâkatâ.

Suddhika-paṭipadâ.

510. Katame dhammâ avyâkatâ?

Yasmiṃ samaye lokuttaraṃ jhânaṃ bhâveti niyyânikaṃ apacayagâmiṃ diṭṭhigatânaṃ pahânâya paṭhamâya bhummiyâpattiyâ vivicceva kâmehi . . . pe . . . paṭhamaṃ jhânaṃ upasampajja viharati suññataṃ—tasmiṃ samaye phasso hoti . . . pe . . . avikkhepo hoti . . . pe . . . ime dhammâ kusalâ: tass' eva lokuttarassa kusalassa jhânassa katattâ bhâvitattâ vipâkaṃ vivicceva kâmehi . . . pe . . . paṭhamaṃ jhânaṃ upasampajja viharati suññataṃ—tasmiṃ samaye phasso hoti . . . pe . . . avikkhepo hoti . . . pe . . . ime dhammâ avyâkatâ.

511. Katame dhammâ avyâkatâ?

Yasmiṃ samaye lokuttaraṃ jhânaṃ bhâveti niyyânikaṃ apacayagâmiṃ diṭṭhigatânaṃ pahânâya paṭhamâya bhummiyâpattiyâ vivicceva kâmehi . . . pe . . . paṭhamaṃ jhânaṃ upasampajja viharati suññataṃ—tasmiṃ samaye phasso hoti . . . pe . . . avikkhepo hoti . . . pe . . . ime dhammâ kusalâ — tass' eva lokuttarassa kusalassa jhânassa katattâ bhâvitattâ vipâkaṃ vivicceva kâmehi . . . pe . . . paṭhamaṃ jhânaṃ upasampajja viharati animittaṃ — tasmiṃ samaye phasso hoti . . . pe . . . avikkhepo hoti . . . pe . . . ime dhammâ avyâkatâ.

512. Katame dhammâ avyâkatâ?

Yasmiṃ samaye lokuttaraṃ jhânaṃ bhâveti niyyânikaṃ apacayagâmiṃ diṭṭhigatânaṃ pahânâya paṭhamâya bhummiyâpattiyâ vivicceva kâmehi . . . pe . . . paṭhamaṃ jhânaṃ upasampajja viharati suññataṃ—tasmiṃ samaye phasso hoti . . . pe . . . avikkhepo hoti . . . pe . . . ime dhammâ kusalâ—tass' eva lokuttarassa kusalassa jhânassa katattâ bhâvitattâ vipâkaṃ vivicceva kâmehi . . . pe . . . paṭhamaṃ jhânaṃ upasampajja viharati appaṇihitaṃ—tasmiṃ samaye phasso hoti . . . pe . . . avikkhepo hoti . . . pe . . . ime dhammâ avyâkatâ.

513. Katame dhammâ avyâkatâ?

Yasmiṃ samaye lokuttaraṃ jhânaṃ bhâveti niyyânikaṃ apacayagâmiṃ diṭṭhigatânaṃ pahânâya paṭhamâya bhummiyâpattiyâ vitakkavicârânaṃ vûpasamâ . . . pe . . . dutiyaṃ jhânaṃ . . . pe . . . tatiyaṃ jhânaṃ . . . pe . . . catutthaṃ jhânaṃ . . . pe . . . paṭhamaṃ jhânaṃ . . . pe . . . pañcamaṃ jhânaṃ upasampajja viharati suññatan ti kusalaṃ . . . pe . . . suññatan ti vipâko . . . pe . . . suññatan ti kusalaṃ . . . pe . . . animittan ti vipâko . . . pe . . . suññatan ti kusalaṃ . . . pe . . . appaṇihitan ti vipâko—tasmiṃ samaye phasso hoti . . . pe . . . avikkhepo hoti . . . pe . . . ime dhammâ avyâkatâ.

Suddhikasuññataṃ.

514. Katame dhammâ avyâkatâ?

Yasmiṃ samaye lokuttaraṃ jhânaṃ bhâveti niyyânikaṃ apacayagâmiṃ diṭṭhigatânaṃ pahânâya paṭhamâya bhummiyâpattiyâ vivicceva kâmehi . . . pe . . . paṭhamaṃ jhânaṃ upasampajja viharati dukkhâpaṭipadaṃ dandhâbhiññaṃ suññataṃ: tasmiṃ samaye phasso hoti . . . pe . . avikkhepo hoti . . . pe . . . ime dhammâ kusalâ: tass' eva lokuttarassa [kusalassa] jhânassa katattâ bhâvitattâ vipâkaṃ vivicceva kâmehi . . . pe . . . paṭhamaṃ jhânaṃ upasampajja viharati dukkhâpaṭipadaṃ dandhâbhiññaṃ suññataṃ—tasmiṃ samaye phasso hoti . . . pe . . . avikkhepo hoti . . . pe . . . ime dhammâ avyâkatâ.

515. Katame dhammâ avyâkatâ?

Yasmiṃ samaye lokuttaraṃ jhânaṃ bhâveti niyyânikaṃ apacayagâmiṃ diṭṭhigatânaṃ pahânâya paṭhamâya bhummiyâpattiyâ vivicceva kâmehi . . . pe . . . paṭhamaṃ jhânaṃ upasampajja viharati dukkhâpaṭipadaṃ dandhâbhiññaṃ suññataṃ: tasmiṃ samaye phasso hoti . . . pe . . . avikkhepo hoti . . . pe . . . ime dhammâ kusalâ: tass' eva lokuttarassa kusalassa jhânassa katattâ bhâvitattâ vipâkaṃ vivicceva kâmehi . . . pe . . . paṭhamaṃ jhânaṃ upasampajja viharati dukkhâpaṭipadaṃ dandhâbhiññaṃ animittaṃ: tasmiṃ samaye phasso hoti . . . pe . . . avikkhepo hoti . . . pe . . . ime dhammâ avyâkatâ.

516. Katame dhammâ avyâkatâ?

Yasmiṃ samaye lokuttaraṃ jhânaṃ bhâveti niyyânikaṃ apacayagâmiṃ diṭṭhigatânaṃ pahânâya paṭhamâya bhummiyâpattiyâ vivicceva kâmehi . . . pe . . . paṭhamaṃ jhânaṃ upasampajja viharati dukkhâpaṭipadaṃ dandhâbhiññaṃ suññataṃ — tasmiṃ samaye phasso hoti . . . pe . . . avikkhepo hoti . . . pe . . . ime dhammâ kusalâ: tass' eva lokuttarassa kusalassa jhânassa katattâ bhâvitattâ vipâkaṃ vivicceva kâmehi paṭhamaṃ jhânaṃ upasampajja viharati dukkhâpaṭipadaṃ dandhâbiññaṃ appaṇihitaṃ — tasmiṃ samaye phasso hoti . . . pe . . . avikkhepo hoti . . . pe . . . ime dhammâ avyâkatâ.

517. Katame dhammâ avyâkatâ?

Yasmiṃ samaye lokuttaraṃ jhânaṃ bhâveti niyyânikaṃ apacayagâmiṃ diṭṭhigatânaṃ pahânâya paṭhamâya bhummiyâpattiyâ vitakkavicârânaṃ vûpasamâ . . . pe . . . dutiyaṃ jhânaṃ . . . pe . . . tatiyaṃ jhânaṃ . . . pe . . . catutthaṃ jhânaṃ . . . pe . . . paṭhamaṃ jhânaṃ . . . pe . . . pañcamaṃ jhânaṃ upasampajja viharati dukkhâpaṭipadaṃ dandhâbhiññaṃ suññatan ti kusalaṃ . . . pe . . . dukkhâpaṭipadaṃ dandhâbhiññaṃ suññatan ti vipâko . . . pe . . . dukkhâpaṭipadaṃ dandhâbhiññaṃ suññatan ti kusalaṃ . . . pe . . . dukkhâpaṭipadaṃ dandhâbhiññaṃ animittan ti vipâko . . . pe . . . dukkhâpaṭipadaṃ dandhâbhiññaṃ suññatan ti kusalaṃ . . . pe . . . dukkhâpaṭipadaṃ dandhâbhiññaṃ appaṇihitan ti vipâko—tasmiṃ samaye phasso hoti . . . pe . . . avikkhepo hoti . . . pe . . . ime dhammâ avyâkatâ.

518. Katame dhammâ avyâkatâ?

Yasmiṃ samaye lokuttaraṃ jhânaṃ bhâveti niyyânikaṃ apacayagâmiṃ diṭṭhigatânaṃ pahânâya paṭhamâya bhummiyâpattiyâ vivicceva kâmehi . . . pe . . . paṭhamaṃ jhânaṃ upasampajja viharati dukkhâpaṭipadaṃ khippâbhiññaṃ suññataṃ . . . pe . . . sukhâpaṭipadaṃ dandhâbhiññaṃ suññataṃ . . . pe . . . sukhâpaṭipadaṃ khippâbhiññaṃ suññataṃ . . . pe . . . dutiyaṃ jhânaṃ . . . pe . . . tatiyaṃ jhânaṃ . . . pe . . . catutthaṃ jhânaṃ . . . pe . . . paṭhamaṃ jhânaṃ . . . pe . . . pañcamaṃ jhânaṃ upasampajja viharati sukhâpaṭipadaṃ khippâbhiññaṃ suññatan ti kusalaṃ . . . pe . . . sukhâpaṭipadaṃ khippâbhiññaṃ suññatan ti vipâko . . . pe . . . sukhâpaṭipadaṃ khippâbhiññaṃ suññatan ti kusalaṃ . . . pe . . . sukhâpaṭipadaṃ khippâbhiññaṃ animittan ti vipâko . . . pe . . . sukhâpaṭipadaṃ khippâbhiññaṃ suññatan ti kusalaṃ . . . pe . . . sukhâpaṭipadaṃ khippâbhiññaṃ appaṇihitan ti vipâko : tasmiṃ samaye phasso hoti . . . pe . . . avikkhepo hoti—ime dhammâ avyâkatâ.

Suññapaṭipadâ.

519. Katame dhammâ avyâkatâ?

Yasmiṃ samaye lokuttaraṃ jhânaṃ bhâveti niyyânikaṃ apacayagâmiṃ diṭṭhigatânaṃ pahânâya paṭhamâya bhummiyâpattiyâ vivicceva kâmehi . . . pe . . . paṭhamaṃ jhânaṃ upasampajja viharati appaṇihitaṃ—tasmiṃ samaye phasso hoti . . . pe . . . avikkhepo hoti . . . pe . . . ime dhammâ kusalâ : tass' eva lokuttarassa kusalassa jhânassa katattâ bhâvitattâ vipâkaṃ vivicceva kâmehi . . . pe . . . paṭhamaṃ jhânaṃ upasampajja viharati appaṇihitaṃ—tasmiṃ samaye phasso hoti . . . pe . . . avikkhepo hoti . . . pe . . . ime dhammâ avyâkatâ.

520. Katame dhammâ avyâkatâ?

Yasmiṃ samaye lokuttaraṃ jhânaṃ bhâveti niyyânikaṃ apacayagâmiṃ diṭṭhigatânaṃ pahânâya paṭhamâya bhummiyâpattiyâ vivicceva kâmehi . . . pe . . . paṭhamaṃ jhânaṃ upasampajja viharati appaṇihitaṃ—tasmiṃ samaye phasso hoti . . . pe . . . avikkhepo hoti . . . pe . . . ime dhammâ kusalâ : tass' eva lokuttarassa kusalassa jhânassa katattâ bhâvitattâ vipâkaṃ vivicceva kâmehi . . . pe . . . paṭhamaṃ jhânaṃ upasampajja viharati animittaṃ—tasmiṃ samaye phasso hoti . . . pe . . . avikkhepo hoti—ime dhammâ avyâkatâ.

521. Katame dhammâ avyâkatâ?

Yasmiṃ samaye lokuttaraṃ jhânaṃ bhâveti niyyânikaṃ apacayagâmiṃ diṭṭhigatânaṃ pahânâya paṭhamâya bhummiyâpattiyâ vivicceva kâmehi . . . pe . . . paṭhamaṃ jhânaṃ upasampajja viharati appaṇihitaṃ : tasmiṃ samaye phasso hoti . . . pe . . . avikkhepo hoti . . . pe . . . ime dhammâ kusalâ : tass' eva lokuttarassa kusalassa jhânassa katattâ bhâvitattâ vipâkaṃ vivicceva kâmehi . . . pe . . . paṭhamaṃ jhânaṃ upasampajja viharati suññataṃ — tasmiṃ samaye phasso hoti . . . pe . . . avikkhepo hoti . . . pe . . . ime dhammâ avyâkatâ.

522. Katame dhammâ avyâkatâ?

Yasmiṃ samaye lokuttaraṃ jhânaṃ bhâveti niyyânikaṃ apacayagâmiṃ diṭṭhigatânaṃ pahânâya paṭhamâya bhummiyâpattiyâ vitakkavicârânaṃ vûpasamâ . . . pe . . . dutiyaṃ jhânaṃ . . . pe . . . tatiyaṃ jhânaṃ . . . pe . . . catutthaṃ jhânaṃ . . . pe . . . paṭhamaṃ jhânaṃ . . . pe . . . pañcamaṃ jhânaṃ upasampajja viharati appaṇihitan ti kusalaṃ . . . pe . . . appaṇihitan ti vipâko . . . pe . . . appaṇihitan ti kusalaṃ . . . pe . . . animittan ti vipâko . . . pe . . . appaṇihitan ti kusalaṃ . . . pe . . . suññatan ti vipâko—tasmiṃ samaye phasso hoti . . . pe . . . avikkhepo hoti . . . pe . . . ime dhammâ avyâkatâ.

Suddhika-appaṇihitaṃ.

523. Katame dhammâ avyâkatâ?

Yasmiṃ samaye . . . pe . . . pattiyâ vivicceva kâmehi . . . pe . . . paṭhamaṃ jhânaṃ upasampajja viharati dukkhâpaṭipadaṃ dandhâbhiññaṃ appaṇihitaṃ—tasmiṃ samaye phasso hoti . . . pe . . . avikkhepo hoti—ime dhammâ kusalâ—tass' eva lokuttarassa kusalassa jhânassa katattâ bhâvitattâ vipâkaṃ vivicceva kâmehi . . . pe . . . paṭhamaṃ jhânaṃ upasampajja viharati dukkhâpaṭipadaṃ dandhâbhiññaṃ appaṇihitaṃ—tasmiṃ samaye phasso hoti . . . pe . . . avikkhepo hoti . . . pe . . . ime dhammâ avyâkatâ.

524. Katame dhammâ avyâkatâ?

Yasmiṃ samaye . . . pe . . . pattiyâ vivicceva kâmehi

. . . pe . . . paṭhamaṃ jhânaṃ upasampajja viharati dukkhâpaṭipadaṃ dandhâbhiññaṃ appaṇihitaṃ—tasmiṃ samaye phasso hoti . . . pe . . . avikkhepo hoti . . . pe . . . ime dhammâ kusalâ: tass' eva lokuttarassa kusalassa jhânassa katattâ bhâvitattâ vipâkaṃ vivicceva kâmehi . . . pe . . . paṭhamaṃ jhânaṃ upasampajja viharati dukkhâpaṭipadaṃ dandhâbhiññaṃ animittaṃ—tasmiṃ samaye phasso hoti . . . pe . . . avikkhepo hoti . . . pe . . . ime dhammâ avyâkatâ.

525. Katame dhammâ avyâkatâ?

Yasmiṃ . . . pe . . . pattiyâ vivicceva kâmehi . . . pe . . . paṭhamaṃ jhânaṃ upasampajja viharati dukkhâpaṭipadaṃ dandhâbhiññaṃ appaṇihitaṃ: tasmiṃ samaye phasso hoti . . . pe . . . avikkhepo hoti . . . pe . . . ime dhammâ kusalâ: tass' eva lokuttarassa kusalassa jhânassa katattâ bhâvitattâ vipâkaṃ vivicceva kâmehi . . . pe . . . paṭhamaṃ jhânaṃ upasampajja viharati dukkhâpaṭipadaṃ dandhâbhiññaṃ suññataṃ—tasmiṃ samaye phasso hoti . . . pe . . . avikkhepo hoti . . . pe . . . ime dhammâ avyâkatâ.

526. Katame dhammâ avyâkatâ?

Yasmiṃ samaye . . . pe . . . pattiyâ vivicceva kâmehi . . . pe . . . dutiyaṃ jhânaṃ . . . pe . . . tatiyaṃ jhânaṃ . . . pe . . . catutthaṃ jhânaṃ . . . pe . . . paṭhamaṃ jhânaṃ . . . pe . . . pañcamaṃ jhânaṃ upasampajja viharati dukkhâpaṭipadaṃ dandhâbhiññaṃ appaṇihitan ti kusalaṃ . . . pe . . . dukkhâpaṭipadaṃ dandhâbhiññaṃ appaṇihitan ti vipâko . . . pe . . . dukkhâpaṭipadaṃ dandhâbhiññaṃ appaṇihitan ti kusalaṃ . . . pe . . . dukkhâpaṭipadaṃ dandhâbhiññaṃ appaṇihitan ti vipâko . . . pe . . . dukkhâpaṭipadaṃ dandhâbhiññaṃ appaṇihitan ti kusalaṃ . . . pe . . . dukkhâpaṭipadaṃ dandhâbhiññaṃ ti vipâko—tasmiṃ samaye phasso hoti . . . pe . . . avikkhepo hoti . . . pe . . . ime dhammâ avyâkatâ.

527. Katame dhammâ avyâkatâ?

Yasmiṃ samaye . . . pe . . . pattiyâ vivicceva kâmehi . . . pe . . . paṭhamaṃ jhânaṃ upasampajja viharati dukkhâpaṭipadaṃ khippâbhiññaṃ appaṇihitaṃ . . . pe . . . sukhâpaṭipadaṃ dandhâbhiññaṃ appaṇihitaṃ . . . pe . . . sukhâpaṭipadaṃ khippâbhiññaṃ appaṇihitaṃ . . . pe . . . dutiyaṃ jhânaṃ . . . pe . . . tatiyaṃ jhânaṃ . . . pe . . . catutthaṃ jhânaṃ . . . pe . . . paṭhamaṃ jhânaṃ . . . pe . . . pañcamaṃ jhânaṃ upasampajja viharati sukhâpaṭipadaṃ khippâbhiññaṃ appaṇihitan ti kusalaṃ . . . pe . . . sukhâpaṭipadaṃ khippâbhiññaṃ appaṇihitan ti vipâko . . . pe . . . sukhâpaṭipadaṃ khippâbhiññaṃ appaṇihitan ti kusalaṃ . . . pe . . . sukhâpaṭipadaṃ khippâbhiññaṃ appaṇihitan ti nimittan ti vipâko . . . pe . . . sukhâpaṭipadaṃ khippâbhiññaṃ appaṇihitan ti kusalaṃ . . . pe . . . sukhâpaṭipadaṃ khippâbhiññaṃ suññatan ti vipâko—tasmiṃ samaye phasso hoti . . . pe . . . avikkhepo hoti . . . pe . . . ime dhammâ avyâkatâ.

Appaṇihitapaṭipadâ.

528. Katame dhammâ avyâkatâ?

Yasmiṃ samaye lokuttaraṃ maggaṃ bhâveti . . . pe . . . lokuttaraṃ satipaṭṭhânaṃ bhâveti . . . pe . . . lokuttaraṃ sammappadhânaṃ bhâveti . . . pe . . . lokuttaraṃ iddhippâdaṃ bhâveti . . . pe . . . lokuttaraṃ indriyaṃ bhâveti . . . pe . . . lokuttaraṃ balaṃ bhâveti . . . pe . . . lokuttaraṃ bojjhaṅgaṃ bhâveti . . . pe . . . lokuttaraṃ saccaṃ bhâveti . . . pe . . . lokuttaraṃ samathaṃ bhâveti . . . pe . . . lokuttaraṃ dhammaṃ bhâveti . . . pe . . . lokuttaraṃ khandhaṃ bhâveti . . . pe . . . lokuttaraṃ âyatanaṃ bhâveti . . . pe . . . lokuttaraṃ dhâtuṃ bhâveti . . . pe . . . lokuttaraṃ âhâraṃ bhâveti . . . pe . . . lokuttaram phassaṃ bhâveti . . . pe . . . lokuttaraṃ vedanaṃ bhâveti . . . pe . . . lokuttaraṃ saññaṃ bhâveti . . . pe . . . lokuttaraṃ cetanaṃ bhâveti . . . pe . . . lokuttaraṃ cittaṃ bhâveti niyyânikaṃ apacayagâmiṃ diṭṭhigatânaṃ pahânâya paṭhamâya bhummiyâpattiyâ vivicceva kâmehi . . . pe . . . paṭhamaṃ jhânaṃ upasampajja viharati dukkhâpaṭipadaṃ dandhâbhiññaṃ—tasmiṃ samaye phasso hoti . . . pe . . . avikkhepo hoti—ime dhammâ kusalâ: tass' eva lokuttarassa kusalassa cittassa katattâ bhâvitattâ vipâkaṃ viviccева kâmehi . . . pe . . . paṭhamaṃ jhânaṃ upasampajja viharati dukkhâpaṭipadaṃ dandhâbhiññaṃ suññataṃ . . . pe . . .

animittaṃ . . . pe . . . appaṇihitaṃ tasmiṃ samaye phasso hoti . . . pe . . . avikkhepo hoti . . . pe . . . ime dhammâ avyâkatâ.

Vîsati mahânayâ.

529. Katame dhammâ avyâkatâ?

Yasmiṃ samaye lokuttaraṃ jhânaṃ bhâveti niyyânikaṃ . . . pe . . . pattiyâ vivicceva kâmehi . . . pe . . . paṭhamaṃ jhânaṃ upasampajja viharati dukkhâpaṭipadaṃ dandhâbhiññaṃ chandâdhipateyyaṃ: tasmiṃ samaye phasso hoti . . . pe . . . avikkhepo hoti . . . pe . . . ime dhammâ kusalâ: tass' eva lokuttarassa kusalassa jhânassa katattâ bhâvitattâ vipâkaṃ vivicceva kâmehi . . . pe . . . paṭhamaṃ jhânaṃ upasampajja viharati dukkhâpaṭipadaṃ dandhâbhiññaṃ suññataṃ chandâdhipateyyaṃ — tasmiṃ samaye phasso hoti . . . pe . . . avikkhepo hoti . . . pe . . . ime dhammâ avyâkatâ.

530. Katame dhammâ avyakatâ?

Yasmiṃ samaye lokuttaraṃ jhânaṃ bhâveti niyyânikaṃ . . . pe . . . pattiyâ vivicceva kâmehi . . . pe . . . paṭhamaṃ jhânaṃ upasampajja viharati dukkhâpaṭipadaṃ dandhâbhiññaṃ chandâdhipateyyaṃ: tasmiṃ samaye phasso hoti . . . pe . . . avikkhepo hoti . . . pe . . . ime dhammâ kusalâ—tass' eva lokuttarassa kusalassa jhânassa katattâ bhâvitattâ vipâkaṃ vivicceva kâmehi . . . pe . . . paṭhamaṃ jhânaṃ upasampajja viharati dukkhâpaṭipadaṃ dandhâbhiññaṃ appanimittaṃ chandâdhipateyyaṃ—tasmiṃ samaye phasso hoti . . . pe . . . avikkhepo hoti . . . pe . . . ime dhammâ avyâkatâ.

531. Katame dhammâ avyâkatâ?

Yasmiṃ samaye lokuttaraṃ . . . pe . . . pattiyâ vivicceva kâmehi . . . pe . . . paṭhamaṃ jhânaṃ upasampajja viharati dukkhâpaṭipadaṃ dandhâbhiññaṃ chandâdhipateyyaṃ: tasmiṃ samaye phasso hoti . . . pe . . . avikkhepo hoti . . . pe . . . ime dhammâ kusalâ — tass' eva lokuttarassa kusalassa jhânassa katattâ bhâvitattâ vipâkaṃ vivicceva kâmehi . . . pe . . . paṭhamaṃ jhânaṃ upasampajja viharati dukkhâpaṭipadaṃ dandhâbhiññaṃ appaṇihitaṃ chandâdhipateyyaṃ—tasmiṃ samaye phasso hoti . . . pe . . . avikkhepo hoti . . . pe . . . ime dhammâ avyâkatâ.

532. Katame dhammâ avyâkatâ ?

Yasmiṃ samaye lokuttaraṃ . . . pe . . . pattiyâ vitakka-vicârânaṃ vûpasamâ . . . pe . . . dutiyaṃ jhânaṃ . . . pe . . . tatiyaṃ jhânaṃ . . . pe . . . catutthaṃ jhânaṃ . . . pe . . . paṭhamaṃ jhânaṃ . . . pe . . . pañcamaṃ jhânaṃ upasampajja viharati dukkhâpaṭipadaṃ dandhâbhiññaṃ chandâdhipateyyan ti kusalaṃ . . . pe . . . dukkhâpaṭipadaṃ dandhâbhiññaṃ suññataṃ chandâdhipateyyan ti vipâko . . . pe . . . dukkhâpaṭipadaṃ dandhâbhiññaṃ chandâdhipateyyan ti kusalaṃ . . . pe . . . dukkhâpaṭipadaṃ dandhâbhiññaṃ animittaṃ chandâdhipateyyan ti vipâko . . . pe . . . dukkhâ-paṭipadaṃ dandhâbhiññaṃ chandâdhipateyyan ti kusalaṃ . . . pe . . . dukkhâpaṭipadaṃ dandhâbhiññaṃ appaṇihitaṃ chandâdhipateyyan ti vipâko—tasmiṃ samaye phasso hoti . . . pe . . . avikkhepo hoti . . . pe . . . ime dhammâ avyâkatâ.

533. Katame dhammâ avyâkatâ ?

Yasmiṃ samaye lokuttaraṃ . . . pe . . . pattiyâ vivicceva kâmehi . . . pe . . . paṭhamaṃ jhânaṃ upasampajja viharati dukkhâpaṭipadaṃ khippâbhiññaṃ chandâdhipateyyaṃ . . . pe . . . sukhâpaṭipadaṃ dandhâbhiññaṃ chandâdhipateyyaṃ . . . pe . . . sukhâpaṭipadaṃ khippâbhiññaṃ chandâdhipa-teyyaṃ . . . pe . . . dutiyaṃ jhânaṃ . . . pe . . . tatiyaṃ jhânaṃ . . . pe . . . catutthaṃ jhânaṃ . . . pe . . . paṭha-maṃ jhânaṃ . . . pe . . . pañcamaṃ jhânaṃ upasampajja viharati sukhâpaṭipadaṃ khippâbhiññaṃ chandâdhipateyyan ti kusalaṃ . . . pe . . . sukhâpaṭipadaṃ khippâbhiññaṃ suññataṃ chandâdhipateyyan ti vipâko . . . pe . . . sukhâ-paṭipadaṃ khippâbhiññaṃ chandâdhipateyyan ti kusalaṃ . . . pe . . . sukhâpaṭipadaṃ khippâbhiññaṃ animittaṃ chandâdhipateyyan ti vipâko . . . pe . . . sukhâpaṭipadaṃ khippâbhiññaṃ chandâdhipateyyan ti kusalaṃ . . . pe . . . sukhâpaṭipadaṃ khippâbhiññaṃ appaṇihitaṃ chandâdhipa-teyyan ti vipâko—tasmiṃ samaye phasso hoti . . . pe . . . avikkhepo hoti . . . pe . . . ime dhammâ avyâkatâ.

Chandâdhipateyyaṃ suddhikapaṭipadâ.

534. Katame dhammâ avyâkatâ?

Yasmiṃ samaye . . . pe . . . pattiyâ vivicceva kâmehi . . . pe . . . paṭhamaṃ jhânaṃ upasampajja viharati suññataṃ chandâdhipateyyaṃ—tasmiṃ samaye phasso hoti . . . pe . . . avikkhepo hoti . . . pe . . . ime dhammâ kusalâ—tass' eva lokuttarassa kusalassa jhânassa katattâ bhâvitattâ vipâkaṃ vivicceva kâmehi . . . pe . . . paṭhamaṃ jhânaṃ upasampajja viharati suññataṃ chandâdhipateyyaṃ—tasmim samaye phasso hoti . . . pe . . . avikkhepo hoti . . . pe . . . ime dhammâ avyâkatâ.

535. Katame dhammâ avyâkatâ?

Yasmiṃ samaye . . . pe . . . pattiyâ vivicceva kâmehi . . . pe . . . paṭhamaṃ jhânaṃ upasampajja viharati suññataṃ chandâdhipateyyaṃ: tasmiṃ samaye phasso hoti . . . pe . . . avikkhepo hoti . . . pe . . . ime dhammâ kusalâ—tass' eva lokuttarassa kusalassa jhânassa katattâ bhâvitattâ vipâkaṃ vivicceva kâmehi . . . pe . . . paṭhamaṃ jhânaṃ upasampajja viharati animittaṃ chandâdhipateyyaṃ—tasmiṃ samaye phasso hoti . . . pe . . . avikkhepo hoti . . . pe . . . ime dhammâ avyâkatâ.

536. Katame dhammâ avyâkatâ?

Yasmiṃ samaye . . . pe . . . pattiyâ vivicceva kâmehi . . . pe . . . paṭhamaṃ jhânaṃ upasampajja viharati suññataṃ chandâdhipateyyaṃ—tasmiṃ samaye phasso hoti . . . pe . . . avikkhepo hoti . . . pe . . . ime dhammâ kusalâ: tass' eva lokuttarassa kusalassa jhânassa katattâ bhâvitattâ vipâkaṃ vivicceva kâmehi . . . pe . . . paṭhamaṃ jhânaṃ upasampajja viharati appaṇihitaṃ chandâdhipateyyaṃ—tasmiṃ samaye phasso hoti . . . pe . . . avikkhepo hoti—ime dhammâ avyâkatâ.

537. Katame dhammâ avyâkatâ?

Yasmiṃ samaye lokuttaraṃ . . . pe . . . pattiyâ vitakkavicârânaṃ vûpasamâ . . . pe . . . dutiyaṃ jhânaṃ . . . pe . . . tatiyaṃ jhânaṃ . . . pe . . . catutthaṃ jhânaṃ . . . pe . . . paṭhamaṃ jhânaṃ . . . pe . . . pañcamaṃ jhânaṃ upasampajja viharati suññataṃ chandâdhipateyyan ti kusalaṃ . . . pe . . . suññataṃ chandâdhipateyyaṃ ti vipâko . . . pe . . . suññataṃ chandâdhipateyyan ti kusalaṃ . . . pe . . . animittaṃ chandâdhipateyyan ti vipâko . . . pe . . . suññataṃ chandâdhipateyyan ti kusalaṃ . . . pe . . . appaṇihitaṃ chandâdhipateyyan ti vipâko—tasmiṃ samaye phasso hoti . . . pe . . . avikkhepo hoti . . . pe . . . ime dhammâ avyâkatâ.

Chandâdhipateyyaṃ suddhikasuññatâ.

538. Katame dhammâ avyâkatâ?

Yasmiṃ samaye lokuttaraṃ . . . pe . . . pattiyâ vivicceva kâmehi . . . pe . . . paṭhamaṃ jhânaṃ upasampajja viharati dukkhâpaṭipadaṃ dandhâbhiññaṃ suññataṃ chandâdhipateyyaṃ—tasmiṃ samaye phasso hoti . . . pe . . . avikkhepo hoti . . . pe . . . ime dhammâ kusalâ: tass' eva lokuttarassa kusalassa jhânassa katattâ bhâvitattâ vipâkaṃ vivicceva kâmehi . . . pe . . . paṭhamam jhânaṃ upasampajja viharati dukkhâpaṭipadaṃ dandhâbhiññaṃ suññataṃ chandâdhipateyyaṃ—tasmiṃ samaye phasso hoti . . . pe . . . avikkhepo hoti . . . pe . . . ime dhammâ avyâkatâ.

539. Katame dhammâ avyâkatâ?

Yasmiṃ samaye lokuttaraṃ . . . pe . . . pattiyâ vivicceva kâmehi . . . pe . . . paṭhamaṃ jhânaṃ upasampajja viharati dukkhâpaṭipadaṃ dandhâbhiññaṃ suññataṃ chandâdhipateyyaṃ—tasmiṃ samaye phasso hoti . . . pe . . . avikkhepo hoti . . . pe . . . ime dhammâ kusalâ—tass' eva lokuttarassa kusalassa jhânassa katattâ bhâvitattâ vipâkaṃ vivicceva kâmehi . . . pe . . . paṭhamaṃ jhânaṃ upasampajja viharati dukkhâpaṭipadaṃ dandhâbhiññaṃ suññataṃ chandâdhipateyyaṃ: tasmiṃ samaye phasso hoti . . . pe . . . avikkhepo hoti . . . pe . . . ime dhammâ avyâkatâ.

540. Katame dhammâ avyâkatâ?

Yasmiṃ samaye . . . pe . . . pattiyâ vivicceva kâmehi . . . pe . . . paṭhamaṃ jhânaṃ upasampajja viharati dukkhâpaṭipadaṃ dandhâbhiññaṃ suññataṃ chandâdhipateyyaṃ—tasmiṃ samaye lokuttaro phasso hoti . . . pe . . . avikkhepo hoti—ime dhammâ kusalâ: tass' eva lokuttarassa kusalassa jhânassa katattâ bhâvitattâ vipâkaṃ vivicceva kâmehi . . . pe . . . paṭhamaṃ jhânaṃ upasampajja viharati dukkhâpaṭipadaṃ dandhâbhiññaṃ appaṇihitaṃ chandâdhipateyyaṃ—

tasmiṃ samaye phasso hoti . . . pe . . . avikkhepo hoti . . . pe . . . ime dhammâ avyâkatâ.

541. Katame dhammâ avyâkatâ?

Yasmiṃ samaye lokuttaraṃ jhânaṃ . . . pe . . . pattiyâ vitakkavicârânaṃ vûpasamâ . . . pe . . . dutiyaṃ jhânaṃ . . . pe . . . tatiyaṃ jhânaṃ . . . pe . . . catutthaṃ jhânaṃ . . . pe . . . paṭhamaṃ jhânaṃ . . . pe . . . pañcamaṃ jhânaṃ upasampajja viharati dukkhâpaṭipadaṃ dandhâbhiññaṃ suññataṃ chandâdhipateyyan ti kusalaṃ . . . pe . . . dukkhâpaṭipadaṃ dandhâbhiññaṃ suññataṃ chandâdhipateyyan ti vipâko . . . pe . . . dukkhâpaṭipadaṃ dandhâbhiññaṃ suññataṃ chandâdhipateyyan ti kusalaṃ . . . pe . . . dukkhâpaṭipadaṃ dandhâbhiññaṃ animittaṃ chandâdhipateyyan ti vipâko . . . pe . . . dukkhâpaṭipadaṃ dandhâbhiññaṃ suññataṃ chandâdhipateyyan ti kusalaṃ . . . pe . . . dukkhâpaṭipadaṃ dandhâbhiññaṃ appaṇihitaṃ chandâdhipateyyan ti vipâko—tasmiṃ samaye phasso hoti . . . pe . . . avikkhepo hoti . . . pe . . . ime dhammâ avyâkatâ.

542. Katame dhammâ avyâkatâ?

Yasmiṃ samaye lokuttaraṃ . . . pe . . . pattiyâ vivicceva kâmehi . . . pe . . . paṭhamaṃ jhânaṃ upasampajja viharati dukkhâpaṭipadaṃ khippâbhiññaṃ suññataṃ chandâdhipateyyaṃ . . . pe . . . sukhâpaṭipadaṃ dandhâbhiññaṃ suññataṃ chandâdhipateyyaṃ . . . pe . . . sukhâpaṭipadaṃ khippâbhiññaṃ suññataṃ chandâdhipateyyaṃ . . . pe . . . dutiyaṃ jhânaṃ . . . pe . . . tatiyaṃ jhânaṃ . . . pe . . . catutthaṃ jhânaṃ . . . pe . . . paṭhamaṃ jhânaṃ . . . pe . . . pañcamaṃ jhânaṃ upasampajja viharati sukhâpaṭipadaṃ khippâbhiññaṃ suññataṃ chandâdhipateyyan ti kusalaṃ . . . pe sukhâpaṭipadaṃ khippâbhiññaṃ suññataṃ chandâdhipateyyan ti vipâko . , . pe . . . sukhâpaṭipadaṃ khippâbhiññaṃ suññataṃ chandâdhipateyyan ti kusalaṃ . . . pe . . . sukhâpaṭipadaṃ khippâbhiññaṃ animittaṃ chandâdhipateyyan ti vipâko . . . pe . . . sukhâpaṭipadaṃ khippâbhiññaṃ suññataṃ chandâdhipateyyan ti kusalaṃ . . . pe . . . sukhâpaṭipadaṃ khippâbhiññaṃ appaṇihitaṃ chandâdhipateyyan ti vipâko—tasmiṃ samaye phasso hoti . . . pe . . . avikkhepo hoti . . . pe . . . ime dhammâ avyâkatâ.

543. Katame dhammâ avyâkatâ?

Yasmiṃ samaye lokuttaraṃ . . . pe . . . pattiyâ vivicceva kâmehi . . . pe . . . paṭhamaṃ jhânaṃ upasampajja viharati appaṇihitaṃ chandâdhipateyyaṃ—tasmiṃ samaye phasso hoti . . . pe . . . avikkhepo hoti . . . pe . . . ime dhammâ kusalâ—tass' eva lokuttarassa kusalassa jhânassa katattâ bhâvitattâ vipâkaṃ vivicceva kâmehi . . . pe . . . paṭhamaṃ jhânaṃ upasampajja viharati appaṇihitaṃ chandâdhipateyyaṃ: tasmiṃ samaye phasso hoti . . . pe . . . avikkhepo hoti . . . pe . . . ime dhammâ avyâkatâ.

544. Katame dhammâ avyâkatâ?

Yasmiṃ samaye lokuttaraṃ jhânaṃ . . . pe . . . pattiyâ vivicceva kâmehi . . . pe . . . paṭhamaṃ jhânaṃ upasampajja viharati appaṇihitaṃ chandâdhipateyyaṃ: tasmiṃ samaye phasso hoti . . . pe . . . avikkhepo hoti . . . pe . . . ime dhammâ kusalâ: tass' eva lokuttarassa kusalassa jhânassa katattâ bhâvitattâ vipâkaṃ vivicceva kâmehi . . . pe . . . paṭhamaṃ jhânaṃ upasampajja viharati animittaṃ chandâdhipateyyaṃ: tasmiṃ samaye phasso hoti . . . pe . . . avikkhepo hoti . . . pe . . . ime dhammâ avyâkatâ.

545. Katame dhammâ avyâkatâ?

Yasmiṃ samaye lokuttaraṃ . . . pe . . . pattiyâ vivicceva kâmehi . . . pe . . . paṭhamaṃ jhânaṃ upasampajja viharati appaṇihitaṃ chandâdhipateyyaṃ—tasmiṃ samaye phasso hoti . . . pe . . . avikkhepo hoti . . . pe . . . ime dhammâ kusalâ: tass' eva lokuttarassa kusalassa jhânassa katattâ bhâvitattâ vipâkaṃ vivicceva kâmehi . . . pe . . . paṭhamaṃ jhânaṃ upasampajja viharati suññataṃ chandâdhipateyyaṃ—tasmiṃ samaye phasso hoti . . . pe . . . avikkhepo hoti . . . pe . . . ime dhammâ avyâkatâ.

546. Katame dhammâ avyâkatâ?

Yasmiṃ samaye lokuttaraṃ . . . pe . . . pattiyâ vitakka-vicârânaṃ vûpasamâ . . . pe . . . dutiyaṃ jhânaṃ . . . pe . . . tatiyaṃ jhânaṃ . . . pe . . . catutthaṃ jhânaṃ . . . pe . . . paṭhamaṃ jhânaṃ . . . pe . . . pañcamaṃ jhânaṃ upasampajja viharati appaṇihitaṃ chandâdhipateyyan ti kusalaṃ . . . pe . . . appaṇihitaṃ chandâdhipateyyan ti vipâko . . . pe . . . appaṇihitaṃ chandâdhipateyyan ti kusalaṃ . . . pe . . . animittaṃ chandâdhipateyyan ti vipâko . . . pe . . . appaṇihitaṃ chandâdhipateyyan ti kusalaṃ . . . pe . . . suññataṃ chandâdhipateyyan ti vipâko : tasmiṃ samaye phasso hoti . . . pe . . . avikkhepo hoti . . . pe . . . ime dhammâ avyâkatâ.

547. Katame dhammâ avyâkatâ?

Yasmiṃ samaye lokuttaraṃ jhânaṃ . . . pe . . . pattiyâ vivicceva kâmehi . . . pe . . . paṭhamaṃ jhânaṃ upasampajja viharati dukkhâpaṭipadaṃ dandhâbhiññaṃ appaṇihitaṃ chandâdhipateyyaṃ—tasmiṃ samaye phasso hoti . . . pe . . . avikkhepo hoti . . . pe . . . ime dhammâ kusalâ; tass' eva lokuttarassa kusalassa jhânassa katattâ bhâvitattâ vipâkaṃ vivicceva kâmehi . . . pe . . . paṭhamaṃ jhânaṃ upasampajja viharati dukkhâpaṭipadaṃ dandhâbhiññaṃ appaṇihitaṃ chandâdhipateyyaṃ—tasmim samaye phasso hoti . . . pe . . . avikkhepo hoti . . . pe . . . ime dhammâ avyâkatâ.

548. Katame dhammâ avyâkatâ?

Yasmiṃ samaye lokuttaraṃ jhânaṃ . . . pe . . . pattiyâ vivicceva kâmehi . . . pe . . . paṭhamaṃ jhânaṃ upasampajja viharati dukkhâpaṭipadaṃ dandhâbhiññaṃ appaṇihitaṃ chandâdhipateyyaṃ—tasmiṃ samaye phasso hoti . . . pe . . . avikkhepo hoti . . . pe . . . ime dhammâ kusalâ—tass' eva lokuttarassa kusalassa jhânassa katattâ bhâvitattâ vipâkaṃ vivicceva kâmehi . . . pe . . . paṭhamaṃ jhânaṃ upasampajja viharati dukkhâpaṭipadaṃ dandhâbhiññaṃ animittaṃ chandâdhipateyyaṃ—tasmiṃ samaye phasso hoti . . . pe . . . avikkhepo hoti . . . pe . . . ime dhammâ avyâkatâ.

549. Katame dhammâ avyâkatâ?

Yasmiṃ samaye lokuttaraṃ jhânaṃ . . . pe . . . pattiyâ vivicceva kâmehi . . . pe . . . paṭhamaṃ jhânaṃ upasampajja viharati dukkhâpaṭipadaṃ dandhâbhiññaṃ appaṇihitaṃ chandâdhipateyyaṃ—tasmiṃ samaye phasso hoti . . . pe . . . avikkhepo hoti—ime dhammâ kusalâ—tass' eva lokuttarassa kusalassa jhânassa katattâ bhâvitattâ vipâkaṃ vivicceva kâmehi paṭhamaṃ jhânaṃ upasampajja viharati dukkhâpaṭipadaṃ dandhâbhiññaṃ suññataṃ chandâdhipateyyaṃ: tasmiṃ samaye phasso hoti . . . pe . . . avikkhepo hoti . . . pe . . . ime dhammâ avyâkatâ.

550. Katame dhammâ avyâkatâ?

Yasmiṃ samaye lokuttaraṃ jhânaṃ . . . pe . . . pattiyâ vitakkavicârânaṃ vûpasamâ . . . pe . . . dutiyaṃ jhânaṃ . . . pe . . . tatiyaṃ jhânaṃ . . . pe . . . catutthaṃ jhânaṃ . . . pe . . . paṭhamaṃ jhânaṃ . . . pe . . . pañcamaṃ jhânaṃ upasampajja viharati dukkhâpaṭipadaṃ dandhâbhiññaṃ appaṇihitaṃ chandâdhipateyyan ti kusalaṃ . . . pe . . . dukkhâpaṭipadaṃ dandhâbhiññaṃ appaṇihitaṃ chandâdhipateyyan ti vipâko . . . pe . . . dukkhâpaṭipadaṃ dandhâbhiññaṃ appaṇihitaṃ chandâdhipateyyan ti kusalaṃ . . . pe . . . dukkhâpaṭipadaṃ dandhâbhiññaṃ animittaṃ chandâdhipateyyan ti vipâko . . . pe . . . dukkhâpaṭipadaṃ dandhâbhiññaṃ appaṇihitaṃ chandâdhipateyyan ti kusalaṃ . . . pe . . . dukkhâpaṭipadaṃ dandhâbhiññaṃ suññataṃ chandâdhipateyyan ti vipâko: tasmiṃ samaye phasso hoti . . . pe . . . avikkhepo hoti . . . pe . . . ime dhammâ avyâkatâ.

551. Katame dhammâ avyâkatâ?

Yasmiṃ samaye lokuttaraṃ jhânaṃ bhâveti . . . pe . . . pattiyâ vivicceva kâmehi . . . pe . . . paṭhamaṃ jhânaṃ upasampajja viharati dukkhâpaṭipadaṃ khippâbiññaṃ appaṇihitaṃ chandâdhipateyyaṃ . . . pe . . . sukhâpaṭipadaṃ dandhâbhiññaṃ appaṇihitaṃ chandâdhipateyyaṃ . . . pe . . . sukhâpaṭipadaṃ khippâbhiññaṃ appaṇihitaṃ chandâdhipateyyaṃ . . . pe . . . dutiyaṃ jhânaṃ . . . pe . . . tatiyaṃ jhânaṃ . . . pe . . . catutthaṃ jhânaṃ . . . pe . . . paṭhamaṃ jhânaṃ . . . pe . . . pañcamaṃ jhânaṃ upasampajja viharati sukhâpaṭipadaṃ khippâbhiññaṃ appaṇihitaṃ chandâdhipateyyan ti kusalaṃ . . . pe . . . sukhâpaṭipadaṃ khippâbhiññaṃ appaṇihitaṃ chandâdhipateyyan ti vipâko . . . pe . . . sukhâpaṭipadaṃ khippâbhiññaṃ appaṇihitaṃ chandâdhipateyyan ti kusalaṃ . . . pe . . . sukhâpaṭipadaṃ khippâbhiññaṃ animittaṃ chandâdhipateyyan ti vipâko . . . pe . . . sukhâpaṭipadaṃ khippâbhiññaṃ appaṇihitaṃ chandâdhipateyyan ti kusalaṃ . . . pe . . . sukhâpaṭipadaṃ khippâbhiññaṃ suññataṃ chandâdhipateyyan ti vipâko—tasmiṃ samaye phasso hoti . .

pe . . . avikkhepo hoti . . . pe . . . ime dhammâ avyâkatâ.

552. Katame dhammâ avyâkatâ?

Yasmiṃ samaye lokuttaraṃ maggaṃ bhâveti . . . pe . . . lokuttaraṃ satipaṭṭhânaṃ bhâveti . . . pe . . . lokuttaraṃ sammappadhânaṃ bhâveti . . . pe . . . lokuttaraṃ iddhipâdaṃ bhâveti . . . pe . . . lokuttaraṃ indriyaṃ bhâveti . . . pe . . . lokuttaraṃ balaṃ bhâveti . . . pe . . . lokuttaraṃ bojjhaṅgaṃ bhâveti . . . pe . . . lokuttaraṃ saccaṃ bhâveti . . . pe . . . lokuttaraṃ samathaṃ bhâveti . . . pe . . . lokuttaraṃ dhammaṃ bhâveti . . . pe . . . lokuttaraṃ khandhaṃ bhâveti . . . pe . . . lokuttaraṃ âyatanaṃ bhâveti . . . pe . . . lokuttaraṃ dhâtum bhâveti . . . pe . . . lokuttaraṃ âhâraṃ bhâveti . . . pe . . . lokuttaraṃ phassaṃ bhâveti . . . pe . . . lokuttaraṃ vedanaṃ bhâveti . . . pe . . . lokuttaraṃ saññaṃ bhâveti . . . pe . . . lokuttaraṃ cetanaṃ bhâveti . . . pe . . . lokuttaraṃ cittaṃ bhâveti niyyânikaṃ apacayagâmiṃ diṭṭhigatânaṃ pahânâya paṭhamâya bhummiyâpattiyâ vivicceva kâmehi . . . pe . . . paṭhamaṃ jhânaṃ upasampajja viharati dukkhâpaṭipadaṃ dandhâbhiññaṃ chandâdhipateyyaṃ—tasmiṃ samaye phasso hoti . . . pe . . . avikkhepo hoti . . . pe . . . ime dhammâ kusalâ—tass' eva lokuttarassa kusalassa jhânassa katattâ bhâvitattâ vipâkaṃ vivicceva kâmehi . . . pe . . . paṭhamaṃ jhânaṃ upasampajja viharati dukkhâpaṭipadaṃ dandhâbhiññaṃ suññataṃ . . . pe . . . animittaṃ . . . pe . . . appaṇihitaṃ chandâdhipateyyaṃ . . . pe . . . viriyâdhipateyyaṃ . . . pe . . . cittâdhipateyyaṃ . . . pe . . . vimaṃsâdhipateyyaṃ—tasmiṃ samaye phasso hoti . . . pe . . . avikkhepo hoti . . . pe . . . ime dhammâ avyâkatâ.

Paṭhamamaggavipâko.

553. Katame dhammâ avyâkatâ?

Yasmiṃ samaye lokuttaraṃ jhânaṃ bhâveti niyyânikaṃ apacayagâmiṃ kâmarâgavyâpâdânaṃ patanubhâvâya dutiyâya bhummiyâpattiyâ vivicceva kâmehi . . . pe . . . vimaṃsâdhipateyyaṃ : tasmiṃ samaye phasso hoti . . . pe . . . kâmarâgavyâpâdânaṃ anavasesappahânâya tatiyâya bhummiyâpattiyâ . . . pe . . . rûparâga-arûparâgamâna-uddhacca-avijjâya anavasesappahânâya catutthâya bhummiyâpattiyâ viviceeva kâmehi . . . pe . . . paṭhamaṃ jhânaṃ upasampajja viharati dukkhâpaṭipadaṃ dandhâbhiññaṃ tasmiṃ samaye phasso hoti . . . pe . . . aññindriyaṃ hoti . . . pe . . . avikkhepo hoti . . . pe . . . ime dhammâ avyâkatâ—tass' eva lokuttarassa kusalassa jhânassa katattâ bhâvitattâ vipâkaṃ viviceeva kâmehi . . . pe . . . paṭhamaṃ jhânaṃ upasampajja viharati dukkhâpaṭipadaṃ dandhâbhiññaṃ suññataṃ — tasmiṃ samaye phasso hoti . . . pe . . . aññâtâvindriyaṃ hoti . . . pe . . . avikkhepo hoti . . . pe . . . ye vâ pana tasmiṃ samaye aññe pi atthi paṭiccasamuppannâ arûpino dhammâ—ime dhammâ avyâkatâ.

554. Katamo tasmiṃ samaye phasso hoti?

Yo tasmiṃ samaye phasso phusanâ samphusanâ samphusitattaṃ—ayaṃ tasmiṃ samaye phasso hoti . . . pe . . .

555. Katamaṃ tasmiṃ samaye aññâtâvindriyaṃ hoti?

Yâ tesaṃ aññâtâvînaṃ dhammânaṃ aññâ paññâ pajânanâ vicayo pavicayo dhammavicayo sallakkhaṇâ upalakkhaṇâ paccupalakkhaṇâ paṇḍiccaṃ kosallaṃ nepuññaṃ vebhavyâ cintâ upaparikkhâ bhûrî medhâ pariṇâyikâ vipassanâ sampajaññaṃ patodo paññâ paññindriyaṃ paññâbalaṃ paññâsatthaṃ paññâpâsâdo paññâ-âloko paññâ-obhâso paññâpajjoto paññâratanaṃ amoho dhammavicayo sammâdiṭṭhi dhammavicayasambojjhaṅgo maggaṅgaṃ maggapariyâpannaṃ, idaṃ tasmiṃ samaye aññâtâvindriyaṃ hoti . . . pe . . . avikkhepo hoti . . . pe . . . ye vâ pana tasmiṃ samaye aññe pi atthi paṭiccasamuppannâ arûpino dhammâ—ime dhammâ avyâkatâ.

Lokuttaravipâko.

556. Katame dhammâ avyâkatâ?

Yasmiṃ samaye akusalassa kammassa katattâ upacitattâ vipâkaṃ cakkhuviññâṇaṃ uppannaṃ hoti upekkhâsahagataṃ rûpârammaṇaṃ . . . pe . . . sotaviññâṇaṃ uppannaṃ hoti upekkhâsahagataṃ saddârammaṇaṃ . . . pe . . . ghânaviññâṇaṃ uppannaṃ hoti upekkhâsahagataṃ gandhârammaṇaṃ . . . pe . . . jivhâviññâṇaṃ uppannaṃ hoti upekkhâsahagataṃ rasârammaṇaṃ . . . pe . . . kâyaviññâṇaṃ uppannaṃ hoti dukkhâsahagataṃ phoṭṭhabbârammaṇaṃ—tasmiṃ samaye phasso hoti vedanâ hoti saññâ hoti cetanâ hoti cittaṃ hoti dukkhaṃ hoti cittass' ekaggatâ hoti manindriyaṃ hoti, dukkhindriyaṃ hoti jîvitindriyaṃ hoti . . . pe . . . ye vâ pana tasmiṃ samaye aññe pi atthi paṭiccasamuppannâ arûpino dhammâ—ime dhammâ avyâkatâ.

557. Katamo tasmiṃ samaye phasso hoti?

Yo tasmiṃ samaye phasso . . . pe . . . ayaṃ tasmiṃ samaye phasso hoti.

558. Katamâ tasmiṃ samaye vedanâ hoti?

Yaṃ tasmiṃ samaye tajjâ kâyaviññâṇadhâtu samphassajaṃ kâyikaṃ asâtaṃ kâyikaṃ dukkhaṃ kâyasamphassajaṃ asâtaṃ dukkhaṃ vedayitaṃ kâyasamphassajâ asâtâ dukkhâ vedanâ—ayaṃ tasmiṃ samaye vedanâ hoti.

559. Katamaṃ tasmiṃ samaye dukkhaṃ hoti?

Yaṃ tasmiṃ samaye kâyikaṃ asâtaṃ kâyikaṃ dukkhaṃ kâyasamphassajaṃ asâtaṃ dukkhaṃ vedayitaṃ kâyasamphassajâ asâtâ dukkhâ vedanâ—idaṃ tasmiṃ samaye dukkhaṃ hoti.

560. Katamaṃ tasmiṃ samaye dukkhindriyaṃ hoti?

Yaṃ tasmiṃ samaye kâyikaṃ . . . pe . . . dukkhâ vedanâ —idaṃ tasmiṃ samaye dukkhindriyaṃ hoti . . . pe . . . ye vâ pana tasmiṃ samaye aññe pi atthi paṭiccasamuppannâ arûpino dhammâ—ime dhammâ avyâkatâ.

Tasmiṃ kho pana samaye cattâro khandhâ honti, dvâyatanâni honti, dve dhâtuyo honti, tayo âhârâ honti, tîṇindriyâni honti, eko phasso hoti . . . pe . . . ekâ manoviññânadhâtu hoti, ekaṃ dhammâyatanaṃ hoti, ekâ dhammadhâtu hoti—ye vâ pana tasmiṃ samaye aññe pi atthi paṭiccasamuppannâ arûpino dhammâ—ime dhammâ avyâkatâ . . . pe . . .

561. Katamo tasmiṃ samaye saṅkhârakkhandho hoti?

Phasso, cetanâ vitakko vicâro cittass' ekaggatâ, jîvitindriyaṃ; ye vâ pana tasmiṃ samaye aññe pi atthi paṭiccasamuppannâ arûpino dhammâ—ṭhapetvâ vedanâkkhandhaṃ, ṭhapetvâ saññâkkhandaṃ, ṭhapetvâ viññâṇakkhandhaṃ—

ayaṃ tasmiṃ samaye saṅkhârakkhandho hoti . . . pe . . . ime dhammâ avyâkatâ . . . pe . . .

562. Katame dhammâ avyâkatâ?

Yasmiṃ samaye akusalassa kammassa katattâ upacitattâ vipâkâ manodhâtu uppannâ hoti upekkhâsahagatâ rûpârammaṇâ vâ . . . pe . . . phoṭṭhabbârammaṇâ vâ—yaṃ yaṃ vâ panârabbha—tasmiṃ samaye phasso hoti, vedanâ hoti, saññâ hoti, cetanâ hoti, cittaṃ hoti, vitakko hoti, vicâro hoti, upekkhâ hoti, cittass' ekaggatâ hoti, manindriyaṃ hoti, upekkhindriyaṃ hoti, jîvitindriyaṃ hoti; ye vâ pana tasmiṃ samaye aññe pi atthi paṭiccasamuppannâ arûpino dhammâ—ime dhammâ avyâkatâ . . . pe . . .

Tasmiṃ kho pana samaye cattâro khandhâ honti, dvâyatanâni honti, dve dhâtuyo honti, tayo âhârâ honti, tîṇindriyâni honti, eko phasso hoti . . . pe . . . ekâ manodhâtu hoti, ekaṃ dhammâyatanaṃ hoti, ekâ dhammadhâtu hoti —ye vâ pana tasmiṃ samaye aññe pi atthi paṭiccasamuppannâ arûpino dhammâ—ime dhammâ avyâkatâ . . . pe . . .

563. Katamo tasmiṃ samaye saṅkhârakkhandho hoti?

Phasso cetanâ vitakko vicâro cittass' ekaggatâ jîvitindriyaṃ—ye vâ pana tasmiṃ samaye aññe pi atthi paṭiccasamuppannâ arûpino dhammâ—ṭhapetvâ vedanâkkhandhaṃ ṭhapetvâ saññâkkhandhaṃ ṭhapetvâ viññâṇakkhandhaṃ—ayaṃ tasmiṃ samaye saṅkhârakkhandho hoti . . . pe . . . ime dhammâ avyâkatâ.

564. Katame dhammâ avyâkatâ?

Yasmiṃ samaye akusalassa kammassa katattâ upacitattâ vipâkâ manoviññâṇadhâtu uppannâ hoti upekkhâsahagatâ rûpârammaṇâ vâ . . . pe . . . dhammârammaṇâ vâ—yaṃ yaṃ vâ panârabbha—tasmiṃ samaye phasso hoti, vedanâ hoti, saññâ hoti, cetanâ hoti, cittaṃ hoti, vitakko hoti, vicâro hoti, upekkhâ hoti, cittass' ekaggatâ hoti, manindriyaṃ hoti, upekkhindriyaṃ hoti, jîvitindriyaṃ hoti, ye vâ pana tasmiṃ samaye aññe pi atthi paṭiccasamuppannâ arûpino dhammâ—ime dhammâ avyâkatâ . . . pe . . .

Tasmiṃ kho pana samaye cattâro khandhâ honti, dvâyatanâni honti, dve dhâtuyo honti, tayo âhârâ honti, tîṇindriyâni honti, eko phasso hoti . . . pe . . . ekâ manoviññâṇadhâtu hoti, ekaṃ dhammâyatanaṃ hoti, ekâ dhammadhâtu hoti—ye vâ pana tasmiṃ samaye aññe pi atthi paṭiccasamuppannâ arûpino dhammâ—ime dhammâ avyâkatâ . . . pe . . .

565. Katamo tasmiṃ samaye saṅkhârakkhandho hoti?

Phasso cetanâ vitakko vicâro cittass' ekaggatâ jîvitindriyaṃ—ye vâ pana tasmiṃ samaye aññe pi atthi paṭiccasamuppannâ arûpino dhammâ—ṭhapetvâ vedanâkkhandhaṃ, ṭhapetvâ saññâkkhandhaṃ ṭhapetvâ viññâṇakkhandhaṃ—ayaṃ tasmiṃ samaye saṅkhârakkhandho hoti . . . pe . . . ime dhammâ avyâkatâ.

Akusalavipâkâ avyâkatâ.

566. Katame dhammâ avyâkatâ?

Yasmiṃ samaye manodhâtu uppannâ hoti kiriyâ neva kusalâ nâkusalâ na ca kammavipâkâ upekkhâsahagatâ rûpârammaṇâ vâ . . . pe . . . phoṭṭhabbârammaṇâ vâ—yaṃ yaṃ vâ panârabbha—tasmiṃ samaye phasso hoti, vedanâ hoti, saññâ hoti, cetanâ hoti, cittaṃ hoti, vitakko hoti, vicâro hoti, upekkhâ hoti, cittass' ekaggatâ hoti, manindriyaṃ hoti, upekkhindriyaṃ hoti, jîvitindriyaṃ hoti, ye vâ pana tasmiṃ samaye aññe pi atthi paṭiccasamuppannâ arûpino dhammâ—ime dhammâ avyâkatâ . . . pe . . . tasmiṃ kho pana samaye cattâro khandhâ honti, dvâyatanâni honti, dve dhâtuyo honti, tayo âhârâ honti, tîṇindriyâni honti, eko phasso hoti . . . pe . . . ekâ manodhâtu hoti, ekaṃ dhammâyatanaṃ hoti, ekâ dhammadhâtu hoti, ye vâ pana tasmiṃ samaye aññe pi atthi paṭiccasamuppannâ arûpino dhammâ—ime dhammâ avyâkatâ.

567. Katamo tasmiṃ samaye saṅkhârakkhando hoti?

Phasso cetanâ vitakko vicâro cittass' ekaggatâ jîvitindriyaṃ—ye vâ pana tasmiṃ samaye aññe pi atthi paṭiccasamuppannâ arûpino dhammâ—ṭhapetvâ vedanâkkhandhaṃ ṭhapetvâ saññâkkhandhaṃ ṭhapetvâ viññâṇakkhandhaṃ—ayaṃ tasmiṃ samaye saṅkhârakkhandho hoti . . . pe . . . ime dhammâ avyâkatâ.

568. Katame dhammâ avyâkatâ?

Yasmiṃ samaye manoviññâṇadhâtu uppannâ hoti kiriyâ

neva kusalâ nâkusalâ na ca kammavipâkâ somanassasahagatâ rûpârammaṇâ vâ . . . pe . . . dhammârammaṇâ vâ—yaṃ yaṃ vâ panârabbha—tasmiṃ samaye phasso hoti, vedanâ hoti, saññâ hoti, cetanâ hoti, cittaṃ hoti, vitakko hoti, vicâro hoti, pîti hoti, sukhaṃ hoti, cittass' ekaggatâ hoti, viriyindriyaṃ hoti, samâdhindriyaṃ hoti, manindriyaṃ hoti, somanassindriyaṃ hoti, jîvitindriyaṃ hoti, yo vâ pana tasmiṃ samaye añño pi atthi paṭiccasamuppannâ arûpino dhammâ—ime dhammâ avyâkatâ.

569. Katamo tasmiṃ samaye phasso hoti?

Yo tasmiṃ samaye phasso phusanâ samphusanâ samphusitattaṃ—ayaṃ tasmiṃ samaye phasso hoti . . . pe . . .

570. Katamâ tasmiṃ samaye cittass' ekaggatâ hoti?

Yâ tasmiṃ samaye cittassa ṭhiti saṇṭhiti avaṭhiti avisâhâro avikkhepo avisâhaṭamanasatâ samatho samâdhindriyaṃ samâdhibalaṃ — ayaṃ tasmiṃ samaye cittass' ekaggatâ hoti.

571. Katamaṃ tasmiṃ samaye viriyindriyaṃ hoti?

Yo tasmiṃ samaye cetasiko viriyârambho nikkamo parakkamo uyyâmo vâyâmo ussâho ussoḷhi thâmo dhiti asithilaparakkamatâ anikkhittachandatâ anikkhittadhuratâ dhurasampaggâho viriyaṃ viriyindriyaṃ viriyabalaṃ—idaṃ tasmiṃ samaye viriyindriyaṃ hoti.

572. Katamaṃ tasmiṃ samaye samâdhindriyaṃ hoti?

Yâ tasmiṃ samaye cittassa ṭhiti . . . pe . . . samâdhibalaṃ—idaṃ tasmiṃ samaye samâdhindriyaṃ hoti . . . pe . . . yo vâ pana tasmiṃ samaye añño pi atthi paṭiccasamuppannâ arûpino dhammâ—ime dhammâ avyâkatâ.

Tasmiṃ kho pana samaye cattâro khandhâ honti, dvâyatanâni honti, dve dhâtuyo honti, tayo âhârâ honti, pañcindriyâni honti, eko phasso hoti . . . pe . . . ekâ manoviññâṇadhâtu hoti, ekaṃ dhammâyatanaṃ hoti, ekâ dhammadhâtu hoti; yo vâ pana tasmiṃ samaye añño pi atthi paṭiccasamuppannâ arûpino dhammâ—ime dhammâ avyâkatâ.

573. Katamo tasmiṃ samaye saṅkhârakkhandho hoti?

Phasso cetanâ vitakko vicâro pîti cittass' ekaggatâ viriyindriyaṃ samâdhindriyaṃ jîvitindriyaṃ—ye vâ pana tasmiṃ samaye añño pi atthi paṭiccasamuppannâ arûpino dhammâ—

ṭhapetvâ vedanâkkhandhaṃ ṭhapetvâ saññâkkhandhaṃ ṭhapetvâ viññâṇakkhandhaṃ—ayaṃ tasmiṃ samaye saṅkhârakkhandho hoti . . . pe . . . ime dhammâ avyâkatâ.

574. Katame dhammâ avyâkatâ?

Yasmiṃ samaye manoviññâṇadhâtu uppannâ hoti kiriyâ neva kusalâ nâkusalâ na ca kammavipâkâ upekkhâsahagatâ rûpârammaṇâ vâ . . . pe . . . dhammârammaṇâ vâ—yaṃ yaṃ vâ panârabbha—tasmiṃ samaye phasso hoti vedanâ hoti, saññâ hoti, cetanâ hoti, cittaṃ hoti, vitakko hoti, vicâro hoti, upekkhâ hoti, cittass' ekaggatâ hoti, viriyindriyaṃ hoti, samâdhindriyaṃ hoti, manindriyaṃ hoti, upekkhindriyaṃ hoti, jîvitindriyaṃ hoti—ye vâ pana tasmiṃ samaye aññe pi atthi paṭiccasamuppannâ arûpino dhammâ—ime dhammâ avyâkatâ . . . pe . . . Tasmiṃ kho pana samaye cattâro khandhâ honti, dvâyatanâni honti, dve dhâtuyo honti, tayo âhârâ honti, pañcindriyâni honti, eko phasso hoti . . : pe . . . ekâ manoviññâṇadhâtu hoti, ekaṃ dhammâyatanaṃ hoti, ekâ dhammadhâtu hoti; ye vâ pana tasmiṃ samaye aññe pi atthi paṭiccasamuppannâ arûpino dhammâ—ime dhammâ avyâkatâ . . . pe . . .

575. Katamo tasmiṃ samaye saṅkhârakkhandho hoti?

Phassò cetanâ vitakko vicâro cittass' ekaggatâ viriyindriyaṃ samâdhindriyaṃ jîvitindriyaṃ—ye vâ pana tasmiṃ samaye aññe pi atthi paṭiccasamuppannâ arûpino dhammâ—ṭhapetvâ vedanâkkhandhaṃ ṭhapetvâ saññâkkhandhaṃ ṭhapetvâ viññâṇakkhandhaṃ—ayaṃ tasmiṃ samaye saṅkhârakkhandho hoti . . . pe . . . ime dhammâ avyâkatâ.

576. Katame dhammâ avyâkatâ?

Yasmiṃ samaye manoviññâṇadhâtu uppannâ hoti kiriyâ neva kusalâ nâkusalâ na ca kammavipâkâ somanassasahagatâ ñâṇasampayuttâ . . . pe . . . somanassasahagatâ ñâṇasampayuttâ sasaṅkhârena . . . pe . . . somanassasahagatâ ñâṇavippayuttâ . . . pe . . . somanassasahagatâ nâṇavippayuttâ sasaṅkhârena . . . pe . . . upekkhâsahagatâ ñâṇasampayuttâ . . . pe . . . upekkhâsahagatâ ñâṇasampayuttâ sasaṅkhârena . . . pe . . . upekkhâsahagatâ ñâṇavippayuttâ . . . pe . . . upekkhâsahagatâ ñâṇavippayuttâ sasaṅkhârena rûpârammaṇâ vâ . . . pe . . . dhammârammaṇâ vâ—yaṃ yaṃ vâ panârabbha—tasmiṃ samaye phasso hoti . . . pe . . . avikkhepo hoti . . . pe . . . ime dhammâ avyâkatâ . . . pe . . .

Alobho avyâkatamûlaṃ . . . pe . . . adoso avyâkatamûlaṃ . . . pe . . . amoho avyâkatamûlaṃ . . . pe . . . ime dhammâ avyâkatâ.

Kâmâvacarakiriyâ.

577. Katame dhammâ avyâkatâ?

Yasmiṃ samaye rûpâvacaraṃ jhânaṃ bhâveti kiriyaṃ neva kusalaṃ nâkusalaṃ na ca kammavipâkaṃ diṭṭhidhammasukhavihâraṃ vivicceva kâmehi . . . pe . . . paṭhamaṃ jhânaṃ upasampajja viharati pathavîkasiṇaṃ—tasmiṃ samaye phasso hoti . . . pe . . . avikkhepo hoti . . . pe . . . ime dhammâ avyâkatâ.

578. Katame dhammâ avyâkatâ?

Yasmiṃ samaye rûpâvacaraṃ jhânaṃ bhâveti kiriyaṃ neva kusalaṃ nâkusalaṃ na ca kammavipâkaṃ diṭṭhidhammasukhavihâraṃ vitakkavicârâṇaṃ vûpasamâ . . . pe . . . dutiyaṃ jhânaṃ . . . pe . . . tatiyaṃ jhânaṃ. . . pe . . . catutthaṃ jhânaṃ . . . pe . . . paṭhamaṃ jhânaṃ . . . pe . . . pañcamaṃ jhânaṃ upasampajja viharati pathavîkasiṇaṃ—tasmiṃ samaye phasso hoti . . . pe . . . avikkhepo hoti . . . pe . . . ime dhammâ avyâkatâ.

Rûpâvacarakiriyâ.

579. Katame dhammâ avyâkatâ?

Yasmiṃ samaye arûpâvacaraṃ jhânaṃ bhâveti kiriyaṃ neva kusalaṃ nâkusalaṃ na ca kammavipâkaṃ diṭṭhidhammasukhavihâraṃ sabbaso rûpasaññânaṃ samatikkamâ paṭighasaññânaṃ atthaṅgamânânattasaññânaṃ amanasikârâ âkâsânañcâyatanasaññâsahagataṃ sukhassa ca pahânâ . . . pe . . . catutthaṃ jhânaṃ upasampajja viharati—tasmiṃ samaye phasso hoti . . . pe . . . avikkhepo hoti . . . pe . . . ime dhammâ avyâkatâ.

580. Katame dhammâ avyâkatâ?

Yasmiṃ samaye arûpâvacaraṃ jhânaṃ bhâveti kiriyaṃ

neva kusalaṃ nâkusalaṃ na ca kammavipâkaṃ diṭṭhidhammasukhavihâraṃ sabbaso âkâsânañcâyatanaṃ samatikkamâ viññâṇañcâyatanasaññâsahagataṃ sukhassa ca pahânâ . . . pe . . . catutthaṃ jhânaṃ upasampajja viharati—tasmiṃ samaye phasso hoti . . . pe . . . avikkhepo hoti ime dhammâ avyâkatâ.

581. Katame dhammâ avyâkatâ?

Yasmiṃ samaye arûpâvacaraṃ jhânaṃ bhâveti kiriyaṃ neva kusalaṃ nâkusalaṃ na ca kammavipâkaṃ diṭṭhidhammasukhavihâraṃ sabbaso viññâṇañcâyatanaṃ samatikkamâ âkiñcaññâyatanasaññâsahagataṃ sukhassa ca pahânâ . . . pe . . . catutthaṃ jhânaṃ upasampajja viharati—tasmiṃ samaye phasso hoti . . . pe . . . avikkhepo hoti . . . pe . . . ime dhammâ avyâkatâ.

582. Katame dhammâ avyâkatâ?

Yasmiṃ samaye arûpâvacaraṃ . . . pe . . . sabbaso âkiñcaññâyatanaṃ samatikkamâ neva saññânâsaññâyatanasaññâsahagataṃ sukhassa ca pahânâ . . . pe . . . catutthaṃ jhânaṃ upasampajja viharati—tasmiṃ samaye phasso hoti . . . pe . . . avikkhepo hoti . . . pe . . . ime dhammâ avyâkatâ . . . pe . . . alobho avyâkatamûlaṃ . . . pe . . . adoso avyâkatamûlaṃ . . . pe . . . amoho avyâkatamûlaṃ . . . pe . . . ime dhammâ avyâkatâ.

Arûpâvacarakiriyâ.

CITTUPPÂDAKAṆḌAṂ.

583. Katame dhammâ avyâkatâ?

Kusalâkusalânaṃ dhammânaṃ vipâkâ kâmâvacarâ, rûpâvacarâ, arûpâvacarâ apariyâpannâ vedanâkkhandho saññâkkhandho saṅkhârakkhandho viññâṇakkhandho ye ca dhammâ kiriyâ neva kusalâ nâkusalâ na ca kammavipâkâ sabbañ ca rûpaṃ asaṅkhatâ ca dhâtu—ime dhammâ avyâkatâ.

584. Tattha katamaṃ sabbaṃ rûpaṃ?

Cattâro ca mahâbhûtâ catunnañ ca mahâbhûtânaṃ upâdâya rûpaṃ—idaṃ vuccati sabbaṃ rûpaṃ.

Sabbaṃ rûpaṃ na hetu ahetukaṃ hetuvippayuttaṃ

sappaccayaṃ saṅkhataṃ rûpiyaṃ lokiyaṃ sâsavaṃ saṃyojaniyaṃ ganthaniyaṃ oghaniyaṃ yoganiyaṃ nivaraṇiyaṃ parâmaṭṭhaṃ upâdâniyaṃ saṅkilesikaṃ avyâkataṃ anârammaṇaṃ acetasikaṃ cittavippayuttaṃ neva vipâkanavipâkadhammadhammaṃ asaṅkiliṭṭhasaṅkilesikaṃ na savitakkasavicâraṃ na avitakkavicâramattaṃ avitakka-avicâraṃ na pîtisahagataṃ na sukhasahagataṃ na upekkhâsahagataṃ neva dassanena na bhâvanâya pahâtabbaṃ neva dassanena na bhâvanâya pahâtabbahetukaṃ neva âcayagâmiṃ na apacayagâmiṃ neva sekkhaṃ nâsekkhaṃ parittaṃ kâmâvacaraṃ na rûpâvacaraṃ na arûpâvacaraṃ pariyâpannaṃ na apariyâpannaṃ aniyataṃ aniyyânikaṃ uppannaṃ chahi viññâṇehi viññeyyaṃ aniccaṃ jarâbhibhûtaṃ evaṃ ekavidhena rûpasaṅgaho.

Ekakaṃ.

585. Duvidhena rûpasaṅgaho: atthi rûpaṃ upâdâ, atthi rûpaṃ no upâdâ, atthi rûpaṃ upâdiṇṇaṃ, atthi rûpaṃ anupâdiṇṇaṃ, atthi rûpaṃ upâdiṇṇupâdâniyaṃ, atthi rûpaṃ anupâdiṇṇupâdâniyaṃ, atthi rûpaṃ sanidassanaṃ, atthi rûpaṃ anidassanaṃ atthi rûpaṃ sappaṭighaṃ, atthi rûpaṃ appaṭighaṃ, atthi rûpaṃ indriyaṃ, atthi rûpaṃ na indriyaṃ, atthi rûpaṃ mahâbhûtaṃ atthi rûpaṃ na mahâbhûtaṃ, atthi rûpaṃ viññatti, atthi rûpaṃ na viññatti, atthi rûpaṃ cittasamuṭṭhânaṃ, atthi rûpaṃ na cittasamuṭṭhânaṃ, atthi rûpaṃ cittasahabhû, atthi rûpaṃ na cittasahabhû, atthi rûpaṃ cittânuparivatti, atthi rûpaṃ na cittânuparivatti, atthi rûpaṃ ajjhatikaṃ, atthi rûpaṃ bâhiraṃ, atthi rûpaṃ oḷârikaṃ, atthi rûpaṃ sukhumaṃ, atthi rûpaṃ dûre, atthi rûpaṃ santike, atthi rûpaṃ cakkhusamphassassa vatthu, atthi rûpaṃ cakkhusamphassassa na vatthu, atthi rûpaṃ cakkhusamphassajâya vedanâya . . . pe . . . saññâya . . . pe . . . cetanâya . . . pe . . . cakkhuviññâṇassa vatthu, atthi rûpaṃ cakkhuviññâṇassa na vatthu, atthi rûpaṃ sotasamphassassa . . . pe . . . ghânasamphassassa . . . pe . . . jivhâsamphassassa . . . pe . . . kâyasamphassassa vatthu, atthi rûpaṃ kâyasamphassassa na vatthu, atthi rûpaṃ kâyasamphassajâya vedanâya . . . pe . . . saññâya . . . pe . . .

cetanâya . . . pe . . . kâyaviññâṇassa vatthu, atthi rûpaṃ kâyaviññâṇassa na vatthu, atthi rûpaṃ cakkhusamphassassa ârammaṇaṃ, atthi rûpaṃ cakkhusamphassassa nârammaṇaṃ, atthi rûpaṃ cakkhusamphassajâya vedanâya . . . pe . . . saññâya . . . pe . . . cetanâya . . . pe . . . cakkhuviññâṇassa ârammaṇaṃ, atthi rûpaṃ cakkhuviññâṇassa nârammaṇaṃ, atthi rûpaṃ sotasamphassassa . . . pe . . . ghânasamphassassa . . . pe . . . jivhâsamphassassa . . . pe . . . kâyasamphassassa ârammaṇaṃ—atthi rûpaṃ kâyasamphassassa nârammaṇaṃ, atthi rûpaṃ kâyasamphassajâya vedanâya . . . pe . . . saññâya . . . pe . . . cetanâya . . . pe . . . kâyaviññâṇassa ârammaṇaṃ—atthi rûpaṃ kâyaviññâṇassa nârammaṇaṃ, atthi rûpaṃ cakkhâyatanaṃ atthi rûpaṃ na cakkhâyatanaṃ, atthi rûpaṃ sotâyatanaṃ . . . pe . . . ghânâyatanaṃ . . . pe . . . jivhâyatanaṃ . . . pe . . . kâyâyatanaṃ, atthi rûpaṃ kâyâyatanaṃ, atthi rûpaṃ rûpâyatanaṃ, atthi rûpaṃ na rûpâyatanaṃ, atthi rûpaṃ saddâyatanaṃ . . . pe . . . gandhâyatanaṃ . . . pe . . . rasâyatanaṃ . . . pe . . . phoṭṭhabbâyatanaṃ atthi rûpaṃ na phoṭṭhabbâyatanaṃ, atthi rûpaṃ cakkhudhâtu, atthi rûpaṃ na cakkhudhâtu, atthi rûpaṃ sotadhâtu . . . pe . . . ghânadhâtu . . . pe . . . jivhâdhâtu . . . pe . . . kâyadhâtu, atthi rûpaṃ na kâyadhâtu atthi rûpaṃ rûpadhâtu atthi rûpaṃ na rûpadhâtu atthi rûpaṃ saddadhâtu . . . pe . . . gandhadhâtu . . . pe . . . rasadhâtu . . . pe . . . phoṭṭhabbadhâtu . . . pe . . . atthi rûpaṃ na phoṭṭhabbadhâtu . . . pe . . . atthi rûpaṃ cakkhundriyaṃ atthi rûpaṃ na cakkhundriyaṃ atthi rûpaṃ sotindriyaṃ . . . pe . . . ghânindriyaṃ . . . pe . . . jivhindriyaṃ . . . pe . . . kâyindriyaṃ atthi rûpaṃ na kâyindriyaṃ atthi rûpaṃ itthindriyaṃ atthi rûpaṃ na itthindriyaṃ atthi rûpaṃ purisindriyaṃ atthi rûpaṃ na purisindriyaṃ atthi rûpaṃ jîvitindriyaṃ atthi rûpaṃ na jîvitindriyaṃ atthi rûpaṃ kâyaviññatti atthi rûpaṃ na kâyaviññatti atthi rûpaṃ vacîviññatti atthi rûpaṃ na vacîviññatti, atthi rûpaṃ âkâsadhâtu, atthi rûpaṃ na âkâsadhâtu, atthi rûpaṃ âpodhâtu, atthi rûpaṃ na âpodhâtu, atthi rûpaṃ rûpassa lahutâ, atthi rûpaṃ na rûpassa lahutâ, atthi rûpaṃ rûpassa mudutâ atthi rûpaṃ rûpassa na mudutâ, atthi rûpaṃ rûpassa kammaññatâ, atthi rûpaṃ rûpassa na kammaññatâ, atthi rûpaṃ rûpassa upacayo, atthi rûpaṃ rûpassa na upacayo, atthi rûpaṃ rûpassa santati atthi rûpaṃ rûpassa na santati, atthi rûpaṃ rûpassa jaratâ, atthi rûpaṃ rûpassa na jaratâ atthi rûpaṃ aniccatâ atthi rûpaṃ na aniccatâ atthi rûpaṃ kabaḷiṅkâro âhâro, atthi rûpaṃ na kabaḷiṅkâro âhâro, evaṃ duvidhena rûpasaṅgaho.

Dukaṃ.

586. Tividhena rûpasaṅgaho?

Yan taṃ rûpaṃ ajjhattikaṃ, taṃ upâdâ, yan taṃ rûpaṃ bâhiraṃ, taṃ atthi upâdâ, atthi nopâdâ, yan taṃ rûpaṃ ajjhattikaṃ, taṃ upâdiṇṇaṃ, yan taṃ rûpaṃ bâhiraṃ taṃ atthi upâdiṇṇaṃ, atthi anupâdiṇṇaṃ, yan taṃ rûpaṃ ajjhattikaṃ tam upâdiṇṇupâdâniyaṃ, yan taṃ rûpaṃ bâhiraṃ, taṃ atthi upâdiṇṇupâdâniyaṃ, atthi anupâdiṇṇupâdâniyaṃ, yan taṃ rûpaṃ ajjhattikaṃ, taṃ anidassanaṃ, yan taṃ rûpaṃ bâhiraṃ, taṃ atthi sanidassanaṃ, atthi anidassanaṃ, yan taṃ rûpaṃ ajjhattikaṃ, taṃ sappaṭighaṃ, yan taṃ rûpaṃ bâhiraṃ, taṃ atthi sappaṭighaṃ, atthi appaṭighaṃ, yan taṃ rûpaṃ ajjhattikaṃ, taṃ indriyaṃ, yan taṃ rûpaṃ bâhiraṃ, taṃ atthi indriyaṃ, atthi na indriyaṃ, yan taṃ rûpaṃ ajjhattikaṃ, taṃ na mahâbhûtaṃ, yan taṃ rûpaṃ bâhiraṃ taṃ atthi mahâbhûtaṃ, atthi na mahâbhûtaṃ, yan taṃ rûpaṃ ajjhattikaṃ, taṃ na viññatti, yan taṃ rûpaṃ bâhiraṃ, taṃ atthi viññatti, atthi na viññatti, yan taṃ rûpaṃ ajjhattikaṃ, taṃ na cittasamuṭṭhânaṃ, yan taṃ rûpaṃ bâhiraṃ, taṃ atthi cittasamuṭṭhânaṃ atthi na cittasamuṭṭhânaṃ, yan taṃ rûpaṃ ajjhattikaṃ, taṃ na cittasahabhû, yan taṃ rûpaṃ bâhiraṃ taṃ atthi cittasahabhû, atthi na cittasahabhû, yan taṃ rûpaṃ ajjhattikaṃ, taṃ na cittânuparivatti, yan taṃ rûpaṃ bâhiraṃ, taṃ atthi cittânuparivatti, atthi na cittânuparivatti, yan taṃ rûpaṃ ajjhattikaṃ, taṃ oḷârikaṃ yan taṃ rûpaṃ bâhiraṃ, taṃ atthi oḷârikaṃ, atthi sukhumaṃ, yan taṃ rûpaṃ ajjhattikaṃ, taṃ santike, yan taṃ rûpaṃ bâhiraṃ, taṃ atthi dûre, atthi santike, yan taṃ rûpaṃ bâhiraṃ, taṃ cakkhusamphassassa na vatthu, yan taṃ rûpaṃ ajjhattikaṃ, taṃ atthi cakkhusamphassassa vatthu, atthi cakkhusamphassassa na vatthu, yan taṃ rûpaṃ bâhiraṃ, taṃ cakkhusamphassajâya vedanâya . . . pe . . . saññâya . . . pe . . . cetanâya . . . pe . . . cakkhuviññâṇassa na vatthu, yan taṃ rûpaṃ ajjhattikaṃ, taṃ atthi cakkhuviññâṇassa vatthu, atthi cakkhuviññâṇassa na vatthu, yan taṃ rûpaṃ bâhiraṃ, taṃ sotasamphassassa . . . pe . . . ghânasamphassassa . . . pe . . . jivhâsamphassassa . . . pe . . . kâyasamphassassa na vatthu, yan taṃ rûpaṃ ajjhattikaṃ, taṃ atthi kâyasamphassassa vatthu, atthi kâyasamphassassa na vatthu, yan taṃ rûpaṃ bâhiraṃ taṃ kâyasamphassajâya vedanâya . . . pe . . . saññâya . . . pe . . . cetanâya . . . pe . . . kâyaviññâṇassa na vatthu, yan taṃ rûpaṃ ajjhattikaṃ, taṃ atthi kâyaviññâṇassa vatthu, atthi kâyaviññâṇassa na vatthu, yan taṃ rûpaṃ ajjhattikaṃ, taṃ cakkhusamphassassa nârammaṇaṃ, yan taṃ rûpaṃ bâhiraṃ, taṃ atthi cakkhusamphassassa ârammaṇaṃ, atthi cakkhusamphassassa nârammaṇaṃ, yan taṃ rûpaṃ ajjhattikaṃ, taṃ cakkhusamphassajâya vedanâya . . . pe . . . saññâya . . . pe . . . cetanâya . . . pe . . . cakkhuviññâṇassa nârammaṇaṃ, yan taṃ rûpaṃ bâhiraṃ, taṃ atthi cakkhuviññâṇassa ârammaṇaṃ atthi cakkhuviññâṇassa nârammaṇaṃ, yan taṃ rûpaṃ ajjhattikaṃ, taṃ sotasamphassassa . . . pe . . . ghâṇasamphassassa . . . pe . . . jivhâsamphassassa . . . pe . . . kâyasamphassassa nârammaṇaṃ, yan taṃ rûpaṃ bâhiraṃ, taṃ atthi kâyasamphassassa ârammaṇaṃ, atthi kâyasamphassassa nârammaṇaṃ, yan taṃ rûpaṃ ajjhattikaṃ taṃ kâyasamphassajâya vedanâya . . . pe . . . saññâya . . . pe . . . cetanâya . . . pe . . . kâyaviññâṇassa nârammaṇam, yan taṃ rûpaṃ bâhiraṃ, taṃ atthi kâyaviññâṇassa ârammanaṃ, atthi kâyaviññâṇassa nârammaṇaṃ, yan taṃ rûpaṃ bâhiraṃ, taṃ na cakkhâyatanaṃ, yan taṃ rûpaṃ ajjhattikaṃ, taṃ atthi cakkhâyatanaṃ, atthi na cakkhâyatanaṃ, yan taṃ rûpaṃ bâhiraṃ, taṃ na sotâyatanaṃ . . . pe . . . na ghâṇâyatanaṃ . . . pe . . . na jivhâyatanaṃ . . . pe . . . na kâyâyatanaṃ, yan taṃ rûpaṃ ajjhattikaṃ, taṃ atthi kâyâyatanaṃ, atthi na kâyâyatanaṃ, yan taṃ rûpaṃ ajjhattikaṃ, taṃ na rûpâyatanaṃ, yan taṃ rûpaṃ bâhiraṃ, taṃ atthi rûpâyatanaṃ, atthi na rûpâyatanaṃ, yan taṃ rûpaṃ ajjhattikaṃ, taṃ na saddâyatanaṃ . . . pe . . . na gandhâyatanaṃ . . . pe . . . na rasâyatanaṃ . . . pe . . . na phoṭṭhabbâyatanaṃ, yan taṃ rûpaṃ bâhiraṃ, taṃ atthi phoṭṭhabbâyatanaṃ, atthi na phoṭṭhabbâyatanaṃ, yan taṃ rûpaṃ bâhiraṃ, taṃ na cakkhudhâtu, yan taṃ rûpaṃ ajjhattikaṃ, taṃ atthi cakkhudhâtu, atthi na cakkhudhâtu, yan taṃ rûpaṃ bâhiraṃ, taṃ na sotadhâtu . . . pe . . . na ghânadhâtu . . . pe . . . na jivhâdhâtu . . . pe . . . na kâyadhâtu . . . pe . . . yan taṃ rûpaṃ ajjhattikaṃ, taṃ atthi kâyadhâtu, atthi na kâyadhâtu yan taṃ rûpaṃ ajjhattikaṃ, taṃ rûpadhâtu, yan taṃ rûpaṃ bâhiraṃ, taṃ atthi rûpadhâtu, atthi na rûpadhâtu, yan taṃ rûpaṃ ajjhattikaṃ, taṃ na saddadhâtu . . . pe . . . na gandhadhâtu . . . pe . . . na rasadhâtu, na phoṭṭhabbadhâtu, yan taṃ rûpaṃ bâhiraṃ, taṃ atthi phoṭṭhabbadhâtu, atthi na phoṭṭhabbadhâtu, yan taṃ rûpaṃ bâhiraṃ, taṃ na cakkhundriyaṃ, yan taṃ rûpaṃ ajjhattikaṃ, taṃ atthi cakkhundriyaṃ atthi na cakkhundriyaṃ, yan taṃ rûpaṃ bâhiraṃ, taṃ na sotindriyaṃ . . . pe . . . na ghânindriyaṃ . . . pe . . . na jivhindriyaṃ . . . pe . . . na kâyindriyaṃ, yan taṃ rûpaṃ ajjhattikaṃ, taṃ atthi kâyindriyaṃ, atthi na kâyindriyaṃ, yan taṃ rûpaṃ ajjhattikaṃ, taṃ na itthindriyaṃ, yan taṃ rûpaṃ bâhiraṃ, taṃ atthi itthindriyaṃ, atthi na itthindriyaṃ yan taṃ rûpaṃ ajjhattikaṃ, taṃ na purisindriyaṃ, yan taṃ rûpaṃ bâhiraṃ, taṃ atthi purisindriyaṃ, atthi na purisindriyaṃ, yan taṃ rûpaṃ ajjhattikaṃ, taṃ na jîvitindriyaṃ, yan taṃ rûpaṃ bâhiraṃ, taṃ atthi jîvitindriyaṃ, atthi na jîvitindriyaṃ, yan taṃ rûpaṃ ajjhattikaṃ, taṃ na kâyaviññatti, yan taṃ rûpaṃ bâhiraṃ, taṃ atthi kâyaviññatti, atthi na kâyaviññatti, yan taṃ rûpaṃ ajjhattikaṃ, taṃ na vacîviññatti, yan taṃ rûpaṃ bâhiraṃ, taṃ atthi vacîviññatti, atthi na vacîviññatti, yan taṃ rûpaṃ ajjhattikaṃ, taṃ na âkâsadhâtu, yan taṃ rûpaṃ bâhiraṃ, taṃ atthi âkâsadhâtu, atthi na âkâsadhâtu, yan taṃ rûpaṃ ajjhattikaṃ, taṃ na âpodhâtu, yan taṃ rûpaṃ bâhiraṃ, taṃ atthi âpodhâtu, atthi na âpodhâtu, yan taṃ rûpaṃ ajjhattikaṃ taṃ rûpassa na lahutâ, yan taṃ rûpaṃ bâhiraṃ, taṃ atthi rûpassa lahutâ, atthi rûpassa na lahutâ, yan taṃ rûpaṃ ajjhattikaṃ taṃ rûpassa na mudutâ, yan taṃ rûpaṃ bâhiraṃ, taṃ atthi rûpassa mudutâ, atthi rûpassa na mudutâ, yan taṃ rûpaṃ ajjhattikaṃ, taṃ rûpassa na kammaññatâ, yan taṃ rûpaṃ bâhiraṃ, taṃ atthi rûpassa kammaññatâ, atthi rûpassa na kammaññatâ, yan taṃ rûpaṃ ajjhattikaṃ, taṃ rûpassa na upacayo, yan taṃ rûpaṃ bâhiraṃ, taṃ atthi rûpassa upacayo, atthi rûpassa na upacayo, yan taṃ rûpaṃ ajjhattikaṃ taṃ rûpassa na santati, yan taṃ rûpaṃ bâhiraṃ, taṃ atthi rûpassa santati, atthi rûpassa na santati, yan taṃ rûpaṃ ajjhattikaṃ, taṃ rûpassa na jaratâ, yan taṃ rûpaṃ bâhiraṃ, taṃ atthi rûpassa jaratâ, atthi rûpassa na jaratâ, yan taṃ rûpaṃ ajjhatikaṃ, taṃ rûpassa na aniccatâ, yan taṃ rûpaṃ bâhiraṃ, taṃ atthi rûpassa aniccatâ, atthi rûpassa na aniccatâ, yan taṃ rûpaṃ ajjhattikaṃ, taṃ na kabaḷiṃkâro âhâro, yan taṃ rûpaṃ bâhiraṃ, taṃ atthi kabaḷiṃkâro âhâro, atthi na kabaḷiṃkâro âhâro. Evaṃ tividhena rûpasaṅgaho.

Tikaṃ.

587. Catubbidhena rûpasaṅgaho:

Yan taṃ rûpaṃ upâdâ, taṃ atthi upâdiṇṇaṃ, atthi anupâdiṇṇaṃ, yan taṃ rûpaṃ anupâdâ, taṃ atthi upâdiṇṇaṃ, atthi anupâdiṇṇaṃ, yan taṃ rûpaṃ upâdâ, taṃ atthi upâdiṇṇupâdâniyaṃ, atthi anupâdiṇṇupâdâniyaṃ, yan taṃ rûpaṃ anupâdâ, taṃ atthi upâdiṇṇupâdâniyaṃ, atthi anupâdiṇṇupâdâniyaṃ, yan taṃ rûpaṃ upâdâ taṃ atthi sappaṭighaṃ, atthi appaṭighaṃ, yan tam rûpaṃ anupâdâ, taṃ atthi sappaṭighaṃ atthi appaṭighaṃ, yan taṃ rûpaṃ upâdâ, taṃ atthi oḷârikaṃ, atthi sukhumaṃ, yan taṃ rûpaṃ nûpâda, taṃ atthi oḷârikaṃ, atthi sukhumaṃ, yan taṃ rûpaṃ upâdâ, taṃ atthi dûre, atthi santike, yan taṃ rûpaṃ nûpâdâ, taṃ atthi dûre, atthi santike, yan taṃ rûpaṃ upâdiṇṇaṃ, taṃ atthi sanidassanaṃ, atthi anidassanaṃ, yan taṃ rûpaṃ anupâdiṇṇaṃ, taṃ atthi sanidassanaṃ, atthi anidassanaṃ, yan taṃ rûpaṃ upâdiṇṇaṃ, taṃ atthi sappaṭighaṃ, atthi appaṭighaṃ, yan taṃ rûpaṃ anupâdiṇṇaṃ, taṃ atthi sappaṭighaṃ, atthi appaṭighaṃ, yan taṃ rûpaṃ upâdiṇṇaṃ, taṃ atthi mahâbhûtaṃ, atthi na mahâbhûtaṃ, yan taṃ rûpaṃ anupâdiṇṇaṃ, taṃ atthi mahâbhûtaṃ, atthi na mahâbhûtaṃ, yan taṃ rûpaṃ upâdiṇṇaṃ, tam atthi oḷârikaṃ, atthi sukhumaṃ, yan taṃ rûpaṃ anupâdiṇṇaṃ, taṃ atthi oḷârikaṃ, atthi sukhumaṃ, yan taṃ rûpaṃ upâdiṇṇaṃ, taṃ atthi dûre, atthi santike, yan taṃ rûpaṃ anupâdiṇṇaṃ, taṃ atthi dûre atthi santike, yan taṃ rûpaṃ upâdiṇṇupâdâniyaṃ, taṃ atthi sanidassanaṃ, atthi anidassanaṃ, yan taṃ rûpaṃ anupâdiṇṇupâdâniyaṃ, taṃ atthi sanidassanaṃ, atthi anidassanaṃ, yan taṃ rûpaṃ upâdiṇṇupâdâniyaṃ, taṃ atthi sappaṭighaṃ, atthi appaṭighaṃ, yan taṃ rûpaṃ anupâdiṇṇupâdâniyaṃ, taṃ atthi sappaṭighaṃ, atthi appaṭighaṃ, yan taṃ rûpaṃ upâdiṇṇupâdâniyaṃ, taṃ atthi mahâbhûtaṃ, atthi na mahâbhûtaṃ, yan taṃ rûpaṃ anupâdiṇṇupâdâniyaṃ, taṃ atthi mahâbhûtaṃ, atthi na mahâbhûtaṃ, yan taṃ rûpaṃ upâdiṇṇupâdâniyaṃ, taṃ atthi oḷârikaṃ, atthi sukhumaṃ, yan taṃ rûpaṃ anupâdiṇṇupâdâniyaṃ, taṃ atthi oḷârikaṃ, atthi sukhumam, yan taṃ rûpaṃ upâdiṇṇupâdâniyaṃ, taṃ atthi dûre, atthi santike, yan taṃ rûpaṃ anupâdiṇṇupâdâniyaṃ, taṃ atthi dûre, atthi santike, yan taṃ rûpaṃ sappaṭighaṃ, taṃ atthi indriyaṃ, atthi na indriyaṃ, yan taṃ rûpaṃ appaṭighaṃ, taṃ atthi indriyaṃ, atthi na indriyaṃ, yan taṃ rûpaṃ sappaṭighaṃ, taṃ atthi mahâbhûtaṃ, atthi na mahâbhûtaṃ, yan taṃ rûpaṃ appaṭighaṃ, taṃ atthi mahâbhûtaṃ, atthi na mahâbhûtaṃ, yan taṃ rûpaṃ indriyaṃ, taṃ atthi oḷârikaṃ, atthi sukhumaṃ, yan taṃ rûpaṃ na indriyaṃ, taṃ atthi oḷârikaṃ, atthi sukhumaṃ, yan taṃ rûpaṃ indriyaṃ, taṃ atthi dûre, atthi santike, yan taṃ rûpaṃ na indriyaṃ, taṃ atthi dûre, atthi santike, yan taṃ rûpaṃ mahâbhûtaṃ, taṃ atthi oḷârikaṃ, atthi sukhumaṃ, yan taṃ rûpaṃ na mahâbhûtaṃ, taṃ atthi oḷârikaṃ, atthi sukhumaṃ, yan taṃ rûpaṃ mahâbhûtaṃ, taṃ atthi dûre, atthi santike, yan taṃ rûpaṃ na mahâbhûtaṃ, taṃ atthi dûre, atthi santike, diṭṭhaṃ sutaṃ mutaṃ viññâtaṃ rûpaṃ. Evaṃ catubbidhena rûpasaṅgaho.

Catukkaṃ.

588. Pañcavidhena rûpasaṅgaho:
Pathavîdhâtu âpodhâtu tejodhâtu vâyodhâtu—yañ ca rûpaṃ upâdâ—evaṃ pañcavidhena rûpasaṅgaho.

Pañcakaṃ.

589. Chabbidhena rûpasaṅgaho:
Cakkhuviññeyyaṃ rûpaṃ—sotaviññeyyaṃ rûpaṃ—ghânaviññeyyaṃ rûpaṃ, jivhâviññeyyaṃ rûpaṃ, kâyaviññeyyaṃ rûpaṃ, manoviññeyyaṃ rûpaṃ—evaṃ chabbidhena rûpasaṅgaho.

Chakkaṃ.

590. Sattavidhena rûpasaṅgaho:
Cakkhuviññeyyaṃ rûpaṃ, sotaviññeyyaṃ rûpaṃ, ghânaviññeyyaṃ rûpaṃ, jivhâviññeyyaṃ rûpaṃ, kâyaviññeyyaṃ rûpaṃ, manoviññeyyaṃ rûpaṃ, dhâtuviññeyyaṃ rûpaṃ—evaṃ sattavidhena rûpasaṅgaho.

Sattakaṃ.

591. Aṭṭhavidhena rûpasaṅgaho:
Cakkhuviññeyyaṃ rûpaṃ, sotaviññeyyaṃ rûpaṃ, ghânaviññeyyaṃ rûpaṃ, jivhâviññeyyaṃ rûpaṃ, kâyaviññeyyaṃ rûpaṃ, atthi sukhasamphassaṃ, atthi dukkhasamphassaṃ—manodhâtuviññeyyaṃ rûpaṃ—manoviññâṇadhâtuviññeyyaṃ rûpaṃ—evaṃ aṭṭhavidhena rûpasaṅgaho.

Aṭṭhakaṃ.

592. Navavidhena rûpasaṅgaho:
Cakkhundriyaṃ, sotindriyaṃ, ghânindriyaṃ, jivhindriyaṃ, kâyindriyaṃ, itthindriyaṃ, purisindriyaṃ, jîvitindriyaṃ yañ ca rûpaṃ na indriyaṃ—evaṃ navavidhena rûpasaṅgaho.

Navakaṃ.

593. Dasavidhena rûpasaṅgaho:
Cakkhundriyaṃ, sotindriyaṃ, ghânindriyaṃ, jivhindriyaṃ, kâyindriyaṃ, itthindriyaṃ, purisindriyaṃ, jîvitindriyaṃ, na indriyaṃ rûpaṃ atthi sappaṭighaṃ—atthi appaṭigham—evaṃ dasavidhena rûpasaṅgaho.

Dasakaṃ.

594. Ekâdasavidhena rûpasaṅgaho:
Cakkhâyatanaṃ, sotâyatanaṃ, ghânâyatanaṃ, jivhâyatanaṃ, kâyâyatanaṃ, rûpâyatanaṃ, saddâyatanaṃ, gandhâyatanaṃ, rasâyatanaṃ, phoṭṭhabbâyatanaṃ yañ ca rûpaṃ anidassanaṃ appaṭighaṃ dhammâyatanapariyâpannaṃ — evaṃ ekâdasavidhena rûpasaṅgaho.

Ekâdasakaṃ.

MÂTIKÂ.

595. Sabbaṃ rûpaṃ na hetum eva ahetukam eva hetuvippayuttam eva sappaccayam eva saṅkhatan eva lokiyam eva sâsavam eva saññojaniyam eva ganthaniyam eva oghaniyam eva yoganiyam eva nivaraṇiyam eva parâmaṭṭham eva upâdâniyaṃ eva saṅkilesikam eva avyâkatam eva anârammaṇam eva acetasikam eva cittavippayuttam eva neva vipâkanavipâkadhammadhammam eva asaṅkiliṭṭhasaṅkilesikam eva na savitakka-savicâram eva na avitakkavicâramattam eva avitakka-avicâram eva na pîtisahagatam eva na sukhasahagatam eva upekkhâsahagatam eva neva dassanena na bhâvanâya pahâtabbam eva neva dassanena na bhâvanâya pahâtabbahetukam eva neva âcayagâminaapacayagâmim eva neva sekkhanâsekkham eva parittaṃ eva kâmâvacaram eva rûpâvacaram eva na arûpâvacaram eva pariyâpannam eva no apariyâpannam eva aniyatam eva aniyyânikam eva uppannaṃ chahi viññânehi viññeyyaṃ eva aniccam eva jarâbhibhûtam eva—evaṃ ekavidhena rûpasaṅgaho.

Ekakaniddeso.

596. Kataman taṃ rûpaṃ upâdâ?

Cakkhâyatanaṃ, sotâyatanaṃ, ghânâyatanaṃ, jivhâyatanaṃ, kâyâyatanaṃ, rûpâyatanaṃ, saddâyatanaṃ, gandhâyatanaṃ, rasâyatanaṃ, itthindriyaṃ, purisindriyaṃ, jîvitindriyaṃ, kâyaviññatti, vacîviññatti, âkâsadhâtu, rûpassa lahutâ, rûpassa mudutâ, rûpassa kammaññatâ, rûpassa upacayo, rûpassa santati, rûpassa jaratâ, rûpassa aniccatâ kabaḷiṅkâro âhâro.

597. Kataman taṃ rûpaṃ cakkhâyatanaṃ?

Yaṃ cakkhuṃ catunnaṃ mahâbhûtânaṃ upâdâya pasâdo attabhâvapariyâpanno anidassano sappaṭigho—yena cakkhunâ anidassanena sappaṭighena rûpaṃ sanidassanaṃ sappaṭighaṃ passi vâ passati vâ passissati vâ passe vâ cakkhuṃ petaṃ cakkhâyatanaṃ petaṃ cakkhudhâtu pesâ cakkhundriyaṃ petaṃ loko peso dvârâ pesâ samuddo peso paṇḍaraṃ petaṃ khettaṃ petaṃ vatthum petaṃ nettaṃ petaṃ nayanaṃ petaṃ oriman tîraṃ petaṃ suñño gâmo peso—idan taṃ rûpaṃ cakkhâyatanaṃ.

598. Kataman taṃ rûpaṃ cakkhâyatanaṃ?

Yaṃ cakkhuṃ . . . pe . . . sappaṭigho yamhi cakkhumhi anidassanamhi sappaṭighamhi rûpaṃ sanidassanaṃ sappaṭighaṃ paṭihaññi vâ paṭihaññati vâ paṭihaññissati vâ paṭihaññe vâ cakkhuṃ petaṃ cakkhâyatanaṃ petaṃ cakkhudhâtu pesâ cakkhundriyaṃ petaṃ loko peso dvârâ pesâ samuddo peso paṇḍaraṃ petaṃ khettaṃ petaṃ vatthum petaṃ nettaṃ petaṃ nayanaṃ petaṃ orimaṃ tîraṃ petaṃ suñño gâmo peso—idaṃ taṃ rûpaṃ cakkhâyatanaṃ.

599. Kataman taṃ rûpaṃ cakkhâyatanaṃ?

Yaṃ cakkhuṃ catunnaṃ . . . pe . . . sappaṭigho—yaṃ cakkhuṃ anidassanaṃ sappaṭighaṃ rûpamhi sanidassanamhi sappaṭighamhi paṭihaññi vâ paṭihaññati vâ paṭihaññissati vâ paṭihaññe vâ cakkhuṃ petaṃ cakkâyatanaṃ petaṃ cakkhudhâtu pesâ cakkhundriyaṃ petaṃ loko peso dvârâ pesâ samuddo peso paṇḍaraṃ petaṃ khettaṃ petaṃ vatthuṃ petaṃ nettaṃ petaṃ nayanaṃ petaṃ oriman tîraṃ petaṃ suñño gâmo peso—idan taṃ rûpaṃ cakkhâyatanaṃ.

600. Kataman taṃ rûpaṃ cakkhâyatanaṃ?

Yaṃ cakkhuṃ catunnaṃ . . . pe . . . sappaṭigho—yaṃ

cakkhuṃ nissâya rûpaṃ ârabbha cakkhusamphasso uppajji vâ uppajjati vâ uppajjissati vâ uppajje vâ yaṃ cakkhuṃ nissâya rûpaṃ ârabbha cakkhusamphassajâ vedanâ . . . pe . . . saññâ . . . pe . . . cetanâ . . . pe . . . cakkhuviññâṇaṃ uppajji vâ uppajjati vâ uppajjissati vâ uppajje vâ cakkhum petaṃ cakkhâyatanaṃ petaṃ cakkhudhâtu pesâ cakkhundriyaṃ petaṃ loko peso dvârâ pesâ samuddo peso paṇḍaraṃ petaṃ khettaṃ petaṃ vatthuṃ petaṃ nettaṃ petaṃ nayanaṃ petaṃ oriman tîraṃ petaṃ suñño gâmo peso—idan taṃ rûpaṃ cakkhâyatanaṃ.

601. Kataman taṃ rûpaṃ sotâyatanaṃ?

Yaṃ sotaṃ catunnaṃ mahâbhûtânaṃ upâdâya pasâdo attabhâvapariyâpanno anidassano sappaṭigho—yena sotena anidassanena sappaṭighena saddaṃ anidassanaṃ sappaṭighaṃ suṇi vâ suṇâti vâ suṇissati vâ suṇe vâ—sotaṃ petaṃ sotâyatanaṃ petaṃ sotadhâtu pesâ sotindriyaṃ petaṃ loko peso dvârâ pesâ samuddo peso paṇḍaraṃ petaṃ khettaṃ petaṃ vatthuṃ petaṃ oriman tîraṃ petaṃ suñño gâmo peso—idaṃ taṃ rûpaṃ sotâyatanaṃ.

602. Kataman taṃ rûpaṃ sotâyatanaṃ?

Yaṃ sotaṃ . . . pe . . . pariyâpanno anidassano sappaṭigho yamhi sotamhi anidassanamhi sappaṭighamhi saddo anidassano sappaṭigho paṭihaññi vâ paṭihaññati vâ paṭihaññissati vâ paṭihaññe vâ—sotaṃ petaṃ sotâyatanaṃ petaṃ sotadhâtu pesâ sotindriyaṃ petaṃ loko peso dvârâ pesâ samuddo peso paṇḍaraṃ petaṃ khettaṃ petaṃ vatthuṃ petaṃ oriman tîraṃ petaṃ suñño gâmo peso—idaṃ taṃ rûpaṃ sotâyatanaṃ.

603. Kataman taṃ rûpaṃ sotâyatanaṃ?

Yaṃ sotaṃ . . . pe . . . pariyâpanno anidassano sappaṭigho—yaṃ sotaṃ anidassanaṃ sappaṭighaṃ saddamhi anidassanamhi sappaṭighamhi paṭihaññi vâ paṭihaññati vâ paṭihaññissati vâ paṭihaññe vâ—sotaṃ petaṃ sotâyatanaṃ petaṃ sotadhâtu pesâ sotindriyaṃ petaṃ loko peso dvârâ pesâ samuddo peso paṇḍaraṃ petaṃ khettaṃ petaṃ vatthuṃ petaṃ oriman tîraṃ petaṃ suñño gâmo peso—idaṃ taṃ rûpaṃ sotâyatanaṃ.

604. Kataman taṃ rûpaṃ sotâyatanaṃ?

Yaṃ sotaṃ . . . pe . . . pariyâpanno anidassano sappaṭigho —yaṃ sotaṃ nissâya saddaṃ ârabbha sotasamphasso uppajji vâ uppajjati vâ uppajjissati vâ uppajje vâ . . . pe . . . yaṃ sotaṃ nissâya saddaṃ ârabbha sotasamphassajâ vedanâ . . . pe . . . saññâ . . . pe . . . cetanâ . . . pe . . . sotaviññâṇaṃ uppajji vâ uppajjati vâ uppajjissati vâ uppajje vâ . . . pe . . . yaṃ sotaṃ nissâya saddârammaṇo sotasamphasso uppajji vâ uppajjati vâ uppajjissati vâ uppajje vâ . . . pe . . . yaṃ sotaṃ nissâya saddârammaṇâ sotasamphassajâ vedanâ . . . pe . . . saññâ . . . pe . . . cetanâ . . . pe . . . sotaviññâṇaṃ uppajji vâ uppajjati vâ uppajjissati vâ uppajje vâ —sotaṃ petaṃ sotâyatanaṃ petaṃ sotadhâtu pesâ sotindriyaṃ petaṃ loko peso dvârâ pesâ samuddo peso paṇḍaraṃ petaṃ khettaṃ petaṃ vatthum petaṃ oriman tîraṃ petaṃ suñño gâmo peso—idaṃ taṃ rûpaṃ sotâyatanaṃ.

605. Kataman taṃ rûpaṃ ghânâyatanaṃ?

Yaṃ ghânaṃ catunnaṃ mahâbhûtânaṃ upâdâya pasâdo attabhâvapariyâpanno anidassano sappaṭigho—yena ghânena anidassanena sappaṭighena gandhaṃ anidassanaṃ sappaṭighaṃ ghâyi vâ ghâyati vâ ghâyissati vâ ghâye vâ ghânaṃ petaṃ ghânâyatanaṃ petaṃ ghânadhâtu pesâ ghânindriyaṃ petaṃ loko peso dvârâ pesâ samuddo peso paṇḍaraṃ petaṃ khettaṃ petaṃ vatthuṃ petaṃ oriman tîraṃ petaṃ suñño gâmo peso—idan taṃ rûpaṃ ghânâyatanaṃ.

606. Kataman taṃ rûpaṃ ghânâyatanaṃ?

Yaṃ ghânaṃ . . . pe . . . pariyâpanno anidassano sappaṭigho—yamhi ghânamhi anidassanamhi sappaṭighamhi gandho anidassano sappaṭigho paṭihaññi vâ paṭihaññati vâ paṭihaññissati vâ paṭihaññe vâ ghânaṃ petaṃ ghânâyatanaṃ petaṃ ghânadhâtu pesâ ghânindriyaṃ petaṃ loko peso dvârâ pesâ samuddo peso paṇḍaraṃ petaṃ khettaṃ petaṃ vatthuṃ petaṃ oriman tîraṃ petaṃ suñño gâmo peso—idan taṃ rûpaṃ ghânâyatanaṃ.

607. Kataman taṃ rûpaṃ ghânâyatanaṃ?

Yaṃ ghânaṃ . . . pe . . . pariyâpanno anidassano sappaṭigho—yaṃ ghânaṃ anidassanaṃ sappaṭighaṃ gandhamhi anidassanamhi sappaṭighamhi paṭihaññi vâ paṭihaññati vâ paṭihaññissati vâ paṭihaññe vâ—ghânaṃ petaṃ ghânâyatanaṃ petaṃ ghânadhâtu pesâ ghânindriyaṃ petaṃ loko peso dvârâ pesâ samuddo peso paṇḍaraṃ petaṃ khettaṃ petaṃ vatthuṃ petaṃ oriman tîraṃ petaṃ suñño gâmo peso—idan taṃ rûpaṃ ghânâyatanaṃ.

608. Kataman taṃ rûpaṃ ghânâyatanaṃ?

Yaṃ ghânaṃ . . . pe . . . pariyâpanno anidassano sappaṭigho yaṃ ghânaṃ nissâya gandhaṃ ârabbha ghânasamphasso uppajji vâ uppajjati vâ uppajjissati vâ uppajje vâ . . . pe . . . yaṃ ghânaṃ nissâya gandhaṃ ârabbha ghânasamphassajâ vedanâ . . . pe . . . saññâ . . . pe . . . cetanâ . . . pe . . . ghânaviññâṇaṃ uppajji vâ uppajjati vâ uppajjissati vâ uppajje vâ . . . pe . . . yaṃ ghânaṃ nissâya gandhârammaṇo ghânasamphasso uppajji vâ uppajjati vâ uppajjissati vâ uppajje vâ . . . pe . . . yaṃ ghânaṃ nissâya gandhârammaṇâ ghânasamphassajâ vedanâ . . . pe . . . saññâ . . . pe . . . cetanâ . . . pe . . . ghânaviññâṇaṃ uppajji vâ uppajjati vâ uppajjissati vâ uppajje vâ—ghânaṃ petaṃ ghânâyatanaṃ petaṃ ghânadhâtu pesâ ghânindriyaṃ petaṃ loko peso dvârâ pesâ samuddo peso paṇḍaraṃ petaṃ khettaṃ petaṃ vatthuṃ petaṃ orimaṃ tîraṃ petaṃ suñño gâmo peso—idan taṃ rûpaṃ ghânâyatanaṃ.

609. Katamaṃ taṃ rûpaṃ jivhâyatanaṃ?

Yâ jivhâ catunnaṃ mahâbhûtânaṃ upâdâya pasâdo attabhâvapariyâpanno anidassano sappaṭigho yâya jivhâya anidassanâya sappaṭighâya rasaṃ anidassanaṃ sappaṭighaṃ sâyi vâ sâyati vâ sâyissati vâ sâye vâ—jivhâ pesâ jivhâyatanaṃ petaṃ jivhâdhâtu pesâ jivhindriyaṃ petaṃ loko peso dvârâ pesâ samuddo peso paṇḍaraṃ petaṃ khettaṃ petaṃ vatthuṃ petaṃ orimaṃ tîraṃ petaṃ suñño gâmo peso—idaṃ taṃ rûpaṃ jivhâyatanaṃ.

610. Kataman taṃ rûpaṃ jivhâyatanaṃ?

Yâ . . . pe . . . pariyâpanno anidassano sappaṭigho yâya jivhâya anidassanâya sappaṭighâya raso anidassano sappaṭigho paṭihaññi vâ paṭihaññati vâ paṭihaññissati vâ paṭihaññe vâ jivhâ pesâ jivhâyatanaṃ petaṃ jivhâdhâtu pesâ jivhindriyaṃ petaṃ loko peso dvârâ pesâ samuddo peso paṇḍaraṃ petaṃ khettaṃ petaṃ vatthuṃ petaṃ oriman tîraṃ petaṃ suñño gâmo peso—idaṃ taṃ rûpaṃ jivhâyatanaṃ.

611. Katamaṃ taṃ rûpaṃ jivhâyatanaṃ?

Yâ . . . pe . . . pariyâpanno anidassano sappaṭigho yâ jivhâ anidassanâ sappaṭighâ rasamhi anidassanamhi sappaṭighamhi paṭihaññi vâ paṭihaññati vâ paṭihaññissati vâ paṭihaññe vâ jivhâ pesâ jivhâyatanaṃ petaṃ jivhâdhâtu pesâ jivhindriyaṃ petaṃ loko peso dvârâ pesâ samuddo peso paṇḍaraṃ petaṃ khettaṃ petaṃ vatthuṃ petaṃ oriman tîraṃ petaṃ suñño gâmo peso—idaṃ taṃ rûpaṃ jivhâyatanaṃ.

612. Kataman taṃ rûpaṃ jivhâyatanam?

Yâ . . . pe . . . pariyâpanno anidassano sappaṭigho yaṃ jivhaṃ nissâya rasaṃ ârabbha jivhâsamphasso uppajji vâ uppajjati vâ uppajjissati vâ uppajje vâ . . . pe . . . yaṃ jivhaṃ nissâya rasaṃ ârabbha jivhâsamphassajâ vedanâ . . . pe . . . saññâ . . . pe . . . cetanâ . . . pe . . jivhâviññâṇaṃ uppajji vâ uppajjati vâ uppajjissati vâ uppajje vâ . . . pe . . . yaṃ jivhaṃ nissâya rasârammaṇo jivhâsamphasso uppajji vâ uppajjati vâ uppajjissati vâ uppajje vâ . . . pe . . . yaṃ jivhaṃ nissâya rasârammaṇâ jivhâ-samphassajâ vedanâ . . . pe . . . saññâ . . . pe . . . cetanâ . . . pe . . . jivhâviññâṇaṃ uppajji vâ uppajjati vâ uppajjissati vâ uppajje vâ jivhâ pesâ jivhâyatanaṃ petaṃ jivhâdhâtu pesâ jivhindriyaṃ petaṃ loko peso dvârâ pesâ samuddo peso paṇḍaraṃ petaṃ khettaṃ petaṃ vatthuṃ petaṃ—oriman tîraṃ petaṃ suñño gâmo peso—idan taṃ rûpaṃ jivhâyatanaṃ.

613. Kataman taṃ rûpaṃ kâyâyatanaṃ?

Yo kâyo catunnaṃ mahâbhûtânaṃ upâdâya pasâdo attabhâvapariyâpanno anidassano sappaṭigho yena kâyena anidassanena sappaṭighena phoṭṭhabbaṃ anidassanaṃ sappaṭighaṃ phusi vâ phusati vâ phusissati vâ phuse vâ—kâyo peso kâyâyatanaṃ petaṃ kâyadhâtu pesâ kâyindriyaṃ petaṃ loko peso dvârâ pesâ samuddo peso paṇḍaraṃ petaṃ khettaṃ petaṃ vatthuṃ petaṃ orimaṃ tîraṃ petaṃ suñño gâmo peso—idan taṃ rûpaṃ kâyâyatanaṃ.

614. Kataman taṃ rûpaṃ kâyâyatanaṃ?

Yo kâyo . . . pe . . . pariyâpanno anidassano sappaṭigho yamhi kâyamhi anidassanamhi sappaṭighamhi phoṭṭhabbo anidassano sappaṭigho paṭihaññi vâ paṭihaññati vâ paṭihaññissati vâ paṭihaññe vâ—kâyo peso . . . pe . . . gâmo peso —idan taṃ rûpaṃ kâyâyatanaṃ.

615. Katamaṃ taṃ rûpaṃ kâyâyatanaṃ?

Yo kâyo . . . pe . . . pariyâpanno anidassano sappaṭigho yo kâyo anidassano sappaṭigho phoṭṭhabbamhi anidassanamhi sappaṭighamhi paṭihaññi vâ paṭihaññati vâ paṭihaññissati vâ paṭihaññe vâ—kâyo peso . . . pe . . . gâmo peso—idan taṃ rûpaṃ kâyâyatanaṃ.

616. Katamaṃ taṃ rûpaṃ kâyâyatanaṃ?

Yo kâyo . . . pe . . . pariyâpanno anidassano sappaṭigho yaṃ kâyaṃ nissâya phoṭṭhabbaṃ ârabbha kâyasamphasso uppajji vâ uppajjati vâ uppajjissati vâ uppajje vâ . . . pe . . . yaṃ kâyaṃ nissâya phoṭṭhabbaṃ ârabbha kâyasamphassajâ vedanâ . . . pe . . . saññâ . . . pe . . . cetanâ . . . pe . . . kâyaviññâṇaṃ uppajji vâ uppajjati vâ uppajjissati vâ uppajje vâ . . . pe . . . yaṃ kâyaṃ nissâya phoṭṭhabbârammaṇo kâyasamphasso uppajji vâ upajjati vâ uppajjissati vâ uppajje vâ . . . pe . . . yaṃ kâyaṃ nissâya phoṭṭhabbârammaṇâ kâyasamphassajâ vedanâ . . . pe . . . saññâ . . . pe . . . cetanâ . . . pe . . . kâyaviññâṇaṃ uppajji vâ uppajjati vâ uppajjissati vâ uppajje vâ—kâyo peso . . . . pe . . . gâmo peso—idan taṃ rûpaṃ kâyâyatanaṃ.

617. Katamaṃ taṃ rûpaṃ rûpâyatanaṃ?

Yaṃ rûpaṃ catunnaṃ mahâbhûtânaṃ upâdâya vaṇṇanibhâsanidassanaṃ sappaṭighaṃ nîlaṃ pîtakaṃ lohitakaṃ odâtaṃ kâḷakaṃ mañjeṭṭhakaṃ harivaṇṇaṃ aṅkuravaṇṇaṃ dîghaṃ rassaṃ aṇuṃ thûlaṃ vaṭṭaṃ parimaṇḍalaṃ caturaṃsaṃ chaḷaṃsaṃ aṭṭhaṃsaṃ soḷasaṃsaṃ ninnathalaṃ chàyâ âtapo âloko andhakâro abbhâ mahikâ dhûmo rajo candamaṇḍalassa vaṇṇanibhâ suriyamaṇḍalassa vaṇṇanibhâ târakarûpânaṃ vaṇṇanibhâ âdâsamaṇḍalassa vaṇṇanibhâ maṇisaṅkhamuttaveḷuriyassa vaṇṇanibhâ jâtarûparajatassa vaṇṇanibhâ—yaṃ vâ panaññam pi atthi rûpaṃ catunnaṃ mahâbhûtânaṃ upâdâya vaṇṇanibhâsanidassanaṃ sappaṭighaṃ—yaṃ rûpaṃ sanidassanaṃ sappaṭighaṃ cakkhunâ anidassanena sappaṭighena passi vâ passati vâ passissati vâ passe vâ rûpaṃ petaṃ rûpâyatanaṃ petaṃ rûpadhâtu pesâ—idaṃ taṃ rûpaṃ rûpâyatanaṃ.

618. Kataman taṃ rûpaṃ rûpâyatanaṃ?

Yaṃ rûpaṃ . . . pe . . sappaṭighaṃ yamhi rûpamhi sanidassanamhi sappaṭighamhi cakkhuṃ anidassanaṃ sappaṭighaṃ paṭihaññi vâ paṭihaññati vâ paṭihaññissati vâ paṭihaññe vâ—rûpaṃ petaṃ rûpâyatanaṃ petaṃ rûpadhâtu pesâ—idan taṃ rûpaṃ rûpâyatanaṃ.

619. Kataman taṃ rûpaṃ rûpâyatanaṃ?

Yaṃ rûpaṃ . . . pe . . . sappaṭighaṃ—yaṃ rûpaṃ sanidassanaṃ sappaṭighaṃ cakkhumhi anidassanamhi sappaṭighamhi paṭihaññi vâ paṭihaññati vâ paṭihaññissati vâ paṭihaññe vâ—rûpaṃ petaṃ rûpâyatanaṃ petaṃ rûpadhâtu pesâ—idan taṃ rûpaṃ rûpâyatanaṃ.

620. Kataman taṃ rûpaṃ rûpâyatanaṃ?

Yaṃ rûpaṃ . . . pe . . . sappaṭighaṃ—yaṃ rûpaṃ ârabbha cakkhuṃ nissâya cakkhusamphasso uppajji vâ uppajjati vâ uppajjissati vâ uppajje vâ . . . pe . . . yaṃ rûpaṃ ârabbha cakkhuṃ nissâya cakkhusamphassajâ vedanâ . . . pe . . . saññâ . . . pe . . . cetanâ . . . pe . . . cakkhuviññâṇaṃ uppajji vâ uppajjati vâ uppajjissati vâ uppajje vâ . . . pe . . . yaṃ rûpârammaṇaṃ cakkhuṃ nissâya cakkhusamphasso uppajji vâ uppajjati vâ uppajjissati vâ uppajje vâ . . . pe . . . yaṃ rûpârammaṇaṃ cakkhuṃ nissâya cakkhusamphassajâ vedanâ . . . pe . . . saññâ . . . pe . . . cetanâ . . . pe . . . cakkhuviññâṇaṃ uppajji vâ uppajjati vâ uppajjissati vâ uppajje vâ—rûpaṃ petaṃ rûpâyatanaṃ petaṃ rûpadhâtu pesâ—idan taṃ rûpaṃ rûpâyatanaṃ.

621. Kataman taṃ rûpaṃ saddâyatanaṃ?

Yo saddo catunnaṃ mahâbhûtânaṃ upâdâya anidassano sappaṭigho bherisaddo mutiṅgasaddo saṅkhasaddo paṇavasaddo gîtasaddo vâditasaddo sammasaddo pâṇisaddo sattânaṃ nigghosasaddo dhâtûnaṃ sannighâtasaddo vâtasaddo udakasaddo manussasaddo amanussasaddo — yo vâ panañño pi atthi saddo catunnaṃ mahâbhûtânaṃ upâdâya anidassano sappaṭigho—yaṃ saddaṃ anidassanaṃ sappaṭighaṃ sotena anidassanena sappaṭighena suṇi vâ suṇâti vâ suṇissati vâ suṇe vâ—saddo peso saddâyatanaṃ petaṃ saddadhâtu pesâ—idan taṃ rûpaṃ saddâyatanaṃ.

622. Kataman taṃ rûpaṃ saddâyatanaṃ?

Yo saddo . . . pe . . . sappaṭigho—yamhi saddamhi anidassanamhi sappaṭighamhi sotaṃ anidassanaṃ sappaṭighaṃ paṭihaññi vâ paṭihaññati vâ paṭihaññissati vâ paṭihaññe vâ—saddo peso saddâyatanaṃ petaṃ saddadhâtu pesâ—idan taṃ rûpaṃ saddâyatanaṃ.

623. Katamam taṃ rûpaṃ saddâyatanaṃ?

Yo saddo . . . pe . . . sappaṭigho—yo saddo anidassano sappaṭigho sotamhi anidassanamhi sappaṭighamhi paṭihaññi vâ paṭihaññati vâ paṭihaññissati vâ paṭihaññe vâ—saddo peso saddâyatanaṃ petaṃ saddadhâtu pesâ—idan taṃ rûpaṃ saddâyatanaṃ.

624. Katamam taṃ rûpaṃ saddâyatanaṃ?

Yo saddo . . . pe . . . sappaṭigho—yaṃ saddaṃ ârabbha sotaṃ nissâya sotasamphasso uppajji vâ uppajjati vâ uppajjissati vâ uppajje vâ . . . pe . . . yaṃ saddaṃ ârabbha sotaṃ nissâya sotasamphassajâ vedanâ . . . pe . . . saññâ . . . pe . . . cetanâ . . . pe . . . sotaviññâṇaṃ uppajji vâ uppajjati vâ uppajjissati vâ uppajje vâ . . . pe . . . yaṃ saddârammaṇaṃ sotaṃ nissâya sotasamphasso uppajji vâ uppajjati vâ uppajjissati vâ uppajje vâ . . . pe . . . yaṃ saddârammaṇaṃ sotaṃ nissâya sotasamphassajâ vedanâ . . . pe . . . saññâ . . . pe . . . cetanâ . . . pe . . . sotaviññâṇaṃ uppajji vâ uppajjati vâ uppajjissati vâ uppajje vâ—saddo peso saddâyatanaṃ petaṃ saddadhâtu pesâ—idaṃ taṃ rûpaṃ saddâyatanaṃ.

625. Katamam taṃ rûpaṃ gandhâyatanaṃ?

Yo gandho catunnaṃ mahâbhûtanaṃ upâdâya anidassano sappaṭigho mûlagandho sâragandho, tacagandho, pattagandho, pupphagandho, phalagandho, âmagandho, vissagandho, sugandho, duggandho yo vâ panañño pi atthi gandho catunnaṃ mahâbhûtânaṃ upâdâya anidassano sappaṭigho—yaṃ gandhaṃ anidassanaṃ sappaṭighaṃ [tena]ghânena anidassanena sappaṭighena ghâyi vâ ghâyati vâ ghâyissati vâ ghâyo vâ—gandho peso gandhâyatanaṃ petaṃ gandhadhâtu pesâ—idan tam rûpaṃ gandhâyatanaṃ.

626. Katamam taṃ rûpaṃ gandhâyatanaṃ?

Yo gandho . . . pe . . . sappaṭigho—yamhi gandhamhi anidassanamhi sappaṭighamhi ghânaṃ anidassanaṃ sappaṭighaṃ paṭihaññi vâ paṭihaññati vâ paṭihaññissati vâ paṭihaññe vâ—gandho peso gandhâyatanaṃ petaṃ gandhadhâtu pesâ—idan taṃ rûpaṃ gandhâyatanaṃ.

627. Katamaṃ taṃ rûpaṃ gandhâyatanaṃ?

Yo gandho . . . pe . . . sappaṭigho—yo gandho anidassano sappaṭigho ghânamhi anidassanamhi sappaṭighamhi paṭihaññi vâ paṭihaññati vâ paṭihaññissati vâ paṭihaññe vâ—gandho peso gandhâyatanaṃ petaṃ gandhadhâtu pesâ—idan taṃ rûpaṃ gandhâyatanaṃ.

628. Katamaṃ taṃ rûpaṃ gandhâyatanaṃ?

Yo gandho . . . pe . . . sappaṭigho—yaṃ gandhaṃ ârabbha ghânaṃ nissâya ghânasamphasso uppajji vâ uppajjati vâ uppajjissati vâ uppajje vâ . . . pe . . . yaṃ gandhaṃ ârabbha ghânaṃ nissâya ghânasamphassajâ vedanâ . . . pe . . . saññâ . . . pe . . . cetanâ . . . pe . . . ghânaviññâṇaṃ uppajji vâ uppajjati vâ uppajjissati vâ uppajje vâ . . . pe . . . yaṃ gandhârammaṇaṃ ghânaṃ nissâya ghânasamphasso uppajji vâ uppajjati vâ uppajjissati vâ uppajje vâ . . . pe . . . yaṃ gandhârammaṇaṃ ghânaṃ nissâya ghânasamphassajâ vedanâ . . . pe . . . saññâ . . . pe . . . cetanâ . . . pe . . . ghânaviññâṇaṃ uppajji vâ uppajjati vâ uppajjissati vâ uppajje vâ—gandho peso gandhâyatanaṃ . . . pe . . . gandhadhâtu pesâ—idan taṃ rûpaṃ gandhâyatanaṃ.

629. Katamaṃ taṃ rûpaṃ rasâyatanaṃ?

Yo raso catunnaṃ mahâbhûtânaṃ upâdâya anidassano sappaṭigho mûlaraso, khandharaso, tacaraso, pattaraso, puppharaso, phalaraso, ambilaṃ, madhuraṃ tittakaṃ kaṭukaṃ loṇikaṃ khârikaṃ lapilaṃ kasâvo sâdu asâdu yo vâ panañño pi atthi raso catunnaṃ mahâbhûtânaṃ upâdâya anidassano sappaṭigho—yaṃ rasaṃ anidassanaṃ sappaṭighaṃ jivhâya anidassanâya sappaṭighâya sâyi vâ sâyati vâ sâyissati vâ sâye vâ—raso peso rasâyatanaṃ petaṃ rasadhâtu pesâ—idan taṃ rûpaṃ rasâyatanaṃ.

630. Katamaṃ taṃ rûpaṃ rasâyatanaṃ?

Yo raso . . . pe . . . sappaṭigho—yamhi rasamhi anidassanamhi sappaṭighamhi jivhâ anidassanâ sappaṭighâ paṭihaññi vâ paṭihaññati vâ paṭihaññissati vâ paṭihaññe vâ—raso peso rasâyatanaṃ petaṃ rasadhâtu pesâ—idan taṃ rûpaṃ rasâyatanaṃ.

631. Katamaṃ taṃ rûpaṃ rasâyatanaṃ?

Yo raso . . . pe . . . sappaṭigho—yo raso anidassano sappaṭigho jivhâya anidassanâya sappaṭighâya paṭihaññi vâ paṭihaññati vâ paṭihaññissati vâ paṭihaññe vâ—raso peso rasâyatanaṃ petaṃ rasadhâtu pesâ—idan taṃ rûpaṃ rasâyatanaṃ.

632. Katamaṃ taṃ rûpaṃ rasâyatanaṃ?

Yo raso . . . pe . . . sappaṭigho—yaṃ rasaṃ ârabbha jivhaṃ nissâya jivhâsamphasso uppajji vâ uppajjati vâ uppajjissati vâ uppajje vâ . . . pe . . . yaṃ rasaṃ ârabbha jivhaṃ nissâya jivhâsamphassajâ vedanâ . . . pe . . . saññâ . . . pe . . . cetanâ . . . pe . . . jivhâviññâṇaṃ uppajji vâ uppajjati vâ uppajjissati vâ uppajje vâ . . . pe . . . yaṃ rasârammaṇaṃ jivhaṃ nissâya jivhâsamphasso uppajji vâ uppajjati vâ uppajjissati vâ uppajje vâ . . . pe . . . yaṃ rasârammaṇaṃ jivhaṃ nissâya jivhâsamphassajâ vedanâ . . . pe . . . saññâ . . . pe . . . cetanâ . . . pe . . . jivhâviññâṇaṃ uppajji vâ uppajjati vâ uppajjissati vâ uppajje vâ—raso peso rasâyatanaṃ petaṃ rasadhâtu pesâ—idan taṃ rûpaṃ rasâyatanaṃ.

633. Katamaṃ taṃ rûpaṃ itthindriyaṃ?

Yaṃ itthiyâ itthiliṅgaṃ itthinimittaṃ itthikuttaṃ itthâkappo itthattaṃ itthibhâvo—idan taṃ rûpaṃ itthindriyaṃ.

634. Katamaṃ taṃ rûpaṃ purisindriyaṃ?

Yaṃ purisassa purisaliṅgaṃ purisanimittaṃ purisakuttaṃ purisâkappo purisattaṃ purisabhâvo—idan taṃ rûpaṃ purisindriyaṃ.

635. Katamaṃ taṃ rûpaṃ jîvitindriyaṃ?

Yo tesaṃ rûpînaṃ dhammânaṃ âyu ṭhiti yapanâ yâpanâ iriyanâ vattanâ pâlanâ jîvitaṃ jîvitindriyaṃ—idan taṃ rûpaṃ jîvitindriyaṃ.

636. Katamaṃ taṃ rûpaṃ kâyaviññatti?

Yâ kusalacittassa vâ akusalacittassa vâ avyâkatacittassa vâ abhikkamantassa vâ paṭikkamantassa vâ âlokentassa vâ vilokentassa vâ sammiñjentassa vâ pasârentassa vâ kâyassa thambhanâ santhambhanâ santhambhitattaṃ viññatti viññâpanâ viññâpitattaṃ idan taṃ rûpaṃ kâyaviññatti.

637. Katamaṃ taṃ rûpaṃ vacîviññatti?

Yâ kusalacittassa vâ akusalacittassa vâ avyâkatacittassa vâ vâcâ girâ vyappatho udîraṇaṃ ghoso ghosakammaṃ vâcâ vacîbhedo—ayaṃ vuccati vâcâ—yâ tâya vâcâya viññatti viññâpanâ viññâpitattaṃ—idan taṃ rûpaṃ vacîviññatti.

638. Kataman taṃ rûpaṃ âkâsadhâtu?

Yo âkâso âkâsaṅgataṃ aghaṃ aghagataṃ vivaro vivaragataṃ asamphuṭṭhaṃ catûhi mahâbhûtehi—idan taṃ rûpaṃ âkâsadhâtu.

639. Kataman taṃ rûpaṃ rûpassa lahutâ?

Yâ rûpassa lahutâ lahupariṇâmatâ adandhanatâ avitthanatâ—idan taṃ rûpaṃ rûpassa lahutâ.

640. Kataman taṃ rûpaṃ rûpassa mudutâ?

Yâ rûpassa mudutâ maddavatâ akakkhaḷatâ akathinatâ—idan taṃ rûpaṃ rûpassa mudutâ.

641. Kataman taṃ rûpaṃ rûpassa kammaññatâ?

Yâ rûpassa kammaññatâ kammaññattaṃ kammaññabhâvo—idan taṃ rûpaṃ rûpassa kammaññatâ.

642. Kataman taṃ rûpaṃ rûpassa upacayo?

Yo âyatanânaṃ âcayo—yo rûpassa upacayo—idan taṃ rûpaṃ rûpassa upacayo.

643. Kataman taṃ rûpaṃ rûpassa santati?

Yo rûpassa upacayo—yâ rûpassa santati—idan taṃ rûpaṃ rûpassa santati.

644. Kataman taṃ rûpaṃ rûpassa jaratâ?

Yâ rûpassa jarâ jîraṇatâ khaṇḍiccaṃ pâliccaṃ valittacatâ âyuno saṃhâni, indriyânaṃ paripâko—idan taṃ rûpaṃ rûpassa jaratâ.

645. Kataman taṃ rûpaṃ rûpassa aniccatâ?

Yo rûpassa khayo vayo bhedo [paribhedo] aniccatâ antaradhânaṃ—idan taṃ rûpaṃ rûpassa aniccatâ.

646. Kataman taṃ rûpaṃ kabaḷiṅkâro âhâro?

Odano kummâso sattu maccho maṃsaṃ khîraṃ dadhi sappi navanîtaṃ telaṃ madhupphâṇitaṃ—yaṃ vâ panaññam pi atthi yamhi yamhi janapade tesaṃ tesaṃ sattânaṃ mukhâsiyaṃ dantavikhâdanaṃ galajjhoharaṇîyaṃ kucchivitthambhanaṃ yâya ojâya sattâ yâpenti—idan taṃ rûpaṃ kabaḷiṅkâro âhâro.

Idan taṃ rûpaṃ upâdâ.

UPÂDÂBHÂJANIYAṂ RÛPAKAṆḌE PAṬHAMABHÂNAVÂRAṂ.

647. Kataman taṃ rûpaṃ no upâdâ?

Phoṭṭhabbâyatanaṃ âpodhâtu—idan taṃ rûpaṃ no upâdâ.

648. Kataman taṃ rûpaṃ phoṭṭhabbâyatanaṃ?

Pathavîdhâtu tejodhâtu vâyodhâtu kakkhaḷaṃ mudukaṃ saṇhaṃ pharusaṃ sukhasamphassaṃ dukkhasamphassaṃ garukaṃ lahukaṃ—yaṃ phoṭṭhabbaṃ anidassanaṃ sappaṭighaṃ kâyena anidassanena sappaṭighena phusi vâ phusati vâ phusissati vâ phuso vâ phoṭṭhabbo peso phoṭṭhabbâyatanaṃ petaṃ phoṭṭhabbadhâtu pesâ—idan taṃ rûpaṃ phoṭṭhabbâyatanaṃ.

649. Kataman taṃ rûpaṃ phoṭṭhabbâyatanaṃ?

Pathavîdhâtu . . . pe . . . lahukaṃ—yamhi phoṭṭhabbamhi anidassanamhi sappaṭighamhi kâyo anidassano sappaṭigho paṭihaññi vâ paṭihaññati vâ paṭihaññissati vâ paṭihaññe vâ—phoṭṭhabbo peso phoṭṭhabbâyatanaṃ petaṃ phoṭṭhabbadhâtu pesâ — idan taṃ rûpaṃ phoṭṭhabbâyatanaṃ.

650. Kataman taṃ rûpaṃ phoṭṭhabbâyatanaṃ?

Pathavîdhâtu . . . pe . . . lahukaṃ—yo phoṭṭhabbo anidassano sappaṭigho kâyamhi anidassanamhi sappaṭighamhi paṭihaññi vâ paṭihaññati vâ paṭihaññissati vâ paṭihaññe vâ—phoṭṭhabbo peso phoṭṭhabbâyatanaṃ petaṃ phoṭṭhabbadhâtu pesâ—idan taṃ rûpaṃ phoṭṭhabbâyatanaṃ.

651. Kataman taṃ rûpaṃ phoṭṭhabbâyatanaṃ?

Pathavîdhâtu . . . pe . . . lahukaṃ—yaṃ phoṭṭhabbaṃ ârabbha kâyaṃ nissâya kâyasamphasso uppajji vâ uppajjati vâ uppajjissati vâ uppajje vâ . . . pe . . . yaṃ phoṭṭhabbaṃ ârabbha kâyaṃ nissâya kâyasamphassajâ vedanâ . . . pe . . . saññâ . . . pe . . . cetanâ . . . pe . . . kâyaviññâṇaṃ uppajji vâ uppajjati vâ uppajjissati vâ uppajje vâ . . . pe . . . yaṃ phoṭṭhabbârammaṇaṃ kâyaṃ nissâya kâyasamphasso uppajji vâ uppajjati vâ uppajjissati vâ uppajje vâ . . . pe . . . yaṃ phoṭṭhabbârammaṇaṃ kâyaṃ nissâya kâyasamphassajâ vedanâ . . . pe . . . saññâ . . . pe . . . cetanâ . . . pe . . . kâyaviññâṇaṃ uppajji vâ uppajjati vâ uppajjissati vâ uppajje vâ—phoṭṭhabbo peso phoṭṭhabbâyatanaṃ petaṃ phoṭṭhabbadhâtu pesâ—idan taṃ rûpaṃ phoṭṭhabbâyatanaṃ.

652. Kataman taṃ rûpaṃ âpodhâtu?

Yaṃ âpo âpogataṃ sineho sinehagataṃ bandhanattaṃ rûpassa idan taṃ rûpaṃ âpodhâtu.

Idan taṃ rûpaṃ no upâdâ.

653. Kataman taṃ rûpaṃ upâdiṇṇaṃ?

Cakkhâyatanaṃ, sotâyatanaṃ, ghâṇâyatanaṃ, jivhâyatanaṃ, kâyâyatanaṃ, itthindriyaṃ, purisindriyaṃ, jîvitindriyaṃ—yaṃ vâ panaññam pi atthi rûpaṃ kammassa katattâ rûpâyatanaṃ, gandhâyatanaṃ, rasâyatanaṃ, phoṭṭhabbâyatanaṃ, âkâsadhâtu, âpodhâtu, rûpassa upacayo rûpasantati kabaḷiṅkâro âhâro—idan taṃ rûpaṃ upâdiṇṇaṃ.

654. Kataman taṃ rûpaṃ anupâdiṇṇaṃ?

Saddâyatanaṃ kâyaviññatti vacîviññatti rûpassa lahutâ rûpassa mudutâ rûpassa kammaññatâ rûpassa jaratâ rûpassa aniccatâ—yaṃ vâ pan' aññam pi atthi rûpaṃ na kammassa katattâ rûpâyatanaṃ gandhâyatanaṃ rasâyatanaṃ phoṭṭhabbâyatanaṃ âkâsadhâtu âpodhâtu rûpassa upacayo rûpassa santati kabaḷiṅkâro âhâro—idan taṃ rupaṃ anupâdiṇṇaṃ.

655. Kataman taṃ rupaṃ upâdiṇṇupâdâniyaṃ?

Cakkhâyatanaṃ . . . pe . . . kâyâyatanaṃ itthindriyaṃ purisindriyaṃ jîvitindriyaṃ—yaṃ vâ pan' aññam pi atthi rûpaṃ kammassa katattâ rûpâyatanaṃ gandhâyatanaṃ rasâyatanaṃ phoṭṭhabbâyatanaṃ âkâsadhâtu, âpodhâtu, rûpassa upacayo rûpasantati kabaḷiṅkâro âhâro—idan taṃ rûpaṃ upâdiṇṇupâdâniyaṃ.

656. Katamaṃ taṃ rûpaṃ anupâdiṇṇupâdâniyaṃ?

Saddâyatamaṃ kâyaviññatti vacîviññatti rûpassa lahutâ rûpassa mudutâ rûpassa kammaññatâ rûpassa jaratâ rûpassa aniccatâ—yaṃ vâ panaññam pi atthi rûpaṃ na kammassa katattâ rûpâyatanaṃ saddâyatanaṃ, gandhâyatanaṃ, rasâyatanaṃ phoṭṭhabbâyatanaṃ, âkâsadhâtu rûpassa upacayo rûpasantati kabaḷiṅkâro âhâro—idan taṃ rûpaṃ anupâdiṇṇupâdâniyaṃ.

657. Kataman taṃ rûpaṃ sanidassanaṃ?

Rûpâyatanaṃ—idan taṃ rûpaṃ sanidassanaṃ.

658. Kataman taṃ rûpaṃ anidassanaṃ.

Cakkhâyatanaṃ . . . pe . . . kabaḷiṅkâro âhâro—idan taṃ rûpaṃ anidassanaṃ.

659. Kataman taṃ rûpaṃ sappaṭighaṃ?
Cakkhâyatanaṃ, sotâyatanaṃ, ghânâyatanaṃ, jivhâyatanaṃ, kâyâyatanaṃ, rûpâyatanaṃ, saddâyatanaṃ, gandhâyatanaṃ, rasâyatanaṃ, phoṭṭhabbâyatanaṃ—idan taṃ rûpaṃ sappaṭighaṃ.

660. Kataman taṃ rûpaṃ appaṭighaṃ?
Itthindriyaṃ . . . pe . . . kabaḷiṅkâro âhâro—idan taṃ rûpaṃ appaṭighaṃ.

661. Kataman taṃ rûpaṃ indriyaṃ?
Cakkhundriyaṃ, sotindriyaṃ, ghânindriyaṃ, jivhindriyaṃ, kâyindriyaṃ, itthindriyaṃ, purisindriyaṃ, jîvitindriyaṃ—idan taṃ rûpaṃ indriyaṃ.

662. Kataman taṃ rûpaṃ na indriyaṃ?
Rûpâyatanaṃ . . . pe . . . kabaḷiṅkâro âhâro—idan taṃ rûpaṃ na indriyaṃ.

663. Kataman taṃ rûpaṃ mahâbhûtaṃ?
Phoṭṭhabbâyatanaṃ âpodhâtu—idan taṃ rûpaṃ mahâbhûtaṃ.

664. Kataman taṃ rûpaṃ na mahâbhûtaṃ?
Cakkhâyatanaṃ . . . pe . . . kabaḷiṅkâro âhâro—idaṃ taṃ rûpaṃ mahâbhûtaṃ.

665. Kataman taṃ rûpaṃ viññatti?
Kâyaviññatti vacîviññatti—idan taṃ rûpaṃ viññatti.

666. Kataman taṃ rûpaṃ na viññatti?
Cakkhâyatanaṃ . . . pe . . . kabaḷiṅkâro âhâro—idan taṃ rûpaṃ na viññatti.

667. Kataman taṃ rûpaṃ cittasamuṭṭhânaṃ?
Kâyaviññatti vacîviññatti—yaṃ vâ pan' aññam pi atthi rûpaṃ cittajaṃ cittahetukaṃ cittasamuṭṭhânaṃ rûpâyatanaṃ saddâyatanaṃ, gandhâyatanaṃ, rasâyatanaṃ, phoṭṭhabbâyatanaṃ, âkâsadhâtu, âpodhâtu, rûpassa lahutâ, rûpassa mudutâ, rûpassa kammaññatâ, rûpassa upacayo, rûpassa santati kabaḷiṅkâro âhâro—idan taṃ rûpaṃ cittasamuṭṭhânaṃ.

668. Kataman taṃ rûpaṃ na cittasamuṭṭhânaṃ?
Cakkhâyatanaṃ . . . pe . . . kâyâyatanaṃ—itthindriyaṃ purisindriyaṃ, jîvitindriyaṃ, rûpassa jaratâ, rûpassa aniccatâ—yaṃ vâ panaññam pi atthi rûpaṃ na cittajaṃ na cittahetukaṃ na cittasamuṭṭhânaṃ rûpâyatanaṃ, saddâyatanaṃ,

gandhâyatanaṃ, rasâyatanaṃ, phoṭṭhabbâyatanaṃ, âkâsadhâtu, âpodhâtu, rûpassa lahutâ, rûpassa mudutâ, rûpassa kammaññatâ, rûpassa upacayo, rûpassa santati, kabaḷiṅkâro âhâro—idan taṃ rûpaṃ na cittasamuṭṭhânaṃ.

669. Katamaṇ taṃ rûpaṃ cittasahabhû?

Kâyaviññatti vacîviññatti—idan taṃ rûpaṃ cittasahabhû.

670. Katamaṇ taṃ rûpaṃ na cittasahabhû?

Cakkhâyatamaṃ . . . pe . . . kabaḷiṅkâro âhâro—idan taṃ rûpaṃ na cittasahabhû.

671. Katamaṇ taṃ rûpaṃ cittânuparivatti?

Kâyaviññatti vacîviññatti—idan taṃ rûpaṃ cittânuparivatti.

672. Katamaṇ taṃ rûpaṃ na cittânuparivatti?

Cakkhâyatanaṃ . . . pe . . . kabaḷiṅkâro âhâro—idan taṃ rûpaṃ na cittânuparivatti.

673. Katamaṇ taṃ rûpaṃ ajjhattikaṃ?

Cakkhâyatanaṃ . . . pe . . . kâyâyatanaṃ—idan taṃ rûpaṃ ajjhattikaṃ.

674. Katamaṇ taṃ rûpaṃ bâhiraṃ?

Rûpâyatanaṃ . . . pe . . . kabaliṅkâro âhâro—idan taṃ rûpaṃ bâhiraṃ.

675. Katamaṇ taṃ rûpaṃ oḷârikaṃ.

Cakkhâyatanaṃ . . . pe . . . phoṭṭhabbâyatanaṃ—idan taṃ rûpaṃ oḷârikaṃ.

676. Katamaṇ taṃ rûpaṃ sukhumaṃ?

Itthindriyaṃ . . . pe . . . kabaliṅkâro âhâro—idan taṃ rûpaṃ sukhumaṃ.

677. Katamaṇ taṃ rûpaṃ dûre?

Itthindriyaṃ . . . pe . . . kabaḷiṅkâro âhâro—idan taṃ rûpaṃ dûre.

678. Katamaṇ taṃ rûpaṃ santike?

Cakkhâyatanaṃ . . . pe . . . phoṭṭhabbâyatanaṃ—idan taṃ rûpaṃ santike.

679. Katamaṇ taṃ rûpaṃ cakhhusamphassassa vatthu?

Cakkhâyatanaṃ—idan taṃ rûpaṃ cakkhusamphassassa vatthu.

680. Katamaṇ taṃ rûpaṃ cakkhusamphassassa na vatthu?

Sotâyatanaṃ . . . pe . . . kabaḷiṅkâro âhâro—idaṃ taṃ rûpaṃ cakkhusamphassassa na vatthu.

681. Kataman taṃ rûpaṃ cakkhusamphassajâya vedanâya . . . pe . . . saññâya . . . pe . . . cetanâya . . . pe . . . cakkhuviññâṇassa vatthu?

Cakkhâyatanaṃ — idaṃ taṃ rûpaṃ cakkhuviññâṇassa vatthu.

682. Kataman taṃ rûpaṃ cakkhuviññâṇassa na vatthu?

Sotâyatanaṃ . . . pe . . . kabaḷiṅkâro âhâro—idan taṃ rûpaṃ cakkhuviññâṇassa na vatthu.

683. Kataman taṃ rûpaṃ sotasamphassassa . . . pe . . . ghânasamphassassa . . . pe . . . kâyasamphassassa vatthu?

Kâyâyatanaṃ—idan taṃ rûpaṃ kâyasamphassassa vatthu.

684. Kataman taṃ rûpaṃ kâyasamphassassa na vatthu?

Cakkhâyatanaṃ . . . pe . . . kabaḷiṅkâro âhâro—idan taṃ rûpaṃ kâyasamphassassa na vatthu.

685. Kataman taṃ rûpaṃ kâyasamphassajâya vedanâya . . . pe . . . saññâya . . . pe . . . cetanâya . . . pe . . . kâyaviññâṇassa vatthu?

Kâyâyatanaṃ—idan taṃ rûpaṃ kâyaviññâṇassa vatthu.

686. Kataman taṃ rûpaṃ kâyaviññâṇassa na vatthu?

Cakkhâyatanaṃ . . . pe . . . kabaḷiṅkâro âhâro—idaṃ taṃ rûpaṃ kâyaviññâṇassa na vatthu.

687. Kataman taṃ rûpaṃ cakkhusamphassassa ârammaṇaṃ?

Rûpâyatanaṃ — idan taṃ rûpaṃ cakkhusamphassassa ârammaṇaṃ.

688. Kataman taṃ rûpam cakkhusamphassassa na ârammaṇaṃ?

Cakkhâyatanaṃ . . . pe . . . kabaḷiṅkâro âhâro—idan taṃ rûpaṃ cakkhusamphassassa na ârammaṇaṃ.

689. Katamaṃ taṃ rûpaṃ cakkhusamphassajâya vedanâya . . . pe . . . saññâya . . . pe . . . cetanâya . . . pe . . . cakkhuviññâṇassa ârammaṇaṃ.

Rûpâyatanaṃ—idan taṃ rûpaṃ cakkhuviññâṇassa ârammaṇaṃ.

690. Kataman taṃ rûpaṃ cakkhuviññâṇassa ârammaṇaṃ?

Cakkhâyatanaṃ—kabaḷiṅkâro âhâro—idan taṃ rûpaṃ cakkhuviññâṇassa ârammaṇaṃ.

691. Kataman taṃ rûpaṃ sotasamphassassa . . . pe . . .

ghânasamphassassa . . . pe . . . jivhâsamphassassa . . . pe . . . kâyasamphassassa ârammaṇaṃ.

Phoṭṭhabbâyatanaṃ—idan taṃ rûpaṃ kâyasamphassassa ârammaṇaṃ.

692. Kataman taṃ rûpaṃ kâyasamphassassa na ârammaṇaṃ?

Cakkhâyatanaṃ . . . pe . . . kabaḷiṅkâro âhâro—idan taṃ rûpaṃ kâyasamphassassa na ârammaṇaṃ.

693. Kataman taṃ rûpaṃ kâyasamphassajâya vedanâya . . . pe . . . saññâya . . . pe . . . cetanâya . . . pe . . . kâyaviññâṇassa ârammaṇaṃ?

Phoṭṭhabbâyatanaṃ—idan taṃ rûpaṃ kâyaviññâṇassa ârammaṇaṃ.

694. Kataman taṃ rûpaṃ kâyaviññâṇassa na ârammaṇaṃ?

Cakkhâyatanaṃ . . . pe . . . kabaḷiṅkâro âhâro—idan taṃ rûpaṃ kâyaviññâṇassa na ârammaṇaṃ.

695. Kataman taṃ rûpaṃ cakkhâyatanaṃ?

Yaṃ cakkhu catunnaṃ mahâbhûtânaṃ upâdâya pasâdo . . . pe . . . suñño gâmo peso—idan taṃ rûpaṃ cakkhâyatanaṃ.

696. Kataman taṃ rûpaṃ na cakkhâyatanaṃ?

Sotâyatanaṃ . . . pe . . . kabaliṅkâro âhâro—idan taṃ rûpaṃ na cakkhâyatanaṃ.

697. Kataman taṃ rûpaṃ sotâyatanaṃ . . . pe . . . ghânâyatanaṃ . . . pe . . . jivhâyatanaṃ . . . pe . . . kâyâyatanaṃ?

Yo kâyo catunnaṃ mahâbhûtânaṃ upâdâya pasâdo . . . pe . . . suñño gâmo peso—idan taṃ rûpaṃ kâyâyatanaṃ.

698. Kataman taṃ rûpaṃ na kâyâyatanaṃ?

Cakkhâyatanaṃ . . . pe . . . kabaḷiṅkâro âhâro—idan taṃ rûpaṃ na kâyâyatanaṃ.

699. Kataman taṃ rûpaṃ rûpâyatanam?

Yaṃ rûpaṃ catunnaṃ mahâbhûtânaṃ upâdâya vaṇṇanibhâ . . . pe . . . rûpadhâtu pesâ—idan taṃ rûpaṃ rûpâyatanaṃ.

700. Kataman taṃ rûpaṃ na rûpâyatanaṃ?

Cakkhâyatanaṃ . . . pe . . . kabaḷiṅkâro âhâro—idan taṃ rûpaṃ na rûpâyatanaṃ.

701. Kataman taṃ rûpaṃ saddâyatanaṃ . . . pe . . .

gandhâyatanaṃ . . . pe . . . rasâyatanaṃ . . . pe . . . phoṭṭhabbâyatanaṃ?

Pathavîdhâtu . . . pe . . . phoṭṭhabbadhâtu pesâ—idaṃ taṃ rûpaṃ phoṭṭhabbadhâtu.

702. Katamaṃ taṃ rûpaṃ na phoṭṭhabbâyatanaṃ?

Cakkhâyatanaṃ . . . pe . . . kabaḷiṅkâro âhâro—idan taṃ rûpaṃ na phoṭṭhabbâyatanaṃ.

703. Katamaṃ taṃ rûpaṃ.cakkhudhâtu.

Cakkhâyatanaṃ—idan taṃ rûpaṃ cakkhudhâtu.

704. Katamaṃ taṃ rûpaṃ na cakkhudhâtu?

Sotâyatanaṃ . . . pe . . . kabaḷiṅkâro âhâro—idan taṃ rûpaṃ na cakkhudhâtu.

705. Katamaṃ taṃ rûpaṃ rûpadhâtu?

Rûpâyatanaṃ—idan taṃ rûpaṃ rûpadhâtu.

706. Katamaṃ taṃ rûpaṃ na rûpadhâtu?

Cakkhâyatanaṃ . . . pe . . . kabaḷiṅkâro âhâro — idan taṃ rûpaṃ na rûpadhâtu.

707. Katamaṃ taṃ rûpaṃ saddadhâtu . . . pe . . . gandhadhâtu . . . pe . . . phoṭṭhabbadhâtu?

Phoṭṭhabbâyatanaṃ—idan taṃ rûpaṃ phoṭṭhabbadhâtu.

708. Katamaṃ taṃ rûpaṃ na phoṭṭhabbadhâtu?

Cakkhâyatanaṃ . . . pe . . . kabaliṅkâro âhâro — idan taṃ rûpaṃ na phoṭṭhabbadhâtu.

709. Katamaṃ taṃ rûpaṃ cakkhundriyaṃ?

Yaṃ cakkhu catunnaṃ mahâbhûtânaṃ upâdâya pasâdo . . . pe . . . suñño gâmo peso—idan taṃ rûpaṃ cakkhundriyaṃ.

710. Katamaṃ taṃ rûpaṃ na cakkhundriyaṃ?

Sotâyatanaṃ . . . pe . . . kabaḷiṅkâro âhâro—idan taṃ rûpaṃ na cakkhundriyaṃ.

711. Katamaṃ taṃ rûpaṃ sotindriyaṃ . . . pe . . . ghâṇindriyaṃ . . . pe . . . jivhindriyaṃ . . . pe . . . kâyindriyaṃ?

Yo kâyo catunnaṃ mahâbhûtânaṃ upâdâya pasâdo . . . pe . . . suñño gâmo peso—idan taṃ rûpaṃ kâyindriyaṃ.

712. Katamaṃ taṃ rûpaṃ na kâyindriyaṃ?

Cakkhâyatanaṃ . . . pe . . . kabaḷiṅkâro âhâro—idan taṃ rûpaṃ na kâyindriyaṃ.

713. Katamaṃ taṃ rûpaṃ itthindriyaṃ?

Yaṃ itthiyâ itthiliṅgaṃ itthinimittaṃ itthikuttaṃ itthâkappo itthattaṃ itthibhâvo—idan taṃ rûpaṃ itthindriyaṃ.

714. Kataman taṃ rûpaṃ purisindriyaṃ ?

Yaṃ purisassa purisaliṅgaṃ purisanimittaṃ purisakuttaṃ purisâkappo purisattaṃ purisabhâvo—idan taṃ rûpaṃ purisindriyaṃ.

715. Kataman taṃ rûpaṃ na purisindriyaṃ ?

Cakkhâyatanaṃ . . . pe . . . kabaḷiṅkâro âhâro—idan taṃ rûpaṃ na purisindriyaṃ.

716. Kataman taṃ rûpaṃ jîvitindriyaṃ ?

Yo tesaṃ rûpînaṃ dhammânaṃ âyu ṭhiti yapanâ yâpanâ iriyanâ vattanâ pâlanâ jîvitaṃ jîvitindriyaṃ—idan taṃ rûpaṃ jîvitindriyaṃ.

717. Kataman taṃ rûpaṃ na jîvitindriyaṃ ?

Cakkhâyatanaṃ . . . pe . . . kabaḷiṅkâro âhâro—idan taṃ rûpaṃ na jîvitindriyaṃ.

718. Kataman taṃ rûpaṃ kâyaviññatti ?

Yâ kusalacittassa vâ akusalacittassa vâ avyâkatacittassa vâ abhikkamantassa vâ paṭikkamantassa vâ âlokentassa vâ vilokentassa vâ sammiñjentassa vâ pasârentassa vâ kâyassa thambhanâ santhambhanâ santhambhitattaṃ viññatti viññâpanâ viññâpitattaṃ: idan taṃ rûpaṃ kâyaviññatti.

719. Kataman taṃ rûpaṃ na kâyaviññatti ?

Cakkhâyatanaṃ . . . pe . . . kabaḷiṅkâro âhâro—idan taṃ rûpaṃ na kâyaviññatti.

720. Kataman taṃ rûpaṃ vacîviññatti ?

Yâ kusalacittassa vâ akusalacittassa vâ avyâkatacittassa vâ vâcâ girâ vyappatho udîraṇaṃ ghoso ghosakammaṃ vâcâ vacîbhedo—ayaṃ vuccati vâcâ—yâ tâya vâcâya viññatti viññâpanâ viññâpitattaṃ—idan taṃ rûpaṃ vacîviññatti.

721. Kataman taṃ rûpaṃ na vacîviññatti ?

Cakkhâyatanaṃ . . . pe . . . kabaḷiṅkâro âhâro—idan taṃ rûpaṃ na vacîviññatti.

722. Kataman taṃ rûpaṃ âkâsadhâtu ?

Yo âkâso âkâsagataṃ aghaṃ aghagataṃ vivaro vivaragataṃ asamphuṭṭhaṃ catûhi mahâbhûtehi—idan taṃ rûpaṃ âkâsadhâtu.

723. Kataman taṃ rûpaṃ na âkâsadhâtu ?

Cakkhâyatanaṃ . . . pe . . . kabaḷiṅkâro âhâro—idan taṃ rûpaṃ âkâsadhâtu.

724. Katamaṃ taṃ rûpaṃ âpodhâtu?

Yaṃ âpo âpogataṃ sineho sinehagataṃ bandhanattaṃ rûpassa—idan taṃ rûpaṃ âpodhâtu.

725. Katamaṃ taṃ rûpaṃ na âpodhâtu?

Cakkhâyatanaṃ . . . pe . . . kabaḷiṅkâro âhâro—idan taṃ rûpaṃ na âpodhâtu.

726. Katamaṃ taṃ rûpaṃ rûpassa lahutâ?

Yâ rûpassa lahutâ lahutapariṇâmatâ adandhanatâ avitthanatâ—idan taṃ rûpaṃ rûpassa lahutâ.

727. Katamaṃ taṃ rûpaṃ rûpassa na lahutâ?

Cakkhâyatanaṃ . . . pe . . . kabaḷiṅkâro âhâro—idan taṃ rûpam rûpassa na lahutâ.

728. Katamaṃ taṃ rûpaṃ rûpassa mudutâ?

Yâ rûpassa mudutâ maddavatâ akakkhaḷatâ akathinatâ—idan taṃ rûpaṃ rûpassa mudutâ.

729. Katamaṃ taṃ rûpaṃ rûpassa na mudutâ?

Cakkhâyatanaṃ . . . pe . . . kabaḷiṅkâro âhâro — idan taṃ rûpaṃ rûpassa na mudutâ.

730. Katamaṃ taṃ rûpaṃ rûpassa kammaññatâ?

Yâ rûpassa kammaññatâ kammaññattaṃ kammaññabhâvo—idan taṃ rûpaṃ rûpassa kammaññatâ.

731. Katamaṃ taṃ rûpaṃ rûpassa na kammaññatâ?

Cakkhâyatanaṃ . . . pe . . . kabaḷiṅkâro âhâro — idan taṃ rûpaṃ rûpassa na kammaññatâ.

732. Katamaṃ taṃ rûpaṃ rûpassa upacayo?

Yo âyatanânaṃ âcayo—so rûpassa upacayo—idan taṃ rûpaṃ rûpassa upacayo.

733. Katamaṃ taṃ rûpaṃ rûpassa na upacayo?

Cakkhâyatanaṃ . . . pe . . . kabaḷiṅkâro âhâro—idan taṃ rûpaṃ rûpassa na upacayo.

734. Katamaṃ taṃ rûpaṃ rûpassa santati?

Yo rûpassa upacayo—sâ rûpassa santati—idaṃ taṃ rûpaṃ rûpassa santati.

735. Katamaṃ taṃ rûpaṃ rûpassa na santati?

Cakkhâyatanaṃ . . . pe . . . kabaḷiṅkâro âhâro — idaṃ taṃ rûpaṃ rûpassa na santati.

736. Kataman taṃ rûpaṃ rûpassa jaratâ?
Yâ rûpassa jarâ jîraṇatâ khaṇḍiccaṃ pâliccaṃ valittacatâ âyuno saṃhâni indriyânaṃ paripâko—idan taṃ rûpaṃ rûpassa jaratâ.

737. Kataman taṃ rûpaṃ rûpassa na jaratâ?
Cakkhâyatanaṃ . . . pe . . . kabaḷiṅkâro âhâro—idaṃ taṃ rûpaṃ rûpassa na jaratâ.

738. Kataman taṃ rûpaṃ rûpassa aniccatâ?
Yo rûpassa khayo vayo bhedo paribhedo aniccatâ antaradhânaṃ: idan taṃ rûpaṃ rûpassa aniccatâ.

739. Kataman taṃ rûpaṃ rûpassa na aniccatâ?
Cakkhâyatanaṃ . . . pe . . . kabaḷiṅkâro âhâro—idaṃ taṃ rûpaṃ rûpassa na aniccatâ.

740. Kataman taṃ rûpaṃ kabaḷiṅkâro âhâro?
Odano kummâso sattu maccho maṃsaṃ khîraṃ dadhi sappi navanîtaṃ telaṃ madhu phâṇitaṃ—yaṃ vâ panaññam pi atthi rûpaṃ yamhi yamhi janapade tesaṃ tesaṃ sattânaṃ mukhâsiyaṃ dantavikhâdanaṃ galajjhoharaṇiyaṃ kucchivitthambhanaṃ—yâya ojâya sattâ yâpenti—idan taṃ rûpaṃ kabaḷiṅkâro âhâro.

741. Kataman taṃ rûpaṃ na kabaḷiṅkâro âhâro?
Cakkhâyatanaṃ . . . pe . . . rûpassa aniccatâ—idan taṃ rûpaṃ na kabaḷiṅkâro âhâro.

Evaṃ duvidhena rûpasaṅgaho. Dukkhaniddeso.

742. Kataman taṃ rûpaṃ ajjhattikaṃ upâdâ?
Cakkhâyatanaṃ . . . pe . . . kâyâyatanaṃ—idaṃ taṃ rûpaṃ ajjhattikaṃ upâdâ.

743. Kataman taṃ rûpaṃ bâhiraṃ upâdâ?
Rûpâyatanaṃ . . . pe . . . kabaḷiṅkâro âhâro—idan taṃ rûpaṃ bâhiraṃ upâdâ.

744. Kataman taṃ rûpaṃ bâhiraṃ no upâdâ?
Phoṭṭhabbâyatanaṃ âpodhâtu—idan taṃ rûpaṃ bâhiraṃ no upâdâ.

745. Kataman taṃ rûpaṃ ajjhattikaṃ upâdiṇṇaṃ?
Cakkhâyatanaṃ . . . pe . . . . kâyâyatanaṃ idan taṃ rûpaṃ ajjhattikaṃ upâdiṇṇaṃ.

746. Kataman taṃ rûpaṃ bâhiraṃ upâdiṇṇaṃ.

Itthindriyaṃ, purisindriyaṃ, jîvitindriyaṃ — yaṃ vâ panaññam pi atthi rûpaṃ kammassa katattâ rûpâyatanaṃ gandhâyatanaṃ rasâyatanaṃ phoṭṭhabbâyatanaṃ âkâsadhâtu âpodhâtu rûpassa upacayo rûpassa santati—kabaḷiṅkâro âhâro idan taṃ rûpaṃ bâhiraṃ upâdiṇṇaṃ.

747. Kataman taṃ rûpaṃ bâhiraṃ anupâdiṇṇaṃ?

Saddâyatanaṃ kâyaviññatti vacîviññatti rûpassa lahutâ rûpassa mudutâ rûpassa kammaññatâ rûpassa jaratâ rûpassa aniccatâ—yaṃ vâ panaññam pi atthi rûpaṃ na kammassa katattâ rûpâyatanaṃ saddâyatanaṃ gandhâyatanaṃ rasâyatanaṃ phoṭṭhabbâyatanaṃ âkâsadhâtu âpodhâtu rûpassa upacayo rûpassa santati kabaḷiṅkâro âhâro—idan taṃ rûpaṃ bâhiraṃ anupâdiṇṇaṃ.

748. Kataman taṃ rûpaṃ ajjhattikaṃ upâdiṇṇupâdâniyaṃ?

Cakkhâyatanaṃ . . . pe . . . kâyâyatanaṃ—idaṃ taṃ rûpaṃ ajjhattikaṃ upâdiṇṇupâdâyaṃ.

749. Kataman taṃ rûpaṃ bâhiraṃ upâdiṇṇupâdâniyaṃ?

Itthindriyaṃ purisindriyaṃ jîvitindriyaṃ—yaṃ vâ panaññaṃ pi atthi rûpaṃ kammassa katattâ rûpâyatanaṃ gandhâyatanaṃ rasâyatanaṃ phoṭṭhabbâyatanaṃ âkâsadhâtu âpodhâtu rûpassa upacayo rûpassa santati kabaḷiṅkâro âhâro—idan taṃ rûpaṃ bâhiraṃ upâdiṇṇupâdâniyaṃ.

750. Kataman taṃ rûpaṃ bâhiraṃ anupâdiṇṇupâdâniyaṃ?

Saddâyatanaṃ kâyaviññatti vacîviññatti rûpassa lahutâ rûpassa mudutâ rûpassa kammaññatâ rûpassa jaratâ rûpassa aniccatâ—yaṃ vâ panaññam pi atthi rûpaṃ na katattâ rûpâyatanaṃ gandhâyatanaṃ rasâyatanaṃ phoṭṭhabbâyatanaṃ âkâsadhâtu âpodhâtu rûpassa upacayo rûpassa santati kabaḷiṅkâro âhâro—idan taṃ rûpaṃ bâhiraṃ anupâdiṇṇupâdâniyaṃ.

751. Kataman taṃ rûpaṃ ajjhattikaṃ anidassanaṃ?

Cakkhâyatanaṃ . . . pe . . . kâyâyatanaṃ—idan taṃ rûpaṃ ajjhattikaṃ anidassanaṃ.

752. Kataman taṃ rûpaṃ bâhiraṃ sanidassanaṃ?

Rûpâyatanaṃ—idaṃ taṃ rûpaṃ bâhiraṃ sanidassanaṃ.

753. Kataman taṃ rûpaṃ bâhiraṃ anidassanaṃ?

Saddâyatanaṃ . . . pe . . . kabaḷiṅkâro âhâro: idaṃ taṃ rûpaṃ bâhiraṃ anidassanaṃ.

754. Katamaṃ taṃ rûpaṃ ajjhattikaṃ sappaṭighaṃ?

Cakkhâyatanaṃ . . . pe . . . kâyâyatanaṃ idaṃ taṃ rûpaṃ ajjhattikaṃ sappaṭighaṃ.

755. Katamaṃ taṃ rûpaṃ bâhiraṃ sappaṭighaṃ?

Rûpâyatanaṃ . . . pe . . . phoṭṭhabbâyatanaṃ—idaṃ taṃ rûpaṃ bâhiraṃ sappaṭighaṃ.

756. Katamaṃ taṃ rûpaṃ bâhiraṃ sappaṭighaṃ?

Itthindriyaṃ . . . pe . . . kabaḷiṅkâro âhâro—idaṃ taṃ rûpaṃ bâhiraṃ sappaṭighaṃ.

757. Katamaṃ taṃ rûpaṃ ajjhattikaṃ indriyaṃ?

Cakkhundriyaṃ . . . pe . . . kâyindriyaṃ—idaṃ taṃ rûpaṃ ajjhattikaṃ indriyaṃ.

758. Katamaṃ taṃ rûpaṃ bâhiraṃ indriyaṃ?

Itthindriyaṃ purisindriyaṃ jîvitindriyaṃ—idaṃ taṃ rûpaṃ bâhiraṃ indriyaṃ.

759. Katamaṃ taṃ rûpaṃ bâhiraṃ na indriyaṃ?

Rûpâyatanaṃ . . . pe . . . kabaḷiṅkâro âhâro—idaṃ taṃ rûpaṃ bâhiraṃ na indriyaṃ.

760. Katamaṃ taṃ rûpaṃ ajjhattikaṃ na mahâbhûtaṃ?

Cakkhâyatanaṃ . . . pe . . . kâyâyatanaṃ—idaṃ taṃ rûpaṃ ajjhattikaṃ na mahâbhûtaṃ.

761. Katamaṃ taṃ rûpaṃ bâhiraṃ mahâbhûtaṃ?

Phoṭṭhabbâyatanaṃ âpodhâtu—idaṃ taṃ rûpaṃ bâhiraṃ mahâbhûtaṃ.

762. Katamaṃ taṃ rûpaṃ bâhiraṃ na mahâbhûtaṃ?

Rûpâyatanaṃ . . . pe . . . kabaḷiṅkâro âhâro—idaṃ taṃ rûpaṃ bâhiraṃ na mahâbhûtaṃ.

763. Katamaṃ taṃ rûpaṃ ajjhattikaṃ na viññatti?

Cakkhâyatanaṃ . . . pe . . . kâyâyatanaṃ—idaṃ taṃ rûpaṃ ajjhattikaṃ na viññatti.

764. Katamaṃ taṃ rûpaṃ bâhiraṃ viññatti?

Kâyaviññatti vacîviññatti.—idaṃ taṃ rûpaṃ bâhiraṃ viññatti.

765. Katamaṃ taṃ rûpaṃ bâhiraṃ na viññatti?

Rûpâyatanaṃ . . . pe . . . kabaḷiṅkâro âhâro—idaṃ taṃ rûpaṃ bâhiraṃ na viññatti.

766. Kataman taṃ rûpaṃ ajjhattikaṃ na cittassa samuṭṭhânaṃ?

Cakkhâyatanaṃ . . . pe . . . kâyâyatanaṃ—idan taṃ rûpaṃ ajjhattikaṃ na cittassa samuṭṭhânaṃ.

767. Kataman taṃ rûpaṃ bâhiraṃ cittasamuṭṭhânaṃ?

Kâyaviññatti vacîviññatti—yaṃ vâ panaññam pi atthi rûpaṃ cittajaṃ cittahetukaṃ cittasamuṭṭhânaṃ rûpâyatanaṃ saddâyatanaṃ gandhâyatanaṃ rasâyatanam phoṭṭhabbâyatanaṃ âkâsadhâtu âpodhâtu rûpassa lahutâ rûpassa mudutâ rûpassa kammaññatâ rûpassa upacayo rûpassa santati kabaḷiṅkâro âhâro—idan taṃ rûpaṃ bâhiraṃ cittasamuṭṭhânaṃ.

768. Kataman taṃ rûpaṃ bâhiraṃ na cittasamuṭṭhânaṃ?

Itthindriyaṃ purisindriyaṃ. jîvitindriyaṃ rûpassa jaratâ rûpassa aniccatâ yaṃ vâ panaññaṃ pi atthi rûpaṃ na cittajaṃ na cittahetukaṃ na cittasamuṭṭhânam rûpâyatanaṃ saddâyatanaṃ gandhâyatanaṃ rasâyatanaṃ phoṭṭhabbâyatanaṃ âkâsadhâtu âpodhâtu rûpassa lahutâ rûpassa mudutâ rûpassa kammaññatâ rûpassa upacayo rûpassa santati kabaḷiṅkâro âhâro—idan taṃ rûpaṃ bâhiraṃ na cittasamuṭṭhânaṃ.

769. Kataman taṃ rûpaṃ ajjhattikaṃ na cittasahabhû?

Cakkhâyatanaṃ . . . pe . . . kâyâyatanaṃ—idan taṃ rûpaṃ ajjhattikaṃ na cittasahabhû.

770. Kataman taṃ rûpaṃ bâhiraṃ cittasahabhû?

Kâyaviññatti vacîviññatti—idan taṃ rûpaṃ bâhiraṃ cittasahabhû.

771. Kataman taṃ rûpaṃ bâhiraṃ na cittasahabhû?

Rûpâyatanaṃ . . . pe . . . kabaḷiṅkâro âhâro—idan taṃ rûpaṃ bâhiraṃ na cittasahabhû.

772. Kataman taṃ rûpaṃ ajjhattikaṃ na cittânuparivatti?

Cakkhâyatanaṃ . . . pe . . . kâyâyatanaṃ—idaṃ taṃ rûpaṃ ajjhattikaṃ na cittânuparivatti.

773. Kataman taṃ rûpaṃ bâhiraṃ cittânuparivatti?

Kâyaviññatti vacîviññatti—idan taṃ rûpaṃ bâhiraṃ cittânuparivatti.

774. Kataman taṃ rûpaṃ bâhiraṃ na cittânuparivatti?

Rûpâyatanaṃ . . . pe . . . kabaḷiṅkâro âhâro—idan taṃ rûpaṃ bâhiraṃ na cittânuparivatti?

775. Kataman taṃ rûpaṃ ajjhattikaṃ oḷârikaṃ?

Cakkhâyatanaṃ . . . pe . . . kâyâyatanaṃ—idan taṃ rûpaṃ ajjhattikaṃ oḷârikaṃ.

776. Kataman taṃ rûpaṃ bâhiraṃ oḷârikaṃ?

Rûpâyatanaṃ . . . pe . . . phoṭṭhabbâyatanaṃ—idan taṃ rûpaṃ bâhiraṃ oḷârikaṃ.

777. Kataman taṃ rûpaṃ bâhiraṃ sukhumaṃ?

Itthindriyaṃ . . . pe . . . kabaḷiṅkâro âhâro—idan taṃ rûpaṃ bâhiraṃ sukhumaṃ.

778. Kataman taṃ rûpaṃ ajjhattikaṃ santike?

Cakkhâyatanaṃ . . . pe . . . kâyâyatanaṃ idan taṃ rûpaṃ ajjhattikaṃ santike.

779. Kataman taṃ rûpaṃ bâhiraṃ dûre?

Itthindriyaṃ . . . pe . . . kabaḷiṅkâro âhâro—idan taṃ rûpaṃ bâhiraṃ dûre.

780. Kataman taṃ rûpaṃ bâhiraṃ santike?

Rûpâyatanaṃ . . . pe . . . phoṭṭhabbâyatanaṃ—idan taṃ rûpaṃ bâhiraṃ santike.

781. Kataman taṃ rûpaṃ bâhiraṃ cakkhusamphassassa na vatthu?

Rûpâyatanaṃ . . . pe . . . kabaḷiṅkâro âhâro—idan taṃ rûpaṃ bâhiraṃ cakkhusamphassassa na vatthu.

782. Kataman taṃ rupaṃ ajjhattikaṃ cakkhusamphassassa vatthu?

Cakkhâyatanaṃ—idan taṃ rûpaṃ ajjhattikaṃ cakkhusamphassassa vatthu.

783. Kataman taṃ rûpaṃ ajjhattikaṃ cakkhusamphassassa na vatthu?

Sotâyatanaṃ . . . pe . . . kâyâyatanaṃ—idan taṃ rûpaṃ ajjhattikaṃ cakkhusamphassassa na vatthu.

784. Kataman taṃ rûpaṃ bâhiraṃ cakkhusamphassajâya vedanâya . . . pe . . . saññâya . . . pe . . . cetanâya . . . pe . . . cakkhuviññâṇassa na vatthu?

Rûpâyatanaṃ . . . pe . . . kabaḷiṅkaro âhâro—idan taṃ rûpaṃ bâhiraṃ cakkhuviññâṇassa na vatthu.

785. Kataman taṃ rûpaṃ ajjhattikaṃ cakkhuviññâṇassa vatthu?

Cakkhâyatanaṃ—idan taṃ rûpaṃ ajjhattikaṃ cakkhuviññâṇassa vatthu.

786. Kataman taṃ rûpaṃ ajjhattikaṃ cakkhuviññâṇassa na vatthu?

Sotâyatanaṃ . . . pe . . . kâyâyatanaṃ—idan taṃ rûpaṃ ajjhattikaṃ cakkhuviññâṇassa na vatthu.

787. Kataman taṃ rûpaṃ bâhiraṃ sotasamphassassa . . . pe . . . ghânasamphassassa . . . pe . . . jivhâsamphassassa . . . pe . . . kâyasamphassassa na vatthu?

Rûpâyatanaṃ . . . pe . . . kabaḷiṅkâro âhâro—idan taṃ rûpaṃ bâhiraṃ kâyasamphassassa na vatthu.

788. Kataman taṃ rûpaṃ ajjhattikaṃ kâyasamphassassa vatthu?

Kâyâyatanaṃ—idan taṃ rûpaṃ ajjhattikaṃ kâyasamphassassa vatthu.

789. Kataman taṃ rûpaṃ ajjhattikaṃ kâyasamphassassa na vatthu?

Cakkhâyatanaṃ . . . pe . . . jivhâyatanaṃ—idan taṃ rûpaṃ ajjhattikaṃ kâyasamphassassa na vatthu.

790. Kataman taṃ rûpaṃ bâhiraṃ kâyasamphassajâya vedanâya . . . pe . . . saññâya . . . pe . . . cetanâya . . . pe . . . kâyaviññâṇassa na vatthu?

Rûpâyatanaṃ . . . pe . . . kabaḷiṅkâro âhâro—idan taṃ rûpaṃ bâhiraṃ kâyaviññâṇassa na vatthu.

791. Kataman taṃ rûpaṃ ajjhattikaṃ kâyaviññâṇassa vatthu?

Kâyâyatanaṃ—idan taṃ rûpaṃ ajjhattikaṃ kâyaviññâṇassa vatthu.

792. Kataman taṃ rûpaṃ ajjhattikaṃ kâyaviññâṇassa na vatthu?

Cakkhâyatanaṃ . . . pe . . . jivhâyatanaṃ—idan taṃ rûpaṃ ajjhattikaṃ kâyaviññâṇassa na vatthu.

793. Kataman taṃ rûpaṃ ajjhattikaṃ cakkhusamphassassa na ârammaṇaṃ?

Cakkhâyatanaṃ . . . pe . . . kâyâyatanaṃ—idan taṃ rûpaṃ cakkhusamphassassa na ârammaṇaṃ.

794. Kataman taṃ rûpaṃ bâhiraṃ cakkhusamphassassa ârammaṇaṃ?

Rûpâyatanaṃ — idan taṃ rûpaṃ cakkhusamphassassa ârammaṇaṃ.

795. Kataman taṃ rûpaṃ bâhiraṃ cakkhusamphassassa na ârammaṇaṃ?

Saddâyatanaṃ . . . pe . . . kabaḷiṅkâro âhâro—idan taṃ rûpaṃ bâhiraṃ cakkhusamphassassa na ârammaṇaṃ?

796. Kataman taṃ rûpaṃ ajjhattikaṃ cakkhusamphassajâya vedanâya . . . pe . . . saññâya . . . pe . . . cetanâya . . . pe . . . cakkhuviññâṇassa na ârammaṇaṃ?

Cakkhâyatanaṃ . . . pe . . . kâyâyatanaṃ . . . pe . . . idan taṃ rûpaṃ ajjhattikaṃ cakkhuviññâṇassa na ârammaṇaṃ.

797. Kataman taṃ rûpaṃ bâhiraṃ cakkhuviññâṇassa ârammaṇaṃ?

Rûpâyatanaṃ—idan taṃ rûpaṃ bâhiraṃ cakkhuviññâṇassa ârammaṇaṃ.

798. Kataman taṃ rûpaṃ bâhiraṃ cakkhuviññâṇassa na ârammaṇaṃ?

Saddâyatanaṃ . . . pe . . . kabaḷiṅkâro âhâro—idan taṃ rûpaṃ bâhiraṃ cakkhuviññâṇassa na ârammaṇaṃ.

799. Kataman taṃ rûpaṃ ajjhattikaṃ sotasamphassassa . . . pe . . . ghânasamphassassa . . . pe . . . jivhâsamphassassa . . . pe . . . kâyasamphassassa na ârammaṇaṃ?

Cakkhâyatanaṃ . . . pe . . . kâyâyatanaṃ—idan taṃ rûpaṃ ajjhattikaṃ kâyasamphassassa na ârammaṇaṃ.

800. Kataman taṃ rûpaṃ bâhiraṃ kâyasamphassassa ârammaṇaṃ?

Phoṭṭhabbâyatanaṃ—idan taṃ rûpaṃ kâyasamphassassa ârammaṇaṃ.

801. Kataman taṃ rûpaṃ bâhiraṃ kâyasamphassassa na ârammaṇaṃ?

Rûpâyatanaṃ . . . pe . . . kabaliṅkâro âhâro—idan taṃ rûpaṃ bâhiraṃ kâyasamphassassa na ârammaṇaṃ.

802. Kataman taṃ rûpaṃ ajjhattikaṃ kâyasamphassajâya vedanâya . . . pe . . . saññâya . . . pe . . . cetanâya . . . pe . . . kâyaviññâṇassa na ârammaṇaṃ?

Cakkhâyatanaṃ . . . pe . . . kâyâyatanaṃ—idan taṃ rûpaṃ ajjhattikaṃ kâyaviññâṇassa na ârammaṇaṃ.

803. Kataman taṃ rûpaṃ bâhiraṃ kâyaviññâṇassa ârammaṇaṃ?

Phoṭṭhabbâyatanaṃ—idan taṃ rûpaṃ bâhiraṃ kâya-viññâṇassa ârammaṇaṃ.

804. Kataman taṃ rûpaṃ bâhiraṃ kâyaviññâṇassa na ârammaṇaṃ?

Rûpâyatanaṃ . . . pe . . . kabaḷiṅkâro âhâro—idan taṃ rûpaṃ bâhiraṃ kâyaviññâṇassa na ârammanaṃ.

805. Kataman taṃ rûpaṃ bâhiraṃ na cakkhâyatanaṃ?

Rûpâyatanaṃ . . . pe . . . kabaḷiṅkâro âhâro—idan taṃ rûpaṃ bâhiraṃ na cakkhâyatanaṃ.

806. Kataman taṃ rûpaṃ ajjhattikaṃ cakkhâyatanaṃ?

Yaṃ cakkhu catunnaṃ mahâbhûtânaṃ upâdâya pasâdo . . . pe . . . suñño gâmo peso—idan taṃ rûpaṃ ajjhattikaṃ cakkhâyatanaṃ.

807. Kataman taṃ rûpaṃ ajjhattikaṃ na cakkhâyatanaṃ?

Sotâyatanaṃ . . . pe . . . kâyâyatanaṃ—idan taṃ rûpaṃ ajjhattikaṃ na cakkhâyatanaṃ.

808. Kataman taṃ rûpaṃ bâhiraṃ na sotâyatanaṃ . . . pe . . . na ghânâyatanaṃ . . . pe . . . na jivhâyatanaṃ . . . pe . . . na kâyâyatanaṃ?

Rûpâyatanaṃ . . . pe . . . kabaḷiṅkâro âhâro—idan taṃ rûpaṃ bâhiraṃ na kâyâyatanaṃ.

809. Kataman taṃ rûpaṃ ajjhattikaṃ kâyâyatanaṃ?

Yo kâyo catunnaṃ mahâbhûtânaṃ upâdâya pasâdo . . . pe . . . suñño gâmo peso—idan taṃ rûpaṃ ajjhattikaṃ kâyâyatanaṃ.

810. Kataman taṃ rûpaṃ ajjhattikaṃ na kâyâyatanaṃ?

Cakkhâyatanaṃ . . . pe . . . jivhâyatanaṃ—idan taṃ rûpaṃ ajjhattikaṃ na kâyâyatanaṃ.

811. Kataman taṃ rûpaṃ ajjhattikaṃ na rûpâyatanaṃ?

Cakkhâyatanaṃ . . . pe . . . kâyâyatanaṃ—idan taṃ rûpaṃ ajjhattikaṃ na rûpâyatanaṃ.

812. Kataman taṃ rûpaṃ bâhiraṃ rûpâyatanaṃ?

Yaṃ rûpaṃ catunnaṃ mahâbhûtânaṃ upâdâya vaṇṇanibhâ . . . pe . . . rûpadhâtu pesâ—idan taṃ rûpaṃ bâhiraṃ rûpâyatanaṃ.

813. Kataman taṃ rûpaṃ bâhiraṃ na rûpâyatanaṃ?

Saddâyatanaṃ . . . pe . . . kabaḷiṅkâro âhâro—idan taṃ rûpaṃ bâhiraṃ na rûpâyatanaṃ.

814. Kataman taṃ rûpaṃ ajjhattikaṃ na saddâyatanaṃ

. . . pe . . . na gandhâyatanaṃ . . . pe . . . na rasâyatanaṃ . . . pe . . . na phoṭṭhabbâyatanaṃ?

Cakkhâyatanaṃ . . . pe . . . kâyâyatanaṃ—idan taṃ rûpaṃ ajjhattikaṃ na phoṭṭhabbâyatanaṃ.

815. Kataman taṃ rûpaṃ bâhiraṃ phoṭṭhabbâyatanaṃ?

Pathavîdhâtu . . . pe . . . phoṭṭhabbadhâtu pesâ—idan taṃ rûpaṃ bâhiraṃ phoṭṭhabbâyatanaṃ.

816. Kataman taṃ rûpaṃ bâhiraṃ na phoṭṭhabbâyatanaṃ?

Rûpâyatanaṃ . . . pe . . . kabaḷiṅkâro âhâro—idan taṃ rûpaṃ bâhiraṃ na phoṭṭhabbâyatanaṃ.

817. Kataman taṃ rûpaṃ bâhiraṃ na cakkhudhâtu?

Rûpâyatanaṃ . . . pe . . . kabaḷiṅkâro âhâro—idan taṃ rûpaṃ bâhiraṃ na cakkhudhâtu.

818. Kataman taṃ rûpaṃ ajjhattikaṃ cakkhudhâtu?

Cakkhâyatanaṃ—idan taṃ rûpaṃ ajjhattikaṃ cakkhudhâtu.

819. Kataman taṃ rûpaṃ ajjhattikaṃ na cakkhudhâtu?

Sotâyatanaṃ . . . pe . . . kâyâyatanaṃ—idan taṃ rûpaṃ ajjhattikaṃ na cakkhudhâtu.

820. Kataman taṃ rûpaṃ bâhiraṃ na sotadhâtu . . . pe . . . na ghânadhâtu, . . . pe . . . na jivhâdhâtu . . . pe . . . na kâyadhâtu?

Rûpâyatanaṃ . . . pe . . . kabaḷiṅkâro âhâro—idan taṃ rûpaṃ bâhiraṃ na kâyadhâtu.

821. Kataman taṃ rûpaṃ ajjhattikaṃ kâyadhâtu?

Kâyâyatanaṃ—idan taṃ rûpaṃ ajjhattikaṃ kâyadhâtu.

822. Kataman taṃ rûpaṃ ajjhattikaṃ na kâyadhâtu?

Cakkhâyatanaṃ . . . pe . . . jivhâyatanaṃ—idan taṃ rûpaṃ ajjhattikaṃ na kâyadhâtu.

823. Kataman taṃ rûpaṃ ajjhattikaṃ na rûpadhâtu?

Cakkhâyatanaṃ . . . pe . . . kâyâyatanaṃ idan taṃ rûpaṃ ajjhattikaṃ na rûpadhâtu.

824. Kataman taṃ rûpaṃ bâhiraṃ rûpadhâtu?

Rûpâyatanaṃ—idan taṃ rûpaṃ bâhiraṃ rûpadhâtu.

825. Kataman taṃ rûpaṃ bâhiraṃ na rûpadhâtu?

Saddâyatanaṃ . . . pe . . . kabaḷiṅkâro âhâro—idan taṃ rûpaṃ bâhiraṃ na rûpadhâtu.

826. Kataman taṃ rûpaṃ ajjhattikaṃ na saddadhâtu

. . . pe . . . na gandhadhâtu . . . pe . . . na rasadhâtu . . . pe . . . na phoṭṭhabbadhâtu?

Cakkhâyatanaṃ . . . pe . . . kâyâyatanaṃ—idan taṃ rûpaṃ ajjhattikaṃ na phoṭṭhabbadhâtu.

827. Katamau taṃ rûpaṃ bâhiraṃ phoṭṭhabbadhâtu?

Phoṭṭhabbâyatanaṃ—idan taṃ rûpaṃ bâhiraṃ phoṭṭhabbadhâtu.

828. Katamau taṃ rûpaṃ bâhiraṃ na phoṭṭhabbadhâtu?

Rûpâyatanaṃ . . . pe . . . kabaḷiṅkaro âhâro—idan taṃ rûpaṃ bâhiraṃ na phoṭṭhabbadhâtu.

829. Katamau taṃ rûpaṃ bâhiraṃ na cakkhundriyaṃ?

Rûpâyatanaṃ . . . pe . . . kabaḷiṅkâro âhâro—idan taṃ rûpaṃ bâhiraṃ na cakkhundriyaṃ.

830. Katamau taṃ rûpaṃ ajjhattikaṃ cakkhundriyaṃ? Yaṃ cakkhu catunnaṃ mahâbhûtânaṃ upâdâya pasâdo . . . pe . . . suñño gâmo peso—idan taṃ rûpaṃ ajjhattikaṃ cakkhundriyaṃ.

831. Katamau taṃ rûpaṃ ajjhattikaṃ na cakkhundriyaṃ?

Sotâyatanaṃ . . . pe . . . kâyâyatanaṃ—idan taṃ rûpaṃ ajjhattikaṃ na cakkhundriyaṃ.

832. Katamau taṃ rûpaṃ bâhiraṃ na sotindriyaṃ . . . pe . . . na ghânindriyaṃ . . . pe . . . na jivhindriyaṃ . . . pe . . . na kâyindriyaṃ?

Rûpâyatanaṃ . . . pe . . . kabaḷiṅkâro âhâro—idan taṃ rûpaṃ bâhiraṃ na kâyindriyaṃ.

833. Katamau taṃ rûpaṃ ajjhattikaṃ kâyindriyaṃ?

Yo kâyo catunnaṃ mahâbhûtânaṃ upâdâya pasâdo . . . pe . . . suñño gâmo peso—idan taṃ rûpaṃ ajjhattikaṃ kâyindriyaṃ.

834. Katamau taṃ rûpaṃ ajjhattikaṃ na kâyindriyaṃ?

Cakkhâyatanaṃ . . . pe . . . jivhâyatanaṃ—idan taṃ rûpaṃ ajjhattikaṃ na kâyindriyaṃ.

835. Katamau taṃ rûpaṃ ajjhattikaṃ na itthindriyaṃ?

Cakkhâyatanaṃ . . . pe . . . kâyâyatanaṃ—idan taṃ rûpaṃ ajjhattikaṃ na itthindriyaṃ.

836. Katamau taṃ rûpaṃ bâhiraṃ itthindriyaṃ?

Yaṃ itthiyâ itthiliṅgaṃ itthinimittaṃ itthikuttaṃ itthâkappo itthattaṃ itthibhâvo — idan taṃ rûpaṃ bâhiraṃ itthindriyaṃ.

837. Kataman taṃ rûpaṃ bâhiraṃ na itthindriyaṃ? Rûpâyatanaṃ . . . pe . . . kabaḷiṅkâro âhâro—idan taṃ rûpaṃ bâhiraṃ na itthindriyaṃ.

838. Kataman taṃ rûpaṃ ajjhattikaṃ na purisindriyaṃ? Cakkhâyatanaṃ . . . pe . . . kâyâyatanaṃ—idan taṃ rûpaṃ ajjhattikaṃ na purisindriyaṃ.

839. Kataman taṃ rûpaṃ bâhiraṃ purisindriyaṃ? Yaṃ purisassa purisaliṅgaṃ purisanimittaṃ purisakuttaṃ purisâkappo purisattaṃ purisabhâvo—idan taṃ rûpaṃ bâhiraṃ purisindriyaṃ.

840. Kataman taṃ rûpaṃ bâhiraṃ na purisindriyaṃ. Rûpâyatanaṃ . . . pe . . . kabaḷiṅkâro âhâro—idan taṃ rûpaṃ bâhiraṃ na purisindriyaṃ.

841. Kataman taṃ rûpaṃ ajjhattikaṃ na jîvitindriyaṃ? Cakkhâyatanaṃ . . . pe . . . kâyâyatanaṃ—idan taṃ rûpaṃ ajjhattikaṃ na jîvitindriyaṃ.

842. Kataman taṃ rûpaṃ bâhiraṃ jîvitindriyaṃ? Yo tesaṃ rûpînaṃ dhammânaṃ âyu ṭhiti yapanâ yâpanâ iriyanâ vattanâ pâlanâ jîvitaṃ jîvitindriyaṃ—idan taṃ rûpaṃ bâhiraṃ jîvitindriyaṃ.

843. Kataman taṃ rûpaṃ bâhiraṃ na jîvitindriyaṃ? Rûpâyatanaṃ . . . pe . . . kabaḷiṅkâro âhâro—idan taṃ rûpaṃ bâhiraṃ na jîvitindriyaṃ.

844. Kataman taṃ rûpaṃ ajjhattikaṃ na kâyaviññatti. Cakkhâyatanaṃ . . . pe . . . kâyâyatanaṃ—idan taṃ rûpaṃ ajjhattikaṃ na kâyaviññatti.

845. Kataman taṃ rûpaṃ bâhiraṃ kâyaviññatti? Yâ kusalacittassa vâ akusalacittassa vâ avyâkatacittassa vâ abhikkamantassa vâ paṭikkamantassa vâ âlokentassa vâ vilokentassa vâ sammiñjentassa vâ pasârentassa vâ kâyassa thambhanâ santhambhanâ santhambhitattaṃ viññatti viññâpanâ viññâpitattaṃ—idan taṃ rûpaṃ bâhiraṃ kâyaviññatti.

846. Kataman taṃ rûpaṃ bâhiraṃ na kâyaviññatti? Rûpâyatanaṃ . . . pe . . . kabaḷiṅkâro âhâro—idan taṃ rûpaṃ bâhiraṃ na kâyaviññatti.

847. Kataman taṃ rûpaṃ ajjhattikaṃ na vacîviññatti? Cakkhâyatanaṃ . . . pe . . . kâyâyatanaṃ—idan taṃ rûpaṃ ajjhattikaṃ na vacîviññatti.

848. Kataman taṃ rûpaṃ bâhiraṃ vacîviññatti?

Yâ kusalacittassa vâ akusalacittassa vâ avyâkatacittassa vâ vâcâ girâ vyappatho udîraṇaṃ ghoso ghosakammaṃ vâcâ vacîbhedo—ayaṃ vuccati vâcâ—yâ tâya vâcâya viññatti viññâpanâ viññâpitattaṃ—idan taṃ rûpaṃ bâhiraṃ vacîviññatti.

849. Kataman taṃ rûpaṃ bâhiraṃ na vacîviññatti.

Rûpâyatanaṃ . . . pe . . . kabaḷiṅkâro âhâro—idan taṃ rûpaṃ bâhiraṃ na vacîviññatti.

850. Kataman taṃ rûpaṃ ajjhattikaṃ na âkâsadhâtu?

Cakkhâyatanaṃ . . . pe . . . kâyâyatanaṃ—idan taṃ rûpaṃ ajjhattikaṃ na âkâsadhâtu.

851. Kataman taṃ rûpaṃ bâhiraṃ âkâsadhâtu?

Yo âkâso âkâsagataṃ aghaṃ aghagataṃ vivaro vivaragataṃ asamphuṭṭhaṃ catûhi mahâbhûtehi—idan taṃ rûpaṃ bâhiraṃ âkâsadhâtu.

852. Kataman taṃ rûpaṃ ajjhattikaṃ na âpodhâtu?

Cakkhâyatanaṃ . . . pe . . . kâyâyatanaṃ—idan taṃ rûpaṃ ajjhattikaṃ na âpodhâtu.

853. Kataman taṃ rûpaṃ bâhiraṃ âpodhâtu?

Yaṃ âpo âpogataṃ sineho sinehagataṃ bandhanattaṃ rûpassa—idan taṃ rûpaṃ bâhiraṃ âpodhâtu.

854. Kataman taṃ rûpaṃ bâhiraṃ na âpodhâtu?

Rûpâyatanaṃ . . . pe . . . kabaḷiṅkâro âhâro—idan taṃ rûpaṃ bâhiraṃ na âpodhâtu.

855. Kataman taṃ rûpaṃ ajjhattikaṃ rûpassa na lahutâ?

Cakkhâyatanaṃ . . . pe . . . kâyâyatanaṃ—idan taṃ rûpaṃ ajjhattikaṃ rûpassa na lahutâ.

856. Kataman taṃ rûpaṃ bâhiraṃ rûpassa lahutâ?

Yâ rûpassa lahutâ lahupariṇâmatâ adandhanatâ avitthanatâ—idan taṃ rûpaṃ bâhiraṃ rûpassa lahutâ.

857. Kataman taṃ rûpam bâhiraṃ rûpassa na lahutâ?

Rûpâyatanaṃ . . . pe . . . kabaḷiṅkâro âhâro—idan taṃ rûpaṃ bâhiraṃ rûpassa na lahutâ.

858. Kataman taṃ rûpaṃ ajjhattikaṃ rûpassa na mudutâ?

Cakkhâyatanaṃ . . . pe . . . kâyâyatanaṃ—idan taṃ rûpaṃ ajjhattikaṃ rûpassa na mudutâ.

859. Kataman taṃ rûpaṃ bâhiraṃ rûpassa mudutâ?

Yâ rûpassa mudutâ maddavatâ akakkhaḷatâ akathinatâ—idan taṃ rûpaṃ bâhiraṃ rûpassa mudutâ.

860. Kataman taṃ rûpaṃ bâhiraṃ rûpassa na mudutâ?

Rûpâyatanaṃ . . . pe . . . kabaḷiṅkâro âhâro—idan taṃ rûpaṃ bâhiraṃ rûpassa na mudutâ.

861. Kataman taṃ rûpaṃ ajjhattikaṃ rûpassa na kammaññatâ?

Cakkhâyatanaṃ . . . pe . . . kâyâyatanaṃ—idan taṃ rûpaṃ ajjhattikaṃ rûpassa na kammaññatâ.

862. Kataman taṃ rûpaṃ bâhiraṃ rûpassa kammaññatâ?

Yâ rûpassa kammaññatâ kammaññattaṃ kammaññabhâvo—idan taṃ rûpaṃ bâhiraṃ rûpassa kammaññatâ.

863. Kataman taṃ rûpaṃ bâhiraṃ rûpassa na kammaññatâ?

Rûpâyatanaṃ . . . pe . . . kabaḷiṅkâro âhâro—idan taṃ rûpaṃ bâhiraṃ rûpassa na kammaññatâ.

864. Kataman taṃ rûpaṃ ajjhattikaṃ rûpassa na upacayo?

Cakkhâyatanaṃ . . . pe . . . kâyâyatanaṃ—idan taṃ rûpaṃ ajjhattikaṃ rûpassa na upacayo.

865. Kataman taṃ rûpaṃ bâhiraṃ rûpassa upacayo?

Yo âyatanânaṃ âcayo—so rûpassa upacayo—idan taṃ rûpaṃ bâhiraṃ rûpassa upacayo.

866. Kataman taṃ rûpaṃ bâhiraṃ rûpassa santati?

Yo rûpassa upacayo—sâ rûpassa santati—idan taṃ rûpaṃ bâhiraṃ rûpassa santati.

867. Kataman taṃ rûpaṃ bâhiraṃ rûpassa na santati?

Rûpâyatanaṃ . . . pe . . . kabaḷiṅkâro âhâro—idan taṃ rûpaṃ bâhiraṃ rûpassa na santati.

868. Kataman taṃ rûpaṃ ajjhattikaṃ rûpassa na jaratâ?

Cakkhâyatanaṃ . . . pe . . . kâyâyatanaṃ—idan taṃ rûpaṃ ajjhattikaṃ rûpassa na jaratâ.

869. Kataman taṃ rûpaṃ bâhiraṃ rûpassa jaratâ?

Yâ rûpassa jarâ jîraṇatâ khaṇḍiccaṃ pâliccaṃ valittacatâ âyuno saṃhâni indriyânaṃ paripâko—idan taṃ rûpaṃ bâhiraṃ rûpassa jaratâ.

870. Kataman taṃ rûpaṃ bâhiraṃ rûpassa na jaratâ?

Rûpâyatanaṃ . . . pe . . . kabaḷiṅkâro âhâro—idan taṃ rûpaṃ bâhiraṃ rûpassa na jaratâ.

871. Kataman taṃ rûpaṃ ajjhattikaṃ rûpassa na aniccatâ? Cakkhâyatanaṃ . . . pe . . . kâyâyatanaṃ—idan taṃ rûpaṃ ajjhattikaṃ rûpassa na aniccatâ.

872. Kataman taṃ rûpaṃ bâhiraṃ rûpassa aniccatâ? Yo rûpassa khayo vayo bhedo paribhedo aniccatâ antaradhânaṃ—idan taṃ rûpaṃ bâhiraṃ rûpassa aniccatâ.

873. Kataman taṃ rûpaṃ bâhiram rûpassa na aniccatâ? Rûpâyatanaṃ . . . pe . . . kabaḷiṅkâro âhâro—idan taṃ rûpaṃ bâhiraṃ rûpassa na aniccatâ.

874. Kataman taṃ rûpaṃ ajjhattikaṃ na kabaḷiṅkâro âhâro?

Cakkhâyatanaṃ . . . pe . . . kâyâyatanaṃ—idan taṃ rûpaṃ ajjhattikaṃ na kabaḷiṅkâro âhâro.

875. Kataman taṃ rûpaṃ bâhiraṃ kabaḷiṅkâro âhâro? Odano kummâso satthu maccho maṃsaṃ khîraṃ dadhi sappi navanîtaṃ telaṃ madhu phâṇitaṃ—yaṃ vâ panaññam pi atthi rûpaṃ yamhi yamhi janapade tesaṃ tesaṃ sattânaṃ mukhâsiyaṃ dantavikhâdanaṃ galajjhoharaṇiyaṃ kucchivitthambhanaṃ—yâya ojâya sattâ yâpenti—idan taṃ rûpaṃ bâhiraṃ kabaḷiṅkâro âhâro.

876. Kataman taṃ rûpaṃ bâhiraṃ na kabaḷiṅkâro âhâro? Rûpâyatanaṃ . . . pe . . . rûpassa aniccatâ—idan taṃ rûpaṃ bâhiraṃ na kabaḷiṅkâro âhâro.

Evaṃ tividhena rûpasaṅgaho.

TIKANIDDESO.

877. Kataman taṃ rûpaṃ upâdâ upâdiṇṇaṃ? Cakkhâyatanaṃ . . . pe . . . kâyâyatanaṃ—itthindriyaṃ purisindriyaṃ jîvitindriyaṃ—yaṃ vâ panaññam pi atthi rûpaṃ kammassa katattâ rûpâyatanaṃ gandhâyatanaṃ rasâyatanaṃ âkâsadhâtu rûpassa upacayo rûpassa santati kabaḷiṅkâro âhâro—idan taṃ rûpaṃ upâdâ upâdiṇṇaṃ.

878. Kataman taṃ rûpaṃ upâdâ anupâdiṇṇaṃ? Saddâyatanaṃ kâyaviññatti vacîviññatti rûpassa lahutâ rûpassa mudutâ rûpassa kammaññatâ rûpassa jaratâ rûpassa aniccatâ yaṃ vâ panaññam pi atthi rûpaṃ na kammassa

katattâ rûpâyatanaṃ gandhâyatanaṃ rasâyatanaṃ âkâsadhâtu rûpassa upacayo rûpassa santati kabaḷiṅkâro âhâro—idan taṃ rûpaṃ upâdâ anupâdiṇṇaṃ.

879. Katamam taṃ rûpaṃ no upâdâ upâdiṇṇaṃ?

Kammassa katattâ phoṭṭhabbâyatanaṃ âpodhâtu—idan taṃ rûpaṃ no upâdâ upâdiṇṇaṃ.

880. Katamam taṃ rûpaṃ no upâdâ anupâdiṇṇaṃ?

Na kammassa katattâ phoṭṭhabbâyatanaṃ âpodhâtu—idan taṃ rûpaṃ no upâdâ anupâdiṇṇaṃ.

881. Katamam taṃ rûpaṃ upâdâ upâdiṇṇupâdâniyaṃ?

Cakkhâyatanaṃ . . . pe . . . kâyâyatanaṃ, itthindriyaṃ purisindriyaṃ jîvitindriyaṃ yaṃ vâ panaññam pi atthi rûpaṃ kammassa katattâ rûpâyatanaṃ gandhâyatanaṃ rasâyatanaṃ âkâsadhâtu rûpassa upacayo rûpassa santati kabaḷiṅkâro âhâro—idan taṃ rûpaṃ upâdâ upâdiṇṇupâdâniyaṃ.

882. Katamam taṃ rûpaṃ upâdâ anupâdiṇṇupâdâniyam?

Saddâyatanaṃ kâyaviññatti vacîviññatti rûpassa lahutâ rûpassa mudutâ rûpassa kammaññatâ rûpassa jaratâ rûpassa aniccatâ—yaṃ vâ panaññam pi atthi rûpaṃ na kammassa katattâ rûpâyatanaṃ gandhâyatanaṃ rasâyatanaṃ âkâsadhâtu rûpassa upacayo rûpassa santati kabaḷiṅkâro âhâro—idan taṃ rûpaṃ upâdâ anupâdiṇṇupâdâniyaṃ.

883. Katamam taṃ rûpaṃ no upâdâ upâdiṇṇupâdâniyaṃ?

Kammassa katattâ phoṭṭhabbâyatanaṃ âpodhâtu—idan taṃ rûpaṃ no upâdâ upâdiṇṇupâdâniyaṃ.

884. Katamam taṃ rûpaṃ no upâdâ anupâdiṇṇupâdâniyaṃ?

Kammassa katattâ phoṭṭhabbâyatanaṃ âpodhâtu—idan taṃ rûpaṃ no upâdâ anupâdiṇṇupâdâniyaṃ.

885. Katamam taṃ rûpaṃ upâdâ sappaṭighaṃ?

Cakkhâyatanaṃ . . . pe . . . rasâyatanaṃ—idan taṃ rûpaṃ upâdâ sappaṭighaṃ.

886. Katamam taṃ rûpaṃ upâdâ appaṭighaṃ?

Itthindriyaṃ . . . pe . . . kabaḷiṅkâro âhâro—idan taṃ rûpaṃ upâdâ appaṭighaṃ.

887. Katamam taṃ rûpaṃ no upâdâ sappaṭighaṃ?

Phoṭṭhabbâyatanaṃ—idan taṃ rûpaṃ no upâdâ sappaṭighaṃ?

888. Kataman taṃ rûpaṃ no upâdâ appaṭighaṃ?
Âpodhâtu—idan taṃ rûpaṃ no upâdâ appaṭighaṃ.
889. Kataman taṃ rûpaṃ upâdâ oḷârikaṃ?
Cakkhâyatanaṃ . . . pe . . . rasâyatanaṃ—idan taṃ rûpaṃ upadâ oḷârikaṃ.
890. Kataman taṃ rûpaṃ upâdâ sukhumaṃ?
Itthindriyaṃ . . . pe . . . kabaḷiṅkâro âhâro—idan taṃ rûpaṃ upâdâ sukhumaṃ.
891. Kataman taṃ rûpaṃ no upâdâ oḷârikaṃ?
Phoṭṭhabbâyatanaṃ—idan taṃ rûpaṃ no upâdâ oḷârikaṃ.
892. Kataman taṃ rûpaṃ no upâdâ sukhumaṃ?
Âpodhâtu—idan taṃ rûpaṃ no upâdâ sukhumaṃ.
893. Kataman taṃ rûpaṃ upâdâ dûre?
Itthindriyaṃ . . . pe . . . kabaḷiṅkâro âhâro—idan taṃ rûpaṃ upâdâ dûre.
894. Kataman taṃ rûpaṃ upâdâ santike?
Cakkhâyatanaṃ . . . pe . . . rasâyatanaṃ—idan taṃ rûpaṃ upâdâ santike.
895. Kataman taṃ rûpaṃ no upâdâ dûre?
Âpodhâtu—idan taṃ rûpaṃ no upâdâ dûre.
896. Kataman taṃ rûpaṃ no upâdâ santike?
Phoṭṭhabbâyatanaṃ—idan taṃ rûpaṃ no upâdâ santike.
897. Kataman taṃ rûpaṃ upâdiṇṇaṃ sanidassanaṃ?
Kammassa katattâ rûpâyatanaṃ—idan taṃ rûpaṃ upâdiṇṇaṃ sanidassanaṃ.
898. Kataman taṃ rûpaṃ upâdiṇṇaṃ anidassanaṃ?
Cakkhâyatanaṃ . . . pe . . . kâyâyatanaṃ—itthindriyaṃ purisindriyaṃ jîvitindriyaṃ—yaṃ vâ panaññam pi atthi rûpaṃ kammassa katattâ gandhâyatanaṃ rasâyatanaṃ phoṭṭhabbâyatanaṃ âkâsadhâtu âpodhâtu rûpassa upacayo rûpassa santati kabaḷiṅkâro âhâro—idan taṃ rûpaṃ upâdiṇṇaṃ anidassanaṃ.
899. Kataman taṃ rûpassa upâdiṇṇaṃ sanidassanaṃ?
Na kammassa katattâ rûpâyatanaṃ—idan taṃ rûpaṃ upâdiṇṇaṃ sanidassanaṃ.
900. Kataman taṃ rûpaṃ anupâdiṇṇaṃ anidassanaṃ?
Saddâyatanaṃ kâyaviññatti vacîviññatti rûpassa lahutâ rûpassa mudutâ rûpassa kammaññatâ rûpassa jaratâ rûpassa

aniccatâ—yaṃ vâ panaññam pi atthi rûpaṃ na kammassa katattâ gandhâyatanaṃ rasâyatanaṃ phoṭṭhabbâyatanaṃ âkâsadhâtu âpodhâtu rûpassa upacayo rûpassa santati kabaḷiṅkâro âhâro—idan taṃ rûpaṃ anupâdiṇṇaṃ anidassanaṃ.

901. Kataman taṃ rûpaṃ upâdiṇṇaṃ sappaṭighaṃ?

Cakkhâyatanaṃ . . . pe . . . kâyâyatanaṃ—yaṃ vâ pan' aññaṃ atthi rûpaṃ kammassa katattâ rûpâyatanaṃ gandhâyatanaṃ rasâyatanaṃ phoṭṭhabbâyatanaṃ—idan taṃ rûpaṃ upâdiṇṇaṃ sappaṭighaṃ.

902. Kataman taṃ rûpaṃ upâdiṇṇaṃ appaṭighaṃ?

Itthindriyaṃ purisindriyaṃ jîvitindriyaṃ—yaṃ vâ panaññaṃ pi atthi rûpaṃ kammassa katattâ âkâsadhâtu âpodhâtu rûpassa upacayo rûpassa santati kabaḷiṅkâro âhâro—idan taṃ rûpaṃ upâdiṇṇaṃ appaṭighaṃ.

903. Kataman taṃ rûpaṃ anupâdiṇṇaṃ sappaṭighaṃ?

Saddâyatanaṃ—yaṃ vâ panaññaṃ pi atthi rûpaṃ na kammassa katattâ rûpâyatanaṃ gandhâyatanaṃ rasâyatanaṃ phoṭṭhabbâyatanaṃ—idan taṃ rûpaṃ anupâdiṇṇaṃ sappaṭighaṃ.

904. Kataman taṃ rûpaṃ anupâdiṇṇaṃ appaṭighaṃ?

Kâyaviññatti vacîviññatti rûpassa lahutâ rûpassa mudutâ rûpassa kammaññatâ rûpassa jaratâ rûpassa aniccatâ—yaṃ vâ panaññam pi atthi rûpaṃ na kammassa katattâ âkâsadhâtu âpodhâtu rûpassa upacayo rûpassa santati kabaḷiṅkâro âhâro—idan taṃ rûpaṃ anupâdiṇṇaṃ appaṭighaṃ.

905. Kataman taṃ rûpaṃ upâdiṇṇaṃ mahâbhûtaṃ?

Kammassa katattâ phoṭṭhabbâyatanaṃ âpodhâtu—idan taṃ rûpaṃ upâdiṇṇaṃ mahâbhûtaṃ.

906. Kataman taṃ rûpaṃ upâdiṇṇaṃ na mahâbhûtaṃ?

Cakkhâyatanaṃ . . . pe . . . kâyâyatanaṃ itthindriyaṃ purisindriyaṃ jîvitindriyaṃ yaṃ vâ panaññam pi atthi rûpaṃ kammassa katattâ rûpâyatanaṃ gandhâyatanaṃ rasâyatanaṃ âkâsadhâtu rûpassa upacayo rûpassa santati kabaḷiṅkâro âhâro—idan taṃ rûpaṃ upâdiṇṇaṃ na mahâbhûtaṃ.

907. Kataman taṃ rûpaṃ anupâdiṇṇaṃ mahâbhûtaṃ?

Na kammassa katattâ phoṭṭhabbâyatanaṃ—âpodhâtu—idan taṃ rûpaṃ anupâdiṇṇaṃ mahâbhûtaṃ.

908. Kataman taṃ rûpaṃ anupâdiṇṇaṃ na mahâbhûtaṃ?

Saddâyatanaṃ kâyaviññatti vacîviññatti rûpassa lahutâ rûpassa mudutâ rûpassa kammaññatâ rûpassa jaratâ rûpassa aniccatâ—yaṃ va panaññaṃ pi atthi rûpaṃ na kammassa katattâ rûpâyatanaṃ gandhâyatanaṃ rasâyatanaṃ âkâsadhâtu rûpassa upacayo rûpassa santati kabaḷiṅkâro âhâro—idan taṃ rûpaṃ anupâdiṇṇaṃ na mahâbhûtaṃ.

909. Kataman taṃ rûpaṃ upâdiṇṇaṃ oḷârikaṃ?

Cakkhâyatanaṃ . . . pe . . . kâyâyatanaṃ—yaṃ vâ panaññaṃ pi atthi rûpaṃ kammassa katattâ rûpâyatanaṃ gandhâyatanaṃ rasâyatanaṃ phoṭṭhabbâyatanaṃ—idan taṃ rûpaṃ upâdiṇṇaṃ oḷârikaṃ.

910. Kataman taṃ rûpaṃ upâdiṇṇaṃ sukhumaṃ?

Itthindriyaṃ, purisindriyaṃ, jîvitindriyaṃ—yaṃ vâ panaññam pi atthi rûpaṃ kammassa katattâ âkâsadhâtu âpodhâtu rûpassa upacayo rûpassa santati kabaḷiṅkâro âhâro—idan taṃ rûpaṃ upâdiṇṇaṃ sukhumaṃ?

911. Kataman taṃ rûpaṃ anupâdiṇṇaṃ oḷârikaṃ?

Saddâyatanaṃ—yaṃ vâ panaññam pi atthi rûpaṃ na kammassa katattâ rûpâyatanaṃ gandhâyatanaṃ rasâyatanaṃ phoṭṭhabbâyatanaṃ—idan taṃ rûpaṃ anupâdiṇṇaṃ oḷârikaṃ.

912. Kataman taṃ rûpaṃ anupâdiṇṇaṃ sukhumaṃ?

Kâyaviññatti vacîviññatti rûpassa lahutâ rûpassa mudutâ, rûpassa kammaññatâ rûpassa jaratâ rûpassa aniccatâ—yaṃ vâ panaññam pi atthi rûpaṃ na kammassa katattâ âkâsadhâtu—rûpassa upacayo rûpassa santati kabaḷiṅkâro âhâro—idan taṃ rûpaṃ anupâdiṇṇaṃ sukhumaṃ.

913. Kataman taṃ rûpaṃ upâdiṇṇaṃ dûre?

Itthindriyaṃ purisindriyaṃ jîvitindriyaṃ—yaṃ vâ panaññam pi atthi rûpaṃ kammassa katattâ âkâsadhâtu âpodhâtu rûpassa upacayo rûpassa santati kabaḷiṅkâro âhâro—idan taṃ rûpaṃ upâdiṇṇaṃ dûre.

914. Kataman taṃ rûpaṃ upâdiṇṇaṃ santike?

Cakkhâyatanaṃ . . . pe . . . kâyâyatanaṃ—yaṃ vâ pan' aññaṃ pi atthi rûpaṃ kammassa katattâ rûpâyatanaṃ gandhâyatanaṃ rasâyatanaṃ phoṭṭhabbâyatanaṃ—idan taṃ rûpaṃ upâdiṇṇaṃ santike.

915. Kataman taṃ rûpaṃ anupâdiṇṇaṃ dûre?

Kâyaviññatti vacîviññatti rûpassa lahutâ rûpassa mudutâ

rûpassa kammaññatâ rûpassa jaratâ rûpassa aniccatâ—yaṃ vâ pan' aññam pi atthi rûpaṃ na kammassa katattâ âkâsadhâtu âpodhâtu rûpassa upacayo rûpassa santati kabaḷiṅkâro âhâro—idan taṃ rûpaṃ anupâdiṇṇaṃ dûre.

916. Kataman taṃ rûpaṃ anupâdiṇṇaṃ santike?

Saddâyatanaṃ—yaṃ vâ pan' aññam pi atthi rûpaṃ na kammassa katattâ rûpâyatanaṃ gandhâyatanaṃ rasâyatanaṃ phoṭṭhabbâyatanaṃ—idan taṃ rûpaṃ anupâdiṇṇaṃ santike.

917. Kataman taṃ rûpaṃ upâdiṇṇupâdâniyaṃ sanidassanaṃ?

Na kammassa katattâ rûpâyatanaṃ—idan taṃ rûpaṃ upâdiṇṇupâdâniyaṃ sanidassanaṃ.

918. Kataman taṃ rûpaṃ upâdiṇṇupâdâniyaṃ anidassanaṃ?

Cakkhâyatanaṃ . . . pe . . . kâyâyatanaṃ—itthindriyaṃ purisindriyaṃ jîvitindriyaṃ—yaṃ vâ panaññam pi atthi rûpaṃ kammassa katattâ gandhâyatanaṃ rasâyatanaṃ phoṭṭhabbâyatanaṃ âkâsadhâtu âpodhâtu rûpassa upacayo rûpassa santati kabaḷiṅkâro âhâro—idan taṃ rûpaṃ upâdiṇṇupâdâniyaṃ anidassanaṃ.

919. Kataman taṃ rûpaṃ anupâdiṇṇupâdâniyaṃ sanidassanaṃ?

Na kammassa katattâ rûpâyatanaṃ—idan taṃ rûpaṃ anupâdiṇṇupâdâniyaṃ sanidassanaṃ.

920. Kataman taṃ rûpaṃ anupâdiṇṇupâdâniyaṃ anidassanaṃ?

Saddâyatanaṃ kâyaviññatti vacîviññatti rûpassa lahutâ rûpassa mudutâ rûpassa kammaññatâ rûpassa jaratâ rûpassa aniccatâ—yaṃ vâ panaññam pi atthi rûpaṃ na kammassa katattâ gandhâyatanaṃ rasâyatanaṃ phoṭṭhabbâyatanaṃ âkâsadhâtu âpodhâtu rûpassa upacayo rûpassa santati kabaḷiṅkâro âhâro—idan taṃ rûpaṃ anupâdiṇṇupâdâniyaṃ anidassanaṃ.

921. Kataman taṃ rûpaṃ upâdiṇṇupâdâniyaṃ sappaṭighaṃ?

Cakkhâyatanaṃ . . . pe . . . kâyâyatanaṃ—yaṃ vâ panaññaṃ pi atthi rûpaṃ kammassa katattâ rûpâyatanaṃ gandhâyatanaṃ rasâyatanaṃ phoṭṭhabbâyatanaṃ—idan taṃ rûpaṃ upâdiṇṇupâdâniyaṃ sappaṭighaṃ.

922. Kataman taṃ rûpaṃ upâdiṇṇupâdâniyaṃ appaṭighaṃ?

Itthindriyaṃ purisindiryaṃ jîvitindriyaṃ—yaṃ vâ panaññam pi atthi rûpaṃ kammassa katattâ âkâsadhâtu apodhâtu rûpassa upacayo rûpassa santati kabaḷiṅkâro âhâro—idan taṃ rûpaṃ upâdiṇṇupâdâniyaṃ appaṭighaṃ.

923. Kataman taṃ rûpaṃ anupâdiṇṇupâdâniyaṃ sappaṭighaṃ?

Saddâyatanaṃ—yam vâ panaññam pi atthi rûpaṃ na kammassa katattâ rûpâyatanaṃ gandhâyatanaṃ rasâyatanaṃ phoṭṭhabbâyatanaṃ—idan taṃ rûpaṃ anupâdiṇṇupâdâniyaṃ sappaṭighaṃ.

924. Kataman taṃ rûpaṃ anupâdiṇṇupâdâniyaṃ appaṭighaṃ?

Kâyaviññatti vacîviññatti rûpassa lahutâ rûpassa mudutâ rûpassa kammaññatâ rûpassa jaratâ rûpassa aniccatâ—yaṃ vâ panaññam pi atthi rûpaṃ na kammassa katattâ âkâsadhâtu âpodhâtu rûpassa upacayo rûpassa santati kabaḷiṅkâro âhâro—idan taṃ rûpaṃ anupâdiṇṇupâdâniyaṃ appaṭighaṃ.

925. Kataman taṃ rûpaṃ upâdiṇṇupâdâniyaṃ mahâbhûtaṃ?

Kammassa katattâ phoṭṭhabbâyatanaṃ âpodhâtu—idan taṃ rûpaṃ upâdiṇṇupâdâniyaṃ mahâbhûtaṃ.

926. Kataman taṃ rûpaṃ upâdiṇṇupâdâniyaṃ na mahâbhûtaṃ?

Cakkhâyatanaṃ . . . pe . . . kâyâyatanaṃ itthindriyaṃ purisindriyaṃ jîvitindriyaṃ—yaṃ vâ panaññam pi atthi kammassa katattâ rûpâyatanaṃ gandhâyatanaṃ rasâyatanaṃ âkâsadhâtu rûpassa upacayo rûpassa santati kabaḷiṅkâro âhâro—idan taṃ rûpaṃ upâdiṇṇupâdâniyaṃ na mahâbhûtaṃ.

927. Kataman taṃ rûpaṃ anupâdiṇṇupâdâniyaṃ mahâbhûtaṃ?

Na kammassa katattâ phoṭṭhabbâyatanaṃ âpodhâtu—idan taṃ rûpaṃ anupâdiṇṇupâdâniyaṃ mahâbhûtaṃ.

928. Kataman taṃ rûpaṃ anupâdiṇṇupâdâniyaṃ na mahâbhûtaṃ?

Saddâyatanaṃ kâyaviññatti vacîviññatti rûpassa lahutâ rûpassa mudutâ rûpassa kammaññatâ rûpassa jaratâ rûpassa aniccatâ—yaṃ vâ pan'aññam pi atthi rûpaṃ na kammassa katattâ rûpâyatanaṃ gandhâyatanaṃ rasâyatanaṃ âkâsadhâtu rûpassa upacayo rûpassa santati kabaḷiṅkâro âhâro—idan taṃ rûpaṃ anupâdiṇṇupâdâniyaṃ na mahâbhûtaṃ.

929. Kataman taṃ rûpaṃ upâdiṇṇupâdâniyaṃ oḷârikaṃ?

Cakkhâyatanaṃ . . . pe . . . kâyâyatanaṃ—yaṃ vâ panaññam pi atthi rûpaṃ kammassa katattâ rûpâyatanaṃ gandhâyatanaṃ rasâyatanaṃ phoṭṭhabbâyatanaṃ—idan taṃ rûpaṃ upâdiṇṇupâdâniyaṃ oḷârikaṃ.

930. Kataman tam rûpaṃ upâdiṇṇupâdâniyaṃ sukhumaṃ?

Itthindriyaṃ purisindriyaṃ jîvitindriyaṃ—yaṃ vâ panaññam pi atthi rûpaṃ kammassa katattâ âkâsadhâtu âpodhâtu rûpassa upacayo rûpassa santati kabaḷiṅkâro âhâro—idan taṃ rûpaṃ upadiṇṇupâdâniyaṃ sukhumaṃ.

931. Kataman taṃ rûpaṃ anupâdiṇṇupâdâniyaṃ oḷârikaṃ?

Saddâyatanaṃ—yaṃ vâ panaññaṃ pi atthi rûpaṃ na kammassa katattâ rûpâyatanaṃ gandhâyatanaṃ rasâyatanaṃ phoṭṭhabbâyatanaṃ—idan taṃ rûpaṃ anupâdiṇṇupâdâniyaṃ oḷârikam.

932. Kataman taṃ rûpaṃ anupâdiṇṇupâdâniyaṃ sukhumaṃ?

Kâyaviññatti vacîviññatti rûpassa lahutâ rûpassa mudutâ rûpassa kammaññatâ rûpassa jaratâ rûpassa aniccatâ—yaṃ vâ panaññaṃ pi atthi rûpaṃ na kammassa katattâ âkâsadhâtu âpodhâtu rûpassa upacayo rûpassa santati kabaḷiṅkâro âhâro—idan taṃ rûpaṃ anupâdiṇṇupâdâniyaṃ sukhumaṃ.

933. Kataman taṃ rûpaṃ upâdiṇṇupâdâniyaṃ dûre?

Itthindriyaṃ purisindriyaṃ jîvitindriyaṃ yaṃ vâ panaññaṃ pi atthi rûpaṃ kammassa katattâ âkâsadhâtu âpodhâtu rûpassa upacayo rûpassa santati kabaḷiṅkâro âhâro—idan taṃ rûpaṃ upâdiṇṇupâdâniyaṃ dûre.

934. Kataman taṃ rûpaṃ upâdiṇṇupâdâniyaṃ santike?

Cakkhâyatanaṃ . . . pe . . . kâyâyatanaṃ—yaṃ vâ panaññaṃ pi atthi rûpaṃ kammassa katattâ rûpâyatanaṃ gandhâyatanaṃ rasâyatanaṃ phoṭṭhabbâyatanaṃ—idan taṃ rûpaṃ upâdiṇṇupâdâniyaṃ santike.

935. Kataman taṃ rûpaṃ anupâdiṇṇupâdâniyaṃ dûre?
Kâyaviññatti vacîviññatti rûpassa lahutâ rûpassa mudutâ rûpassa kammaññatâ rûpassa jaratâ rûpassa aniccatâ—yaṃ vâ panaññaṃ pi atthi rûpaṃ na kammassa katattâ âkâsadhâtu âpodhâtu rûpassa upacayo rûpassa santati kabaḷiṅkâro âhâro—idan taṃ rûpaṃ anupâdiṇṇupâdâniyaṃ dûre.

936. Kataman taṃ rûpaṃ anupâdiṇṇupâdâniyaṃ santike?
Saddâyatanaṃ—yaṃ vâ panaññaṃ pi atthi rûpaṃ na kammassa katattâ rûpâyatanaṃ gandhâyatanaṃ rasâyatanaṃ phoṭṭhabbâyatanaṃ—idan taṃ rûpaṃ anupâdiṇṇupâdâniyaṃ santike.

937. Kataman taṃ rûpaṃ sappaṭighaṃ indriyaṃ?
Cakkhundriyaṃ . . . pe . . . kâyindriyaṃ—idan taṃ rûpaṃ sappaṭighaṃ indriyaṃ.

938. Kataman taṃ rûpaṃ sappaṭighaṃ na indriyaṃ?
Rûpâyatanaṃ . . . pe . . . phoṭṭhabbâyatanaṃ—idan taṃ rûpaṃ sappaṭighaṃ na indriyaṃ.

939. Kataman taṃ rûpaṃ appaṭighaṃ indriyaṃ?
Itthindriyaṃ purisindriyaṃ jîvitindriyaṃ—idan taṃ rûpaṃ appaṭighaṃ indriyaṃ?

940. Kataman taṃ rûpaṃ appaṭighaṃ na indriyaṃ?
Kâyaviññatti . . . pe . . . kabaḷiṅkâro âhâro—idan taṃ rûpaṃ appaṭighaṃ na indriyaṃ.

941. Kataman taṃ rûpaṃ sappaṭighaṃ mahâbhûtaṃ?
Phoṭṭhabbâyatanaṃ—idan taṃ rûpaṃ sappaṭighaṃ mahâbhûtaṃ.

942. Kataman taṃ rûpaṃ sappaṭighaṃ na mahâbhûtaṃ?
Cakkhâyatanaṃ . . . pe . . . rasâyatanaṃ—idan taṃ rûpaṃ sappaṭighaṃ na mahâbhûtaṃ.

943. Kataman taṃ rûpaṃ appaṭighaṃ mahâbhûtaṃ?
Âpodhâtu—idan taṃ rûpaṃ appaṭighaṃ mahâbhûtaṃ.

944. Kataman taṃ rûpaṃ appaṭighaṃ na mahâbhûtaṃ?
Itthindriyaṃ . . . pe . . . kabaḷiṅkâro âhâro—idan taṃ rûpaṃ appaṭighaṃ na mahâbhûtaṃ.

945. Kataman taṃ rûpaṃ indriyaṃ oḷârikaṃ?
Cakkhundriyaṃ . . . pe . . . kâyindriyaṃ—idan taṃ rûpaṃ indriyaṃ oḷârikaṃ.

946. Kataman taṃ rûpaṃ indriyaṃ sukhumaṃ?

Itthindriyaṃ purisindriyaṃ jîvitindriyaṃ — idan taṃ rûpaṃ indriyaṃ sukhumaṃ.

947. Katamaṃ taṃ rûpaṃ na indriyaṃ oḷârikaṃ?

Rûpâyatanaṃ . . . pe . . . phoṭṭhabbâyatanaṃ—idan taṃ rûpaṃ na indriyaṃ oḷârikaṃ.

948. Katamaṃ taṃ rûpaṃ na indriyaṃ sukhumaṃ?

Kâyaviññatti . . . pe . . . kabaḷiṅkâro âhâro—idan taṃ rûpaṃ na indriyaṃ sukhumaṃ.

949. Katamaṃ taṃ rûpaṃ indriyaṃ dûre?

Itthindriyaṃ purisindriyaṃ jîvitindriyaṃ—idan taṃ rûpaṃ indriyaṃ dûre.

950. Katamaṃ taṃ rûpaṃ indriyaṃ santike?

Cakkhundriyaṃ . . . pe . . . kâyindriyaṃ—idan taṃ rûpaṃ indriyaṃ santike.

951. Katamaṃ taṃ rûpaṃ na indriyaṃ dûre?

Kâyaviññatti . . . pe . . . kabaḷiṅkâro âhâro—idan taṃ rûpaṃ na indriyaṃ dûre.

952. Katamaṃ taṃ rûpaṃ na indriyaṃ santike?

Rûpâyatanaṃ . . . pe . . . phoṭṭhabbâyatanaṃ—idan taṃ rûpaṃ na indriyaṃ santike.

953. Katamaṃ taṃ rûpaṃ mahâbhûtaṃ oḷârikaṃ?

Phoṭṭhabbâyatanaṃ — idan taṃ rûpaṃ mahâbhûtaṃ oḷârikaṃ.

954. Katamaṃ taṃ rûpaṃ mahâbhûtaṃ sukhumaṃ?

Âpodhâtu—idan taṃ rûpaṃ mahâbhûtaṃ sukhumaṃ.

955. Katamaṃ taṃ rûpaṃ na mahâbhûtaṃ oḷârikaṃ?

Cakkhâyatanaṃ . . . pe . . . rasâyatanaṃ—idan taṃ rûpaṃ na mahâbhûtaṃ oḷârikaṃ.

956. Katamaṃ taṃ rûpaṃ na mahâbhûtaṃ sukhumaṃ?

Itthindriyaṃ . . . pe . . . kabaḷiṅkâro âhâro—idan taṃ rûpaṃ na mahâbhûtaṃ sukhumaṃ.

957. Katamaṃ taṃ rûpaṃ mahâbhûtaṃ dûre?

Âpodhâtu—idan taṃ rûpaṃ mahâbhûtaṃ dûre.

958. Katamaṃ taṃ rûpaṃ mahâbhûtaṃ santike?

Phoṭṭhabbâyatanaṃ—idan taṃ rûpaṃ mahâbhûtaṃ santike.

959. Katamaṃ taṃ rûpaṃ na mahâbhûtaṃ dûre.

Itthindriyaṃ . . . pe . . . kabaḷiṅkâro âhâro—idan taṃ rûpaṃ na mahâbhûtaṃ dûre.

960. Kataman taṃ rûpaṃ na mahâbhûtaṃ santike?

Cakkhâyatanaṃ . . . pe . . . rasâyatanaṃ—idan taṃ rûpaṃ na mahâbhûtaṃ santike.

961. Rûpâyatanaṃ diṭṭhaṃ saddâyatanaṃ sutaṃ gandhâyatanam rasâyatanaṃ phoṭṭhabbâyatanaṃ mutaṃ—sabbaṃ rûpaṃ manasâ viññâtaṃ rûpaṃ evaṃ catubbidhena rûpasaṅgaho.

Catukkaṃ.

962. Kataman taṃ rûpaṃ pathavîdhâtu?

Yaṃ kakkhaḷaṃ kharagataṃ kakkhaḷattaṃ kakkhaḷabhâvo ajjhattaṃ vâ bahiddhâ vâ upâdiṇṇaṃ vâ anupâdiṇṇaṃ vâ—idan taṃ rûpaṃ pathavîdhâtu.

963. Kataman taṃ rûpaṃ âpodhâtu?

Yaṃ âpo âpogataṃ sineho sinehagataṃ bandhanattaṃ rûpassa ajjhattaṃ vâ bahiddhâ vâ upâdiṇṇaṃ vâ anupâdiṇṇaṃ vâ—idan taṃ rûpaṃ âpodhâtu.

964. Kataman taṃ rûpaṃ tejodhâtu?

Yaṃ tejo tejogataṃ usmâ usmâgataṃ usumaṃ usumâgataṃ ajjhattaṃ vâ . . . pe . . . anupâdiṇṇaṃ vâ—idan taṃ rûpaṃ tejodhâtu.

965. Kataman taṃ rûpaṃ vâyodhâtu?

Yaṃ vâyo vâyogataṃ chambhitattaṃ thambhitattaṃ rûpassa ajjhattaṃ vâ . . . pe . . . anupâdiṇṇaṃ vâ—idan taṃ rûpaṃ vâyodhâtu.

966. Kataman taṃ rûpaṃ upâdâ?

Cakkhâyatanaṃ . . . pe . . . kabaḷiṅkâro âhâro—idan taṃ rûpaṃ upâdâ.

Evaṃ pañcavidhena rûpasaṅgaho.

Pañcakaṃ.

967. Rûpâyatanaṃ cakkhuviññeyyaṃ rûpaṃ — saddâyatanaṃ sotaviññeyyaṃ rûpaṃ — gandhâyatanaṃ ghânaviññeyyaṃ rûpaṃ—rasâyatanaṃ jivhâviññeyyaṃ rûpaṃ—phoṭṭhabbâyatanaṃ kâyaviññeyyaṃ rûpaṃ—sabbaṃ rûpaṃ manoviññeyyaṃ rûpaṃ.

Evaṃ chabbidhena rûpasaṅgaho.

Chakkaṃ.

968. Rûpâyatanaṃ cakkhuviññeyyaṃ rûpaṃ—saddâyatanaṃ sotaviññeyyaṃ rûpaṃ—gandhâyatanaṃ ghânaviññeyyaṃ rûpaṃ — rasâyatanaṃ jivhâviññeyyaṃ rûpaṃ — phoṭṭhabbâyatanaṃ kâyaviññeyyaṃ rûpaṃ.

969. Rûpâyatanaṃ saddâyatanaṃ gandhâyatanaṃ rasâyatayaṃ phoṭṭhabbâyatanaṃ manodhâtuviññeyyaṃ rûpaṃ—sabbaṃ rûpaṃ manoviññâṇadhâtuviññeyyaṃ rûpaṃ.

Evaṃ sattavidhena rûpasaṅgaho.

SATTAKAṂ.

970. Rûpâyatanaṃ cakkhuviññeyyaṃ rûpaṃ — saddâyatanaṃ sotaviññeyyaṃ rûpaṃ—gandhâyatanaṃ ghânaviññeyyaṃ rûpaṃ—rasâyatanaṃ jivhâviññeyyaṃ rûpaṃ.

Manâpiyo phoṭṭhabbo sukhasamphasso kâyaviññeyyaṃ rûpaṃ — amanâpiyo phoṭṭhabbo dukkhasamphasso kâyaviññeyyaṃ rûpaṃ. Rûpâyatanaṃ saddâyatanaṃ gandhâyatanaṃ rasâyatanaṃ phoṭṭhabbâyatanaṃ manodhâtuviññeyyaṃ rûpaṃ — sabbaṃ rûpaṃ manoviññâṇadhâtuviññeyyaṃ rûpaṃ.

Evaṃ aṭṭhavidhena rûpasaṅgaho.

AṬṬHAKAṂ.

971. Kataman taṃ rûpaṃ cakkhundriyaṃ?

Yaṃ cakkhu catunnaṃ mahâbhûtânaṃ upâdâya pasâdo . . . pe . . . suñño gâmo peso—idan taṃ rûpaṃ cakkhundriyaṃ.

972. Kataman taṃ rûpaṃ sotindriyaṃ . . . pe . . . ghânindriyaṃ . . . pe . . . jivhindriyaṃ . . . pe . . . kâyindriyaṃ . . . pe . . . itthindriyaṃ . . . pe . . . purisindriyaṃ . . . pe . . . jîvitindriyaṃ?

Yo tesaṃ rûpînaṃ dhammânaṃ âyu ṭhiti yapanâ yâpanâ iriyanâ vattanâ pâlanâ jîvitaṃ jîvitindriyaṃ—idan taṃ rûpaṃ jîvitindriyaṃ.

973. Kataman taṃ rûpaṃ na indriyaṃ?

Rûpâyatanaṃ . . . pe . . . kabaḷiṅkâro âhâro: idan taṃ rûpaṃ na indriyaṃ.

Evaṃ navavidhena rûpasaṅgaho.

NAVAKAṂ.

974. Kataman taṃ rûpaṃ cakkhundriyaṃ?

Yaṃ cakkhu catunnaṃ mahâbhûtânaṃ upâdâya pasâdo ... pe ... suñño gâmo peso—idan taṃ rûpaṃ cakkhundriyaṃ.

975. Kataman taṃ rûpaṃ sotindriyaṃ . . . pe . . . ghânindriyaṃ . . . pe . . . jivhindriyaṃ . . . pe . . . kâyindriyaṃ . . . pe . . . itthindriyaṃ . . . pe . . . purisindriyaṃ . . . pe . . . jîvitindriyaṃ?

Yo tesaṃ rûpînaṃ dhammânaṃ âyu ṭhiti yapanâ yâpanâ iriyanâ vattanâ pâlanâ jîvitaṃ jîvitindriyaṃ—idan taṃ rûpaṃ jîvitindriyaṃ.

976. Kataman taṃ rûpaṃ na indriyaṃ sappaṭighaṃ?

Rûpâyatanaṃ . . . pe . . . phoṭṭhabbâyatanaṃ—idan taṃ rûpaṃ na indriyaṃ sappaṭighaṃ.

977. Kataman taṃ rûpaṃ na indriyaṃ appaṭighaṃ?

Kâyaviññatti . . . pe . . . kabaḷiṅkâro âhâro—idan taṃ rûpaṃ indriyaṃ appaṭighaṃ.

Evaṃ dasavidhena rûpasaṅgaho.

DASAKAṂ.

978. Kataman taṃ rûpaṃ cakkhâyatanaṃ?

Yaṃ cakkhu catunnaṃ mahâbhûtânaṃ upâdâya pasâdo . . . pe . . . suñño gâmo peso—idan taṃ rûpaṃ cakkhâyatanaṃ.

979. Kataman taṃ rûpaṃ sotâyatanaṃ . . . pe . . . ghânâyatanaṃ . . . pe . . . jivhâyatanaṃ . . . pe . . . kâyâyatanaṃ . . . pe . . . rûpâyatanaṃ . . . pe . . . saddâyatanaṃ . . . pe . . . rasâyatanaṃ. . . pe . . . phoṭṭhabbâyatanaṃ?

Pathavîdhâtu . . . pe . . . phoṭṭhabbadhâtu—idan taṃ rûpaṃ phoṭṭhabbâyatanaṃ.

980. Kataman taṃ rûpaṃ anidassanaṃ appaṭighaṃ dhammâyatanaṃ pariyâpannaṃ?

Itthindriyaṃ . . . pe . . . kabaḷiṅkâro âhâro—idan taṃ rûpaṃ anidassanaṃ appaṭighaṃ dhammâyatanaṃ pariyâpannaṃ.

Evaṃ ekâdasavidhena rûpasaṅgaho.

RÛPAVIBHATTI AṬṬHAMAṂ BHÂṆAVÂRAṂ.

981. Katame dhammâ kusalâ?

Tîṇi kusalamûlâni—alobho adoso amoho—taṃ sabbayutto vedanâkkhandho saññâkkhandho saṅkhârakkhandho viññâṇakkhandho—taṃ samuṭṭhânaṃ kâyakammaṃ vacîkammaṃ—ime dhammâ kusalâ.

982. Katame dhammâ akusalâ?

Tîṇi akusalamûlâni—lobho doso moho—tad ekaṭṭhâ ca kilesâ—taṃ sampayutto vedanâkkhandho saññâkkhandho saṅkhârakkhandho viññâṇakkhandho — taṃ samuṭṭhânaṃ kâyakammaṃ vacîkammaṃ manokammaṃ — ime dhammâ akusalâ.

983. Katame dhammâ avyâkatâ?

Kusalâkusalânaṃ dhammânaṃ vipâkâ kâmâvacarâ rûpâvacarâ arûpâvacarâ apariyâpannâ vedanâkkhandho saññâkkhandho saṅkhârakkhandho viññâṇakkhandho: ye ca dhammâ kiriyâ neva kusalâ nâkusalâ na ca kammavipâkâ—sabbañ ca rûpaṃ saṅkhatâ ca dhâtu—ime dhammâ avyâkatâ.

984. Katame dhammâ sukhâya vedanâya sampayuttâ?

Sukhabhummiyaṃ kâmâvacare rûpâvacare apariyâpanne sukhaṃ vedanaṃ ṭhapetvâ sampayutto saññâkkhandho saṅkhârakkhandho viññâṇakkhandho: ime dhammâ sukhâya vedanâya sampayuttâ.

985. Katame dhammâ dukkhâya vedanâya sampayuttâ?

Dukkhabhummiyaṃ kâmâvacare dukkhaṃ vedanaṃ ṭhapetvâ taṃ sampayutto saññâkkhandho saṅkhârakkhandho viññâṇakkhandho—ime dhammâ dukkhâya vedanâya sampayuttâ.

986. Katame dhammâ adukkhamasukhâya vedanâya sampayuttâ?

Adukkhamasukhabhummiyaṃ kâmâvacare rûpâvacare arûpâvacare apariyâpanne adukkhamasukhaṃ vedanaṃ ṭhapetvâ taṃ sampayutto saññâkkhandho saṅkhârakkhandho viññâṇakkhandho—ime dhammâ adukkhamasukhâya vedanâya sampayuttâ.

987. Katame dhammâ vipâkâ?

Kusalâkusalânaṃ dhammânaṃ vipâkâ kâmâvacarâ rûpâvacarâ arûpâvacarâ apariyâpannâ vedanâkkhandho . . . pe . . . viññâṇakkhandho: ime dhammâ vipâkâ.

988. Katame dhammâ vipâkadhammadhammâ?
Kusalâkusalâ dhammâ kâmâvacarâ rûpâvacarâ arûpâvacarâ apariyâpannâ vedanâkkhandho . . . pe . . . viññâṇakkhandho—ime dhammâ vipâkadhammadhammâ.

989. Katame dhammâ neva vipâkanavipâkadhammadhammâ?
Ye ca dhammâ kiriyâ neva kusalâ nâkusalâ na ca kammavipâkâ—sabbañ ca rûpaṃ asaṅkhatâ ca dhâtu—ime dhammâ neva vipâkanavipâkadhammadhammâ.

990. Katame dhammâ upâdiṇṇupâdâniyâ?
Sâsavâ kusalâkusalânaṃ dhammânaṃ vipâkâ kâmâvacarâ rûpâvacarâ arûpâvacarâ vedanâkkhandho . . . pe . . . viññâṇakkhandho—yañ ca rûpaṃ kammassa katattâ—ime dhammâ upâdiṇṇupâdâniyâ.

991. Katame dhammâ anupâdiṇṇupâdâniyâ?
Sâsavâ kusalâkusalâ dhammâ kâmâvacarâ rûpâvacarâ arûpâvacarâ vedanâkkhandho . . . pe . . . viññâṇakkhandho—ye ca dhammâ kiriyâ—neva kusalâ nâkusalâ na ca kammavipâkâ—yañ ca rûpaṃ na kammassa katattâ—ime dhammâ anupâdiṇṇupâdâniyâ.

992. Katame dhammâ anupâdiṇṇânupâdâniyâ?
Apariyâpannâ maggâ ca maggaphalâni asaṅkhatâ ca dhâtu: ime dhammâ anupâdiṇṇânupâdâniyâ.

993. Katame dhammâ saṅkiliṭṭhasaṅkilesikâ?
Tîṇi akusalamûlâni lobho doso moho—tadekaṭṭhâ ca kilesâ—taṃ sampayutto vedanâkkhandho . . . pe . . . viññâṇakkhandho taṃ samuṭṭhânaṃ—kâyakammaṃ vacîkammaṃ manokammaṃ—ime dhammâ saṅkiliṭṭhasaṅkilesikâ.

994. Katame dhammâ asaṅkiliṭṭhasaṅkilesikâ?
Sâsavâ kusalâ vyâkatâ dhammâ kâmâvacarâ rûpâvacarâ arûpâvacarâ rûpakkhandho vedanâkkhandho saññâkkhandho saṅkhârakkhandho viññâṇakkhandho—ime dhammâ asaṅkiliṭṭhasaṅkilesikâ.

995. Katame dhammâ asaṅkiliṭṭâhsaṅkilesikâ?
Apariyâpannâ maggâ ca maggaphalâni ca asaṅkhatâ ca dhâtu—ime dhammâ asaṅkiliṭṭhâsaṅkilesikâ.

996. Katame dhammâ savitakkasavicârâ?
Savitakkasavicârabhummiyaṃ kâmâvacaro rûpâvacaro

apariyâpanne vitakkavicâre ṭhapetvâ sampayutto vedanâkkhandho . . . pe . . . viññâṇakkhandho—ime dhammâ savitakkasavicârâ.

997. Katame dhammâ avitakkavicâramattâ?

Avitakkavicâramattabhummiyaṃ rûpâvacare apariyâpanne vicâraṃ ṭhapetvâ taṃ sampayutto vedanâkkhandho . . . pe . . . viññâṇakkhandho—ime dhammâ avitakkavicâramattâ.

998. Katame dhammâ avitakka-avicârâ?

Avitakka-avicârabhummiyaṃ kâmâvacare rûpâvacare arûpâvacare apariyâpanne vedanâkkhandho . . . pe . . . viññâṇakkhandho—sabbañ ca rûpaṃ asaṅkhatâ ca dhâtu—ime dhammâ avitakka-avicârâ.

999. Katame dhammâ pîtisahagatâ?

Pîtibhummiyaṃ kâmâvacare rûpâvacare apariyâpanne pîtiṃ ṭhapetvâ taṃ sampayutto vedanâkkhandho . . . pe . . . viññâṇakkhandho—ime dhammâ pîtisahagatâ.

1000. Katame dhammâ sukhasahagatâ?

Sukhabhummiyaṃ kâmâvacare rûpâvacare apariyâpanne sukhaṃ ṭhapetvâ taṃ sampayutto saññâkkhandho saṅkhârakkhandho viññâṇakkhandho—ime dhammâ sukhasahagatâ.

1001. Katame dhammâ upekkhâsahagatâ?

Upekkhâbhummiyaṃ kâmâvacare rûpâvacare arûpâvacare apariyâpanne upekkhaṃ ṭhapetvâ—taṃ sampayutto saññâkkhandho saṅkhârakkhandho viññâṇakkhandho — ime dhammâ upekkhâsahagatâ.

1002. Katame dhammâ dassanena pahâtabbâ?

Tîṇi saññojanâni — sakkâyadiṭṭhi, vicikicchâ, sîlabbataparâmâso.

1003. Tattha katamâ sakkâyadiṭṭhi?

Idha assutavâ puthujjano ariyânaṃ adassâvî ariyadhammassa akovido ariyadhamme avinîto sappurisânaṃ adassâvi sappurisadhammassa akovido sappurisadhamme avinîto rûpaṃ attato samanupassati — rûpavantaṃ vâ attânaṃ attani vâ rûpaṃ rûpasmiṃ vâ attânaṃ—vedanaṃ attato samanupassati —vedanâvantaṃ vâ attânaṃ attani vâ vedanaṃ vedanâya vâ attânaṃ—saññaṃ attato samanupassati—saññâvantaṃ vâ attânaṃ attani vâ saññaṃ saññâya vâ attânaṃ—saṅkhâre attato samanupassati saṅkhâravantaṃ vâ attânaṃ attani vâ saṅkhâre saṅkhâresu vâ attânaṃ—viññâṇaṃ attato samanupassati—viññâṇavantaṃ vâ attânaṃ attani vâ viññâṇaṃ viññâṇasmiṃ vâ attânaṃ—yâ evarûpâ diṭṭhi diṭṭhigataṃ diṭṭhigahanaṃ diṭṭhikantâro diṭṭhivisûkâyikaṃ diṭṭhivipphanditaṃ diṭṭhisaññojanaṃ gâho paṭiggâho abhiniveso parâmâso kummaggo micchâpatho micchattaṃ titthâyatanaṃ vipariyesaggâho—ayaṃ vuccati sakkâyadiṭṭhi.

1004. Tattha katamâ vicikicchâ?

Satthari kaṅkhati vicikicchati—dhamme kaṅkhati vicikicchati—saṅghe kaṅkhati vicikicchati—sikkhâya kaṅkhati vicikicchati—pubbante kaṅkhati vicikicchati—aparante kaṅkhati vicikicchati—pubbantâparante kaṅkhati vicikicchati idappaccayatâ paticcasamuppannesu dhammesu kaṅkhati vicikicchati—yâ evarûpâ kaṅkhâ kaṅkhâyanâ kaṅkhâyitattaṃ vimati vicikicchâ dveḷhakaṃ dvedhâpatho saṃsayo anekaṃsagâho âsappanâ parisappanâ apariyogâhanâ thambhitattaṃ cittassa mano vilekho—ayaṃ vuccati vicikicchâ.

1005. Tattha katamo sîlabbataparâmâso?

Ito bahiddhâ samaṇabrahmaṇânaṃ sîlena suddhivatena suddhisîlabbatena suddhîti—evarûpâ diṭṭhi diṭṭhigataṃ diṭṭhigahaṇaṃ diṭṭhikantâro diṭṭhivisûkâyikaṃ diṭṭhivipphanditaṃ diṭṭhisaññojanaṃ—gâho paṭiggâho abhiniveso parâmâso kummaggo micchâpatho micchattaṃ titthâyatanaṃ vipariyesagâho—ayaṃ vuccati sîlabbataparâmâso.

1006. Imâni tîni saññojanâni—tadekaṭṭhâ ca kilesâ—taṃ sampayutto vedanâkkhandho . . . pe . . . viññâṇakkhandho—taṃ samuṭṭhânaṃ kâyakammaṃ vacîkammaṃ manokammaṃ—ime dhammâ dassanena pahâtabbâ.

1007. Katame dhammâ bhâvanâya pahâtabbâ?

Avaseso lobho doso moho—tad ekaṭṭhâ ca kilesâ—taṃ sampayutto vedanâkkhandho . . . pe . . . viññâṇakkhandho—taṃ samuṭṭhânaṃ kâyakammaṃ vacîkammaṃ manokammaṃ—ime dhammâ bhâvanâyâ pahâtabbâ.

1008. Katame dhammâ neva dassanena na bhâvanâya pahâtabbâ?

Kusalâ vyâkatâ dhammâ—kâmâvacarâ rûpâvacarâ arûpâvacarâ apariyâpannâ—vedanâkkhandho . . . pe . . . viññâṇakkhandho—sabbañ ca rûpaṃ asaṅkhatâ ca dhâtu—ime dhammâ neva dassanena na bhâvanâya pahâtabbâ.

1009. Katame dhammâ dassanena pahâtabbahetukâ?

Tîṇi saññojanâni sakkâyadiṭṭhi vicikicchâ sîlabbataparâmâso. Tattha sakkâyadiṭṭhi vicikicchâ sîlabbataparâmâso.

1010. Imâni tîṇi saññojanâni—tad ekaṭṭhâ ca kilesâ—taṃ sampayutto vedanâkkhandho . . . pe . . . viññâṇakkhandho —taṃ samuṭṭhânaṃ kâyakammaṃ vacîkammaṃ manokammaṃ—ime dhammâ dassanena pahâtabbahetukâ.

1011. Katame dhammâ bhâvanâya pahâtabbahetukâ?

Avaseso lobho doso moho—ime dhammâ bhâvanâya pahâtabbahetukâ tad ekaṭṭhâ ca kilesâ—taṃ sampayutto vedanâkkhandho . . . pe . . . viññâṇakkhandho—taṃ samuṭṭhânaṃ kâyakammaṃ vacîkammaṃ manokammaṃ — ime dhammâ bhâvanâya pahâtabbahetukâ.

1012. Katame dhammâ neva dassanena na bhâvanâya pahâtabbahetukâ?

Te dhamme ṭhapetvâ avasesâ kusalâkusalâ vyâkatâ dhammâ kâmâvacarâ rûpâvacarâ arûpâvacarâ apariyâpannâ—vedanâkkhandho saññâkkhandho saṅkhârakkhandho viññâṇakkhandho—sabbañ ca rûpaṃ asaṅkhatâ ca dhâtu—ime dhammâ neva dassanena na bhâvanâya pahâtabbahetukâ.

1013. Katame dhammâ âcayagâmino?

Sâsavâ kusalâkusalâ dhammâ kâmâvacarâ rûpâvacarâ arûpâvacarâ vedanâkkhandho . . . pe . . . viññâṇakkhandho—ime dhammâ âcayagâmino.

1014. Katame dhammâ apacayagâmino?

Cattâro maggâ apariyâpannâ—ime dhammâ apacayagâmino.

1015. Katame dhammâ neva âcayagâmino na apacayagâmino?

Kusalâkusalânaṃ dhammânaṃ vipâkâ kâmâvacarâ rûpâvacarâ arûpâvacarâ apariyâpannâ—vedanâkkhandho . . . pe . . . viññâṇakkhandho—ye ca dhammâ kiriyâ neva kusalâ nâkusalâ na ca kammavipâkâ sabbañ ca rûpaṃ asaṅkhatâ ca dhâtu—ime dhammâ neva âcayagâmino na apacayagâmino.

1016. Katame dhammâ sekkhâ?

Cattâro maggâ apariyâpannâ heṭṭhimâni ca tîṇi sâmaññaphalâni—ime dhammâ sekkhâ.

1017. Katame dhammâ asekkhâ?
Uparitthimaṃ arahattaphalaṃ—ime dhammâ asekkhâ.
1018. Katame dhammâ neva sekkhâ na asekkhâ?
Te dhamme ṭhapetvâ avasesâ kusalâkusalâvyâkatâ dhammâ kâmâvacarâ rûpâvacarâ arûpâvacarâ vedanâkkhandho . . . pe . . . viññâṇakkhandho—sabbañ ca rûpaṃ asaṅkhatâ ca dhâtu—ime dhammâ neva sekkhâ na asekkhâ.
1019. Katame dhammâ parittâ?
Sabbeva kâmâvacarâ kusalâkusalâvyâkatâ dhammâ—rûpakkhandho . . . pe . . . viññâṇakkhandho—ime dhammâ parittâ.
1020. Katame dhammâ mahaggatâ?
Rûpâvacarâ arûpâvacarâ kusalâkusalâvyâkatâ dhammâ—vedanâkkhandho . . . pe . . . viññâṇakkhandho—ime dhammâ mahaggatâ.
1021. Katame dhammâ appamâṇâ?
Apariyâpannâ maggâ ca maggaphalâni ca asaṅkhatâ ca dhâtu—ime dhammâ appamâṇâ.
1022. Katame dhammâ parittârammaṇâ?
Paritte dhamme ârabbha ye uppajjanti cittacetasikâ dhammâ—ime dhammâ parittârammaṇâ.
1023. Katame dhammâ mahaggatârammaṇâ?
Mahaggate dhamme ârabbha ye uppajjanti cittacetasikâ dhammâ—ime dhammâ mahaggatârammaṇâ.
1024. Katame dhammâ appamâṇârammaṇâ?
Appamâṇe dhamme ârabbha ye uppajjanti cittacetasikâ dhammâ—ime dhammâ appamâṇârammaṇâ.
1025. Katame dhammâ hînâ?
Tîṇi akusalamûlâni—lobho doso moho—tad ekaṭṭhâ ca kilesâ—taṃ sampayutto vedanâkkhando . . . pe . . . viññâṇakkhandho—taṃ samuṭṭhânaṃ kâyakammaṃ vacîkammaṃ manokammaṃ—ime dhammâ hînâ.
1026. Katame dhammâ majjhimâ?
Sâsavâ kusalâkusalâvyâkatâ dhammâ—kâmâvacarâ rûpâvacarâ arûpâvacarâ rûpakkhandho . . . pe . . . viññâṇakkhandho—ime dhammâ majjhimâ.
1027. Katame dhammâ paṇîtâ?
Apariyâpannâ maggâ ca maggaphalâni ca asaṅkhatâ ca dhâtu—ime dhammâ paṇîtâ.

1028. Katame dhammâ micchattaniyatâ?

Pañca kammâni anantarakâni yâ ca micchâdiṭṭhi niyatâ—ime dhammâ micchattaniyatâ.

1029. Katame dhammâ sampattaniyatâ?

Cattâro maggâ apariyâpannâ—ime dhammâ sampattaniyatâ.

1030. Katame dhammâ aniyatâ?

Te dhamme ṭhapetvâ avasesâ kusalâkusalâvyâkatâ dhammâ kâmâvacarâ rûpâvacarâ arûpâvacarâ apariyâpannâ — vedanâkkhandho . . . pe . . . viññâṇakkhandho—sabbañ ca rûpaṃ asaṅkhatâ ca dhâtu—ime dhammâ aniyatâ.

1031. Katame dhammâ maggârammaṇâ?

Ariyamaggaṃ ârabbha ye uppajjanti cittacetasikâ dhammâ ime dhammâ maggârammaṇâ.

1032. Katame dhammâ maggahetukâ?

Ariyamaggasamaṅgissa maggaṅgâni ṭhapetvâ taṃ sampayutto vedanâkkhandho . . . pe . . . viññâṇakkhandho—ime dhammâ maggahetukâ.

1033. Ariyamaggasamaṅgissa sammâdiṭṭhi maggo ceva hetu ca sammâdiṭṭhiṃ ṭhapetvâ taṃ sampayutto vedanâkkhandho . . . pe . . . viññâṇakkhandho — ime dhammâ maggahetukâ.

Ariyamaggasamaṅgissa alobho adoso amoho—ime dhammâ maggahetukâ — taṃ sampayutto vedanâkkhandho . . . pe . . . viññâṇakkhandho—ime dhammâ maggahetukâ.

1034. Katame dhammâ maggâdhipatino?

Ariyamaggaṃ adhipatiṃ karitvâ ye uppajjanti cittacetasikâ dhammâ—ime dhammâ maggâdhipatino—ariyamaggasamaṅgissa vimaṃsâdhipateyyaṃ maggaṃ bhâvayantassa vimaṃsaṃ ṭhapetvâ taṃ sampayutto vedanâkkhandho . . . pe . . . viññâṇakkhandho—ime dhammâ maggâdhipatino.

1035. Katame dhammâ uppannâ?

Ye dhammâ jâtâ bhûtâ sañjâtâ nippattâ abhinippattâ pâtubhûtâ uppannâ samuppannâ uṭṭhitâ samuṭṭhitâ uppannâ uppannaṃsena saṅgahitâ rûpâ vedanâ saññâ saṅkhârâ viññâṇaṃ—ime dhammâ uppannâ.

1036. Katame dhammâ anuppannâ?

Ye dhammâ ajâtâ abhûtâ asañjâtâ anippattâ anabhinippattâ

apâtubhûtâ anuppannâ asamuppannâ anuṭṭhitâ asamuṭṭhitâ anuppannâ anuppannaṃsena saṅgahitâ rûpâ vedanâ saññâ saṅkhârâ viññâṇaṃ—ime dhammâ anuppannâ.

1037. Katame dhammâ uppâdino?

Kusalâkusalânaṃ dhammânaṃ vipâkâ kâmâvacarâ rûpâvacarâ arûpâvacarâ apariyâpannâ vedanâkkhandho . . . pe . . . viññâṇakkhandho—yañ ca rûpaṃ kammassa katattâ uppajjissati—ime dhammâ uppâdino.

1038. Katame dhammâ atîtâ?

Ye dhammâ atîtâ niruddhaṅgatâ vipariṇatâ—atthaṅgatâ abbhatthaṅgatâ uppajjitvâ vigatâ atîtâ atîtaṃsena saṅgahitâ rûpâ vedanâ saññâ saṅkhârâ viññâṇaṃ—ime dhammâ atîtâ.

1039. Katame dhammâ anâgatâ?

Ye dhammâ ajâtâ abhûtâ asañjâtâ anippattâ anabhinippattâ apâtubhûtâ anuppannâ asamuppannâ anuṭṭhitâ asamuṭṭhitâ anâgatâ anâgataṃsena saṅgahitâ rûpâ vedanâ saññâ saṅkhârâ viññâṇaṃ—ime dhammâ anâgatâ.

1040. Katame dhammâ paccuppannâ?

Ye dhammâ jâtâ bhûtâ sañjâtâ nippattâ pâtubhûtâ uppannâ samuppannâ uṭṭhitâ samuṭṭhitâ paccuppannâ paccuppannaṃsena saṅgahitâ rûpâ vedanâ saññâ saṅkhârâ viññâṇaṃ—ime dhammâ paccuppannâ.

1041. Katame dhammâ atîtârammaṇâ?

Atîte dhamme ârabbha ye uppajjanti cittacetasikâ dhammâ—ime dhammâ atîtârammaṇâ.

1042. Katame dhammâ anâgatârammaṇâ?

Anâgate dhamme ârabbha ye uppajjanti cittacetasikâ dhammâ—ime dhammâ anâgatârammaṇâ.

1043. Katame dhammâ paccuppannârammaṇâ?

Paccuppanne dhamme ârabbha ye uppajjanti cittacetasikâ dhammâ—ime dhammâ paccuppannârammaṇâ.

1044. Katame dhammâ ajjhattâ?

Ye dhammâ tesaṃ tesaṃ sattânaṃ ajjhattaṃ paccattaṃ niyatâ paṭipuggalikâ upâdiṇṇâ rûpâ vedanâ saññâ saṅkhârâ viññâṇaṃ—ime dhammâ ajjhattâ.

1045. Katame dhammâ bahiddhâ?

Ye dhammâ tesaṃ tesaṃ parasattânaṃ parapuggalânaṃ

ajjhattaṃ paccattaṃ niyatâ paṭipuggalikâ . . . pe . . . viññâṇaṃ ime dhammâ bahiddhâ.

1046. Katame dhammâ ajjhattabahiddhâ?

Tad ubhayaṃ—ime dhammâ ajjhattabahiddhâ.

1047. Katame dhammâ ajjhattârammaṇâ?

Ajjhatte dhamme ârabbha ye uppajjanti cittacetasikâ dhammâ—ime dhammâ ajjhattârammaṇâ.

1048. Katame dhammâ bahiddhârammaṇâ?

Bahiddhâ dhamme ârabbha ye . . . pe . . . dhammâ—ime dhammâ bahiddhârammaṇâ.

1049. Katame dhammâ ajjhattabahiddhârammaṇâ?

Ajjhattabahiddhâ dhamme ârabbha ye . . . pe . . . dhammâ—ime dhammâ ajjhattabahiddhârammaṇâ.

1050. Katame dhammâ sanidassanasappaṭighâ?

Rûpâyatanaṃ—ime dhammâ sanidassanasappaṭighâ.

1051. Katame dhammâ anidassanasappaṭighâ?

Cakkhâyatanaṃ sotâyatanaṃ ghânâyatanaṃ jivhâyatanaṃ kâyâyatanaṃ saddâyatanaṃ gandhâyatanaṃ rasâyatanaṃ phoṭṭhabbâyatanaṃ—ime dhammâ anidassanasappaṭighâ.

1052. Katame dhammâ anidassana-appaṭighâ?

Vedanâkkhandho saññâkkhandho saṅkhârakkhandho viññâṇakkhandho—yañ ca rûpaṃ anidassanaṃ appaṭighaṃ dhammâyatanapariyâpannaṃ asaṅkhatâ ca dhâtu—ime dhammâ anidassana-appaṭighâ.

Tikkaṃ.

1053. Katame dhammâ hetû?

Tayo kusalahetû, tayo akusalahetû, tayo avyâkatahetû—nava kâmâvacarahetû, cha rûpâvacarahetû, cha arûpâvacarahetû cha apariyâpannahetû.

1054. Tattha katame tayo kusalahetû?

Alobho adoso amoho.

1055. Tattha katamo alobho?

Yo alobho alubbhanâ alubbhitattaṃ asârâgo asârajjanâ asârajjitattaṃ anabhijjhâ alobho kusalamûlaṃ—ayaṃ vuccati alobho.

1056. Tattha katamo adoso?

Yo adoso adussanâ adussitattaṃ mettaṃ mettâyanâ mettâyitattaṃ anuddâ anuddâyanâ anuddâyitattaṃ hitesitâ anukampâ avyâpâdo avyâpajjo adoso kusalamûlaṃ — ayaṃ vuccati adoso.

1057. Tattha katamo amoho?

Dukkhe ñâṇaṃ, dukkhasamudaye ñâṇaṃ, dukkhanirodhe ñâṇaṃ, dukkhanirodhagâminiyâ paṭipadâya ñâṇaṃ, pubbante ñâṇaṃ, aparante ñâṇaṃ pubbantâparante ñâṇaṃ—idappaccayatâ paṭiccasamuppannesu dhammesu ñâṇaṃ—yâ evarûpâ paññâ pajânanâ vicayo pavicayo dhammavicayo sallakkhaṇâ upalakkhaṇâ paccupalakkhaṇâ paṇḍiccaṃ kosallaṃ nepuññaṃ vebhavyâ cintâ upaparikkhâ bhûri medhâ pariṇâyikâ vipassanâ sampajaññaṃ patodo paññâ paññindriyaṃ paññâbalaṃ paññâsatthaṃ paññâpâsâdo paññâ-âloko paññâ-obhâso paññâ-pajjoto paññâratanaṃ amoho dhammavicayo sammâdiṭṭhi — ayaṃ vuccati amoho.

Ime tayo kusalahetû.

1058. Tattha katame tayo akusalahetû?

Lobho doso moho.

1059. Tattha katamo lobho?

Yo râgo sârâgo anunayo anurodho nandî nandîrâgo cittassa sârâgo—icchâ mucchâ ajjhosânaṃ gedho paligedho saṅgo paṅko ejâ mâyâ janikâ sañjananî sibbinî jâlinî saritâ visattikâ suttaṃ visaṭâ âyûhanî dutiyâ paṇidhi bhavanettî vanaṃ vanatho santhavo sineho apekkhâ paṭibandhu âsâ âsiṃsanâ asiṃsitattaṃ rûpâsâ saddâsâ gandhâsâ rasâsâ phoṭṭhabbâsâ lâbhâsâ dhanâsâ puttâsâ jîvitâsâ jappâ pajappâ abhijappâ jappanâ jappitattaṃ loluppaṃ loluppâyanâ loluppâyitattaṃ puñcikatâ sâdukamyatâ adhammarâgo visamalobho nikanti nikâmanâ patthanâ pihanâ sampatthanâ kâmataṇhâ bhavataṇhâ vibhavataṇhâ rûpataṇhâ arûpataṇhâ nirodhataṇhâ saddataṇhâ gandhataṇhâ rasataṇhâ phoṭṭhabbataṇhâ dhammataṇhâ ogho yogo gantho upâdânaṃ âvaraṇaṃ nîvaraṇaṃ chandânaṃ bandhanaṃ upakkileso anusayo pariyuṭṭhânaṃ latâ veviccham dukkhamûlaṃ dukkhanidânaṃ dukkhappabhavo mârapâso mârabalisaṃ mâravisayo taṇhâ nandîtaṇhâ jâlaṃtaṇhâ gaddulaṃtaṇhâ samuddo abhijjhâ lobho akusalamûlaṃ—ayaṃ vuccati lobho.

1060. Tattha katamo doso?

Anatthaṃ me acarîti âghâto jâyati—anatthaṃ me caratîti âghâto jâyati—anatthaṃ me carissatîti âghâto jâyati—piyassa me manâpassa anatthaṃ acari . . . pe . . . anatthaṃ carati . . . pe . . . anatthaṃ carissatîti âghâto jâyati appiyassa me amanâpassa atthaṃ acari . . . pe . . . atthaṃ carati . . . pe . . . atthaṃ carissatîti âghâto jâyati—aṭṭhâne vâ pana âghâto jâyati—yo evarûpo cittassa âghâto paṭighâto paṭighaṃ paṭivirodho kopo pakopo sampakopo doso padoso sampadoso cittassa vyâpatti manopadoso kodho kujjhanâ kujjhitattaṃ doso dussanâ dussitattaṃ vyâpatti vyâpajjanâ vyâpajjitattaṃ virodho paṭivirodho caṇḍikkaṃ asuropo anattamanatâ cittassa—ayaṃ vuccati doso.

1061. Tattha katamo moho?

Dukkhe aññâṇaṃ dukkhasamudaye aññâṇaṃ dukkhanirodhe aññâṇaṃ dukkhanirodhagâminiyâ paṭipadâya aññâṇaṃ pubbante aññâṇaṃ aparante aññâṇaṃ pubbantâparante aññâṇaṃ idappaccayatâ paṭiccasamuppannesu dhammesu aññâṇaṃ—yaṃ evarûpaṃ aññâṇaṃ adassanaṃ anabhisamayo ananubodho asambodho appaṭivedho asaṅgâhanâ apariyogâhanâ asamapekkhanâ apaccavekkhanâ apaccakkhakammaṃ—dummejjhaṃ balyaṃ asampajaññaṃ moho pamoho sammoho avijjâ avijjogho avijjâyogo avijjânusayo avijjâpariyuṭṭhânaṃ avijjâlaṅgî moho akusalamûlaṃ—ayaṃ vuccati moho.

Ime tayo akusalahetû.

1062. Tattha katame tayo avyâkatahetû?

Kusalânaṃ dhammânaṃ vipâkato kiriyâ vyâkatesu vâ dhammesu alobho adoso amoho—ime tayo avyâkatahetû.

1063. Tattha katame nava kâmâvacarahetû?

Tayo kusalahetû tayo akusalahetû tayo avyâkatahetû—ime nava kâmâvacarahetû.

1064. Tattha katame cha rûpâvacarahetû?

Tayo kusalahetû, tayo avyâkatahetû—ime cha rûpâvacarahetû.

1065. Tattha katame cha arûpâvacarahetû?

Tayo kusalahetû tayo avyâkatahetû—ime cha arûpâvacarahetû.

1066. Tattha katame cha apariyâpannahetû?

Tayo kusalahetû tayo avyâkatahetû—ime cha apariyâpannahetû.

1067. Tattha katame tayo kusalahetû?

Alobho adoso amoho.

1068. Tattha katamo alobho . . . pe . . .

1069. Tattha katamo adoso?

Adussanâ adussitattaṃ avyâpâdo avyâpajjo adoso kusalamûlaṃ—ayaṃ vuccati adoso.

1070. Tattha katamo amoho?

Dukkhe ñâṇaṃ . . . pe . . . yâ evarûpâ paññâ pajânanâ vicayo pavicayo dhammavicayo sallakkhaṇâ upalakkhaṇâ paccupalakkhaṇâ paṇḍiccaṃ kosallaṃ nepuññaṃ vebhavyâ cintâ upaparikkhâ bhûri medhâ . . . pe . . . amoho dhammavicayo sammâdiṭṭhi dhammavicayasambojjhaṅgo maggaṅgaṃ maggapariyâpannaṃ—ayaṃ vuccati amoho.

Ime tayo kusalahetû.

1071. Tattha katame tayo avyâkatahetû?

Kusalânaṃ dhammânaṃ vipâkato alobho adoso amoho—ime tayo avyâkatahetû—ime cha apariyâpannahetû.

Ime dhammâ hetû.

1072. Katame dhammâ na hetû?

Te dhamme ṭhapetvâ avasesâ kusalâkusalâ avyâkatâ dhammâ kâmâvacarâ rûpâvacarâ arûpâvacarâ—apariyâpannâ vedanâkkhandho . . . pe . . . viññâṇakkhandho—sabbañ ca rûpaṃ asaṅkhatâ ca dhâtu—ime dhammâ na hetû.

1073. Katame dhammâ sahetukâ?

Tehi dhammehi ye dhammâ sahetukâ vedanâkkhandho— . . . pe . . . viññâṇakkhandho—ime dhammâ sahetukâ.

1074. Katame dhammâ ahetukâ?

Tehi dhammehi ye dhammâ ahetukâ vedanâkkhandho . . . pe . . . viññâṇakkhandho—sabbañ ca rûpaṃ asaṅkhatâ ca dhâtu—ime dhammâ ahetukâ.

1075. Katame dhammâ hetusampayuttâ?

Tehi dhammehi ye dhammâ sampayuttâ—vedanâkkhandho . . . pe . . . viññâṇakkhandho— ime dhammâ hetusampayuttâ.

1076. Katame dhammâ hetuvippayuttâ?

Tehi dhammehi ye dhammâ vippayuttâ—vedanâkkhandho . . . pe . . . viññâṇakkhandho—sabbañ ca rûpaṃ asaṅkhatâ ca dhâtu—ime dhammâ hetuvippayuttâ.

1077. Katame dhammâ hetû ceva sahetukâ ca?

Lobho mohena hetu ceva sahetuko ca—moho lobhena hetu ceva sahetuko ca—doso mohena hetu ceva sahetuko—moho dosena hetu ceva sahetuko ca.

Alobho adoso amoho—te aññamaññaṃ hetû ceva sahetukâ ca—ime dhammâ hetû ceva sahetukâ ca.

1078. Katame dhammâ sahetukâ ceva na ca hetû?

Tehi dhammehi ye dhammâ sahetukâ—te dhamme ṭhapetvâ vedanâkkhandho . . . pe . . . viññâṇakkhandho . . . pe . . . ime dhammâ sahetukâ ceva na ca hetû.

1079. Katame dhammâ hetû ceva hetusampayuttâ ca?

Lobho mohena hetu ceva hetusampayutto ca—moho lobhena hetu ceva hetusampayutto ca—doso mohena hetu ceva hetusampayutto ca—moho dosena hetu ceva hetusampayutto ca.

Alobho adoso amoho—te aññamaññaṃ hetû ceva hetusampayuttâ ca—ime dhammâ hetû ceva hetusampayuttâ ca.

1080. Katame dhammâ hetusampayuttâ ceva na ca hetû?

Tehi dhammehi ye dhammâ sampayuttâ—te dhamme ṭhapetvâ vedanâkkhandho . . . pe . . . viññâṇakkhandho—ime dhammâ . . . pe . . . hetû.

1081. Katame dhammâ na hetukâ?

Tehi dhammehi ye dhammâ na hetû sahetukâ—vedanâkkhandho . . . pe . . . viññâṇakkhandho—ime dhammâ na hetukâ.

1082. Katame dhamnâ na hetû ahetukâ?

Tehi dhammehi ye dhammâ na hetû ahetukâ—vedanâkkhandho . . . pe . . . viññâṇakkhandho—sabbañ ca rûpaṃ asaṅkhatâ ca dhâtu—ime dhammâ na hetû ahetukâ.

1083. Katame dhammâ sappaccayâ?

Pañca khandhâ—rûpakkhandho, vedanâkkhandho, saññâkkhando, saṅkhârakkhandho, viññâṇakkhandho — ime dhammâ sappaccayâ.

1084. Katame dhammâ appaccayâ?

Asaṅkhatâ ca dhâtu—ime dhammâ appaccayâ.

1085. Katame dhammâ saṅkhatâ?

Yeva te dhammâ sappaccayâ—teva te dhammâ saṅkhatâ.

1086. Katame dhammâ asaṅkhatâ?

Yo eva so dhammo appaccayo—so eva so dhammo asaṅkhato.

1087. Katame dhammâ sanidassanâ?

Rûpâyatanaṃ—ime dhammâ sanidassanâ.

1088. Katame dhammâ anidassanâ?

Cakkhâyatanaṃ . . . pe . . . phoṭṭhabbâyatanaṃ vedanâkkhandho . . . pe . . . viññâṇakkhandho—yañ ca rûpaṃ anidassanaṃ appaṭighaṃ dhammâyatanaṃ pariyâpannaṃ—asaṅkhatâ ca dhâtu—ime dhammâ anidassanâ.

1089. Katame dhammâ sappaṭighâ?

Cakkhâyatanaṃ . . . pe . . . phoṭṭhabbâyatanaṃ—ime dhammâ sappaṭighâ.

1090. Katame dhammâ appaṭighâ?

Vedanâkkhandho . . . pe . . . viññâṇakkhandho—yañ ca rûpaṃ anidassanaṃ appaṭighaṃ dhammâyatanaṃ pariyâpannaṃ asaṅkhatâ ca dhâtu—ime dhammâ appaṭighâ.

1091. Katame dhammâ rûpino?

Cattâro ca mahâbhûtâ catunnañ ca mahâbhûtânaṃ upâdâya rûpaṃ—ime dhammâ rûpino.

1092. Katame dhammâ arûpino?

Vedanâkkhandho . . . pe . . . viññâṇakkhandho asaṅkhatâ ca dhâtu—ime dhammâ arûpino.

1093. Katame dhammâ lokiyâ?

Sâsavâ kusalâkusalâ vyâkatâ dhammâ kâmâvacarâ rûpâvacarâ arûpâvacarâ — rûpakkhandho . . . pe . . . viññâṇakkhandho—ime dhammâ lokiyâ.

1094. Katame dhammâ lokuttarâ?

Apariyâpannâ maggâ ca maggaphalâni va asaṅkhatâ ca dhâtu—ime dhammâ lokuttarâ.

1095. Katame dhammâ kenaci viññeyyâ kenaci na viññeyyâ?

Ye te dhammâ cakkhuviññeyyâ, na te dhammâ sotaviññeyyâ, ye vâ pana te dhammâ sotaviññeyyâ, na te dhammâ cakkhuviññeyyâ, ye te dhammâ cakkhuviññeyyâ, na te dhammâ ghânaviññeyyâ, ye vâ pana te dhammâ ghânaviññeyyâ, na te dhammâ cakkhuviññeyyâ, ye te dhammâ cakkhuviññeyyâ, na te dhammâ jivhâviññeyyâ, ye vâ pana te dhammâ jivhâviññeyyâ, na te dhammâ cakkhuviññeyyâ, ye te dhammâ cakkhuviññeyyâ, na te dhammâ kâyaviññeyyâ, ye vâ pana te dhammâ kâyaviññeyyâ, na te dhammâ cakkhuviññeyyâ, ye te dhammâ sotaviññeyyâ, na te dhammâ ghânaviññeyyâ, ye vâ pana te dhammâ ghânaviññeyyâ, na te dhammâ sotaviññeyyâ, ye te dhammâ sotaviññeyyâ, na te dhammâ jivhâviññeyyâ, ye vâ pana te dhammâ jivhâviññeyyâ, na te dhammâ sotaviññeyyâ, ye te dhammâ sotaviññeyyâ, na te dhammâ kâyaviññeyyâ, ye vâ pana te dhammâ kâyaviññeyyâ, na te dhammâ sotaviññeyyâ, ye te dhammâ sotaviññeyyâ, na te dhammâ cakkhuviññeyyâ, ye vâ pana te dhammâ cakkhuviññeyyâ, na te dhammâ sotaviññeyyâ, ye te dhammâ ghânaviññeyyâ, na te dhammâ jivhâviññeyyâ, ye vâ pana te dhammâ jivhâviññeyyâ, na te dhammâ ghânaviññeyyâ, ye te dhammâ ghânaviññeyyâ, na te dhammâ kâyaviññeyyâ, ye vâ pana te dhammâ kâyaviññeyyâ, na te dhammâ ghânaviññeyyâ, ye te dhammâ ghânaviññeyyâ, na te dhammâ cakkhuviññeyyâ, ye vâ pana te dhammâ cakkhuviññeyyâ, na te dhammâ ghânaviññeyyâ, ye te dhammâ ghânaviññeyyâ, na te dhammâ sotaviññeyyâ, ye vâ pana te dhammâ sotaviññeyyâ, na te dhammâ ghânaviññeyyâ, ye te dhammâ jivhâviññeyyâ, na te dhammâ kâyaviññeyyâ, ye vâ pana te dhammâ kâyaviññeyyâ, na te dhammâ jivhâviññeyyâ, ye te dhammâ jivhâviññeyyâ, na te dhammâ cakkhuviññeyyâ, ye vâ pana te dhammâ cakkhuviññeyyâ, na te dhammâ jivhâviññeyyâ, ye te dhammâ jivhâviññeyyâ, na te dhammâ sotaviññeyyâ, ye vâ pana te dhammâ sotaviññeyyâ, na te dhammâ jivhâviññeyyâ, ye te dhammâ jivhâviññeyyâ, na te dhammâ ghânaviññeyyâ, ye vâ pana te dhammâ ghânaviññeyyâ, na te dhammâ jivhâviññeyyâ, ye te dhammâ kâyaviññeyyâ, na te dhammâ cakkhuviññeyyâ, ye vâ pana te dhammâ cakkhuviññeyyâ, na te dhammâ kâyaviññeyyâ, ye te dhammâ kâyaviññeyyâ, na te dhammâ sotaviññeyyâ, ye vâ pana te dhammâ sotaviññeyyâ, na te dhammâ kâyaviññeyyâ, ye te dhammâ kâyaviññeyyâ, na te dhammâ ghânaviññeyyâ ye vâ pana te dhammâ ghânaviññeyyâ, na te dhammâ kâyaviññeyyâ, ye te dhammâ kâyaviññeyyâ, na te dhammâ jivhâviññeyyâ, ye vâ pana te dhammâ jivhâviññeyyâ, na te dhammâ kâyaviññeyyâ—ime dhammâ kenaci viññeyyâ—kenaci na viññeyyâ.

1096. Katame dhammâ âsavâ?

Cattâro âsavâ—kâmâsavo bhavâsavo diṭṭhâsavo avijjâsavo.

1097. Tattha katamo kâmâsavo?

Yo kâmesu kâmacchando kâmarâgo kâmanandî kâmataṇhâ kâmasineho kâmapipâso kâmapariḷâho kâmamucchâ kâmajjhosânaṃ—ayaṃ vuccati kâmâsavo.

1098. Tattha katamo bhavâsavo?

Yo bhavesu bhavacchando bhavarâgo bhavanandî—bhavataṇhâ bhavasineho bhavapariḷâho bhavamucchâ bhavajjhosânam ayaṃ vuccati bhavâsavo.

1099. Tattha katamo diṭṭhâsavo?

Sassato loko ti vâ asassato loko ti vâ antavâ loko ti vâ anantavâ loko ti vâ, taṃ jîvan taṃ sarîran ti vâ aññaṃ jîvaṃ aññaṃ sarîran ti vâ hoti tathâgato paraṃ maraṇâ ti vâ, na hoti tathâgato paraṃ maraṇâ ti vâ, hoti ca na ca hoti tathâgato paraṃ maraṇâ ti vâ, neva hoti na na hoti tathâgato paraṃ maraṇâ ti vâ, yâ evarûpâ diṭṭhi diṭṭhigataṃ diṭṭhigahaṇaṃ diṭṭhikantâro diṭṭhivisûkâyikaṃ diṭṭhivipphanditaṃ diṭṭhisaññojanaṃ gâho paṭiggâho abhiniveso parâmâso kummaggo micchâpatho micchattaṃ titthâyatanaṃ vipariyesaggâho—ayaṃ vuccati diṭṭhâsavo—sabbâpi micchâdiṭṭhi diṭṭhâsavo.

1100. Tattha katamo avijjâsavo?

Dukkhe aññâṇaṃ dukkhudaye aññâṇaṃ dukkhanirodhagâminiyâ paṭipadâya aññâṇaṃ—pubbante aññâṇaṃ aparante aññâṇaṃ pubbantâparante aññâṇaṃ—idappaccayatâ paṭiccasamuppannesu dhammesu aññâṇaṃ yaṃ evarûpaṃ aññâṇaṃ adassanaṃ anabhisamayo ananubodho asambodho appaṭivedho asaṅgâhanâ apariyogâhanâ asamapekkhanâ apaccavekkhanâ apaccakkhakammaṃ dummejjhaṃ balyaṃ asampajaññaṃ moho pamoho sammoho avijjâ avijjogho avijjâyogo avijjânusayo avijjâpariyuṭṭhânaṃ avijjâlangî moho akusalamûlaṃ —ayaṃ vuccati avijjâsavo—Ime dhammâ âsavâ.

1101. Katame dhammâ anâsavâ?

Apariyâpannâ maggâ ca maggaphalâni ca asaṅkhatâ ca dhâtu—ime dhammâ anâsavâ.

1102. Katame dhammâ no âsavâ?

Te dhamme ṭhapetvâ avasesâ kusalâ vyâkatâ dhammâ kâmâvacarâ rûpâvacarâ arûpâvacarâ apariyâpannâ—vedanâkkhandho . . . pe . . . viññâṇakkhandho — sabbañ ca rûpaṃ asaṅkhatâ ca dhâtu—ime dhammâ no âsavâ.

1103. Katame dhammâ sâsavâ?

Kusalâkusalâvyâkatâ dhammâ kâmâvacarâ rûpâvacarâ arûpâvacarâ rûpakkhandho . . . pe . . . viññâṇakkhandho —ime dhammâ sâsavâ.

1104. Katame dhammâ anâsavâ?

Apariyâpannâ maggâ ca maggaphalâni ca asaṅkhatâ ca dhâtu—ime dhammâ anâsavâ.

1105. Katame dhammâ âsavasampayuttâ?

Tehi dhammehi ye dhammâ sampayuttâ vedanâkkhandho . . . pe . . . viññâṇakkhandho—ime dhammâ âsavasampayuttâ.

1106. Katame dhammâ âsavavippayuttâ?

Tehi dhammehi ye dhammâ vippayuttâ—vedanâkkhandho . . . pe . . . viññâṇakkhandho—sabbañ ca rûpaṃ asaṅkhatâ ca dhâtu—ime dhammâ âsavavippayuttâ.

1107. Katame dhammâ âsavâ ceva sâsavâ ca?

Te ca âsavâ âsavâ ceva sâsavâ ca.

1108. Katame dhammâ sâsavâ ceva no ca âsavâ?

Tehi dhammehi ye dhammâ sâsavâ te dhamme ṭhapetvâ avasesâ sâsavâ kusalâkusalâvyâkatâ dhammâ kâmâvacarâ rûpâvacarâ arûpâvacarâ rûpakkhandho . . . pe . . . viññâṇakkhandho—ime dhammâ sâsavâ ceva no ca âsavâ.

1109. Katame dhammâ âsavâ ceva âsavasampayuttâ ca?

Kâmâsavo avijjâsavena âsavo ceva âsavasampayutto ca— avijjâsavo kâmâsavena âsavo ceva âsavasampayutto ca — bhavâsavo avijjâsavena âsavo ceva âsavasampayutto ca avijjâsavo bhavâsavena âsavo ceva âsavasampayutto ca diṭṭhâsavo avijjâsavena âsavo ceva âsavasampayutto ca avijjâsavo diṭṭhâsavena âsavo ceva âsavasampayutto ca—ime dhammâ âsavâ ceva âsavasampayuttâ ca.

1110. Katame dhammâ âsavasampayuttâ ceva no ca âsavâ? Tehi dhammehi ye dhammâ sampayuttâ—te dhamme ṭhapetvâ vedanâkkhandho . . . pe . . . viññâṇakkhandho—ime dhammâ âsavasampayuttâ ceva no ca âsavâ.

1111. Katame dhammâ âsavavippayuttâ sâsavâ? Tehi dhammehi ye dhammâ vippayuttâ sâsavâ kusalâkusalâvyâkatâ dhammâ kâmâvacarâ rûpâvacarâ arûpâvacarâ rûpakkhandho . . . pe . . . viññâṇakkhandho—ime dhammâ âsavavippayuttâ sâsavâ.

1112. Katame dhammâ âsavavippayuttâ anâsavâ? Apariyâpannâ maggâ ca maggaphalâni ca asaṅkhatâ ca dhâtu—ime dhammâ âsavavippayuttâ anâsavâ.

1113. Katame dhammâ saññojanâ? Dasa saññojanâni—kâmarâgasaññojanaṃ paṭighasaññojanaṃ mânasaññojanaṃ diṭṭhisaññojanaṃ vicikicchâsaññojanaṃ sîlabbataparâmâsasaññojanaṃ bhavarâgasaññojanaṃ issâsaññojanaṃ macchariyasaññojanaṃ avijjâsaññojanaṃ.

1114. Tattha—katamaṃ kâmarâgasaññojanaṃ? Yo kâmesu kâmachando kâmarâgo kâmanandî kâmataṇhâ kâmasineho kâmapariḷâho kâmamucchâ kâmajjhosânaṃ idaṃ vuccati kâmarâgasaññojanaṃ.

1115. Tattha katamaṃ paṭighasaññojanaṃ? Anatthaṃ me acarîti âghâto jâyati—anatthaṃ me caratîti âghâto jâyati—anatthaṃ me carissatîti âghâto jâyati—piyassa me manâpassa anatthaṃ acari . . . pe . . . anatthaṃ carati . . . pe . . . anatthaṃ carissatîti âghâto jâyati—apiyassa amanâpassa atthaṃ acari . . . pe . . . atthaṃ carati . . . pe . . . atthaṃ carissatîti âghâto jâyati—aṭṭhâne vâ pana âghâto jâyati—yo evarûpo cittena âghâto paṭighâto paṭighaṃ paṭivirodho kopo pakopo sampakopo doso padoso sampadoso cittassa vyâpatti manopadoso kodho kujjhanâ kujjhitattaṃ doso dussanâ dussitattaṃ vyâpatti vyâpajjanâ vyâpajjitattaṃ virodho paṭivirodho caṇḍikkaṃ asuropo anattamanatâ cittassa—idaṃ vuccati paṭighasaññojanaṃ.

1116. Tattha katamaṃ mânasaññojanaṃ? Seyyo 'hamasmîti mâno—sadiso 'hamasmîti mâno—hîno 'hamasmîti mâno—yo evarûpo mâno maññanâ maññitattaṃ uṇṇati uṇṇamo dhajo sampaggâho ketukamyatâ cittassa—idaṃ vuccati mânasaññojanaṃ.

1117. Tattha katamaṃ diṭṭhisaññojanaṃ?

Sassato loko ti vâ asassato loko ti vâ antavâ loko ti vâ anantavâ loko ti vâ taṃ jîvan taṃ sarîran ti vâ aññaṃ jîvaṃ aññaṃ sarîran ti vâ—hoti tathâgato param maraṇâ ti vâ na hoti tathâgato param maraṇâ ti vâ, hoti ca na ca hoti tathâgato param maraṇâ ti vâ, neva hoti na na hoti tathâgato param maraṇâ ti vâ, yâ evarûpâ diṭṭhi diṭṭhigataṃ diṭṭhigahanaṃ diṭṭhikantâro diṭṭhivisûkâyikaṃ diṭṭhivipphanditaṃ diṭṭhisaññojanaṃ gâho paṭiggâho abhiniveso parâmâso kummaggo micchâpatho micchattaṃ titthâyatanaṃ vipariyesagâho—idaṃ vuccati diṭṭhisaññojanaṃ—ṭhapetvâ sîlabbataparâmâsasaññojanaṃ sabbâ pi micchâdiṭṭhi diṭṭhisaññojanaṃ.

1118. Tattha katamaṃ vicikicchâsaññojanaṃ?

Satthari kaṅkhati vicikicchati, dhamme kaṅkhati vicikicchati, saṅghe kaṅkhati vicikicchati, sikkhâya kaṅkhati vicikicchati, pubbante kaṅkhati vicikicchati, aparante kaṅkhati vicikicchati, pubbantâparante kaṅkhati vicikicchati, idappaccayatâ paṭiccasamuppannesu dhammesu kaṅkhati vicikicchati, yâ evarûpâ kaṅkhâ kaṅkhâyanâ kaṅkhâyitattaṃ vimati vicikicchâ dveḷhakaṃ dvedhâpatho saṃsayo anekaṃsagâho âsappanâ parisappanâ apariyogâhanâ thambhitattaṃ cittassa manovilekho—idaṃ vuccati vicikicchâsaññojanaṃ.

1119. Tattha katamaṃ sîlabbataparâmâsasaññojanaṃ?

Ito bahiddhâ samaṇabrahmaṇânaṃ sîlena suddhivatena suddhisîlabbatena suddhîti yâ evarûpâ diṭṭhi diṭṭhigataṃ diṭṭhigahanaṃ diṭṭhikantâro diṭṭhivisûkâyikaṃ diṭṭhivipphanditaṃ diṭṭhisaññojanaṃ gâho paṭiggâho abhiniveso parâmâso kummaggo micchâpatho micchattaṃ titthâyatanaṃ vipariyesagâho—idaṃ vuccati sîlabbataparâmâsasaññojanaṃ.

1120. Tattha katamaṃ bhavarâgasaññojanaṃ?

Yo bhavesu bhavachando bhavarâgo bhavanandî bhavataṇhâ bhavasineho bhavapariḷâho bhavamucchâ bhavajjhosânaṃ—idaṃ vuccati bhavarâgasaññojanaṃ.

1121. Tattha katamaṃ issâsaññojanaṃ?

Yâ paralobhasakkâragarukâramânanavandanapûjanâsu issâ

issâyanâ issâyitattaṃ usuyyâ usuyyanâ usuyitattaṃ—idaṃ vuccati issâsaññojanaṃ.

1122. Tattha katamaṃ macchariyasaññojanaṃ?

Pañca macchariyâni—âvâsamacchariyaṃ kusalamacchariyaṃ lâbhamacchariyaṃ vaṇṇamacchariyaṃ dhammamacchariyaṃ—yaṃ evarûpaṃ maccharaṃ maccharâyanâ maccharâyitattaṃ vevicchaṃ kadariyaṃ kaṭakañcukatâ aggahitattaṃ cittassa—idaṃ vuccati macchariyasaññojanaṃ.

1123. Tattha katamaṃ avijjâsaññojanaṃ?

Dukkhe aññâṇaṃ . . . pe . . . dukkhanirodhagâminiyâ paṭipadâya aññâṇaṃ, pubbante aññâṇaṃ, aparante aññâṇaṃ pubbantâparante aññâṇaṃ, idappaccayatâ paṭiccasamuppannesu dhammesu aññâṇaṃ—yaṃ evarûpaṃ aññâṇaṃ adassanaṃ anabhisamayo ananubodho asambodho appaṭivedho asaṅgâhanâ apariyogâhanâ asamapekkhanâ apaccavekkhanâ apaccakkhakammaṃ dummejjhaṃ balyaṃ asampajaññaṃ moho pamoho sammoho avijjâ avijjogho avijjâyogo avijjânusayo avijjâpariyuṭṭhânaṃ avijjâlaṅgî moho akusalamûlaṃ—idaṃ vuccati avijjâsaññojanaṃ—Ime dhammâ saññojanâ.

1124. Katame dhammâ no saññojanâ?

Te dhamme ṭhapetvâ avasesâ kusalâkusalâvyâkatâ dhammâ kâmâvacarâ rûpâvacarâ arûpâvacarâ apariyâpannâ vedanâkkhandho . . . pe . . . viññâṇakkhandho—sabbañ ca rûpaṃ asaṅkhatâ ca dhâtu—ime dhammâ no saññojanâ.

1125. Katame dhammâ saññojaniyâ?

Sâsavâ kusalâkusalâvyâkatâ dhammâ kâmâvacarâ rûpâvacarâ arûpâvacarâ—rûpakkhandho . . . pe . . . viññâṇakkhandho—ime dhammâ saññojaniyâ.

1126. Katame dhammâ asaññojaniyâ?

Apariyâpannâ maggâ ca maggaphalâni ca asaṅkhatâ ca dhâtu—ime dhammâ asaññojaniyâ.

1127. Katame dhammâ saññojanasampayuttâ?

Tehi dhammehi ye dhammâ sampayuttâ vedanâkkhandho . . . pe . . . viññâṇakkhandho—ime dhammâ saññojanasampayuttâ.

1128. Katame dhammâ saññojanavippayuttâ?

Tehi dhammehi ye dhammâ vippayuttâ vedanâkkhandho . . . pe . . . viññâṇakkhandho sabbañ ca rûpaṃ asaṅkhatâ ca dhâtu—ime dhammâ saññojanavippayuttâ.

1129. Katame dhammâ saññojanâ ceva saññojaniyâ ca?

Tâneva saññojanâni saññojanâ ceva saññojaniyâ ca.

1130. Katame dhammâ saññojaniyâ ceva no ca saññojanâ?

Tehi dhammehi ye dhammâ saññojaniyâ—te dhamme ṭhapetvâ avasesâ sâsavâ kusalâkusalâvyâkatâ dhammâ kâmâvacarâ rûpâvacarâ arûpâvacarâ rûpakkhandho . . . pe . . . viññâṇakkhandho—ime dhammâ saññojaniyâ ceva no ca saññojanâ.

1131. Katame dhammâ saññojanâ ceva saññojanasampayuttâ ca?

Kâmarâgasaññojanaṃ avijjâsaññojanena saññojanañ ceva saññojanasampayuttañ ca—avijjâsaññojanaṃ kâmarâgasaññojanena saññojanañ ceva saññojanasampayuttañ ca; paṭighasaññojanaṃ avijjâsaññojanena saññojanañ ceva saññojanasampayuttañca; avijjâsaññojanaṃ paṭighasaññojanena saññojanañ ceva saññojanasampayuttañ ca; mânasaññojanaṃ avijjâsaññojanena saññojanañ ceva saññojanasampayuttañ ca—avijjâsaññojanaṃ mânasaññojanena saññojanañ ceva saññojanasampayuttañ ca — diṭṭhisaññojaṃ avijjâsaññojanena saññojanañ ceva saññojanasampayuttañ ca.

Avijjâsaññojanaṃ diṭṭhisaññojanena saññojanañ ceva saññojanasampayuttañ ca, vicikicchâsaññojanaṃ avijjâsaññojanena saññojanañ ceva saññojanasampayuttañ ca, avijjâsaññojanaṃ vicikicchâsaññojanena saññojanañ ceva saññojanasampayuttañ ca, sîlabbataparâmâsasaññojanaṃ avijjâsaññojanena saññojanañ ceva saññojanasampayuttañ ca, avijjâsaññojanaṃ sîlabbataparâmâsasaññojanena saññojanañ ceva saññojanasampayuttañ ca, bhavarâgasaññojanaṃ avijjâsaññojanena saññojanañ ceva saññojanasampayuttañ ca, avijjâsaññojanaṃ bhavarâgasaññojanena saññojanañ ceva saññojanasampayuttañ ca, issâsaññojanaṃ avijjâsaññojanena saññojanañ ceva saññojanasampayuttañ ca, avijjâsaññojanaṃ issâsaññojanena saññojanañ ceva saññojanasampayuttañ ca, macchariyasaññojanaṃ avijjâsaññojanena saññojanañ ceva saññojanasampayuttañ ca, avijjâsaññojanaṃ macchariyasaññojanena saññojanañ ceva saññojanasampayuttañ ca—ime dhammâ saññojanâ ceva saññojanasampayuttâ ca.

1132. Katame dhammâ saññojanasampayuttâ ceva no ca saññojanâ?

Tehi dhammehi ye dhammâ sampayuttâ—te dhamme ṭhapetvâ vedanâkkhandho . . . pe . . viññâṇakkhandho—ime dhammâ saññojanasampayuttâ ceva no ca saññojanâ.

1133. Katame dhammâ saññojanavippayuttâ saññojaniyâ?

Tehi dhammehi ye dhammâ vippayuttâ sâsavâ kusalâkusalâ vyâkatâ dhammâ kâmâvacarâ rûpâvacarâ arûpâvacarâ—rûpakkhandho . . . pe . . . viññâṇakkhandho—ime dhammâ saññojanavippayuttâ saññojaniyâ.

1134. Katame dhammâ saññojanavippayuttâ saññojaniyâ?

Apariyâpannâ maggâ ca maggaphalâni ca asaṅkhatâ ca dhâtu—ime dhammâ saññojanavippayuttâ saññojaniyâ.

1135. Katame dhammâ ganthâ?

Cattâro ganthâ abhijjhâkâyagantho vyâpâdo kâyagantho sîlabbataparâmâso kâyagantho idaṃ saccâbhiniveso kâyagantho.

1136. Tattha katamo abhijjhâkâyagantho?

Yo râgo sârâgo anunayo anurodho nandî nandîrâgo cittassa sârâgo—icchâ mucchâ ajjhosânaṃ gedho paligedho saṅgo paṅko ejâ mâyâ janikâ sañjananî sibbinî jâlinî saritâ visattikâ suttaṃ visaṭâ âyûhanî dutiyâ paṇidhi bhavanetti vanaṃ vanatho santhavo sineho apekkhâ paṭibandhu âsâ âsiṃsanâ âsiṃsitattaṃ rûpâsâ saddâsâ gandhâsâ rasâsâ phoṭṭhabbâsâ lâbhâsâ dhanâsâ puttâsâ jîvitâsâ jappâ pajappâ abhijappâ jappanâ jappitattaṃ loluppaṃ loluppâyanâ loluppâyitattaṃ puñcikatâ sâdukamyatâ adhammarâgo visamalobho nikanti nikâmanâ patthanâ pihanâ sampatthanâ kâmataṇhâ bhavataṇhâ vibhavataṇhâ rûpataṇhâ arûpataṇhâ nirodhataṇhâ saddataṇhâ gandhataṇhâ rasataṇhâ phoṭṭhabbataṇhâ dhammataṇhâ ogho yogo gantho upâdânaṃ âvaraṇaṃ nîvaraṇaṃ chandanaṃ bandhanaṃ upakkileso anusayo pariyuṭṭhânaṃ latâ vevicchaṃ dukkhamûlaṃ dukkhanidânaṃ dukkhappabhavo mârapâso mârabaḷisaṃ mâravisayo taṇhâ nandîtaṇhâ jâlaṃtaṇhâ gaddulaṃtaṇhâ samuddo abhijjhâlobho akusalamûlaṃ—ayaṃ vuccati abhijjhâkâyagantho.

1137. Tattha katamo vyâpâdo kâyagantho?

Anatthaṃ me acarîti âghâto jâyati—anatthaṃ me caratîti

âghâto jâyati, anatthaṃ me carissatîti âghâto jâyati, piyassa
me manâpassa anatthaṃ acari . . . pe . . . anatthaṃ carati
. . . pe . . . anatthaṃ carissatîti âghâto jâyati, appiyassa
me amanâpassa atthaṃ acari . . . pe . . . atthaṃ carati
. . . pe . . . atthaṃ carissatîti âghâto jâyati, aṭṭhâne vâ
pana âghâto jâyati, yo evarûpo cittassa âghâto paṭighâto
paṭighaṃ paṭivirodho kopo pakopo sampakopo doso padoso
sampadoso cittassa vyâpatti manopadoso kodho kujjhanâ
kujjhitattaṃ doso dussanâ dussitattaṃ vyâpatti vyâpajjanâ
vyâpajjitattaṃ virodho paṭivirodho caṇḍikkaṃ asuropo anattamanatâ cittassa—ayaṃ vuccati vyâpâdo kâyagantho.

1138. Tattha katamo sîlabbataparâmâso kâyagantho ?

Ito bahiddhâ samaṇabrahmaṇânaṃ sîlena suddhivatena
suddhisîlabbatena suddhîti yâ evarûpâ diṭṭhi diṭṭhigataṃ
diṭṭhigahaṇaṃ diṭṭhikantâro diṭṭhivisûkâyikaṃ diṭṭhivipphanditaṃ diṭṭhisaññojanaṃ gâho paṭiggâho abhiniveso parâmâso kummaggo micchâpatho micchattaṃ titthâyatanaṃ
vipariyesagâho—ayaṃ vuccati sîlabbataparâmâso kâyagantho.

1139. Tattha katamo idaṃ saccâbhiniveso kâyagantho ?

Sassato loko idam eva saccaṃ moghaṃ aññan ti vâ ; asassato
loko, idam eva saccaṃ moghaṃ aññan ti vâ ; antavâ loko,
idam eva saccaṃ mogham aññan ti vâ ; anantavâ loko, idam
eva saccaṃ mogham aññan ti vâ ; jîvan taṃ sarîraṃ idam eva
saccaṃ mogham aññan ti vâ ; aññaṃ jîvaṃ aññaṃ sarîraṃ
idam eva saccaṃ mogham aññan ti vâ ; hoti tathâgato paraṃ
maraṇâ idam eva saccaṃ mogham aññan ti vâ, na hoti
tathâgato paraṃ maraṇâ idam eva saccaṃ mogham aññan ti
vâ, hoti ca na ca hoti tathâgato paraṃ maraṇâ, idam eva
saccaṃ mogham aññan ti vâ, neva hoti na na hoti tathâgato
paraṃ maraṇâ idam eva saccaṃ mogham aññan ti vâ, yâ
evarûpâ diṭṭhi diṭṭhigataṃ diṭṭhigahaṇaṃ diṭṭhikantâro
diṭṭhivisûkâyikaṃ diṭṭhivipphanditaṃ diṭṭhisaññojanaṃ
gâho patiggâho abhiniveso parâmâso kummaggo micchâpatho
micchattaṃ titthâyatanaṃ vipariyesagâho, ayaṃ vuccati
idam saccâbhiniveso kâyagantho, ṭhapetvâ sîlabbataparâ-
mâsaṃ kâyaganthaṃ sabbâ pi micchâdiṭṭhi, idaṃ saccâbhiniveso kâyagantho—Ime dhammâ ganthâ.

1140. Katame dhammâ no ganthâ ?

Te dhamme ṭhapetvâ avasesâ kusalâkusalâvyakatâ dhammâ kâmâvacarâ rûpâvacarâ arûpâvacarâ apariyâpannâ vedanâkkhando . . . pe . . . viññâṇakkhandho sabbañ ca rûpaṃ asaṅkhatâ ca dhâtu—ime dhammâ no ganthâ.

1141. Katame dhammâ ganthaniyâ?

Sâsavâ kusalâkusalâvyâkatâ dhammâ kâmâvacarâ rûpâvacarâ arûpâvacarâ—rûpakkhandho . . . pe . . . viññâṇakkhandho—ime dhammâ ganthaniyâ.

1142. Katame dhammâ aganthaniyâ?

Apariyâpannâ maggâ ca maggaphalâni ca asaṅkhatâ ca dhâtu—ime dhammâ aganthaniyâ.

1143. Katame dhammâ ganthasampayuttâ?

Tehi dhammehi ye dhammâ sampayuttâ—vedanâkkhandho . . . pe . . . viññâṇakkhandho—ime dhammâ ganthasampayuttâ.

1144. Katame dhammâ ganthavippayuttâ?

Tehi dhammehi ye dhammâ vippayuttâ vedanâkkhandho . . . pe . . . viññâṇakkhandho—ime dhammâ ganthavippayuttâ.

1145. Katame dhammâ ganthâ ceva ganthaniyâ ca?

Teva ganthâ ganthâ ceva ganthaniyâ ca.

1146. Katame dhammâ ganthaniyâ ceva no ca ganthâ?

Tehi dhammehi ye dhammâ ganthaniyâ — te dhamme ṭhapetvâ avasesâ sâsavâ kusalâkusalâvyâkatâ dhammâ kâmâvacarâ rûpâvacarâ arûpâvacarâ—rûpakkhandho . . . pe . . . viññâṇakkhandho—ime dhammâ ganthaniyâ ceva no ca ganthâ.

1147. Katame dhammâ ganthâ ceva ganthasampayuttâ ca?

Sîlabbataparâmâso kâyagantho, abhijjhâkâyaganthena gantho ceva ganthasampayutto ca — abhijjhâkâyagantho sîlabbataparâmâsakâyaganthena gantho ceva ganthasampayutto ca, idaṃ saccâbhiniveso kâyagantho abhijjhâkâyaganthena gantho ceva ganthasampayutto ca, abhijjhâkâyagantho idaṃ saccâbhinivesakâyaganthena gantho ceva ganthasampayutto ca—ime dhammâ ganthâ ceva ganthasampayuttâ ca.

1148. Katame dhammâ ganthasampayuttâ ceva no ca ganthâ?

Tehi dhammehi ye dhammâ sampayuttâ—te dhamme ṭhapetvâ vedanâkkhandhaṃ . . . pe . . . viññâṇakkhandhaṃ—ime dhammâ . . . pe . . . no ca ganthâ.

1149. Katame dhammâ ganthavippayuttâ ganthaniyâ?

Tehi dhammehi ye dhammâ vippayuttâ sâsavâ kusalâkusalâ vyâkatâ dhammâ kâmâvacarâ rûpâvacarâ arûpâvacarâ, rûpakkhandho . . . pe . . . viññâṇakkhandho—ime dhammâ ganthavippayuttâ ganthaniyâ.

1150. Katame dhammâ ganthavippayuttâ aganthaniyâ?

Apariyâpannâ maggâ ca maggaphalâni ca asaṅkhatâ ca dhâtu—ime dhammâ ganthavippayuttâ ganthaniyâ.

1151. Katame dhammâ oghâ . . . pe . . .

Katame dhammâ yogâ . . . pe . . .

1152. Katame dhammâ nîvaraṇâ?

Cha nîvaraṇâ, kâmacchandanîvaraṇaṃ, vyâpâdanîvaranaṃ, thînamiddhanîvaraṇaṃ, uddhaccakukkuccanîvaranaṃ, vicikicchânîvaraṇaṃ, avijjânîvaraṇaṃ.

1153. Tattha katamaṃ kâmacchandanîvaraṇaṃ?

Yo kâmesu kamacchando kâmarâgo kâmanandî kâmataṇhâ kâmasineho kâmapariḷâho kâmamucchâ kâmajjhosânaṃ—idam vuccati kâmacchandanîvaraṇaṃ.

1154. Tattha katamaṃ vyâpâdanîvaraṇaṃ?

Anatthaṃ me acarîti âghâto jâyati, anatthaṃ me caratîti âghâto jâyati, anatthaṃ me carissatîti âghâto jâyati, piyassa me manâpassa anatthaṃ acari . . . pe . . . anatthaṃ carati . . . pe . . . anatthaṃ carissatîti âghâto jâyati, appiyassa me amanâpassa atthaṃ acari . . . pe . . . atthaṃ carati . . . pe . . . atthaṃ carissatîti âghâto jâyati aṭṭhâne vâ pana âghâto jâyati, yo evarûpo cittassa âghâto paṭighâto paṭighaṃ virodho kopo pakopo sampakopo doso padoso sampadoso cittassa vyâpatti manopadoso kodho kujjhanâ kujjhitattaṃ doso dussanâ dussitattaṃ vyâpatti vyâpajjanâ vyâpajjitattaṃ virodho paṭivirodho caṇḍikkaṃ asuropo anattamanatâ cittassa, idaṃ vuccati vyâpâdanîvaraṇaṃ.

1155. Tattha katamaṃ thînamiddhanîvaraṇaṃ?

Atthi thînaṃ atthi middhaṃ.

1156. Tattha katamaṃ thînaṃ?

Yâ cittassa akalyatâ akammaññatâ olîyanâ sallîyanâ lînaṃ

lîyanâ lîyitattaṃ thînaṃ thîyanâ thîyitattaṃ cittassa—idaṃ vuccati thînaṃ.

1157. Tattha katamaṃ middhaṃ?

Yâ kâyassa akalyatâ akammaññatâ onâho pariyonâho anto samorodho middhaṃ soppaṃ pacalâyikâ soppaṃ supinâ supitattaṃ, idaṃ vuccati middhaṃ. Iti idañ ca thînaṃ idañ ca middhaṃ idaṃ vuccati thînamiddhanîvaraṇaṃ.

1158. Tattha katamaṃ uddhaccakukkuccanîvaraṇaṃ?

Atthi uddhaccaṃ atthi kukkuccaṃ.

1159. Tattha katamaṃ uddhaccaṃ?

Taṃ cittassa uddhaccaṃ avûpasamo cetaso vikkhepo bhantattaṃ cittassa—idaṃ vuccati uddhaccaṃ.

1160. Tattha katamaṃ kukkuccaṃ?

Akappiye kappiyasaññitâ, kappiye akappiyasaññitâ, avajje vajjasaññitâ, vajje avajjasaññitâ, yaṃ evarûpaṃ kukkuccaṃ kukkuccâyanâ kukkuccâyitattaṃ cetaso vippaṭisâro manovilekho, idaṃ vuccati kukkuccaṃ. Iti, idañ ca uddhaccaṃ idañ ca kukkuccaṃ—idaṃ vuccati uddhaccakukkuccanîvaraṇaṃ.

1161. Tattha katamaṃ vicikicchânîvaraṇaṃ?

Satthari kaṅkhati vicikicchati dhamme kaṅkhati vicikicchati, saṅghe kaṅkhati vicikicchati, sikkhâya kaṅkhati vicikicchati, pubbante kaṅkhati vicikicchati, aparante kaṅkhati vicikicchati, pubbantâparante kaṅkhati vicikicchati, idappaccayatâ paṭiccasamuppannesu dhammesu kaṅkhati vicikicchati, yâ evarûpâ kaṅkhâ kaṅkhâyanâ kaṅkhâyitattaṃ vimati vicikicchâ dveḷhakaṃ dvedhâpatho saṃsayo anekaṃsagâho âsappanâ parisappanâ apariyogâhanâ thambhitattaṃ cittassa manovilekho—idaṃ vuccati vicikicchânîvaraṇaṃ.

1162. Tattha katamaṃ avijjânîvaraṇaṃ?

Dukkhe aññâṇaṃ . . . pe . . . pubbante aññâṇaṃ aparante aññâṇaṃ pubbantâparante aññâṇaṃ idappaccayatâ paṭiccasamuppannesu dhammesu aññâṇaṃ—yaṃ evarûpaṃ aññâṇaṃ adassanaṃ anabhisamayo ananubodho asambodho appaṭivedho asaṅgâhanâ apariyogâhanâ asamapekkhanâ apaccavekkhaṇâ apaccakkhakammaṃ dummejjham balyaṃ asampajaññaṃ moho pamoho sammoho avijjâ avijjogho avijjâyogo avijjânusayo avijjâpariyuṭṭhânaṃ avijjâlangî moho akusalamûlaṃ—idaṃ vuccati avijjânîvaraṇaṃ—ime dhammâ nîvaraṇâ.

1163. Katame dhammâ no nîvaranâ?

Te dhamme ṭhapetvâ avasesâ kusalâkusalâvyâkatâ dhammâ kâmâvacarâ rûpâvacarâ arûpâvacarâ apariyâpannâ—vedanâkkhandho . . . pe . . . viññâṇakkhandho—sabbañ ca rûpaṃ asaṅkhatâ ca dhâtu—ime dhammâ no nîvaraṇâ.

1164. Katame dhammâ nîvaraṇiyâ?

Sâsavâ kusalâkusalâvyâkatâ dhammâ kâmâvacarâ rûpâvacarâ arûpâvacarâ—rûpakkhandho . . . pe . . . viññâṇakkandho—ime dhammâ nîvaraṇiyâ.

1165. Katame dhammâ anîvaraṇiyâ?

Apariyâpannâ maggâ ca maggaphalâni ca asaṅkhatâ ca dhâtu—ime dhammâ aṇîvaraṇiyâ.

1166. Katame dhammâ nîvaraṇasampayuttâ?

Tehi dhammehi ye dhammâ sampayuttâ—vedanâkkhandho . . . pe . . . viññâṇakkhandho—ime dhammâ nîvaraṇasampayuttâ?

1167. Katame dhammâ nîvaraṇavippayuttâ?

Ṭehi dhammehi ye dhammâ vippayuttâ vedanâkkhandho . . . pe . . . viññâṇakkhandho—sabbañ ca rûpaṃ asaṅkhatâ ca dhâtu—ime dhammâ nîvaraṇavippayuttâ.

1168. Katame dhammâ nîvaraṇâ ceva nîvaraṇiyâ ca?

Tâneva nîvaraṇâni nîvaraṇâ ceva nîvaraṇiyâ ca.

1169. Katame dhammâ nîvaraṇiyâ ceva no ca nîvaraṇâ?

Tehi dhammehi ye dhammâ nîvaraṇiyâ, te dhamme ṭhapetvâ avasesâ sâsavâ kusalâkusalâvyâkatâ dhammâ kâmâvacarâ rûpâvacarâ arûpâvacarâ, rûpakkhandho . . . pe . . . viññâṇakkhandho—ime dhammâ nîvaraṇiyâ ceva no ca nîvaraṇâ.

1170. Katame dhammâ nîvaraṇâ ceva nîvaraṇasampayuttâ ca?

Kâmacchandanîvaraṇaṃ avijjânîvaraṇena nîvaraṇañ ceva nîvaraṇasampayuttañ ca, avijjânîvaraṇaṃ kâmacchandanîvaraṇena nîvaraṇañ ceva nîvaraṇasampayuttañ ca, vyâpâdanîvaraṇaṃ avijjânîvaraṇena nîvaraṇañ ceva nîvaraṇasampayuttañ ca, avijjânîvaranaṃ vyâpâdanîvaraṇena nîvaraṇañ ceva nîvaraṇasampayuttañ ca, thînamiddhanîvaraṇaṃ avijjânîvaraṇena nîvaraṇañ ceva nîvaraṇasampayuttañ ca, avijjânîvaraṇaṃ thînamiddhanîvaraṇena nîvaraṇañ ceva nîvaraṇasampayuttañ ca, uddhaccanîvaraṇaṃ avijjânîvaraṇena nîvaraṇañ ceva nîvaraṇasampayuttañ ca, avijjânîvaraṇaṃ uddhaccanîvaraṇena nîvaraṇañ ceva nîvaraṇasampayuttañ ca, kukkuccanîvaraṇaṃ avijjânîvaraṇena nîvaraṇañ ceva nîvaraṇasampayuttañ ca, avijjânîvaraṇaṃ kukkuccanîvaraṇena nîvaraṇañ ceva nîvaraṇasampayuttañ ca, vicikicchânîvaraṇaṃ avijjânîvaraṇena nîvaraṇañ ceva nîvaraṇasampayuttañ ca, avijjânîvaraṇaṃ vicikicchânîvaraṇena nîvaraṇañ ceva nîvaraṇasampayuttañ ca, kâmacchandanîvaraṇaṃ uddhaccanîvaraṇena nîvaraṇañ ceva nîvaraṇasampayuttañ ca, uddhaccanîvaraṇaṃ kâmacchandanîvaraṇena nîvaraṇañ ceva nîvaraṇasampayuttañ ca, vyâpâdânîvaraṇaṃ uddhaccanîvaraṇena nîvaraṇañ ceva nîvaraṇasampayuttañ ca, uddhaccanîvaraṇaṃ vyâpâdanîvaraṇena nîvaraṇañ ceva nîvaraṇasampayuttañ ca, thînamiddhanîvaraṇaṃ uddhaccanîvaraṇena nîvaraṇañ ceva nîvaraṇasampayuttañ ca, uddhaccanîvaraṇaṃ thînamiddhanîvaraṇena nîvaraṇañ ceva nîvaraṇasampayuttañ ca, kukkuccanîvaraṇaṃ uddhaccanîvaraṇena nîvaraṇañ ceva nîvaraṇasampayuttañ ca, uddhaccanîvaraṇaṃ kukkuccanîvaraṇena nîvaraṇañ ceva nîvaraṇasampayuttañ ca, vicikicchânîvaraṇaṃ uddhaccanîvaraṇena nîvarañ ceva nîvaraṇasampayuttañ ca, uddhaccanîvaraṇaṃ vicikicchânîvaraṇena nîvaraṇañ ceva nîvaraṇasampayuttañ ca, avijjânîvaraṇaṃ uddhaccanîvaraṇena nîvaraṇañ ceva nîvaraṇasampayuttañ ca, uddhaccanîvaraṇaṃ avijjânîvaraṇena nîvaraṇañ ceva nîvaraṇasampayuttañ ca—Ime dhammâ nîvaraṇâ ceva nîvaraṇasampayuttâ ca.

1171. Katame dhammâ nîvaraṇasampayuttâ ceva no ca nîvaraṇâ?

Tehi dhammehi ye dhammâ sampayuttâ—te dhamme ṭhapetvâ vedanâkkhandho . . . pe . . . viññâṇakkhandho—ime dhammâ nîvaraṇasampayuttâ ceva no ca nîvaraṇâ.

1172. Katame dhammâ nîvaraṇavippayuttâ nîvaraṇiyâ?

Tehi dhammehi ye dhammâ vippayuttâ sâsavâ kusalâkusalâvyâkatâ dhammâ kâmâvacarâ rûpâvac arâarûpâvacarâ rûpakkhandho . . . pe . . . viññâṇakkhandho—ime dhammâ nîvaraṇavippayuttâ nîvaraṇiyâ.

1173. Katame dhammâ nîvaraṇavippayuttâ anîvaraṇiyâ?

Apariyâpannâ maggâ ca maggaphalâni ca asaṅkhatâ ca dhâtu—ime dhammâ nîvaraṇavippayuttâ anîvaraṇiyâ.

1174. Katame dhammâ parâmâsâ?

Diṭṭhiparâmâso.

1175. Tattha katamo diṭṭhiparâmâso?

Sassato loko ti vâ asassato loko ti vâ antavâ loko ti vâ anantavâ loko ti vâ taṃ jîvan taṃ sarîran ti vâ aññaṃ jîvaṃ aññaṃ sarîran ti vâ, hoti tathâgato param maraṇâ ti vâ na hoti tathâgato param maraṇâ ti vâ, hoti ca na ca hoti tathâgato param maraṇâ ti vâ, neva hoti na na hoti tathâgato param maraṇâ ti vâ, yâ evarûpâ diṭṭhi diṭṭhigataṃ diṭṭhigahaṇaṃ diṭṭhikantâro diṭṭhivisûkâyikaṃ diṭṭhivipphanditaṃ diṭṭhisaññojanaṃ gâho paṭiggâho abhiniveso parâmâso kummaggo micchâpatho micchattaṃ titthâyatanaṃ vipariyesagâho — ayaṃ vuccati diṭṭhiparâmâso — sabbâ pi micchâdiṭṭhi diṭṭhiparâmâso—ime dhammâ parâmâsâ.

1176. Katame dhammâ no parâmâsâ?

Te dhamme ṭhapetvâ avasesâ kusalâkusalâvyâkatâ dhammâ kâmâvacarâ rûpâvacarâ arûpâvacarâ apariyâpannâ—vedanâkkhandho . . . pe . . . viññâṇakkhandho—sabbañ ca rûpaṃ asaṅkhatâ ca dhâtu—ime dhammâ no parâmâsâ.

1177. Katame dhammâ parâmaṭṭhâ?

Sâsavâ kusalâkusalâvyâkatâ dhammâ kâmâvacarâ rûpâvacarâ arûpâvacarâ—rûpakkhandho . . . pe . . . viññâṇakkhandho—ime dhammâ parâmaṭṭhâ.

1178. Katame dhammâ aparâmaṭṭhâ?

Apariyâpannâ maggâ ca maggaphalâni ca asaṅkhatâ ca dhâtu—ime dhammâ aparâmaṭṭhâ.

1179. Katame dhammâ parâmâsasampayuttâ?

Tehi dhammehi ye dhammâ sampayuttâ—vedanâkkhandho . . . pe . . . viññâṇakkhandho — ime dhammâ parâmâsasampayuttâ.

1180. Katame dhammâ parâmâsavippayuttâ?

Tehi dhammehi ye dhammâ vippayuttâ—vedanâkkhandho . . . pe . . . viññâṇakkhandho—sabbañ ca rûpaṃ asaṅkhatâ ca dhâtu—ime dhammâ parâmâsavippayuttâ.

1181. Katame dhammâ parâmâsâ ceva parâmaṭṭhâ ca?

Sveva parâmâso parâmâso ceva parâmaṭṭho ca.

1182. Katame dhammâ parâmaṭṭhâ ceva no ca parâmâsâ?

Tehi dhammehi ye dhammâ parâmaṭṭhâ te dhamme

ṭhapetvâ avasesâ sâsavâ kusalâkusalâvyâkatâ dhammâ kâmâvacarâ rûpâvacarâ arûpâvacarâ—rûpakkhandho . . . pe . . . viññâṇakkhandho—ime dhammâ parâmaṭṭhâ ceva no ca parâmâsâ.

1183. Katame dhammâ parâmâsavippayuttâ parâmaṭṭhâ?

Tehi dhammehi ye dhammâ vippayuttâ sâsavâ kusalâkusalâvyâkatâ dhammâ kâmâvacarâ rûpâvacarâ arûpâvacarâ—rûpakkhandho . . . pe . . . viññâṇakkhandho — ime dhammâ parâmâsavippayuttâ parâmaṭṭhâ.

1184. Katamo dhammâ parâmâsavippayuttâ aparâmaṭṭhâ?

Apariyâpannâ maggâ ca maggaphalâni ca asaṅkhatâ ca dhâtu—ime dhammâ parâmâsavippayuttâ aparâmaṭṭhâ.

1185. Katame dhammâ sârammaṇâ?

Vedanâkkhandho saññâkkhandho saṅkhârakkhandho viññâṇakkhandho—ime dhammâ sârammaṇâ.

1186. Katame dhammâ anârammaṇâ?

Sabbañ ca rûpaṃ asaṅkhatâ ca dhâtu—ime dhammâ anârammaṇâ.

1187. Katame dhammâ cittâ?

Cakkhuviññâṇaṃ sotaviññâṇaṃ ghânaviññâṇaṃ jivhâviññâṇaṃ kâyaviññâṇaṃ manodhâtu manoviññâṇadhâtu—ime dhammâ cittâ.

1188. Katame dhammâ no cittâ?

Vedanâkkhandho saññâkkhandho saṅkhârakkhandho—sabbañ ca rûpaṃ asaṅkhatâ ca dhâtu—ime dhammâ no cittâ.

1189. Katame dhammâ cetasikâ?

Vedanâkkhandho saññâkkhandho saṅkhârakkhandho—ime dhammâ cetasikâ.

1190. Katame dhammâ acetasikâ?

Cittañ ca sabbañ ca rûpaṃ asaṅkhatâ ca dhâtu—ime dhammâ acetasikâ.

1191. Katame dhammâ cittasampayuttâ?

Vedanâkkhandho saññâkkhandho saṅkhârakkhandho—ime dhammâ cittasampayuttâ.

1192. Katame dhammâ cittavippayuttâ?

Sabbañ ca rûpaṃ asaṅkhatâ ca dhâtu—ime dhammâ cittavippayuttâ.

Cittaṃ na vattabbaṃ cittena sampayuttan ti pi cittena vippayuttan ti pi.

1193. Katame dhammâ cittasaṃsaṭṭhâ?

Vedanâkkhandho saññâkkhandho saṅkhârakkhandho—ime dhammâ cittasaṃsaṭṭhâ.

1194. Katame dhammâ cittavisaṃsaṭṭhâ?

Sabbañ ca rûpaṃ asaṅkhatâ ca dhâtu—ime dhammâ cittavisaṃsaṭṭhâ.

Cittaṃ na vattabbaṃ cittena samsaṭṭhan ti pi cittena visaṃsaṭṭhan ti pi.

1195. Katame dhammâ cittasamuṭṭhânâ?

Vedanâkkhandho saññâkkhandho saṅkhârakkhandho kâyaviññatti vacîviññatti—taṃ vâ panaññam pi atthi rûpaṃ cittajaṃ cittahetukaṃ cittasamuṭṭhânaṃ rûpâyatanaṃ saddâyatanaṃ gandhâyatanaṃ phoṭṭhabbâyatanaṃ âkâsadhâtu âpodhâtu rûpassa lahutâ rûpassa mudutâ rûpassa kammaññatâ rûpassa upacayo rûpassa santati kabaḷiṅkâro âhâro —ime dhammâ cittasamuṭṭhânâ.

1196. Katame dhammâ no cittasamuṭṭhânâ?

Cittañ ca avasesañ ca rûpaṃ asaṅkhatâ ca dhâtu—ime dhammâ no cittasamuṭṭhânâ.

1197. Katame dhammâ cittasahabhuno?

Vedanâkkhandho saññâkkhandho saṅkhârakkhandho kâyaviññatti vacîviññatti—ime dhammâ cittasahabhuno.

1198. Katame dhammâ no cittasahabhuno?

Cittañ ca avasesañ ca rûpaṃ asaṅkhatâ ca dhâtu—ime dhammâ no cittasahabhuno.

1199. Katame dhammâ cittânuparivattino?

Vedanâkkhandho saññâkkhandho saṅkhârakkhandho kâyaviññatti vacîviññatti—ime dhammâ cittânuparivattino.

1200. Katame dhammâ no cittânuparivattino?

Cittañ ca avasesañ ca rûpaṃ asaṅkhatâ ca dhâtu—ime dhammâ no cittânuparivattino.

1201. Katame dhammâ cittasaṃsaṭṭhasamuṭṭhânâ?

Vedanâkkhandho saññâkkhandho saṅkhârakkhandho—ime dhammâ cittasaṃsaṭṭhasamuṭṭhânâ.

1202. Katame dhammâ no cittasaṃsaṭṭhasamuṭṭhânâ?

Cittañ ca sabbañ ca rûpaṃ asaṅkhatâ ca dhâtu—ime dhammâ no cittasaṃsaṭṭhasamuṭṭhânâ.

1203. Katame dhammâ cittasaṃsaṭṭhasamuṭṭhânasahabhuno?

Vedanâkkhandho saññâkkhandho saṅkhârakkhandho — ime dhammâ cittasaṃsaṭṭhasamuṭṭhânasahabhuno.

1204. Katame dhammâ no cittasaṃsaṭṭhasamuṭṭhânasahabhuno.

Cittañ ca sabbañ ca rûpaṃ asaṅkhatâ ca dhâtu—ime dhammâ no cittasaṃsaṭṭhasamuṭṭhânasahabhuno.

1205. Katame dhammâ cittasaṃsaṭṭhasamuṭṭhânânuparivattino?

Vedanâkkhandho saññâkkhandho saṅkhârakkhandho — ime dhammâ cittasaṃsaṭṭhasamuṭṭhânânuparivattino.

1206. Katame dhammâ no cittasaṃsaṭṭhasamuṭṭhânânuparivattino.

Cittañ ca sabbañ ca rûpaṃ asaṅkhatâ ca dhâtu—ime dhammâ no cittasaṃsaṭṭhasamuṭṭhânânuparivattino.

1207. Katame dhammâ ajjhattikâ?

Cakkhâyatanaṃ . . . pe . . . manâyatanaṃ—ime dhammâ ajjhattikâ.

1208. Katame dhammâ bâhirâ?

Rûpâyatanaṃ . . . pe . . . dhammâyatanaṃ—ime dhammâ bâhirâ.

1209. Katame dhammâ upâdâ?

Cakkhâyatanaṃ . . . pe . . . kabaḷiṅkâro âhâro — ime dhammâ upâdâ.

1210. Katame dhammâ no upâdâ?

Vedanâkkhandho, saññâkkhandho, saṅkhârakkhandho, viññâṇakkhandho, cattâro mahâbhûtâ, asaṅkhatâ ca dhâtu—ime dhammâ no upâdâ.

1211. Katame dhammâ upâdiṇṇâ?

Sâsavâ kusalâkusalânaṃ dhammânaṃ vipâkâ kâmâvacarâ rûpâvacarâ arûpâvacarâ vedanâkkhandho . . . pe . . . viññâṇakkhandho—yañ ca rûpaṃ kammassa katattâ—ime dhammâ upâdiṇṇâ.

1212. Katame dhammâ anupâdiṇṇâ?

Sâsavâ kusalâkusalâ dhammâ kâmâvacarâ rûpâvacarâ arûpâvacarâ vedanâkkhandho . . . pe . . . viññâṇakkhandho, ye ca dhammâ kiriyâ neva kusalâ nâkusalâ na ca kammavipâkâ, yañ ca rûpaṃ na kammassa katattâ, apariyâpannâ maggâ ca maggaphalâni ca asaṅkhatâ ca dhâtu—ime dhammâ anupâdiṇṇâ.

1213. Katame dhammâ upâdânâ?

Cattâri upâdânâni—kâmupâdânaṃ diṭṭhupâdânaṃ sîlabbatupâdânaṃ attavâdupâdânaṃ.

1214. Tattha katamaṃ kâmupâdânaṃ?

Yo kâmesu kâmacchando kâmarâgo kâmanandî kâmataṇhâ kâmasineho kâmapariḷâho kâmamucchâ kâmajjhosânaṃ—idaṃ vuccati kâmupâdânaṃ.

1215. Tattha katamaṃ diṭṭhupâdânaṃ?

Natthi diṇṇaṃ, natthi yiṭṭhaṃ, natthi hutaṃ, natthi sukaṭadukkaṭânaṃ kammânaṃ phalaṃ vipâko, natthi ayaṃ loko, natthi paraloko, natthi mâtâ, natthi pitâ, natthi sattâ opapâtikâ, natthi loke samaṇabrahmaṇâ sammaggatâ sammâpaṭipannâ, ye imañ ca lokaṃ parañ ca lokaṃ sayaṃ abhiññâ sacchîkatvâ pavedentîti—yâ evarûpâ diṭṭhi diṭṭhigataṃ diṭṭhigahanaṃ diṭṭhikantâro diṭṭhivisûkâyikaṃ diṭṭhivipphanditaṃ diṭṭhisaññojanaṃ gâho patiggâho abhiniveso parâmâso kummaggo micchâpatho micchattaṃ titthâyatanaṃ vipariyesagâho—idaṃ vuccati diṭṭhupâdânaṃ, ṭhapetvâ sîlabbatupâdânaṃ ca attavâdupâdânañ ca, sabbâpi micchâdiṭṭhi diṭṭhupâdânaṃ.

1216. Tattha katamaṃ sîlabbatupâdânaṃ?

Ito bahiddhâ samaṇabrahmaṇânaṃ sîlena suddhivatena suddhisîlabbatena suddhîtiyâ evarûpâ diṭṭhi diṭṭhigataṃ diṭṭhigahanaṃ diṭṭhikantâro diṭṭhivisûkâyikaṃ diṭṭhivipphanditaṃ diṭṭhisaññojanaṃ gâho patiggâho abhiniveso parâmâso kummaggo micchâpatho micchattaṃ titthâyatanaṃ vipariyesagâho—idaṃ vuccati sîlabbatupâdânaṃ.

1217. Tattha katamaṃ attavâdupâdânaṃ?

Idha assutavâ puthujjano, ariyânaṃ adassâvî ariyadhammassa akovido ariyadhamme avinîto sappurisânaṃ adassâvî sappurisadhammassa akovido sappurisadhamme avinîto rûpaṃ attato samanupassati, rûpavantaṃ vâ attânaṃ attani vâ rûpaṃ, rûpasmiṃ vâ attânaṃ vedanaṃ . . . pe . . . saññaṃ . . . pe . . . saṅkhâre . . . pe . . . viññâṇaṃ attato samanupassati, viññâṇavantaṃ vâ attânaṃ, attani vâ viññaṇaṃ, viññâṇasmiṃ vâ attânaṃ, yâ evarûpâ diṭṭhi diṭṭhigataṃ diṭṭhigahaṇaṃ diṭṭhikantâro diṭṭhivisûkâyikaṃ diṭṭhivipphanditaṃ diṭṭhisaññojanaṃ gâho patiggâho abhiniveso parâmâso kummaggo micchâpatho micchattaṃ titthâyatanaṃ vipariyesaggâho, idaṃ vuccati attavâdupâdânaṃ—ime dhammâ upâdânâ.

1218. Katame dhammâ no upâdânâ?

Te dhamme ṭhapetvâ avasesâ kusalâkusalâvyâkatâ dhammâ kâmâvacarâ rûpâvacarâ arûpâvacarâ apariyâpannâ vedanâkkhandho . . . pe . . . viññâṇakkhandho sabbañ ca rûpaṃ asaṅkhatâ ca dhâtu—ime dhammâ no upâdânâ.

1219. Katame dhammâ upâdâniyâ?

Sâsavâ kusalâkusalâvyâkatâ dhammâ kâmâvacarâ rûpâvacarâ arûpâvacarâ, rûpakkhandho . . . pe . . . viññâṇakkhandho—ime dhammâ upâdâniyâ.

1220. Katame dhammâ anupâdâniyâ?

Apariyâpannâ maggâ ca maggaphalâni ca asaṅkhatâ ca dhâtu—ime dhammâ anupâdâniyâ?

1221. Katame dhammâ upâdânasampayuttâ?

Tehi dhammehi ye dhammâ sampayuttâ vedanâkkhandho . . . pe . . . viññâṇakkhandho—ime dhammâ upâdânasampayuttâ.

1222. Katame dhammâ upâdânavippayuttâ?

Tehi dhammehi ye dhammâ vippayuttâ, vedanâkkhandho . . . pe . . . viññâṇakkhandho, sabbañ ca rûpaṃ asaṅkhatâ ca dhâtu—ime dhammâ upâdânavippayuttâ.

1223. Katame dhammâ upâdânâ ceva upâdâniyâ ca?

Tâneva upâdânâni upâdânâ ceva upâdâniyâ ca.

1224. Katame dhammâ upâdâniyâ ceva no ca upâdânâ?

Tehi dhammehi ye dhammâ upâdâniyâ—te dhamme ṭhapetvâ avasesâ sâsavâ kusalâkusalâvyâkatâ dhammâ kâmâvacarâ rûpâvacarâ arûpâvacarâ rûpakkhandho . . . pe . . . viññâṇakkhandho—ime dhammâ upâdâniyâ ceva no ca upâdânâ.

1225. Katame dhammâ upâdânâ ceva upâdânasampayuttâ ca?

Diṭṭhupâdânaṃ kâmupâdânena upâdânañ ceva upâdânasampayuttañ ca—kâmupâdânaṃ diṭṭhupâdânena upâdânañ ceva upâdânasampayuttañ ca—sîlabbatupâdânaṃ kâmupâdânena upâdânañ ceva upâdânasampayuttañ ca—kamupâdânaṃ sîlabbatupâdânena upâdânañ ceva upâdânasampayuttañ ca—attavâdupâdânaṃ kâmupâdânena upâdânañ ceva upâdânasampayuttañ ca kâmupâdânaṃ attavâdupâdânena upâdânañ ceva upâdânasampayuttañ ca—ime dhammâ upâdânâ ceva upâdânasampayuttâ ca.

1226. Katame dhammâ upâdânasampayuttâ ceva no ca upâdânâ?

Tehi dhammehi ye dhammâ sampayuttâ—te dhamme ṭhapetvâ vedanâkkhandho . . . pe . . . viññâṇakkhandho—ime dhammâ upâdânasampayuttâ ceva no ca upâdânâ.

1227. Katame dhammâ upâdânavippayuttâ upâdâniyâ ca?

Tehi dhammehi ye dhammâ vippayuttâ sâsavâ kusalâkusalâvyâkatâ dhammâ kâmâvacarâ rûpâvacarâ arûpâvacarâ—rûpakkhandho . . . pe . . . viññâṇakkhandho—ime dhammâ upâdânavippayuttâ upâdâniyâ ca.

1228. Katame dhammâ upâdânavippayuttâ anupâdâniyâ?

Apariyâpannâ maggâ ca maggaphalâni ca asaṅkhatâ ca dhâtu—ime dhammâ upâdânavippayuttâ anupâdâniyâ?

1229. Katame dhammâ kilesâ?

Dasa kilesavatthûni — Lobho doso moho mâno, diṭṭhi, vicikicchâ, thînaṃ, uddhaccaṃ, ahirikaṃ, anottappam.

1230. Tattha katamo lobho?

Yo râgo sârâgo anunayo anurodho nandî nandîrâgo cittassa sârâgo—icchâ mucchâ ajjhosânaṃ gedho paligedho saṅgo paṅko ejâ mâyâ janikâ sañjananî sibbinî jâlinî saritâ visattikâ suttaṃ visaṭâ âyûhanî dutiyâ paṇidhi bhavanetti vanaṃ vanatho santhavo sineho apekkhâ paṭibandhu âsâ âsiṃsanâ âsiṃsitattaṃ rûpâsâ saddâsâ gandhâsâ rasâsâ phoṭṭhabbâsâ lâbhâsâ dhanâsâ puttâsâ jîvitâsâ jappâ pajappâ abhijappâ jappanâ jappitattaṃ loluppaṃ loluppâyanâ loluppâyitattaṃ—puñcikatâ sâdukamyatâ adhammarâgo visamalobho nikantî nikâmanâ patthanâ pihanâ sampatthanâ kâmataṇhâ bhavataṇhâ vibhavataṇhâ rûpataṇhâ, arûpataṇhâ nirodhataṇhâ saddataṇhâ gandhataṇhâ rasataṇhâ phoṭṭhabbataṇhâ dhammataṇhâ ogho yogo gantho upâdânaṃ âvaraṇaṃ nîvaraṇaṃ chandanaṃ bandhanaṃ upakkileso anusayo pariyuṭṭhânaṃ latâ vevicchaṃ dukkhamûlaṃ dukkhanidânaṃ dukkhappabhavo mârapâso mârabaḷisaṃ mâravisayo taṇhâ nandîtaṇhâ jâlaṃtaṇhâ gaddulaṃtaṇhâ samuddo abhijjhâlobho akusalamûlaṃ—ayaṃ vuccati lobho.

1231. Tattha katamo doso?

Anatthaṃ me acarîti âghâto jâyati, anatthaṃ me caratîti âghâto jâyati, anatthaṃ me carissatîti âghâto jâyati, piyassa me manâpassa anatthaṃ acari . . . pe . . . anatthaṃ carati . . . pe . . . anatthaṃ carissatîti âghâto jâyati, appiyassa me amanâpassa atthaṃ acari . . . pe . . . atthaṃ carati . . . pe . . . atthaṃ carissatîti âghâto jâyati, aṭṭhâne vâ pana âghâto jâyati, yo evarûpo cittassa âghâto paṭighâto paṭighaṃ paṭivirodho kopo pakopo sampakopo doso padoso sampadoso cittassa vyâpatti manopadoso kodho kujjhanâ kujjhitattaṃ doso dussanâ dussitattaṃ vyâpatti vyâpajjanâ vyâpajjitattaṃ virodho paṭivirodho caṇḍikkaṃ asuropo anukkamanatâ cittassa—ayaṃ vuccati doso.

1232. Tattha katamo moho?

Dukkhe aññâṇaṃ . . . pe . . . pubbante aññâṇaṃ aparante aññâṇaṃ pubbantâparante aññâṇaṃ idappaccayatâ paṭiccasamuppannesu dhammesu aññâṇaṃ—yaṃ evarûpaṃ aññâṇaṃ adassanaṃ anabhisamayo ananubodho asambodho appaṭivedho asaṅgâhanâ apariyogâhanâ asamapekkhanâ apaccavekkhanâ apaccakkhakammaṃ dummejjhaṃ balyaṃ asampajaññaṃ moho pamoho sammoho avijjâ avijjogho avijjâyogo avijjânusayo avijjâpariyuṭṭhânaṃ avijjâlaṅgî moho akusalamûlaṃ—ayaṃ vuccati moho.

1233. Tattha katamo mâno?

Seyyo 'hamasmîti mâno, sadiso 'hamasmîti mâno, hîno 'hamasmîti mâno, yo evarûpo mâno maññanâ maññitattaṃ unnati unnamo dhajo sampaggâho ketukamyatâ cittassa—ayaṃ vuccati mâno.

1234. Tattha katamâ diṭṭhi?

Sassato loko ti vâ asassato loko ti vâ antavâ loko ti vâ anantavâ loko ti vâ taṃ jîvan taṃ sarîran ti vâ aññaṃ jîvaṃ aññaṃ sarîran ti vâ, hoti tathâgato paraṃ maraṇâ ti vâ na hoti tathâgato param maraṇâ ti vâ, hoti ca na ca hoti tathâgato param maraṇâ ti vâ, neva hoti na na hoti tathâgato param maraṇâ ti vâ, yâ evarûpâ diṭṭhi diṭṭhigataṃ diṭṭhigahaṇaṃ diṭṭhikantâro diṭṭhivisûkâyikaṃ diṭṭhivipphanditaṃ diṭṭhisaññojanaṃ gâho paṭiggâho abhiniveso parâmâso kummaggo micchâpatho micchattaṃ titthâyatanaṃ vipariyesagâho — ayaṃ vuccati diṭṭhi—sabbâ pi micchâdiṭṭhi diṭṭhi.

1235. Tattha katamâ vicikicchâ?

Satthari kaṅkhati vicikicchati, dhamme kaṅkhati vicikicchati, saṅghe kaṅkhati vicikicchati, sikkhâya kaṅkhati vicikicchati, pubbante kaṅkhati vicikicchati, aparante kaṅkhati vicikicchati, pubbantâparante kaṅkhati vicikicchati, idappaccayatâ paṭiccasamuppannesu dhammesu kaṅkhati vicikicchati, yâ evarûpâ kaṅkhâ kaṅkhâyanâ kaṅkhâyitattaṃ vimati vicikicchâ dveḷhakaṃ dvedhâpatho saṃsayo, anekaṃsagâho âsappanâ parisappanâ apariyogâhanâ thambhitattaṃ cittassa manovilekho—ayaṃ vuccati vicikicchâ.

1236. Tattha katamaṃ thînaṃ?

Yâ cittassa akalyatâ akammaññatâ olîyanâ sallîyanâ lînaṃ lîyanâ lîyitattaṃ thînaṃ thîyanâ thîyitattaṃ cittassa—idaṃ vuccati thînaṃ.

1237. Tattha katamaṃ uddhaccaṃ?

Yaṃ cittassa uddhaccaṃ vûpasamo cetaso vikkhepo bhantattaṃ cittassa—idaṃ vuccati uddhaccaṃ.

1238. Tattha katamaṃ ahirikaṃ?

Yaṃ na hiriyati hiriyitabbena—na hiriyati pâpakânaṃ akusalânaṃ dhammânaṃ samâpattiyâ—idaṃ vuccati ahirikaṃ.

1239. Tattha katamaṃ anottappaṃ?

Yaṃ na ottappati ottappitabbena—na ottappati pâpakânaṃ akusalânaṃ dhammânaṃ samâpattiyâ—idaṃ vuccati anottappaṃ.

Ime dhammâ kilesâ.

1240. Katame dhammâ no kilesâ?

Te dhamme ṭhapetvâ avasesâ kusalâkusalâvyâkatâ dhammâ kâmâvacarâ rûpâvacarâ arûpâvacarâ apariyâpannâ—vedanâkkhandho . . . pe . . . viññâṇakkhandho—sabbañ ca rûpaṃ asaṅkhatâ ca dhâtu—ime dhammâ no kilesâ.

1241. Katame dhammâ saṅkilesikâ?

Sâsavâ kusalâkusalâvyâkatâ dhammâ kâmâvacarâ rûpâvacarâ arûpâvacarâ apariyâpannâ, rûpakkhandho . . . pe . . . viññâṇakkhandho—ime dhammâ saṅkilesikâ.

1242. Katame dhammâ asaṅkilesikâ?

Apariyâpannâ maggâ ca maggaphalâni ca—asaṅkhatâ ca dhâtu—ime dhammâ asaṅkilesikâ.

1243. Katame dhammâ saṅkiliṭṭhâ?

Tîṇi akusalamûlâni, lobho doso moho, tadekaṭṭhâ ca kilesâ taṃ sampayutto vedanâkkhandho . . . pe . . . viññâṇakkhandho taṃ samuṭṭhânaṃ kâyakammaṃ vacîkammaṃ manokammaṃ—ime dhammâ saṅkiliṭṭhâ.

1244. Katame dhammâ kilesasampayuttâ?

Tehi dhammehi ye dhammâ sampayuttâ vedanâkkhandho . . . pe . . . viññâṇakkhandho—ime dhammâ kilesasampayuttâ.

1245. Katame dhammâ kilesavippayuttâ?

Tehi dhammehi ye dhammâ vippayuttâ, vedanâkkhandho . . . pe . . . viññâṇakkhandho, sabbañ ca rûpaṃ asaṅkhatâ ca dhâtu—ime dhammâ kilesavippayuttâ.

1246. Katame dhammâ kilesâ ceva saṅkilesikâ ca?

Teva kilesâ kilesâ ceva saṅkilesikâ ca.

1247. Katame dhammâ saṅkilesikâ ceva no ca kilesâ?

Tehi dhammehi ye dhammâ saṅkilesikâ, te dhamme ṭhapetvâ avasesâ sâsavâ kusalâkusalâvyâkatâ dhammâ kâmâvacarâ rûpâvacarâ arûpâvacarâ, rûpakkhandho . . . pe . . . viññâṇakkhandho—ime dhammâ saṅkilesikâ ceva no ca kilesâ.

1248. Katame dhammâ kilesâ ceva saṅkiliṭṭhâ ca?

Teva kilesâ kilesâ ceva saṅkiliṭṭhâ ca.

1249. Katame dhammâ saṅkiliṭṭhâ ceva no ca kilesâ?

Tehi dhammehi ye dhammâ saṅkiliṭṭhâ te dhamme ṭhapetvâ vedanâkkhandho . . . pe . . . viññâṇakkhandho—ime dhammâ saṅkiliṭṭhâ ceva no ca kilesâ.

1250. Katame dhammâ kilesâ ceva kilesasampayuttâ ca?

Lobho mohena kileso ceva kilesasampayutto ca, moho

lobhena kileso ceva kilesasampayutto ca, doso mohena kileso ceva kilesasampayutto ca, moho dosena kileso ceva kilesasampayutto ca, mâno mohena kileso ceva kilesasampayutto ca, moho mânena kileso ceva kilesasampayutto ca, diṭṭhi mohena kileso ceva kilesasampayuttâ ca, moho diṭṭhiyâ kileso ceva kilesasampayutto ca, vicikicchâ mohena kileso ceva kilesasampayuttâ ca, moho vicikicchâya kileso ceva kilesasampayutto ca, thînaṃ mohena kileso ceva kilesesampayuttañ ca, moho thînena kileso ceva kilesasampayutto ca, uddhaccaṃ mohena kileso ceva kilesasampayuttañ ca. Moho uddhaccena kileso ceva kilesasampayutto ca, ahirikaṃ mohena kileso ceva kilesasampayutto ca, moho ahirikena kileso ceva kilesasampayutto ca, anottappaṃ mohena kileso ceva kilesasampayuttañ ca, moho anottappena kileso ceva kilesasampayutto ca.

Lobho uddhaccena kileso ceva kilesasampayutto ca, uddhaccaṃ lobhena kileso ceva kilesasampayuttañ ca, doso uddhaccena kileso ceva kilesasampayutto ca, uddhaccaṃ dosena kileso ceva kilesasampayuttañ ca, moho uddhaccena kileso ceva kilesasampayutto ca, uddhaccaṃ mohena kileso ceva kilesasampayuttañ ca, mâno uddhaccena kileso ceva kilesasampayutto ca, uddhaccaṃ mânena kileso ceva kilesasampayuttañ ca, diṭṭhi uddhaccena kileso ceva kilesasampayuttâ ca, uddhaccaṃ diṭṭhiyâ kileso ceva kilesasampayuttañ ca, vicikicchâ uddhaccena kileso ceva kilesasampayuttâ ca, uddhaccaṃ vicikicchâya kileso ceva kilesasampayuttañ ca, thînaṃ uddhaccena kileso ceva kilesasampayuttañ ca, uddhaccaṃ thînena kileso ceva kilesasampayuttañ ca, ahirikaṃ uddhaccena kileso ceva kilesasampayuttañ ca, uddhaccaṃ ahirikena kileso ceva kilesasampayuttañ ca, anottappaṃ uddhaccena kileso ceva kilesasampayuttañ ca, uddhaccaṃ anottappena kileso ceva kilesasampayuttañ ca, lobho ahirikena kileso ceva kilesasampayutto ca.

Ahirikaṃ lobhena kileso ceva kilesasampayuttañ ca, doso ahirikena kileso ceva kilesasampayutto ca, ahirikaṃ dosena kileso ceva kilesasampayuttañ ca, moho ahirikena kileso ceva kilesasampayutto ca, ahirikaṃ mohena kileso ceva kilesasampayuttañ ca, mâno ahirikena kileso ceva kilesasampayutto ca, ahirikaṃ mânena kileso ceva kilesasampayuttañ ca, diṭṭhi ahirikena kileso ceva kilesasampayuttâ ca, ahirikaṃ diṭṭhiyâ kileso ceva kilesasampayuttañ ca, vicikicchâ ahirikena kileso ceva kilesasampayuttâ ca, ahirikaṃ vicikicchâya kileso ceva kilesasampayuttañ ca, thînaṃ ahirikena kileso ceva kilesasampayuttañ ca, ahirikaṃ thînena kileso ceva kilesasampayuttañ ca, uddhaccaṃ ahirikena kileso ceva kilesasampayuttañ ca, ahirikaṃ uddhaccena kileso ceva kilesasampayuttañ ca, anottappaṃ ahirikena kileso ceva kilesasampayuttañ ca, ahirikaṃ anottappena kileso ceva kilesasampayuttañ ca, lobho anottappena kileso ceva kilesasampayutto ca, anottappaṃ lobhena kileso ceva kilesasampayuttañ ca, doso anottappena kileso ceva kilesasampayutto ca, anottappaṃ dosena kileso ceva kilesasampayuttañ ca, moho anottappena kileso ceva kilesasampayutto ca, anottappaṃ mohena kileso ceva kilesasampayuttañ ca, mâno anottappena kileso ceva kilesasampayutto ca, anottappaṃ mânena kileso ceva kilesasampayuttañ ca, diṭṭhi anottappena kileso ceva kilesasampayuttâ ca, anottappaṃ diṭṭhiyâ kileso ceva kilesasampayuttañ ca, vicikicchâ anottappena kileso ceva kilesasampayuttâ ca, anottappaṃ vicikicchâya kileso ceva kilesasampayuttañ ca, thînaṃ anottappena kileso ceva kilesasampayuttañ ca, anottappaṃ thînena kileso ceva kilesasampayuttañ ca, uddhaccaṃ anottappena kileso ceva kilesasampayuttañ ca, anottappaṃ uddhaccena kileso ceva kilesasampayuttañ ca, ahirikaṃ anottappena kileso ceva kilesasampayuttañ ca, anottappaṃ ahirikena kileso ceva kilesasampayuttañ ca.

Ime dhammâ kilesâ ceva kilesasampayuttâ ca.

1251. Katame dhammâ kilesasampayuttâ ceva no ca kilesâ?

Tehi dhammehi ye dhammâ sampayuttâ—te dhamme ṭhapetvâ vedanâkkhandho . . . pe . . . viññâṇakkhandho—ime dhammâ kilesasampayuttâ ceva no ca kilesâ.

1252. Katame dhammâ kilesavippayuttâ saṅkilesikâ?

Tehi dhammehi vippayuttâ sâsavâ kusalâkusalâvyâkatâ dhammâ kâmâvacarâ rûpâvacarâ arûpâvacarâ rûpakkhandho

. . . pe . . . viññâṇakkhandho—ime dhammâ kilesavippayuttâ saṅkilesikâ.

1253. Katame dhammâ kilesavippayuttâ asaṅkilesikâ?

Apariyâpannâ maggâ ca maggaphalâni asaṅkhatâ ca dhâtu—ime dhammâ kilesavippayuttâ asaṅkilesikâ.

1254. Katame dhammâ dassanena pahâtabbâ?

Tîṇi saññojanâni—sakkâyadiṭṭhi vicikicchâ sîlabbataparâmâso.

1255. Tattha katamâ sakkâyadiṭṭhi?

Idha assutavâ puthujjano ariyânaṃ adassâvî ariyadhammassa akovido ariyadhamme avinîto sappurisânaṃ adassâvî sappurisadhammassa akovido sappurisadhamme avinîto rûpaṃ attato samanupassati, rûpavantaṃ vâ attânaṃ, attani vâ rûpaṃ rûpasmiṃ vâ attânaṃ, vedanaṃ . . . pe . . . saññaṃ . . . pe . . . saṅkhâre . . . pe . . . viññâṇaṃ attato samanupassati viññâṇavantaṃ vâ attânaṃ attani vâ viññâṇaṃ, viññâṇasmiṃ vâ attânaṃ, yâ evarûpâ diṭṭhi diṭṭhigataṃ . . . pe . . . vipariyesagâho—ayaṃ vuccati sakkâyadiṭṭhi.

1256. Tattha katamâ vicikicchâ?

Satthari kaṅkhati vicikicchati . . . pe . . . thambhitattaṃ cittassa manovilekho—ayaṃ vuccati vicikicchâ.

1257. Tattha katamo sîlabbataparâmâso?

Ito bahiddhâ samaṇabrahmaṇânaṃ sîlena suddhivatena suddhisîlabbatena suddhîtiyâ evarûpâ diṭṭhi diṭṭhigataṃ . . . pe . . . vipariyesagâho—ayaṃ vuccati sîlabbataparâmâso.

Imâni tîṇi saññojanâni tad ekaṭṭhâ ca kilesâ—taṃ sampayutto vedanâkkhandho . . . pe . . . viññâṇakkhandho—taṃ samuṭṭhânaṃ kâyakammaṃ vacîkammaṃ manokammaṃ—ime dhammâ dassanena pahâtabbâ.

1258. Katame dhammâ na dassanena pahâtabbâ?

Te dhamme ṭhapetvâ avasesâ kusalâkusalâvyâkatâ dhammâ kâmâvacarâ rûpâvacarâ arûpâvacarâ apariyâpannâ—vedanâkkhandho . . . pe . . . viññâṇakkhandho—sabbañ ca rûpaṃ asaṅkhatâ ca dhâtu—ime dhammâ na dassanena pahâtabbâ.

1259. Katame dhammâ bhâvanâya pahâtabbâ?

Avaseso lobho doso moho, tad ekaṭṭhâ ca kilesâ, taṃ sampayutto vedanâkkhandho . . . pe . . . viññâṇakkhandho, taṃ samuṭṭhânaṃ kâyakammaṃ vacîkammaṃ manokammaṃ—ime dhammâ bhâvanâya pahâtabbâ.

1260. Katame dhammâ na bhâvanâya pahâtabbâ?

Te dhamme ṭhapetvâ avasesâ kusalâkusalâvyâkatâ dhammâ, kâmâvacarâ rûpâvacarâ arûpâvacarâ apariyâpannâ, vedanâkkhandho . . . pe . . . viññâṇakkhandho, sabbañ ca rûpaṃ asaṅkhatâ ca dhâtu—ime dhammâ na bhâvanâya pahâtabbâ.

1261. Katame dhammâ dassanena pahâtabbahetukâ?

Tîni saññojanâni—sakkâyadiṭṭhi vicikicchâ sîlabbataparâmâso.

1262. Tattha katamâ sakkâyadiṭṭhi?

Idha assutavâ puthujjano ariyânaṃ adassâvî ariyadhammassa akovido ariyadhamme avinîto sappurisânaṃ adassâvî sappurisadhammassa akovido sappurisadhamme avinîto rûpaṃ attato samanupassati rûpavantaṃ vâ attânaṃ attani vâ rûpaṃ rûpasmiṃ vâ attânaṃ, vedanaṃ . . . pe . . . saññaṃ . . . pe . . . saṅkhâre . . . pe . . . viññâṇaṃ attato samanupassati, viññâṇavantaṃ vâ attânaṃ, attani vâ viññâṇaṃ viññâṇasmiṃ vâ attânaṃ, yâ evarûpâ diṭṭhi diṭṭhigataṃ . . . pe . . . vipariyesagâho—ayaṃ vuccati sakkâyadiṭṭhi.

1263. Tattha katamâ vicikicchâ?

Satthari kaṅkhati vicikicchati . . . pe . . . thambhittaṃ cittassa manovilekho—ayaṃ vuccati vicikicchâ.

1264. Tattha katamo sîlabbataparâmâso?

Ito bahiddhâ samaṇabrahmaṇânaṃ sîlena suddhivatena suddhisîlabbatena suddhîtiyâ evarûpâ diṭṭhi diṭṭhigataṃ . . . pe . . . vipariyesagâho, ayaṃ vuccati sîlabbataparâmâso, imâni tîṇi saṃyojanâni, tad ekaṭṭhâ ca kilesâ, taṃ sampayutto vedanâkkhandho . . . pe . . . viññâṇakkhandho, taṃ samuṭṭhânaṃ kâyakammaṃ vacîkammaṃ manokammaṃ, ime dhammâ dassanena pahâtabbahetukâ, tîni saññojanâni sakkâyadiṭṭhi vicikicchâ sîlabbataparâmâso, ime dhammâ dassanena pahâtabbahetukâ, tad ekaṭṭho ca lobho doso moho, ime dhammâ dassanena pahâtabbahetukâ, tad ekaṭṭhâ ca kilesâ, taṃ sampayutto vedanâkkhandho . . . pe . . . viññâṇakkhando, taṃ samuṭṭhânaṃ kâyakammaṃ vacikammaṃ manokammaṃ—ime dhammâ dassanena pahâtabbahetukâ.

1265. Katame dhammâ na dassanena pahâtabbahetukâ?

Te dhamme ṭhapetvâ avasesâ kusalâkusalâvyâkatâ dhammâ

kâmâvacarâ rûpâvacarâ arûpâvacarâ apariyâpannâ—vedanâkkhandho . . . pe . . . viññâṇakkhandho—sabbañ ca rûpaṃ asaṅkhatâ ca dhâtu—ime dhammâ na dassanena pahâtabbahetukâ.

1266. Katame dhammâ bhâvanâya pahâtabbahetukâ?

Avaseso lobho doso moho—ime dhammâ bhâvanâya pahâtabbahetukâ—tad ekaṭṭhâ ca kilesâ—taṃ sampayutto vedanâkkhandho . . . pe . . . viññâṇakkhandho — taṃ samuṭṭhânaṃ kâyakammaṃ vacîkammaṃ manokammaṃ—ime dhammâ bhâvanâya pahâtabbahetukâ.

1267. Katame dhammâ na bhâvanâya pahâtabbahetukâ?

Te dhamme ṭhapetvâ avasesâ kusalâkusalâvyâkatâ dhammâ kâmâvacarâ rûpâvacarâ arûpâvacarâ apariyâpannâ—vedanâkkhandho . . . pe . . . viññâṇakkhandho—sabbañ ca rûpaṃ asaṅkhatâ ca dhâtu—ime dhammâ na bhâvanâya pahâtabbahetukâ.

1268. Katame dhammâ savitakkâ?

Savitakkabhummiyaṃ kâmâvacare rûpâvacare arûpâvacare pariyâpanne vitakkaṃ ṭhapetvâ taṃ sampayutto vedanâkkhandho . . . pe . . . viññâṇakkhandho — ime dhammâ savitakkâ.

1269. Katame dhammâ avitakkâ?

Avitakkabhummiyaṃ kâmâvacare rûpâvacare arûpâvacare apariyâpanne vedanâkkhandho . . . pe . . . viññâṇakkhandho —vitakko ca sabbañ ca rûpaṃ asaṅkhatâ ca dhâtu—ime dhammâ avitakkâ.

1270. Katame dhammâ savicârâ?

Savicârabhummiyaṃ—kâmâvacare rûpâvacare arûpâvacare apariyâpanne vicâraṃ ṭhapetvâ taṃ sampayutto vedanâkkhandho saññâkkhandho, saṅkhârakkhandho, viññâṇakkhandho—ime dhammâ savicârâ.

1271. Katame dhammâ avicârâ?

Avicârabhummiyaṃ kâmâvacare rûpâvacare arûpâvacare apariyâpanne vedanâkkhandho . . . pe . . . viññâṇakkhandho —vicâro sabbañ ca rûpaṃ asaṅkhatâ ca dhâtu—ime dhammâ avicârâ.

1272. Katame dhammâ sappîtikâ?

Sappîtikabhummiyaṃ kâmâvacare rûpâvacare arûpâvacare

apariyâpanne pîtiṃ ṭhapetvâ taṃ sampayutto vedanâkkhandho . . . pe . . . viññâṇakkhandho—ime dhammâ sappîtikâ.

1273. Katame dhammâ appîtikâ?

Appîtikabhummiyaṃ kâmâvacare rûpâvacare arûpâvacare apariyâpanne vedanâkkhandho . . . pe . . . viññâṇakkhandho —pîti ca sabbañ ca rûpaṃ asaṅkhatâ ca dhâtu—ime dhammâ appîtikâ.

1274. Katame dhammâ pîtisahagatâ?

Pîtibhummiyaṃ kâmâvacare rûpâvacare arûpâvacare apariyâpanne pîtiṃ ṭhapetvâ taṃ sampayutto vedanâkkhandho . . . pe . . . viññâṇakkhandho—ime dhammâ pîtisahagatâ.

1275. Katame dhammâ na pîtisahagatâ?

Na pîtibhummiyaṃ kâmâvacare rûpâvacare arûpâvacare apariyâpanne vedanâkkhandho . . . pe . . . viññâṇakkhandho pîti ca sabbañ ca rûpaṃ asaṅkhatâ ca dhâtu—ime dhammâ na pîtisahagatâ.

1276. Katame dhammâ sukhasahagatâ?

Sukhabhummiyaṃ kâmâvacare rûpâvacare arûpâvacare apariyâpanne sukhaṃ ṭhapetvâ taṃ sampayutto saññâkkhandho saṅkhârakkhandho viññâṇakkhandho — ime dhammâ sukhasahagatâ.

1277. Katame dhammâ na sukhasahagatâ?

Na sukhabhummiyaṃ kâmâvacare rûpâvacare arûpâvacare apariyâpanne vedanâkkhandho . . . pe . . . viññâṇakkhandho —sukhañ ca sabbañ ca rûpaṃ asaṅkhatâ ca dhâtu—ime dhammâ na sukhasahagatâ.

1278. Katame dhammâ upekkhâsahagatâ?

Upekkhâbhummiyaṃ kâmâvacare rûpâvacare arûpâvacare apariyâpanne upekkhaṃ ṭhapetvâ taṃ sampayutto saññâkkhandho saṅkhârakkhandho viññâṇakkhandho — ime dhammâ upekkhâsahagatâ.

1279. Katame dhammâ na upekkhâsahagatâ?

Na upekkhâbhummiyaṃ kâmâvacare rûpâvacare arûpâvacare apariyâpanne vedanâkkhandho . . . pe . . . viññâṇakkhandho—upekkhâ sabbañ ca rûpaṃ asaṅkhatâ ca dhâtu—ime dhammâ na upekkhâsahagatâ.

1280. Katame dhammâ kâmâvacarâ?

Heṭṭhato avîcinirayaṃ pariyantaṃ karitvâ uparito parinimmitavasavattideve anto karitvâ yaṃ etasmiṃ antare etthâvacarâ etthapariyâpannâ khandhadhâtu âyatanâ rûpâ vedanâ saññâ saṅkhârâ viññâṇaṃ—ime dhammâ kâmâvacarâ.

1281. Katame dhammâ na kâmâvacarâ?

Rûpâvacarâ arûpâvacarâ apariyâpannâ—ime dhammâ na kâmâvacarâ.

1282. Katame dhammâ rûpâvacarâ?

Heṭṭhato brahmalokaṃ pariyantaṃ karitvâ uparito akaniṭṭhadeve anto karitvâ yaṃ etasmiṃ antare etthâvacarâ etthapariyâpannâ samâpannassa vâ uppannassa vâ diṭṭhadhammasukhavihârissa vâ cittacetasikâ dhammâ — ime dhammâ rûpâvacarâ.

1283. Katame dhammâ na rûpâvacarâ?

Kâmâvacarâ arûpâvacarâ apariyâpannâ—ime dhammâ na rûpâvacarâ.

1284. Katame dhammâ arûpâvacarâ?

Heṭṭhato âkâsânañcâyatanupage deve pariyantaṃ karitvâ uparito nevasaññânâsaññâyatanupage deve anto karitvâ yaṃ etasmiṃ antare etthâvacarâ etthapariyâpannâ samâpannassa vâ uppannassa vâ diṭṭhadhammasukhavihârissa vâ cittacetasikâ dhammâ—ime dhammâ arûpâvacarâ.

1285. Katame dhammâ na arûpâvacarâ?

Rûpâvacarâ apariyâpannâ—ime dhammâ na arûpâvacarâ.

1286. Katame dhammâ pariyâpannâ?

Sâsavâ kusalâkusalâvyâkatâ dhammâ kâmâvacarâ rûpâvacarâ arûpâvacarâ rûpakkhandho . . . pe . . . viññâṇakkhandho—ime dhammâ pariyâpannâ.

1287. Katame dhammâ apariyâpannâ?

Maggâ ca maggaphalâni ca asaṅkhatâ ca dhâtu—ime dhammâ apariyâpannâ.

1288. Katame dhammâ niyyânikâ?

Cattâro maggâ apariyâpannâ—ime dhammâ niyyânikâ.

1289. Katame dhammâ aniyyânikâ?

Te dhamme ṭhapetvâ avasesâ kusalâkusalâvyâkatâ dhammâ kâmâvacarâ rûpâvacarâ arûpâvacarâ apariyâpannâ—vedanâkkhandho . . . pe . . . viññâṇakkhandho—sabbañ ca rûpaṃ asaṅkhatâ ca dhâtu—ime dhammâ aniyyânikâ.

1290. Katame dhammâ niyatâ?

Pañca kammâni ânantarikâni yâ ca micchâdiṭṭhi niyatâ cattâro maggâ apariyâpannâ—ime dhammâ niyatâ.

1291. Katame dhammâ aniyatâ?

Te dhamme ṭhapetvâ avasesâ kusalâkusalâvyâkatâ dhammâ kâmâvacarâ rûpâvacarâ arûpâvacarâ apariyâpannâ—vedanâkhandho . . . pe . . . viññâṇakkhandho—sabbañ ca rûpaṃ asaṅkhatâ ca dhâtu—ime dhammâ aniyatâ.

1292. Katame dhammâ sauttarâ?

Sâsavâ kusalâkusalâvyâkatâ dhammâ kâmâvacarâ rûpâvacarâ arûpâvacarâ rûpakkhandho . . . pe . . . viññâṇakkhandho—ime dhammâ sauttarâ.

1293. Katame dhammâ anuttarâ?

Apariyâpannâ maggâ ca maggaphalâni ca asaṅkhatâ ca dhâtu—ime dhammâ anuttarâ.

1294. Katame dhammâ saraṇâ?

Tîṇi akusalamûlâni lobho doso moho—tad ekaṭṭhâ ca kilesâ —taṃ sampayutto vedanâkkhandho . . . pe . . . viññâṇakkhandho taṃ samuṭṭhânaṃ kâyakammaṃ vacîkammaṃ manokammaṃ—ime dhammâ saraṇâ.

1295. Katame dhammâ asaraṇâ?

Kusalâkusalâvyâkatâ dhammâ kâmâvacarâ rûpâvacarâ arûpâvacarâ apariyâpannâ—vedanâkkhandho . . . pe . . . viññâṇakkhandho sabbañ ca rûpaṃ asaṅkhatâ ca dhâtu—ime dhammâ asaraṇâ.

1296. Katame dhammâ vijjâbhâgino?

Vijjâya sampayuttakâ dhammâ—ime dhammâ vijjâbhâgino.

1297. Katame dhammâ avijjâbhâgino?

Avijjâya sampayuttakâ dhammâ—ime dhammâ avijjâbhâgino.

1298. Katame dhammâ vijjûpamâ?

Heṭṭhimesu tîsu ariyamaggesu paññâ—ime dhammâ vijjûpamâ.

1299. Katame dhammâ vajirûpamâ?

Uparitthime arahattamagge paññâ—ime dhammâ vajirûpamâ.

1300. Katame dhammâ bâlâ?

Ahirikañ ca anottappañ ca—ime dhammâ bâlâ—sabbe pi akusalâ bâlâ.

1301. Katame dhammâ paṇḍitâ?

Hiri ca ottappañ ca—ime dhammâ paṇḍitâ—sabbe pi kusalâ dhammâ paṇḍitâ.

1302. Katame dhammâ kaṇhâ?

Ahirikañ ca anottappañ ca—ime dhammâ kaṇhâ—sabbe pi akusalâ dhammâ kaṇhâ.

1303. Katame dhammâ sukkâ?

Hiri ca ottappañ ca—ime dhammâ sukkâ—sabbe pi kusalâ dhammâ sukkâ.

1304. Katame dhammâ tapaniyâ?

Kâyaduccaritaṃ vacîduccaritaṃ manoduccaritaṃ—ime dhammâ tapaniyâ—sabbe pi akusalâ dhammâ tapaniyâ.

1305. Katame dhammâ atapaniyâ?

Kâyasucaritaṃ vacîsucaritaṃ manosucaritaṃ—ime dhammâ atapaniyâ—sabbe pi kusalâ dhammâ atapaniyâ.

1306. Katame dhammâ adhivacanâ?

Yâ tesaṃ tesaṃ dhammânaṃ saṅkhâ samaññâ paññatti vohâro nâmaṃ nâmakammaṃ nâmadheyyaṃ nirutti vyañjanaṃ abhilâpo—ime dhammâ adhivacanâ.

Sabbeva dhammâ adhivacanapathâ.

1307. Katame dhammâ nirutti?

Yâ tesaṃ tesaṃ dhammânaṃ saṅkhâ samaññâ paññatti vohâro nâmaṃ nâmakammaṃ nâmadheyyaṃ nirutti vyañjanaṃ abhilâpo—ime dhammâ nirutti.

Sabbeva dhammâ niruttipathâ.

1308. Katame dhammâ paññatti?

Yâ tesaṃ tesaṃ dhammânaṃ saṅkhâ samaññâ paññatti vohâro nâmaṃ nâmakammaṃ nâmadheyyaṃ nirutti vyañjanaṃ abhilâpo—ime dhammâ paññatti.

Sabbeva dhammâ paññattipathâ.

1309. Tattha katamaṃ nâmaṃ?

Vedanâkkhandho saññâkkhandho saṅkhârakkhandho viññâṇakkhandho—asaṅkhatâ ca dhâtu—idaṃ vuccati nâmaṃ.

✓ 1310. Tattha katamaṃ rûpaṃ?
Cattâro mahâbhûtâ catunnañ ca mahâbhûtânaṃ upâdâya rûpaṃ—idaṃ vuccati rûpaṃ.
1311. Tattha katamâ avijjâ?
Yaṃ aññâṇaṃ adassanaṃ . . . pe . . . avijjâlaṅgî moho akusalamûlaṃ—ayaṃ vuccati avijjâ.
1312. Tattha katamâ bhavataṇhâ?
Yo bhavesu bhavacchando . . . pe . . . bhavajjhosânaṃ—ayaṃ vuccati bhavataṇhâ.
1313. Tattha katamâ bhavadiṭṭhi?
Bhavissati attâ ca loko câti yâ evarûpâ diṭṭhi diṭṭhigataṃ . . . pe . . . vipariyesagâho—ayaṃ vuccati bhavadiṭṭhi?
1314. Tattha katamâ vibhavadiṭṭhi?
Na bhavissati attâ ca loko câti yâ evarûpâ diṭṭhi diṭṭhigataṃ —vipariyesagâho—ayaṃ vuccati vibhavadiṭṭhi.
1315. Tattha katamâ sassatadiṭṭhi?
Sassato attâ ca loko câti yâ evarûpâ diṭṭhi diṭṭhigataṃ . . . pe . . . vipariyesagâho—ayaṃ vuccati sassatadiṭṭhi.
1316. Tattha katamâ ucchedadiṭṭhi?
Ucchijjissati attâ ca loko câti yâ evarûpâ diṭṭhi diṭṭhigataṃ . . . pe . . . vipariyesagâho—ayaṃ vuccati ucchedadiṭṭhi.
1317. Tattha katamâ antavâ diṭṭhi?
Antavâ attâ ca loko câti yâ evarûpâ diṭṭhi diṭṭhigataṃ . . . pe . . . vipariyesagâho—ayaṃ vuccati antavâ diṭṭhi.
1318. Tattha katamâ anantavâ diṭṭhi?
Anantavâ attâ ca loko câti yâ evarûpâ diṭṭhi diṭṭhigataṃ . . . pe . . . vipariyesagâho—ayaṃ vuccati anantavâ diṭṭhi.
1319. Tattha katamâ pubbantânudiṭṭhi?
Pubbantaṃ ârabbha yâ uppajjati diṭṭhi diṭṭhigataṃ . . . pe . . . vipariyesagâho—ayaṃ vuccati pubbantânudiṭṭhi.
1320. Tattha katamâ aparantânudiṭṭhi?
Aparantaṃ ârabbha yâ uppajjati diṭṭhi diṭṭhigataṃ . . . pe . . . vipariyesagâho—ayaṃ vuccati aparantânudiṭṭhi.
1321. Tattha katamaṃ ahirikaṃ?
Yaṃ na hiriyati hiriyitabbena—na hiriyati pâpakânaṃ akusalânaṃ dhammânaṃ samâpattiyâ — idaṃ vuccati ahirikaṃ.
1322. Tattha katamaṃ anottappaṃ?

Yaṃ na ottappati ottappitabbena—na ottappati pâpakânaṃ akusalânaṃ dhammânaṃ samâpattiyâ—idam vuccati anottappaṃ.

1323. Tattha katamâ hiri?

Yaṃ hiriyati hiriyitabbena—hiriyati pâpakânaṃ akusalânaṃ dhammânaṃ samâpattiyâ—ayaṃ vuccati hiri.

1324. Tattha katamaṃ ottappaṃ?

Yaṃ ottappati ottappitabbena—ottappati pâpakânaṃ akusalânaṃ dhammânaṃ samâpattiyâ—idaṃ vuccati ottappaṃ.

1325. Tattha katamâ dovacassatâ?

Sahadhammike vuccamâne dovacassatâyaṃ dovacassiyaṃ dovacassatâ vippaṭikûlagâhitâ vipaccanîkasâtatâ anâdariyaṃ anâdaratâ agâravatâ appaṭissavatâ — ayaṃ vuccati dovacassatâ.

1326. Tattha katamâ pâpamittatâ?

Ye te puggalâ assaddhâ dussîlâ appassutâ macchârino duppaññâ—yâ tesaṃ sevanâ nisevanâ saṃsevanâ bhajanâ sambhajanâ bhatti sambhatti sampavaṅkatâ—ayaṃ vuccati pâpamittatâ.

1327. Tattha katamâ sovacassatâ?

Sahadhammike vuccamâne sovacassatâyaṃ sovacassiyaṃ sovacassatâ appaṭikûlagâhitâ avipaccanîkasâtatâ sagâravatâ sappaṭissavatâ—ayaṃ vuccati sovacassatâ.

1328. Tattha katamâ kalyâṇamittatâ?

Ye te puggalâ saddhâ sîlavanto bahussutâ câgavanto paññâvanto—yâ tesaṃ sevanâ nisevanâ saṃsevanâ bhajanâ sambhajanâ bhatti sambhatti sampavaṅkatâ—ayaṃ vuccati kalyâṇamittatâ.

1329. Tattha katamâ âpattikusalatâ?

Pañca pi âpattikkhandhâ âpattiyo, satta pi âpattikkhandhâ âpattiyo, yâ tâsaṃ âpattînaṃ âpattikusalatâ paññâ pajânanâ . . . pe . . . amoho dhammavicayo sammâdiṭṭhi — ayaṃ vuccati âpattikusalatâ.

1330. Tattha katamâ âpattivuṭṭhânakusalatâ?

Yâ tâhi âpattîhi vuṭṭhânakusalatâ, paññâ pajânanâ, . . . pe . . . amoho dhammavicayo sammâdiṭṭhi—ayaṃ vuccati âpattivuṭṭhânakusalatâ.

1331. Tattha katamâ samâpattikusalatâ?

Atthi savitakkasavicârâ samâpatti, atthi avitakkavicâramattâ samâpatti, atthi avitakka-avicârâ samâpatti, yâ tâsam samâpattînaṃ samâpattikusalatâ paññâ pajânanâ . . . pe . . . amoho dhammavicayo sammâdiṭṭhi—ayaṃ vuccati samâpattikusalatâ.

1332. Tattha katamâ samâpattivuṭṭhânakusalatâ?

Yâ tâhi samâpattîhi vuṭṭhânakusalatâ paññâ pajânanâ . . . pe . . . amoho dhammavicayo sammâdiṭṭhi—ayaṃ vuccati samâpattivuṭṭhânakusalatâ.

1333. Tattha katamâ dhâtukusalatâ?

Aṭṭhârasa dhâtuyo—cakkhudhâtu rûpadhâtu cakkhuviññâṇadhâtu sotadhâtu saddadhâtu sotaviññâṇadhâtu ghânadhâtu gandhadhâtu ghânaviññâṇadhâtu jivhâdhâtu rasadhâtu jivhâviññâṇadhâtu kâyadhâtu phoṭṭhabbadhâtu kâyaviññâṇadhâtu manodhâtu dhammadhâtu manoviññâṇadhâtu yâ tâsaṃ dhâtûnaṃ dhâtukusalatâ paññâ pajânanâ . . . pe . . . amoho dhammavicayo sammâdiṭṭhi—ayaṃ vuccati dhâtukusalatâ.

1334. Tattha katamâ manasikârakusalatâ?

Yâ tâsaṃ dhâtûnaṃ manasikârakusalatâ paññâ pajânanâ . . . pe . . . amoho dhammavicayo sammâdiṭṭhi—ayaṃ vuccati manasikârakusalatâ.

1335. Tattha katamâ âyatanakusalatâ?

Dvâdasâyatanâni — cakkhâyatanaṃ, rûpâyatanaṃ, sotâyatanaṃ, saddâyatanaṃ, ghânâyatanaṃ, gandhâyatanaṃ, jivhâyatanaṃ, rasâyatanaṃ, kâyâyatanaṃ, phoṭṭhabbâyatanaṃ, manâyatanaṃ, dhammâyatanaṃ,—yâ tesaṃ âyatanânaṃ âyatanakusalatâ paññâ pajânanâ. . . pe . . . amoho dhammavicayo sammâdiṭṭhi—ayaṃ vuccati âyatanakusalatâ.

1336. Tattha katamâ paṭiccasamuppâdakusalatâ?

Avijjâpaccayâ saṅkhârâ, saṅkhârapaccayâ viññâṇaṃ, viññâṇapaccayâ nâmarûpaṃ, nâmarûpapaccayâ saḷâyatanaṃ, saḷâyatanapaccayâ phasso, phassapaccayâ vedanâ, vedanâpaccayâ taṇhâ, taṇhâpaccayâ upâdânaṃ, upâdânapaccayâ bhavo, bhavapaccayâ jâti jâtipaccayâ jarâmaraṇaṃ sokaparidevadukkhadomanassupâyâsâ sambhavanti, evam etassa kevalassa dukkhakkhandhassa samudayo hotîti, yâ tattha paññâ pajânanâ . . . pe . . . amoho dhammavicayo sammâdiṭṭhi—ayaṃ vuccati paṭiccasamuppâdakusalatâ.

1337. Tattha katamâ ṭhânakusalatâ?

Ye ye dhammâ yesaṃ yesaṃ dhammânaṃ hetu paccayâ uppâdâya taṃ taṃ ṭhânan ti yâ tattha paññâ pajânanâ . . . pe . . . amoho dhammavicayo sammâdiṭṭhi—ayaṃ vuccati ṭhânakusalatâ.

1338. Tattha katamâ aṭṭhânakusalatâ?

Ye ye dhammâ yesaṃ yesaṃ dhammânaṃ na hetu appaccayâ uppâdâya taṃ taṃ aṭṭhânan ti yâ tattha paññâ pajânanâ . . . pe . . . amoho dhammavicayo sammâdiṭṭhi—ayaṃ vuccati aṭṭhânakusalatâ.

1339. Tattha katamo ajjavo?

Ajjavatâ ajimhatâ avaṅkatâ akuṭilatâ—ayaṃ vuccati ajjavo.

1340. Tattha katamo maddavo?

Yâ mudutâ maddavatâ akakkhaḷatâ—akaṭhinatâ nîcacittatâ—ayaṃ vuccati maddavo.

1341. Tattha katamâ khantî?

Yâ khantî khamanatâ adhivâsanatâ acaṇḍikkaṃ anasuropo attamanatâ cittassa—ayaṃ vuccati khantî.

1342. Tattha katamaṃ soraccaṃ?

Yo kâyiko avîtikkamo vâcasiko avîtikkamo kâyikavâcasiko avîtikkamo—idaṃ vuccati soraccaṃ.

Sabbo pi sîlasaṃvaro soraccaṃ.

1343. Tattha katamaṃ sâkhalyaṃ?

Yâ sâ vâcâ aṇḍakâ asâtâ kakkasâ parakaṭukâ parâbhisajjanikodhasâmantâ asamâdhisaṃvattanikâ — tathârûpiṃ vâcaṃ pahâya yâ sâ vâcâ neḷâ kaṇṇasukhâ pemaniyâ hadayaṃgamâ porî bahujanakantâ bahujanamanâpâ—tathârûpiṃ vâcaṃ bhâsitâ hoti—yâ tattha saṇhavâcatâ sakhilavâcatâ apharusavâcatâ—idaṃ vuccati sâkhalyaṃ.

1344. Tattha katamo paṭisanthâro?

Dve paṭisanthârâ—âmisapaṭisanthâro ca dhammapaṭisanthâro ca—idhekacco paṭisanthârako hoti—âmisapaṭisanthâreṇa vâ dhammapaṭisanthârena vâ—ayaṃ vuccati paṭisanthâro.

1345. Tattha katamâ indriyesu aguttadvâratâ?

Idhekacco puggalo cakkhunâ rûpaṃ disvâ nimittaggâhî hoti anuvyañjanaggâhî, yatvâdhikaraṇam enaṃ cakkhundriyaṃ asaṃvutaṃ viharantaṃ abhijjhâdomanassâ pâpakâ akusalâ dhammâ anvâssaveyyuṃ, tassa saṃvarâya na paṭipajjati na rakkhati cakkhundriyaṃ, cakkhundriye na saṃvaraṃ âpajjati, sotena saddaṃ sutvâ . . . pe . . . ghânena gandhaṃ ghâyitvâ . . . pe . . . jivhâya rasaṃ sâyitvâ . . . pe . . . kâyena phoṭṭhabbaṃ phusitvâ . . . pe . . . manasâ dhammaṃ viññâya nimittaggâhî hoti anuvyañjanaggâhî, yatvâdhikaraṇam enaṃ manindriyaṃ asaṃvutaṃ viharantaṃ abhijjhâdomanassâ pâpakâ akusalâ dhammâ anvâssaveyyuṃ, tassa saṃvarâya na paṭipajjati, na rakkhati manindriyaṃ, manindriye na saṃvaraṃ âpajjati. Yâ imesaṃ channaṃ indriyânaṃ agutti agopanâ anârakkho asaṃvaro—ayaṃ vuccati indriyesu aguttadvâratâ.

1346. Tattha katamâ bhojane amattaññutâ?

Idhekacco appaṭisaṅkhâ ayoniso âhâraṃ âhâreti, davâya madâya maṇḍanâya vibhûsanâya, yâ tattha asantuṭṭhitâ amattaññutâ appaṭisaṅkhâ bhojane—ayaṃ vuccati bhojane amattaññutâ.

1347. Tattha katamâ indriyesu guttadvâratâ?

Idhekacco cakkhunâ rûpaṃ disvâ na nimittaggâhî hoti na anuvyañjanaggâhi, yatvâdhikaraṇam enaṃ cakkhundriyaṃ asaṃvutaṃ viharantaṃ abhijjhâdomanassâ pâpakâ akusalâ dhammâ anvâssaveyyuṃ, tassa saṃvarâya paṭipajjati, rakkhati cakkhundriyaṃ, cakkhundriye saṃvaraṃ âpajjati, sotena saddaṃ sutvâ . . . pe . . . ghânena gandhaṃ ghâyitvâ . . . pe . . . jivhâya rasaṃ sâyitvâ . . . pe . . . kâyena phoṭṭhabbaṃ phusitvâ . . . pe . . . manasâ dhammaṃ viññâya na nimittaggâhi hoti nânuvyañjanaggâhi, yatvâdhikaraṇam enaṃ manindriyaṃ asaṃvutaṃ viharantaṃ abhijjhâdomanassâ pâpakâ akusalâ dhammâ anvâssaveyyuṃ, tassa saṃvarâya paṭipajjati, rakkhati manindriyaṃ manindriye saṃvaraṃ âpajjati; yâ imesaṃ channaṃ indriyânaṃ gutti gopanâ ârakkho saṃvaro—ayaṃ vuccati indriyesu guttadvâratâ.

1348. Tattha katamâ bhojane mattaññutâ?

Idhekacco paṭisaṅkhâ yoniso âhâraṃ âhâreti, neva davâya na madâya na maṇḍanâya na vibhûsanâya yâvad eva imassa kâyassa ṭhitiyâ yâpanâya vihiṃsûparatiyâ brahmacariyânuggahâya iti purâṇañ ca vedanaṃ paṭihaṅkhâmi, navañ ca vedanaṃ na uppâdessâmi, yâtrâ ca me bhavissati anavajjatâ ca phâsuvihâro câti ; yâ tattha santuṭṭhitâ mattaññutâ paṭisaṅkhâ bhojane—ayaṃ vuccati bhojane mattaññutâ.

1349. Tattha katamaṃ muṭṭhasaccaṃ?

Yâ anussati ananussati appaṭissati, asaraṇata adhâraṇatâ apilâpanatâ asammussanatâ—idaṃ vuccati muṭṭhasaccaṃ.

1350. Tattha katamaṃ asampajaññaṃ?

Yam aññâṇaṃ, adassanaṃ . . . pe . . . avijjâlaṅgî moho akusalamûlaṃ—idaṃ vuccati asampajaññaṃ.

1351. Tattha katamâ sati?

Yâ sati anussati paṭissati saraṇatâ dhâraṇatâ apilâpanatâ asammussanatâ sati satindriyaṃ satibalaṃ sammâsati—ayaṃ vuccati sati.

1352. Tattha katamaṃ sampajaññaṃ?

Yâ paññâ pajânanâ . . . pe . . . amoho dhammavicayo sammâdiṭṭhi—idaṃ vuccati sampajaññaṃ.

1353. Tattha katamaṃ paṭisaṅkhânâbalaṃ?

Yâ paññâ pajânanâ . . . pe . . . amoho dhammavicayo sammâdiṭṭhi idaṃ vuccati patisaṅkhânabalaṃ.

1354. Tattha katamaṃ bhâvanâbalaṃ?

Yâ kusalânaṃ dhammânaṃ âsevanâ bhâvanâ bahulîkammaṃ—idaṃ vuccati bhâvanâbalaṃ—satta pi bojjhaṅgâ bhâvanâbalaṃ.

1355. Tattha katamo samatho?

Yâ cittassa ṭhiti . . . pe. . . . sammâsamâdhi—ayaṃ vuccati samatho.

1356. Tattha katamâ vipassanâ?

Yâ paññâ pajânanâ . . . pe . . . amoho dhammavicayo sammâdiṭṭhi—ayaṃ vuccati vipassanâ.

1357. Tattha katamaṃ samathanimittaṃ?

Yâ cittassa ṭhiti . . . pe . . . sammâsamâdhi—idaṃ vuccati samathanimittaṃ.

1358. Tattha katamaṃ paggâhanimittaṃ?

Yo cetasiko viriyârambho . . . pe . . . sammâvâyâmo idaṃ vuccati paggâhanimittaṃ.

1359. Tattha katamo paggâho?

Yo cetasiko viriyârambho . . . pe . . . sammâvâyâmo—ayaṃ vuccati paggâho.

1360. Tattha katamo avikkhepo?

Yâ cittassa ṭhiti . . . pe . . . sammâsamâḍhi—ayaṃ vuccati avikkhepo.

1361. Tattha katamâ sîlavipatti?

Yo kâyiko vîtikkamo vâcasiko vîtikkamo kâyikavâcasiko vîtikkamo—ayaṃ vuccati sîlavipatti—sabbam pi dussîlyaṃ sîlavipatti.

1362. Tattha katamâ diṭṭhivipatti?

Natthi dinnaṃ, natthi yiṭṭhaṃ, natthi hutaṃ, natthi sukaṭadukkaṭânaṃ kammânaṃ phalaṃ vipâko, natthi ayaṃ loko, natthi paraloko, natthi mâtâ, natthi pitâ, natthi sattâ opapâtikâ, natthi loke samaṇabrahmanâ sammaggatâ sammâpaṭipannâ, ye imañ ca lokaṃ parañ ca lokaṃ sayaṃ abhiññâ sacchîkatvâ pavedentîti, yâ evarûpâ diṭṭhi ditthigatam . . . pe . . . vipariyesagâho, ayaṃ vuccati diṭṭhivipatti—sabbâpi micchâdiṭṭhi diṭṭhivipatti.

1363. Tattha katamâ sîlasampadâ?

Kâyiko avîtikkamo vâcasiko avîtikkamo kâyikavâcasiko avîtikkamo—ayaṃ vuccati sîlasampadâ—sabbo pi sîlasaṃvaro sîlasampadâ.

1364. Tattha katamâ diṭṭhisampadâ?

Atthi dinnaṃ, atthi yiṭṭhaṃ, atthi hutaṃ, atthi sukaṭadukkaṭânaṃ kammânaṃ phalaṃ vipâko, atthi ayaṃ loko, atthi paraloko, atthi mâtâ, atthi pitâ atthi sattâ opapâtikâ, atthi loke samaṇabrahmaṇâ sammaggatâ sammâpaṭipannâ, ye imañ ca lokaṃ parañ ca lokaṃ sayaṃ abhiññâ sacchîkatvâ pavedentîti yâ evarûpâ paññâ pajânanâ . . . pe . . . amoho dhammavicayo sammâdiṭṭhi, ayaṃ vuccati diṭṭhisampadâ—sabbâ pi sammâdiṭṭhi diṭṭhisampadâ.

1365. Tattha katamâ sîlavisuddhi?

Kâyiko avîtikkamo vâcasiko avîtikkamo kâyikavâcasiko avîtikkamo—ayaṃ vuccati sîlavisuddhi—sabbo pi sîlasaṃvaro sîlavisuddhi.

1366. Tattha katamâ diṭṭhivisuddhi?

Kammassa katam ñâṇasaccânulomikaṃ ñâṇaṃ maggasamaṅgissa ñâṇaṃ phalasamaṅgissa ñâṇaṃ.

Diṭṭhivisuddhi kho panâti yâ paññâ pajânanâ . . pe . . . amoho dhammavicayo sammâdiṭṭhi.

Yathâ diṭṭhissa ca padhânan ti yo cetasiko viriyârambho . . . pe . . . sammâvâyâmo.

Saṃvego ti jâtibhayaṃ jarâbhayaṃ vyâdhibhayaṃ maraṇabhayaṃ saṃvejaniyaṃ ṭhânan ti jâti jarâ vyâdhi maraṇaṃ.

Saṃviggassa ca yoniso padhânan ti idha bhikkhu anuppannânaṃ pâpakânaṃ akusalânaṃ dhammânaṃ anuppâdâya chandaṃ janeti vâyamati viriyaṃ ârabhati cittaṃ paggaṇhâti padahati—uppannânaṃ pâpakânaṃ akusalânaṃ dhammânaṃ pahânâya chandaṃ janeti vâyamati viriyaṃ ârabhati cittaṃ paggaṇhâti padahati—anuppannânaṃ kusalânaṃ dhammânaṃ uppâdâya chandaṃ janeti vâyamati viriyaṃ ârabhati cittaṃ paggaṇhâti padahati—uppannânaṃ kusalânaṃ dhammânaṃ ṭhitiyâ asammosâya bhiyyobhâvâya vepullâya bhâvanâya pâripûriyâ chandaṃ janeti vâyamati viriyaṃ ârabhati cittaṃ paggaṇhâti padahati.

1367. Asantuṭṭhitâ ca kusalesu dhammesu ti yâ kusalânaṃ dhammânaṃ bhâvanâya asantuṭṭhassa bhiyyokamyatâ.

Appaṭivânitâ ca padhânasmin ti yâ kusalânaṃ dhammânaṃ bhâvanâya sakkaccakiriyatâ sâtaccakiriyatâ aṭṭhitakiriyatâ anolînavuttitâ anikkhittachandatâ anikkhittadhuratâ âsevanâ bhâvanâ bahulîkammaṃ.

Vijjâ ti tisso vijjâ—pubbenivâsânussativiññâṇaṃ vijjâ ; sattânaṃ cutupapâte ñâṇaṃ vijjâ âsavânaṃ khaye ñâṇaṃ vijjâ.

Vimuttîti dve vimuttiyo—cittassa ca adhimutti nibbânañ ca.

Khaye ñâṇan ti—maggasamaṅgissa ñâṇaṃ.
Anuppâde ñâṇan ti—phalasamaṅgissa ñâṇaṃ.

Nikkhepakhaṇḍo niṭṭhito.

1368. Katame dhammâ kusalâ ?

Catûsu bhummîsu kusalaṃ—ime dhammâ kusalâ.

1369. Katame dhammâ akusalâ ?

Dvâdasa akusalacittuppâdâ—ime dhammâ akusalâ.

1370. Katame dhammâ avyâkatâ ?

Catûsu bhummîsu vipâko—tîsu bhummîsu kiriyâvyâkataṃ rûpañ ca nibbânañ ca—ime dhammâ avyâkatâ.

1371. Katame dhammâ sukhâya vedanâya sampayuttâ?

Kâmâvacarakusalato cattâro somanassasahagatacittuppâdâ, akusalato cattâro kâmâvacarassa kusalassa vipâkato cha kiriyato pañca rûpâvacaratikacatukkajjhânâ kusalato ca vipâkato ca kiriyato ca lokuttaratikacatukkajjhânâ kusalato ca vipâkato ca, etth' uppannaṃ sukhaṃ vedanaṃ ṭhapetvâ—imo dhammâ sukhâya vedanâya sampayuttâ.

1372. Katame dhammâ dukkhâya vedanâya sampayuttâ?

Dve domanassasahagatâ cittuppâdâ dukkhasahagataṃ kâyaviññâṇaṃ, etth' uppannaṃ dukkhaṃ vedanaṃ ṭhapetvâ—imo dhammâ dukkhâya vedanâya sampayuttâ.

1373. Katame dhammâ adukkhamasukhâya vedanâya sampayuttâ?

Kâmâvacarakusalato cattâro upekkhâsahagatâ cittuppâdâ akusalato cha, kâmâvacarassa akusalassa vipâkato dasa, akusalassa vipâkato cha, kiriyato cha, rûpâvacaracatutthaṃ jhânaṃ kusalato ca vipâkato ca kiriyato ca, cattâro arûpâvacarâkusalato ca vipâkato ca kiriyato ca, lokuttaraṃ catutthaṃ jhânaṃ kusalato ca vipâkato ca, etth' uppannaṃ adukkhamasukhaṃ vedanaṃ ṭhapetvâ, ime dhammâ adukkhamasukhâya vedanâya sampayuttâ, tisso ca vedanâ rûpañ ca nibbânañ ca, imo dhammâ na vattabbâ sukhâya vedanâya sampayuttâ ti pi, dukkhâya vedanâya sampayuttâ ti pi—adukkhamasukhâya vedanâya sampayuttâ ti pi.

1374. Katame dhammâ vipâkâ?

Catûsu bhummîsu vipâko—imo dhammâ vipâkâ.

1375. Katame dhammâ vipâkadhammadhammâ?

Catûsu bhummîsu kusalaṃ akusalaṃ—imo dhammâ vipâkadhammadhammâ.

1376. Katame dhammâ nevavipâkanavipâkadhammadhammâ?

Tîsu bhummîsu kiriyâvyâkataṃ rûpañ ca nibbânañ ca—imo dhammâ nevavipâkanavipâkadhammadhammâ.

1377. Katame dhammâ upâdiṇṇupâdâniyâ?

Tîsu bhummisu vipâko—yañ ca rûpaṃ kammassa katattâ—imo dhammâ upâdiṇṇupâdâniyâ.

1378. Katame dhammâ anupâdiṇṇupâdâniyâ?

Tisu bhummîsu kusalaṃ akusalaṃ, tîsu bhummîsu kiriyâvyâkataṃ, yañ ca rûpaṃ na kammassa katattâ—ime dhammâ anupâdiṇṇupâdâniyâ.

1379. Katame dhammâ anupâdiṇṇâ anupâdâniyâ?

Cattâro maggâ apariyâpannâ cattâri ca sâmaññaphalâni nibbânañ ca—ime dhammâ anupâdiṇṇâ anupâdâniyâ.

1380. Katame dhammâ saṅkiliṭṭhasaṅkilesikâ?

Dvâdasâkusalacittuppâdâ—ime dhammâ saṅkiliṭṭhasaṅkilesikâ?

1381. Katame dhammâ asaṅkiliṭṭhasaṅkilesikâ?

Tîsu bhummîsu kusalaṃ, tîsu bhummîsu vipâko, tîsu bhummîsu kiriyâvyâkataṃ, sabbañ ca rûpaṃ—ime dhammâ asaṅkiliṭṭhasankilesikâ.

1382. Katame dhammâ asaṅkiliṭṭhâsaṅkilesikâ?

Cattâro maggâ apariyâpannâ, cattâri ca sâmaññaphalâni nibbânañ ca—ime dhammâ asaṅkiliṭṭhâsaṅkilesika.

1383. Katame dhammâ savitakkasavicârâ?

Kâmâvacaraṃ kusalaṃ akusalaṃ—kâmâvacarakusalassa vipâkato ekâdasa cittuppâdâ, akusalassa vipâkato dve, kiriyato ekâdasa, rûpâvacarapaṭhamaṃ jhânaṃ kusalato ca vipâkato ca kiriyato ca, lokuttaraṃ paṭhamaṃ jhânaṃ kusalato ca vipâkato ca etth' uppanne vitakkavicâre ṭhapetvâ—ime dhammâ savitakkasavicârâ.

1384. Katame dhammâ avitakkavicâramattâ?

Rûpâvacarapañcakanaye dutiyaṃ jhânaṃ kusalato ca vipâkato ca kiriyato ca, lokuttarapañcakanaye dutiyaṃ jhânaṃ kusalato ca vipâkato ca, etth' uppannaṃ vicâraṃ ṭhapetvâ vitakko ca—ime dhammâ avitakkavicâramattâ.

1385. Katame dhammâ avitakka-avicârâ?

Dve pañca viññâṇâni rûpâvacaratikatikajjhânâ kusalato ca vipâkato ca kiriyato ca, cattâro âruppâ kusalato ca vipâkato ca kiriyato ca, lokuttaratikatikajjhânâ kusalato ca vipâkato ca, pañcakanaye dutiye jhâne uppanno ca vicâro, rûpañ ca nibbânañ ca—ime dhammâ avitakka-avicârâ.

1386. Vitakkasahajâto vicâro na vattabbo savitakkasavicâro ti pi.

Avitakkavicâramatto ti pi. Avitakka-avicâro ti pi.

1387. Katame dhamme pîtisahagatâ?

Kâmâvacarakusalato cattâro somanassasahagatâ cittuppâdâ, akusalato cattâro, kâmâvacarakusalassa vipâkato pañca, kiriyato pañca, rûpâvacaradukatikajjhânâ kusalato ca vipâkato ca kiriyato ca, lokuttaradukatikajjhânâ kusalato ca vipâkato ca, etth' uppannaṃ pîtiṃ ṭhapetva—ime dhammâ pîtisahagatâ.

1388. Katame dhammâ sukhasahagatâ?

Kâmâvacarakusalato cattâro somanassasahagatacittuppâdâ, akusalato cattâro, kâmâvacarakusalassa vipâkato cha, kiriyato pañca, rûpâvacaratikacatukkajjhânâ kusalato ca vipâkato ca, kiriyato ca, lokuttaratikacatukkajjhânâ kusalato ca vipâkato ca, etth' uppannaṃ sukhaṃ ṭhapetvâ—ime dhammâ sukhasahagatâ.

1389. Katame dhamma upekkhâsahagatâ?

Kâmâvacarakusalato cattâro upekkhâsahagatacittuppâdâ, akusalato cha, kâmâvacarakusalassa vipâkato dasa, akusalavipâkato cha, kiriyato cha, rûpâvacaracatutthaṃ jhânaṃ kusalato ca vipâkato ca kiriyato ca, cattâro âruppâ kusalato ca vipâkato ca kiriyato ca, lokuttaraṃ catutthaṃ jhânaṃ kusalato ca vipâkato ca, etth' uppannaṃ upekkhaṃ ṭhapetvâ—ime dhammâ upekkhâsahagatâ.

Pîti na pîtisahagatâ sukhasahagatâ na upekkhâsahagatâ, sukhaṃ na sukhasahagataṃ siyâ pîtisahagataṃ na upekkhâsahagataṃ, siyâ na vattabbam pîtisahagatan ti pi.

Dve domanassasahagatacittuppâdâ, dukkhasahagataṃ kâyaviññâṇaṃ, yâ ca vedanâ upekkhâ rûpañ ca nibbânañ ca;—ime dhammâ na vattabbâ pîtisahagatâ ti pi sukhasahagatâ ti pi upekkhâsahagatâ ti pi.

1390. Katame dhammâ dassanena pahâtabbâ?

Cattâro diṭṭhigatasampayuttacittuppâdâ—vicikicchâsahagato cittuppâdo—ime dhammâ dassanena pahâtabbâ.

1391. Katame dhammâ bhâvanâya pahâtabbâ?

Uddhaccasahagato cittuppâdo—ime dhammâ bhâvanâya pahâtabbâ.

1392. Cattâro diṭṭhigatavippayuttâ lobhasahagatacittuppâdâ.

Dve domanassasahagatacittuppâdâ—ime dhammâ siyâ dassanena pahâtabbâ siyâ bhâvanâya pahâtabbâ.

1393. Katame dhammâ neva dassanena na bhâvanâya pahâtabbâ?

Catûsu bhummîsu kusalaṃ, catûsu bhummîsu vipâko, tîsu bhummîsu kiriyâvyâkataṃ, rûpañ ca nibbânañ ca—ime dhammâ neva dassanena na bhâvanâya pahâtabbâ.

1394. Katame dhammâ dassanena pahâtabbahetukâ?

Cattâro diṭṭhigatasampayuttacittuppâdâ, vicikicchâsahagato cittuppâdo, etth' uppannaṃ mohaṃ ṭhapetvâ—ime dhammâ dassanena pahâtabbahetukâ.

1395. Katame dhammâ bhâvanâya pahâtabbahetukâ?

Uddhaccasahagato cittuppâdo, etth' uppannaṃ mohaṃ ṭhapetvâ, ime dhammâ bhâvanâya pahâtabbahetukâ, cattâro diṭṭhigatavippayuttâ lobhasahagatacittuppâdâ dve domanassasahagatacittuppâdâ, ime dhammâ siyâ dassanena pahâtabbahetukâ, siyâ bhâvanâya pahâtabbahetukâ.

1396. Katame dhammâ neva dassanena na bhâvanâya pahâtabbahetukâ?

Vicikicchâsahagato moho, uddhaccasahagato moho, catûsu bhummîsu kusalaṃ, catûsu bhummîsu vipâko, tîsu bhummîsu kiriyâyvâkataṃ, rûpañ ca nibbânañ ca—ime dhammâ neva dassanena na bhâvanâya pahâtabbahetukâ.

1397. Katame dhammâ âcayagâmino?

Tîsu bhummîsu kusalaṃ akusalaṃ—ime dhammâ âcayagâmino.

1398. Katame dhammâ apacayagâmino?

Cattâro maggâ apariyâpannâ—ime dhammâ apacayagâmino.

1399. Katame dhammâ nevâcayagâmino nâpacayagâmino?

Catûsu bhummîsu vipâko tîsu bhummîsu kiriyâvyâkataṃ rûpañ ca nibbânañ ca—ime dhammâ nevâcayagâmino nâpacayagâmino.

1400. Katame dhammâ sekkhâ?

Cattâro maggâ apariyâpannâ heṭṭhimâni ca tîṇi sâmaññaphalâni—ime dhammâ sekkhâ.

1401. Katame dhammâ asekkhâ?

Upariṭṭhimaṃ arahattaphalaṃ—ime dhammâ asekkhâ.

1402. Katame dhammâ neva sekkhâ nâsekkhâ?

Tîsu bhummîsu kusalaṃ akusalaṃ—tîsu bhummîsu vipâko tîsu bhummîsu kiriyâvyâkataṃ rûpañ ca nibbânañ ca ime dhammâ neva sekkhâ nâsekkhâ.

1403. Katame dhammâ parittâ?

Kâmâvacarakusalaṃ akusalaṃ sabbo kâmâvacarassa vipâko kâmâvacarakiriyâvyâkataṃ, sabbañ ca rûpaṃ—ime dhammâ parittâ.

1404. Katame dhammâ mahaggatâ?

Rûpâvacarâ arûpâvacarâ kusalâvyâkatâ—ime dhammâ mahaggatâ.

1405. Katame dhammâ appamânâ?

Cattâro maggâ apariyâpannâ cattâri ca sâmaññaphalâni nibbânañ ca—ime dhammâ appamânâ.

1406. Katame dhammâ parittârammaṇâ?

Sabbo kâmâvacarassa vipâko kiriyâ manodhâtu, kiriyâhetukamanoviññâṇadhâtu somanassasahagatâ—ime dhammâ parittârammaṇâ.

1407. Katame dhammâ mahaggatârammaṇâ?

Viññâṇañcâyatanaṃ nevasaññânâsaññâyatanaṃ — ime dhammâ mahaggatârammaṇâ.

1408. Katame dhammâ appamânârammaṇâ?

Cattâro maggâ apariyâpannâ cattâri ca sâmaññaphalâni—ime dhammâ appamânârammaṇâ.

Kâmâvacarakusalato cattâro ñâṇavippayuttacittuppâdâ, kiriyato cattâro ñâṇavippayuttacittuppâdâ, sabbaṃ akusalaṃ, ime dhammâ siyâ parittârammaṇâ, siyâ mahaggatârammaṇâ, na appamânârammaṇâ, siyâ na vattabbâ parittârammaṇâ ti pi mahaggatârammaṇâ ti pi, kâmâvacarakusalato cattâro ñâṇasampayuttâ cittuppâdâ, kiriyato cattâro ñâṇasampayuttâ cittuppâdâ, rûpâvacaracatutthaṃ jhânaṃ kusalato ca kiriyato ca, kiriyâhetukamanoviññâṇadhâtu upekkhâsahagatâ—ime dhammâ siyâ parittârammaṇâ, siyâ mahaggatârammaṇâ, siyâ appamâṇârammaṇâ siyâ na vattabbâ parittârammaṇâ ti pi, mahaggatârammaṇâ ti pi, appamâṇâ ti pi, rûpâvacaratikacatukkajjhânâ kusalato ca vipâkato ca kiriyato ca catutthassa jhânassa vipâko âkâsânañcâyatanaṃ âkiñcaññâyatanaṃ, ime dhammâ na vattabbâ parittârammaṇâ ti pi mahaggatârammaṇâ ti pi appamâṇârammaṇâ ti pi—rûpañ ca nibbânañ ca anârammaṇâ.

1409. Katame dhammâ hînâ?

Dvâdasa akusalacittuppâdâ—ime dhammâ hînâ.

1410. Katame dhammâ majjhimâ?

Tîsu bhummîsu kusalaṃ, tîsu bhummîsu vipâko, tîsu bhummîsu kiriyâvyâkataṃ, sabbañ ca rûpaṃ—ime dhammâ majjhimâ.

1411. Katame dhammâ paṇîtâ?

Cattâro maggâ apariyâpannâ cattâri ca sâmaññaphalâni nibbânañ ca—ime dhammâ paṇîtâ.

1412. Katame dhammâ micchattaniyatâ?

Cattâro diṭṭhigatasampayuttacittuppâdâ, dve domanassasahagatacittuppâdâ—ime dhammâ siyâ micchattaniyatâ siyâ aniyatâ.

1413. Katame dhammâ sampattaniyatâ?

Cattâro maggâ apariyâpannâ—ime dhammâ sampattaniyatâ.

1414. Katame dhammâ aniyatâ?

Cattâro diṭṭhigatavippayuttalobhasahagatacittuppâdâ, vicikicchâsahagato cittuppâdo uddhaccasahagato cittuppâdo, tîsu bhummîsu kusalaṃ, catûsu bhummîsu vipâko, tîsu bhummîsu kiriyâvyâkataṃ rûpañ ca nibbânañ ca—ime dhammâ aniyatâ.

1415. Katame dhammâ maggârammaṇâ?

Kâmâvacarakusalato cattâro ñâṇasampayuttacittuppâdâ kiriyato cattâro ñâṇasampayuttacittuppâdâ, ime dhammâ siyâ maggârammaṇâ, na maggahetukâ, siyâ maggâdhipatino, siyâ na vattabbâ maggârammaṇâ ti pi maggâdhipatino ti pi, cattâro ariyamaggâ na maggârammaṇâ, maggahetukâ, siyâ maggâdhipatino siyâ na vattabbâ maggâdhipatino ti rûpâvacaracatutthaṃ jhânaṃ kusalato ca kiriyato ca kiriyâhetukamanoviññâṇadhâtu upekkhâsahagatâ, ime dhammâ siyâ maggârammaṇâ, na maggahetukâ, na maggâdhipatino siyâ na vattabbâ maggârammaṇâ ti, kâmâvacarakusalato cattâro ñâṇavippayuttacittuppâdâ sabbaṃ akusalaṃ, sabbo kâmâvacarassa vipâko, kiriyato cha cittuppâdâ rûpâvacaratikacatukkajjhânâ kusalato ca vipâkato ca kiriyato ca catutthajhânassa vipâko, cattâro âruppâ kusalato ca vipâkato ca kiriyato ca cattâri ca sâmaññaphalâni—ime dhammâ na vattabbâ maggârammanâ ti pi maggahetukâ ti pi maggâdhipatino ti pi, rûpañ ca nibbânañ ca anârammaṇâ.

1416. Katame dhammâ uppannâ?

Catûsu bhummîsu vipâko, yañ ca rûpaṃ kammassa katattâ

ime dhammâ siyâ uppannâ, siyâ uppâdino, na vattabbâ anuppannâ ti, catûsu bhummîsu kusalaṃ, akusalaṃ, tîsu bhummîsu kiriyâvyâkataṃ, yañ ca rûpaṃ na kammassa katattâ, ime dhammâ siyâ uppannâ, siyâ anuppannâ, na vattabbâ uppâdino ti, nibbânaṃ na vattabbaṃ uppannan ti pi anuppannan ti pi [uppâdîti pi].

Nibbânaṃ ṭhapetvâ sabbe dhammâ siyâ atîtâ, siyâ anâgatâ, siyâ paccuppannâ, nibbânaṃ na vattabbaṃ atîtan ti pi anâgatan ti pi paccuppannan ti pi.

1417. Katame dhammâ atîtârammaṇâ?

Viññâṇañcâyatanaṃ neva saññânâsaññâyatanaṃ — ime dhammâ atîtârammaṇâ.

Niyogâ anâgatârammaṇâ natthi.

1418. Katame dhammâ paccuppannârammaṇâ?

Dve pañca viññâṇâni tisso ca manodhâtuyo ime dhammâ paccuppannârammaṇâ.

Kâmâvacarakusalassa vipâkato dasa cittuppâdâ akusalassa vipâkato manoviññâṇadhâtu upekkhâsahagatâ kiriyahetukâ manoviññâṇadhâtu somanassasahagatâ, ime dhammâ siyâ atîtârammaṇâ, siyâ anâgatârammaṇâ, siyâ paccuppannârammaṇâ, kâmâvacarakusalaṃ akusalaṃ kiriyato na cittuppâdâ, rûpâvacaracatutthaṃ jhânaṃ kusalato ca kiriyato ca, ime dhammâ siyâ atîtârammaṇâ, siyâ anâgatârammaṇâ, siyâ paccuppannârammaṇâ, siyâ na vattabbâ atîtârammaṇâ ti pi anâgatârammaṇâ ti pi paccuppannârammaṇâ ti pi, rûpâvacaratikacatukkajjhânâ kusalato ca, vipâkato ca kiriyato ca catutthassa jhânassa vipâko, âkâsânañcâyatanaṃ âkiñcaññâyatanaṃ cattâro maggâ apariyâpannâ cattâri ca sâmaññaphalâni, ime dhammâ na vattabbâ atîtârammaṇâ ti pi anâgatârammaṇâ ti pi paccuppannârammaṇâ ti pi—rûpañ ca nibbânañ ca anârammaṇâ. Manindriyaṃ baddharûpañ ca nibbânañ ca ṭhapetvâ sabbe dhammâ siyâ ajjhattâ siyâ bahiddhâ, siyâ ajjhattabahiddhâ — manindriyaṃ baddharûpañ ca nibbânañ ca bahiddhâ.

1419. Katame dhammâ ajjhattârammaṇâ?

Viññâṇañcâyatanaṃ neva saññânâsaññâyatanaṃ — ime dhammâ ajjhattârammaṇâ.

1420. Katame dhammâ bahiddhârammaṇâ?

Rûpâvacaratikacatukkajjhânâ kusalato ca vipâkato ca kiriyato ca, catutthassa jhânassa vipâko, âkâsânañcâyatanaṃ, cattâro maggâ apariyâpannâ cattâri ca sâmaññaphalâni—ime dhammâ bahiddhârammaṇâ. Rûpaṃ ṭhapetvâ sabbeva kâmâvacarâ kusalâkusalâvyâkatâ dhammâ, rûpâvacaracatutthajjhânaṃ kusalato ca kiriyato ca, ime dhammâ siyâ ajjhattârammaṇâ, siyâ bahiddhârammaṇâ, siyâ ajjhattabahiddhârammaṇâ, âkiñcaññâyatanaṃ na vattabbaṃ ajjhattârammaṇan ti pi bahiddhârammaṇan ti pi ajjhattabahiddhârammaṇan ti pi—rûpañ ca nibbânañ ca anârammaṇâ.

1421. Katame dhammâ sanidassanasappaṭighâ?

Rûpâyatanaṃ—ime dhammâ sanidassanasappaṭighâ.

1422. Katame dhammâ anidassanasappaṭighâ?

Cakkhâyatanaṃ . . . pe . . . phoṭṭhabbâyatanaṃ—ime dhammâ anidassanasappaṭighâ.

1423. Katame dhammâ anidassana-appaṭighâ?

Catûsu bhummîsu kusalaṃ akusalaṃ catûsu bhummîsu vipâko, tîsu bhummîsu kiriyâvyâkataṃ, yañ ca rûpaṃ anidassanaṃ appaṭighaṃ dhammâyatanapariyâpannaṃ, nibbânañ ca—ime dhammâ anidassana-appaṭighâ.

Tikaṃ.

1424. Katame dhammâ hetû?

Tayo kusalahetû, tayo akusalahetû, tayo avyâkatahetû, alobho kusalahetu, adoso kusalahetu, amoho kusalahetu, catûsu bhummîsu kusalesu uppajjanti, amoho kusalahetu kâmâvacarakusalato cattâro ñâṇavippayuttacittuppâde ṭhapetvâ catûsu bhummîsu kusalesu uppajjati, lobho aṭṭhasu lobhasahagatesu cittuppâdesu uppajjati, doso dvîsu domanassasahagatesu cittuppâdesu uppajjati, moho sabbâkusalesu uppajjati, alobho vipâkahetu, adoso vipâkahetu, kâmâvacarassa vipâkato ahetuke cittuppâde ṭhapetvâ catûsu bhummîsu vipâkesu uppajjanti amoho vipâkahetu kâmâvacarassa vipâkato ahetuke cittuppâde ṭhapetvâ cattâro ñâṇavippayuttacittuppâde ṭhapetvâ catûsu bhummîsu vipâkesu uppajjati, alobho kiriyahetu adoso kiriyahetu kâmâvacarassa kiriyato ahetuke cittuppâde ṭhapetvâ tîsu bhummîsu kiriyesu uppajjanti, amoho kiriyahetu kâmâvacarakiriyato ahetuke cittuppâde ṭhapetvâ cattâro ñâṇavippayuttacittuppâde ṭhapetvâ tîsu bhummîsu kiriyesu uppajjati—ime dhammâ hetû.

1425. Katame dhammâ na hetû?

Ṭhapetvâ hetû catûsu bhummîsu kusalaṃ akusalaṃ—catûsu bhummîsu vipâko—tîsu bhummîsu kiriyâvyâkataṃ—rûpañ ca nibbânañ ca—ime dhammâ na hetû.

1426. Katame dhammâ sahetukâ?

Vicikicchâsahagataṃ uddhaccasahagataṃ mohaṃ ṭhapetvâ avasesaṃ akusalaṃ, catûsu bhummîsu kusalaṃ, kâmâvacarassa vipâkato ahetuke cittuppâde ṭhapetvâ catûsu bhummîsu vipâko kâmâvacarakiriyato ahetuke cittuppâde ṭhapetvâ tîsu bhummîsu kiriyâvyâkataṃ—ime dhammâ sahetukâ.

1427. Katame dhammâ ahetukâ?

Vicikicchâsahagato moho uddhaccasahagato moho dve pañca viññâṇâni—tisso ca manodhâtuyo—pañca ca ahetukamanoviññâṇadhâtuyo rûpañ ca nibbânañ ca—ime dhammâ ahetukâ.

1428. Katame dhammâ hetusampayuttâ?

Vicikicchâsahagataṃ uddhaccasahagataṃ mohaṃ ṭhapetvâ, avasesaṃ akusalaṃ, catûsu bhummîsu kusalaṃ kâmâvacarassa vipâkato ahetuke cittuppâde ṭhapetvâ catûsu bhummîsu vipâko, kâmâvacarakiriyato ahetukacittuppâde ṭhapetvâ tîsu bhummîsu kiriyâvyâkataṃ—ime dhammâ hetusampayuttâ.

1429. Katame dhammâ hetuvippayuttâ?

Vicikicchâsahagato moho uddhaccasahagato moho dve pañca viññâṇâni—tisso ca manodhâtuyo—pañca ca ahetukamanoviññâṇadhâtuyo rûpañ ca nibbânañ ca—ime dhammâ hetuvippayuttâ.

1430. Katame dhammâ hetû ceva sahetukâ ca?

Yattha dve tayo hetû ekato uppajjanti—ime dhammâ hetû ceva sahetukâ ca.

1431. Katame dhammâ sahetukâ ceva na ca hetû?

Catûsu bhummîsu kusalaṃ, akusalaṃ kâmâvacarassa vipâkato ahetuke cittuppâde ṭhapetvâ catûsu bhummîsu vipâko, kâmâvacarakiriyato ahetuke cittuppâde ṭhapetvâ tîsu bhummîsu kiriyâvyâkataṃ, etth' uppanno hetû ṭhapetvâ, ime dhammâ sahetukâ ceva na ca hetû. Ahetukâ dhammâ na vattabbâ hetû ceva sahetukâ ti pi sahetukâ ceva na ca hetû ti pi.

1432. Katame dhammâ hetû ceva hetusampayuttâ ca?

Yattha dve tayo hetû ekato uppajjanti—ime dhammâ hetû ceva hetusampayuttâ ca.

1433. Katame dhammâ hetusampayuttâ ceva na ca hetû?

Catûsu bhummîsu, kusalam akusalaṃ, kâmâvacarassa vipâkato ahetukacittuppâde ṭhapetvâ catûsu bhummîsu vipâko, kâmâvacarakiriyato ahetuke cittuppâde ṭhapetvâ tîsu bhummîsu kiriyâvyâkataṃ, etth' uppanne hetû ṭhapetvâ, ime dhammâ hetusampayuttâ ceva na ca hetû. Hetuvippayuttâ dhammâ na vattabbâ hetû ceva hetusampayuttâ ti pi hetusampayuttâ ceva na ca hetû ti pi.

1434. Katame dhammâ na hetû sahetukâ?

Catûsu bhummîsu kusalaṃ akusalaṃ, kâmâvacarassa vipâkato ahetuke cittuppâde ṭhapetvâ catûsu bhummîsu vipâko, kâmâvacarakiriyato ahetuke cittuppâde ṭhapetvâ tîsu bhummîsu kiriyâvyâkataṃ, etth' uppanne hetû ṭhapetvâ—ime dhammâ na hetû sahetukâ.

1435. Katame dhammâ na hetû ahetukâ?

Dve pañca viññâṇâni, tisso ca manodhâtuyo, pañca ahetukamanoviññâṇadhâtuyo, rûpañ ca nibbânañ ca—ime dhammâ na hetû ahetukâ.

Hetû dhammâ na vattabbâ na hetû sahetukâ ti pi na hetû ahetukâ ti pi.

1436. Katame dhammâ sappaccayâ?

Catûsu bhummîsu kusalaṃ akusalaṃ, catûsu bhummîsu vipâko, tîsu bhummîsu kiriyâvyâkataṃ sabbañ ca rûpaṃ—ime dhammâ sappaccayâ.

1437. Katame dhammâ appaccayâ?

Nibbânaṃ—ime dhammâ appaccayâ.

1438. Katame dhammâ saṅkhatâ?

Catûsu bhummîsu kusalaṃ akusalaṃ catûsu bhummîsu vipâko, tîsu bhummîsu kiriyâvyâkataṃ sabbañ ca rûpaṃ —ime dhammâ saṅkhatâ.

1439. Katame dhammâ asaṅkhatâ?

Nibbânaṃ—ime dhammâ asaṅkhatâ.

1440. Katame dhammâ sanidassanâ?

Rûpâyatanaṃ—ime dhammâ sanidassanâ.

1441. Katame dhammâ anidassanâ?

Cakkhâyatanaṃ . . . pe . . . phoṭṭhabbâyatanaṃ, catûsu bhummîsu kusalaṃ akusalaṃ, catûsu bhummîsu vipâko, tîsu bhummîsu kiriyâvyâkataṃ, yañ ca rûpaṃ anidassanaṃ appaṭighaṃ dhammâyatanapariyâpannaṃ nibbânañ ca—ime dhammâ anidassanâ.

1442. Katame dhammâ sappaṭighâ?

Cakkhâyatanaṃ . . . pe . . . phoṭṭhabbâyatanaṃ—ime dhammâ sappaṭighâ.

1443. Katame dhammâ appaṭighâ?

Catûsu bhummîsu kusalaṃ akusalaṃ catûsu bhummîsu vipâko, tîsu bhummîsu kiriyâvyâkataṃ, yañ ca rûpaṃ anidassanaṃ appaṭighaṃ dhammâyatanapariyâpannaṃ nibbânañ ca—ime dhammâ appaṭighâ.

1444. Katame dhammâ rûpino?

Cattâro ca mahâbhûtâ catunnañ ca mahâbhûtânaṃ upâdâya rûpaṃ—ime dhammâ rûpino.

1445. Katame dhammâ arûpino?

Catûsu bhummîsu kusalaṃ akusalaṃ, catûsu bhummîsu vipâko, tîsu bhummîsu kiriyâvyâkataṃ, nibbânañ ca—ime dhammâ arûpino.

1446. Katame dhammâ lokiyâ.

Tîsu bhummîsu kusalaṃ akusalaṃ, tîsu bhummîsu vipâko, tîsu bhummîsu kiriyâvyâkataṃ sabbañ ca rûpaṃ—ime dhammâ lokiyâ.

1447. Katame dhammâ lokuttarâ?

✓ Cattâro maggâ apariyâpannâ, cattâri ca sâmaññaphalâni nibbânañ ca—ime dhammâ lokuttarâ.

Sabbe dhammâ kenaci viññeyyâ kenaci na viññeyyâ.

1448. Katame dhammâ âsavâ?

Cattâro âsavâ, kâmâsavo bhavâsavo diṭṭhâsavo avijjâsavo.

Kâmâsavo aṭṭhasu lobhasahagatesu cittuppâdesu uppajjati, bhavâsavo catûsu diṭṭhigatavippayuttalobhasahagatesu cittuppâdesu uppajjati, diṭṭhâsavo catûsu diṭṭhigatasampayuttesu cittuppâdesu uppajjati, avijjâsavo sabbâkusalesu uppajjati—ime dhammâ âsavâ.

1449. Katame dhammâ no âsavâ?

Ṭhapetvâ âsave, avasesaṃ akusalaṃ catûsu bhummîsu

kusalaṃ, catûsu bhummîsu vipâko, tîsu bhummîsu kiriyâvyâkataṃ, rûpañ ca nibbânañ ca—ime dhammâ no âsavâ.

1450. Katame dhammâ sâsavâ?

Tîsu bhummîsu kusalaṃ akusalaṃ, tîsu bhummîsu vipâko, tîsu bhummîsu kiriyâvyâkataṃ, sabbañ ca rûpaṃ—ime dhammâ sâsavâ.

1451. Katame dhammâ anâsavâ?

Cattâro maggâ apariyâpannâ cattâri ca sâmaññaphalâni nibbânañ ca—ime dhammâ anâsavâ.

1452. Katame dhammâ âsavasampayuttâ?

Dve domanassasahagatacittuppâdâ, etth' uppannaṃ mohaṃ ṭhapetvâ, vicikicchâsahagataṃ uddhaccasahagataṃ mohaṃ ṭhapetvâ avasesaṃ akusalaṃ—ime dhammâ âsavasampayuttâ.

1453. Katame dhammâ âsavavippayuttâ?

Dvîsu domanassasahagatesu cittuppâdesu uppanno moho, vicikicchâsahagato moho uddhaccasahagato moho, catûsu bhummîsu kusalaṃ, catûsu bhummîsu vipâko tîsu bhummîsu kiriyâvyâkataṃ, rûpaṃ ca nibbânañ ca—ime dhammâ âsavavippayuttâ.

1454. Katame dhammâ âsavâ ceva sâsavâ ca?

Teva âsavâ âsavâ ceva sâsavâ ca.

1455. Katame dhammâ sâsavâ ceva no ca âsavâ?

Ṭhapetvâ âsave avasesaṃ akusalaṃ, tîsu bhummîsu kusalaṃ, tîsu bhummîsu vipâko, tîsu bhummîsu kiriyâvyâkataṃ, sabbañ ca rûpaṃ, ime dhammâ sâsavâ ceva no ca âsavâ. Anâsavâ dhammâ na vattabbâ âsavâ ceva sâsavâ ti pi sâsavâ ceva no ca âsavâ ti pi.

1456. Katame dhammâ âsavâ ceva âsavasampayuttâ ca?

Yattha dve tayo âsavâ ekato uppajjanti—ime dhammâ âsavâ ceva âsavasampayuttâ ca.

1457. Katame dhammâ âsavasampayuttâ ceva no ca âsavâ?

Ṭhapetvâ âsave avasesaṃ akusalaṃ, ime dhammâ âsavasampayuttâ no ca âsavâ. Âsavavippayuttâ dhammâ na vattabbâ âsavâ ceva âsavasampayuttâ ti pi—âsavasampayuttâ ceva no ca âsavâ ti pi.

1458. Katame dhammâ âsavavippayuttâ sâsavâ?

Dvîsu domanassasahagatesu cittuppâdesu uppanno moho vicikicchâsahagato moho uddhaccasahagato moho sutî bhummîsu kusalaṃ tîsu bhummîsu vipâko tîsu bhummîsu kiriyâvyâkataṃ, sabbañ ca rûpaṃ—ime dhammâ âsavavippayuttâ sâsavâ.

1459. Katame dhammâ âsavavippayuttâ anâsavâ?

Cattâro maggâ apariyâpannâ cattâri ca sâmaññaphalâni nibbânañ ca—ime dhammâ âsavavippayuttâ anâsavâ—âsavasampayuttâ dhammâ na vattabbâ âsavavippayuttâ sâsavâ ti pi âsavavippayuttâ anâsavâ ti pi.

1460. Katame dhammâ saññojanâ?

Dasa saññojanâni, kâmarâgasaññojanaṃ, paṭighasaññojanaṃ, mânasaññojanaṃ, diṭṭhisaññojanaṃ, vicikicchâsaññojanaṃ, sîlabbataparâmâsasaññojanaṃ, bhavarâgasaññojanaṃ, issâsaññojanaṃ, macchariyasaññojanaṃ, avijjâsaññojanaṃ.

Kâmarâgasaññojanaṃ aṭṭhasu lobhasahagatesu cittuppâdesu uppajjati, paṭighasaññojanaṃ dvîsu domanassasahagatesu cittuppâdesu uppajjati, mânasaññojanaṃ catûsu diṭṭhigatavippayuttalobhasahagatesu cittuppâdesu uppajjati, diṭṭhisaññojanaṃ catûsu diṭṭhigatasampayuttesu cittuppâdesu uppajjati, vicikicchâsaññojanaṃ vicikicchâsahagatacittuppâde uppajjati, sîlabbataparâmâsasaññojanaṃ catûsu diṭṭhigatasampayuttesu cittuppâdesu uppajjati, bhavarâgasaññojanaṃ catûsu diṭṭhigatavippayuttalobhasahagatesu cittuppâdesu uppajjati, issâsaññojanañ ca macchariyasaññojanañ ca dvîsu domanassasahagatesu cittuppâdesu uppajjanti, avijjâsaññojanaṃ sabbâkusalesu uppajjati—ime dhammâ saññojanâ.

1461. Katame dhammâ no saññojanâ?

Ṭhapetvâ saññojane avasesaṃ akusalaṃ catûsu bhummîsu kusalaṃ catûsu bhummîsu vipâko tîsu bhummîsu kiriyâvyâkataṃ rûpañ ca nibbânañ ca—ime dhammâ no saññojanâ.

1462. Katame dhammâ saññojaniyâ?

Tîsu bhummîsu kusalaṃ akusalaṃ—tîsu bhummîsu vipâko tîsu bhummîsu kiriyâvyâkataṃ sabbañ ca rûpaṃ—ime dhammâ saññojaniyâ.

1463. Katame dhammâ asaññojaniyâ?

Cattâro maggâ apariyâpannâ cattâri ca sâmaññaphalâni nibbânañ ca—ime dhammâ asaññojaniyâ.

1464. Katame dhammâ saññojanasampayuttâ?

Uddhaccasahagataṃ mohaṃ ṭhapetvâ avasesaṃ akusalaṃ —ime dhammâ saññojanasampayuttâ.

1465. Katame dhammâ saññojanavippayuttâ?

Uddhaccasahagato moho catûsu bhummîsu kusalaṃ catûsu bhummîsu vipâko tîsu bhummîsu kiriyâvyâkataṃ rûpañ ca nibbânañ ca—ime dhammâ saññojanavippayuttâ.

1466. Katame dhammâ saññojanâ ceva saññojaniyâ ca?

Tâneva saññojanâni saññojanâ ceva saññojaniyâ ca.

1467. Katame dhammâ saññojaniyâ ceva no ca saññojanâ?

Ṭhapetvâ saññojane avasesaṃ akusalaṃ, tîsu bhummîsu kusalaṃ tîsu bhummîsu vipâko, tîsu bhummîsu kiriyâvyâkataṃ sabbañ ca rûpaṃ — ime dhammâ saññojaniyâ ceva no ca saññojanâ. Asaññojaniyâ dhammâ na vattabbâ saññojanâ ceva saññojaniyâ ti pi asaññojaniyâ ceva no ca saññojanâ ti pi.

1468. Katame dhammâ saññojanâ ceva saññojanasampayuttâ ca?

Yattha dve tîṇi saññojanâni ekato uppajjanti — ime dhammâ saññojanâ ceva saññojanasampayuttâ ca.

1469. Katame dhammâ saññojanasampayuttâ ceva no ca saññojanâ?

Ṭhapetvâ saññojane avasesaṃ akusalaṃ—ime dhammâ saññojanasampayuttâ ceva no ca saññojanâ.

Saññojanavippayuttâ dhammâ na vattabbâ saññojanâ ceva saññojanasampayuttâ ti pi—saññojanasampayuttâ ceva no ca saññojanâ ti pi.

1470. Katame dhammâ saññojanavippayuttâ saññojaniyâ?

Uddhaccasahagato moho tîsu bhummîsu kusalaṃ tîsu bhummîsu vipâko tîsu bhummîsu kiriyâvyâkataṃ sabbañ ca rûpaṃ—ime dhammâ saññojanavippayuttâ saññojaniyâ.

1471. Katame dhammâ saññojanavippayuttâ asaññojaniyâ?

Cattâro maggâ apariyâpannâ cattâri ca sâmaññaphalâni nibbânañ ca—ime dhammâ saññojanavippayuttâ asaññojaniyâ.

Saññojanasampayuttâ dhammâ na vattabbâ saññojanavippayuttâ saññojaniyâ ti pi saññojanavippayuttâ asaññojaniyâ ti pi.

1472. Katame dhammâ ganthâ?

Cattâro ganthâ, abhijjhâkâyagantho, vyâpâdo kâyagantho sîlabbataparâmâso kâyagantho, idaṃ saccâbhiniveso kâyagantho.

Abhijjhâkâyagantho aṭṭhasu lobhasahagatesu cittuppâdesu uppajjati, vyâpâdo kâyagantho dvîsu domanassasahagatesu cittuppâdesu uppajjati, sîlabbataparâmâso kâyagantho ca idaṃ saccâbhiniveso kâyagantho ca catûsu diṭṭhigatasampayuttesu cittuppâdesu uppajjanti—ime dhammâ ganthâ.

1473. Katame dhammâ no ganthâ?

Ṭhapetvâ ganthe avasesaṃ akusalaṃ catûsu bhummîsu kusalaṃ catûsu bhummîsu vipâko tîsu bhummîsu kiriyâvyâkataṃ sabbañ ca rûpaṃ nibbânañ ca—ime dhammâ no ganthâ.

1474. Katame dhammâ ganthaniyâ?

Tîsu bhummîsu kusalaṃ akusalaṃ tîsu bhummîsu vipâko tîsu bhummîsu kiriyâvyâkataṃ sabbañ ca rûpaṃ—ime dhammâ ganthaniyâ.

1475. Katame dhammâ aganthaniyâ?

Cattâro maggâ apariyâpannâ, cattâri ca sâmaññaphalâni nibbânañ ca—ime dhammâ aganthaniyâ.

1476. Katame dhammâ ganthasampayuttâ?

Cattâro diṭṭhigatasampayuttacittuppâdâ, cattâro diṭṭhigatavippayuttâ lobhasahagatacittuppâdâ, etth' uppannaṃ lobhaṃ ṭhapetvâ dve domanassasahagatacittuppâdâ, etth' uppannaṃ paṭighaṃ ṭhapetvâ—ime dhammâ ganthasampayuttâ.

1477. Katame dhammâ ganthavippayuttâ?

Catûsu diṭṭhigatavippayuttalobhasahagatesu cittuppâdesu uppanno lobho, dvîsu domanassasahagatesu cittuppâdesu uppannaṃ paṭighaṃ, vicikicchâsahagato cittuppâdo uddhaccasahagato cittuppâdo catûsu bhummîsu kusalaṃ catûsu bhummîsu vipâko tîsu bhummîsu kiriyâvyâkataṃ rûpañ ca nibbânañ ca—ime dhammâ ganthavippayuttâ.

1478. Katame dhammâ ganthâ ceva ganthaniyâ ca?

Te va ganthâ ganthâ ceva ganthaniyâ ca.

1479. Katame dhammâ ganthaniyâ ceva no ca ganthâ?

Ṭhapetvâ ganthe avasesaṃ akusalaṃ tîsu bhummîsu kusalaṃ tîsu bhummîsu vipâko tîsu bhummîsu kiriyâvyâkataṃ sabbañ ca rûpaṃ, ime dhammâ ganthaniyâ ceva no ca ganthâ, aganthaniyâ dhammâ na vattabbâ ganthâ ceva ganthaniyâ ti pi ganthaniyâ ceva no ca ganthâ ti pi.

1480. Katame dhammâ ganthâ ceva ganthasampayuttâ ca?

Yattha diṭṭhi ca lobho ca ekato uppajjanti—ime dhammâ ganthâ ceva ganthasampayuttâ ca.

1481. Katame dhammâ ganthasampayuttâ ceva no ca ganthâ?

Aṭṭha lobhasahagatacittuppâdâ, dve domanassasahagatacittuppâdâ, etth' uppanne ganthe ṭhapetvâ, ime dhammâ ganthasampayuttâ ceva no ca ganthâ. Ganthavippayuttâ dhammâ na vattabbâ ganthâ ceva ganthasampayuttâ ti pi—ganthasampayuttâ ceva no ca ganthâ ti pi.

1482. Katame dhammâ ganthavippayuttâ ganthaniyâ?

Catûsu diṭṭhigatavippayuttalobhasahagatesu cittuppâdesu uppanno lobho dvîsu domanassasahagatesu cittuppâdesu uppannaṃ paṭighaṃ vicikicchâsahagato cittuppâdo uddhaccasahagato cittuppâdo tîsu bhummîsu kusalaṃ tîsu bhummîsu vipâko tîsu bhummîsu kiriyâvyâkataṃ sabbañ ca rûpaṃ—ime dhammâ ganthavippayuttâ ganthaniyâ.

1483. Katame dhammâ ganthavippayuttâ aganthaniyâ?

Cattâro maggâ apariyâpannâ cattâri ca sâmaññaphalâni nibbânañ ca, ime dhammâ ganthavippayuttâ aganthaniyâ. Ganthasampayuttâ dhammâ na vattabbâ ganthavippayuttâ ganthaniyâ ti pi ganthavippayuttâ aganthaniyâ ti pi.

1484. Katame dhammâ oghâ . . . pe . . .

1485. Katame dhammâ yogâ . . . pe . . .

1486. Katame dhammâ nîvaraṇâ?

Cha nîvaraṇâni, kâmacchandanîvaraṇaṃ, vyâpâdanîvaraṇaṃ thînamiddhanîvaraṇaṃ, uddhaccakukkuccanîvaraṇaṃ, vicikicchânîvaraṇaṃ avijjânîvaraṇaṃ.

Kâmacchandanîvaraṇaṃ aṭṭhasu lobhasahagatesu cittuppâdesu uppajjati, vyâpâdanîvaraṇaṃ dvîsu domanassasahagatesu cittuppâdesu uppajjati, thînamiddhanîvaraṇaṃ sasaṅkhârike akusale uppajjati, uddhaccanîvaraṇaṃ uddhaccasahagate cittuppâde uppajjati, kukkuccanîvaraṇaṃ dvîsu domanassasahagatesu cittuppâdesu uppajjati, vicikicchânîvaraṇaṃ vicikicchâsahagate cittuppâde uppajjati, avijjânîvaraṇaṃ sabbâkusalesu uppajjati—ime dhammâ nîvaraṇâ.

1487. Katame dhammâ no nîvaraṇâ?

Ṭhapetvâ nîvaraṇe avasesaṃ akusalaṃ catûsu bhummîsu akusalaṃ catûsu bhummîsu vipâko tîsu bhummîsu kiriyâvyâkataṃ rûpañ ca nibbânañ ca—ime dhammâ no nîvaraṇâ.

1488. Katame dhammâ nîvaraniyâ?

Tîsu bhummîsu kusalaṃ akusalaṃ tîsu bhummîsu vipâko tîsu bhummîsu kiriyâvyâkataṃ sabbañ ca rûpaṃ—ime dhammâ nîvaraniyâ.

1489. Katame dhammâ anîvaraṇiyâ?

Cattâro maggâ apariyâpannâ cattâri ca sâmaññaphalâni nibbânañ ca—ime dhammâ anîvaraṇiyâ.

1490. Katame dhammâ nîvaraṇasampayuttâ?

Dvâdasa akusalacittuppâdâ—ime dhammâ nîvaraṇasampayuttâ.

1491. Katame dhammâ nîvaraṇavippayuttâ?

Catûsu bhummîsu kusalaṃ catûsu bhummîsu vipâko tîsu bhummîsu kiriyâvyâkataṃ rûpañ ca nibbânañ ca—ime dhammâ nîvaraṇavippayuttâ.

1492. Katame dhammâ nîvaraṇâ ceva nîvaraṇiyâ ca?

Tâneva nîvaraṇâni nîvaraṇâ ceva nîvaraṇiyâ ca.

1493. Katame dhammâ nîvaraṇiyâ ceva no ca nîvaraṇâ?

Ṭhapetvâ nîvaraṇe avasesaṃ akusalaṃ tîsu bhummîsu kusalaṃ tîsu bhummîsu vipâko tîsu bhummîsu kiriyâvyâkataṃ sabbañ ca rûpaṃ—ime dhammâ nîvaraṇiyâ ceva no ca nîvaraṇâ.

Anîvaraṇiyâ dhammâ na vattabbâ nîvaraṇâ ceva nîvaraṇiyâ ti pi nîvaraṇiyâ ceva no ca nîvaraṇâ ti pi.

1494. Katame dhammâ nîvaraṇâ ceva nîvaraṇasampayuttâ ca.

Yattha dve tîṇi nîvaraṇâni ekato uppajjanti—ime dhammâ nîvaraṇâ ceva nîvaraṇasampayuttâ ca.

1495. Katame dhammâ nîvaraṇasampayuttâ ceva no ca nîvaraṇâ.

Ṭhapetvâ nîvaraṇe avasesaṃ akusalaṃ, ime dhammâ nîvaraṇasampayuttâ ceva no ca nîvaraṇâ, nîvaraṇavippayuttâ dhammâ na vattabbâ nîvaraṇâ ceva nîvaraṇasampayuttâ ti pi—nîvaraṇasampayuttâ ceva no ca nîvaraṇâ ti pi.

1496. Katame dhammâ nîvaraṇavippayuttâ nîvaraṇiyâ?

Tîsu bhummîsu kusalaṃ tîsu bhummîsu vipâko tîsu bhummîsu kiriyâvyâkataṃ sabbañ ca rûpaṃ—ime dhammâ nîvaraṇavippayuttâ nîvaraṇiyâ.

1497. Katame dhammâ nîvaraṇavippayuttâ anîvaraṇiyâ?

Cattâro maggâ apariyâpannâ cattâri ca sâmaññaphalâni nibbânañ ca—ime dhammâ nîvaraṇavippayuttâ anîvaraṇiyâ.

Nîvaraṇasampayuttâ dhammâ na vattabbâ nîvaraṇavippayuttâ nîvaraṇiyâ ti pi nîvaraṇavippayuttâ anîvaraṇiyâ ti pi.

1498. Katame dhammâ parâmâsâ?

Diṭṭhiparâmâso catûsu diṭṭhigatasampayuttesu cittuppâdesu uppajjati—ime dhammâ parâmâsâ.

1499. Katame dhammâ no parâmâsâ?

Ṭhapetvâ parâmâsaṃ avasesaṃ akusalaṃ catûsu bhummîsu kusalaṃ catûsu bhummîsu vipâko tîsu bhummîsu kiriyâvyâkataṃ rûpañ ca nibbânañ ca—ime dhammâ no parâmâsâ.

1500. Katame dhammâ parâmaṭṭhâ?

Tîsu bhummîsu kusalaṃ akusalaṃ tîsu bhummîsu vipâko tîsu bhummîsu kiriyâvyâkataṃ sabbañ ca rûpaṃ—ime dhammâ parâmaṭṭhâ.

1501. Katame dhammâ aparâmaṭṭhâ?

Cattâro maggâ apariyâpannâ cattâri ca sâmaññaphalâni nibbânañ ca—ime dhammâ aparâmaṭṭhâ.

1502. Katame dhammâ parâmâsasampayuttâ?

Cattâro diṭṭhigatasampayuttacittuppâdâ, etth' uppannaṃ parâmâsaṃ ṭhapetvâ—ime dhammâ parâmâsasampayuttâ.

1503. Katame dhammâ parâmâsavippayuttâ?

Cattâro diṭṭhigatavippayuttalobhasahagatacittuppâdâ, dve domanassasahagatacittuppâdâ vicikicchâsahagato cittuppâdo uddhaccasahagato cittuppâdo catûsu bhummîsu kusalaṃ catûsu bhummîsu vipâko tîsu bhummîsu kiriyâvyâkataṃ rûpañ ca nibbânañ ca, ime dhammâ parâmâsavippayuttâ. Parâmâso na vattabbo parâmâsasampayutto ti pi parâmâsavippayutto ti pi.

1504. Katame dhammâ parâmâsâ ceva parâmaṭṭhâ ca?

So eva parâmâso parâmâso ceva parâmaṭṭho ca.

1505. Katame dhammâ parâmaṭṭhâ ceva no ca parâmâsâ?

Ṭhapetvâ parâmâsaṃ avasesaṃ akusalaṃ tîsu bhummîsu kusalaṃ tîsu bhummîsu vipâko tîsu bhummîsu kiriyâvyâkataṃ sabbañ ca rûpaṃ, ime dhammâ parâmaṭṭhâ ceva no ca parâmâsâ. Aparâmaṭṭhâ dhammâ na vattabbâ parâmâsâ ceva parâmaṭṭhâ ti pi—parâmaṭṭhâ ceva no ca parâmâsâ ti pi.

1506. Katame dhammâ parâmâsavippayuttâ parâmaṭṭhâ?

Cattâro diṭṭhigatavippayuttâ lobhasahagatacittuppâdâ dve domanassasahagatacittuppâdâ vicikicchâsahagato cittuppâdo uddhaccasahagato cittuppâdo tîsu bhummîsu kusalaṃ tîsu bhummîsu vipâko tîsu bhummîsu kiriyâvyâkataṃ sabbañ ca rûpaṃ—ime dhammâ parâmâsavippayuttâ parâmaṭṭhâ.

1507. Katame dhammâ parâmâsavippayuttâ aparâmaṭṭhâ?

Cattâro maggâ apariyâpannâ cattâri ca sâmaññaphalâni nibbânañ ca, ime dhammâ parâmâsavippayuttâ aparâmaṭṭhâ. Parâmâsâ ceva parâmâsasampayuttâ ca dhammâ na vattabbâ parâmâsavippayuttâ parâmaṭṭhâ ti pi—parâmâsavippayuttâ aparâmaṭṭhâ ti pi.

1508. Katame dhammâ sârammaṇâ?

Catûsu bhummîsu kusalaṃ akusalaṃ catûsu bhummîsu vipâko tîsu bhummîsu kiriyâvyâkataṃ—ime dhammâ sârammaṇâ.

1509. Katame dhammâ anârammaṇâ?

Rûpañ ca nibbânañ ca—ime dhammâ anârammaṇâ.

1510. Katame dhammâ cittâ?

Cakkhuviññâṇaṃ, sotaviññâṇaṃ, ghânaviññâṇaṃ, jivhâviññâṇaṃ, kâyaviññâṇaṃ, manodhâtu manoviññâṇadhâtu—ime dhammâ cittâ.

1511. Katame dhammâ no cittâ?

Vedanâkkhandho, saññâkkhandho, saṅkhârakkhandho, rûpañ ca nibbânañ ca—ime dhammâ no cittâ.

1512. Katame dhammâ cetasikâ?

Vedanâkkhandho, saññâkkhandho, saṅkhârakkhandho—ime dhammâ cetasikâ.

1513. Katame dhammâ acetasikâ?

Cittañ ca rûpañ ca nibbânañ ca—ime dhammâ acetasikâ.

1514. Katame dhammâ cittasampayuttâ?
Vedanâkkhandho, saññâkkhandho, saṅkhârakkhandho—ime dhammâ cittasampayuttâ.
1515. Katame dhammâ cittavippayuttâ?
Rûpañ ca nibbânañ ca, ime dhammâ cittavippayuttâ. Cittaṃ na vattabbaṃ cittena sampayuttan ti pi cittena vippayuttan ti pi.
1516. Katame dhammâ cittasaṃsaṭṭhâ?
Vedanâkkhandho, saññâkkhandho, saṅkhârakkhandho—ime dhammâ cittasaṃsaṭṭhâ.
1517. Katame dhammâ cittavisaṃsaṭṭhâ?
Rûpañ ca nibbânañ ca—ime dhammâ cittavisaṃsaṭṭhâ.
Cittaṃ na vattabbaṃ cittena saṃsaṭṭhan ti pi cittena visaṃsaṭṭhan ti pi.
1518. Katame dhammâ cittasamuṭṭhânâ?
Vedanâkkhandho saññâkkhandho saṅkhârakkhandho, kâyaviññatti vacîviññatti, yaṃ vâ panaññaṃ pi atthi rûpaṃ cittajaṃ cittahetukaṃ cittasamuṭṭhânaṃ rûpâyatanaṃ saddâyatanaṃ gandhâyatanaṃ rasâyatanaṃ, phoṭṭabbâyatanaṃ, âkâsadhâtu, âpodhâtu, rûpassa lahutâ, rûpassa mudutâ, rûpassa kammaññatâ, rûpassa upacayo, rûpassa santati, kabaḷinkâro âhâro—ime dhammâ cittasamuṭṭhânâ.
1519. Katame dhammâ no cittasamuṭṭhânâ?
Cittañ ca avasesañ ca rûpañ ca nibbânañ ca—ime dhammâ no cittasamuṭṭhânâ.
1520. Katame dhammâ cittasahabhuno?
Vedanâkkhandho saññâkkhandho saṅkhârakkhandho kâyaviññatti vacîviññâtti—ime dhammâ cittasahabhuno.
1521. Katame dhammâ no cittasahabhuno?
Cittañ ca avasesañ ca rûpaṃ nibbânañ ca—ime dhammâ no cittasahabhuno.
1522. Katame dhammâ cittânuparivattino?
Vedanâkkhandho, saññâkkhandho, saṅkhârakkhandho, kâyaviññatti, vacîviññatti—ime dhammâ cittânuparivattino.
1523. Katame dhammâ no cittânuparivattino?
Cittañ ca avasesañ ca rûpañ ca nibbânañ ca—ime dhammâ no cittânuparivattino.
1524. Katame dhammâ cittasaṃsaṭṭhasamuṭṭhânâ?

Vedanâkkhandho, saññâkkhandho, saṅkhârakkhandho—ime dhammâ cittasaṃsaṭṭhasamuṭṭhânâ.

1525. Katame dhammâ no cittasaṃsaṭṭhasamuṭṭhânâ?

Cittañ ca rûpañ ca nibbânañ ca—ime dhammâ no cittasaṃsaṭṭhasamuṭṭhânâ.

1526. Katame dhammâ cittasaṃsaṭṭhasamuṭṭhânasahabhuno?

Vedanâkkhandho saññâkkhandho saṅkhârakkhandho—ime dhammâ cittasaṃsaṭṭhasamuṭṭhânasahabhuno.

1527. Katame dhammâ no cittasaṃsaṭṭhasamuṭṭhânasahabhuno?

Cittañ ca rûpañ ca nibbânañ ca—ime dhammâ no cittasaṃsaṭṭhasamuṭṭhânasahabhuno.

1528. Katame dhammâ cittasaṃsaṭṭhasamuṭṭhânânuparivattino?

Vedanâkkhandho, saññâkkhandho, saṅkhârakkhandho—ime dhammâ cittasaṃsaṭṭhasamuṭṭhânânuparivattino.

1529. Katame dhammâ no cittasaṃsaṭṭhasamuṭṭhânânuparivattino?

Cittañ ca rûpañ ca nibbânañ ca—ime dhammâ no cittasaṃsaṭṭhasamuṭṭhânânuparivattino.

1530. Katame dhammâ ajjhattikâ?

Cakkhâyatanaṃ . . . pe . . . manâyatanaṃ—ime dhammâ ajjhattikâ.

1531. Katame dhammâ bâhirâ?

Rûpâyatanaṃ . . . pe . . . dhammâyatanaṃ—ime dhammâ bâhirâ.

1532. Katame dhammâ upâdâ?

Cakkhâyatanaṃ . . . pe . . . kabaḷiṅkâro âhâro—ime dhammâ upâdâ.

1533. Katame dhammâ no upâdâ?

Catûsu bhummîsu kusalaṃ akusalaṃ catûsu bhummîsu vipâko, tîsu bhummîsu kiriyâvyâkataṃ cattâro ca mahâbhûtâ nibbânañ ca—ime dhammâ no upâdâ.

1534. Katame dhammâ upâdiṇṇâ?

Tîsu bhummîsu vipâko yañ ca rûpaṃ kammassa katattâ—ime dhammâ upâdiṇṇâ.

1535. Katame dhammâ anupâdiṇṇâ?

Tîsu bhummîsu kusalaṃ akusalaṃ tîsu bhummîsu kiriyâvyâkataṃ, yañ ca rûpaṃ na kammassa katattâ, cattâro maggâ apariyâpannâ cattâri ca sâmaññaphalâni nibbânañ ca—ime dhammâ anupâdiṇṇâ.

1536. Katame dhammâ upâdânâ ?

Cattâri upâdânâni, kâmupâdânaṃ diṭṭhupâdânaṃ sîlabbatupâdânaṃ attavâdupâdânaṃ—kâmupâdânaṃ aṭṭhasu lobhasahagatesu cittuppâdesu uppajjati, diṭṭhupâdânañ ca sîlabbatupâdânañ ca attavâdupâdânañ ca catûsu diṭṭhigatasampayuttesu cittuppâdesu uppajjanti—ime dhammâ upâdânâ.

1537. Katame dhammâ no upâdânâ ?

Ṭhapetvâ upâdâne avasesaṃ akusalaṃ catûsu bhummîsu kusalaṃ catûsu bhummîsu vipâko tîsu bhummîsu kiriyâvyâkataṃ rûpañ ca nibbânañ ca—ime dhammâ no upâdânâ.

1538. Katame dhammâ upâdâniyâ ?

Tîsu bhummîsu kusalaṃ akusalaṃ tîsu bhummîsu vipâko tîsu bhummîsu kiriyâvyâkataṃ sabbañ ca rûpaṃ—ime dhammâ upâdâniyâ.

1539. Katame dhammâ anupâdâniyâ ?

Cattâro maggâ apariyâpannâ cattâri ca sâmaññaphalâni nibbânañ ca—ime dhammâ anupâdâniyâ.

1540. Katame dhammâ upâdânasampayuttâ ?

Cattâro diṭṭhigatasampayuttâ lobhasahagatacittuppâdâ, cattâro diṭṭhigatavippayuttâ lobhasahagatacittupâdâ, etth'uppannaṃ lobhaṃ ṭhapetvâ—ime dhammâ upâdânasampayuttâ.

1541. Katame dhammâ upâdânavippayuttâ ?

Catûsu diṭṭhigatavippayuttalobhasahagatesu cittuppâdesu uppanno lobho dve domanassasahagatacittuppâdâ vicikicchâsahagato cittuppâdo uddhaccasahagato cittuppâdo catûsu bhummîsu kusalaṃ catûsu bhummîsu vipâko tîsu bhummîsu kiriyâvyâkataṃ rûpañ ca nibbânañ ca—ime dhammâ upâdânavippayuttâ.

1542. Katame dhammâ upâdânâ ceva upâdâniyâ ca ?

Tâneva upâdânâni upâdânâ ceva upâdâniyâ ca.

1543. Katame dhammâ upâdâniyâ ceva no ca upâdânâ ?

Ṭhapetvâ upâdâne avasesaṃ akusalaṃ tîsu bhummîsu kusalaṃ tîsu bhummîsu vipâko tîsu bhummîsu kiriyâvyâkataṃ sabbañ ca rûpaṃ—ime dhammâ upâdâniyâ ceva no ca upâdânâ. Anupâdâniyâ dhammâ na vattabbâ upâdânâ ceva upâdâniyâ ti pi—upâdâniyâ ceva no ca upâdânâ ti pi.

1544. Katame dhammâ upâdânâ ceva upâdânasampayuttâ ca?

Yattha diṭṭhi ca lobho ca ekato uppajjanti—ime dhammâ upâdânâ ceva upâdânasampayuttâ ca.

1545. Katame dhammâ upâdânasampayuttâ ceva no ca upâdânâ?

Aṭṭha lobhasahagatacittuppâdâ—etth' uppanne upâdâne ṭhapetvâ—ime dhammâ upâdânasampayuttâ ceva no ca upâdânâ.

Upâdânavippayuttâ dhammâ na vattabbâ upâdânâ ceva upâdânasampayuttâ ti pi—upâdânasampayuttâ ceva no ca upâdânâ ti pi.

1546. Katame dhammâ upâdânavippayuttâ upâdâniyâ?

Catûsu diṭṭhigatavippayuttalobhasahagatesu cittuppâdesu uppanno lobho dve domanassasahagatâ cittuppâdâ vicikicchâsahagato cittuppâdo uddhaccasahagato cittuppâdo tîsu bhummîsu kusalaṃ tîsu bhummîsu vipâko tîsu bhummîsu kiriyâvyâkataṃ sabbañ ca rûpaṃ—ime dhammâ upâdânavippayuttâ upâdâniyâ.

1547. Katame dhammâ upâdânavippayuttâ anupâdâniyâ?

Cattâro maggâ apariyâpannâ cattâri sâmaññaphalâni nibbânañ ca—ime dhammâ upâdânavippayuttâ anupâdâniyâ. Upâdânasampayuttâ dhammâ na vattabbâ upâdânavippayuttâ upâdâniyâ ti pi—upâdânavippayuttâ anupâdâniyâ ti pi.

1548. Katame dhammâ kilesâ?

Dasa kilesavatthûni, lobho, doso, moho, mâno, diṭṭhi, vicikicchâ, thînaṃ, uddhaccaṃ, ahirikaṃ, anottappaṃ. Lobho aṭṭhasu lobhasahagatesu cittuppâdesu uppajjati, doso dvîsu domanassasahagatesu cittuppâdesu uppajjati, moho sabbâkusalesu uppajjati, mâno catûsu diṭṭhigatavippayuttalobhasahagatesu cittuppâdesu uppajjati, diṭṭhi catûsu diṭṭhigatasampayuttesu cittuppâdesu uppajjati, vicikicchâ vicikicchâsahagatesu cittuppâdesu uppajjati, thînaṃ sasaṅkhârike akusale uppajjati, uddhaccañ ca ahirikañ ca anottappañ ca sabbâkusalesu uppajjanti—ime dhammâ kilesâ.

1549. Katame dhammâ no kilesâ?

Ṭhapetvâ kilese avasesaṃ akusalaṃ catûsu bhummîsu kusalaṃ catûsu bhummîsu vipâko tîsu bhummîsu kiriyâvyâkataṃ rûpañ ca nibbânañ ca—ime dhammâ no kilesâ.

1550. Katame dhammâ saṅkilesikâ?

Tîsu bhummîsu kusalaṃ akusalaṃ tîsu bhummîsu vipâko tîsu bhummîsu kiriyâvyâkataṃ sabbañ ca rûpaṃ—ime dhammâ saṅkilesikâ.

1551. Katame dhammâ asaṅkilesikâ?

Cattâro maggâ apariyâpannâ cattâri ca sâmaññaphalâni nibbânañ ca—ime dhammâ asaṅkilesikâ.

1552. Katame dhammâ saṅkiliṭṭhâ?

Dvâdasa akusalacittuppâdâ—ime dhammâ saṅkiliṭṭhâ.

1553. Katame dhammâ asaṅkiliṭṭhâ?

Catûsu bhummîsu kusalaṃ catûsu bhummîsu vipâko tîsu bhummîsu kiriyâvyâkataṃ rûpañ ca nibbânañ ca—ime dhammâ asaṅkiliṭṭhâ.

1554. Katame dhammâ kilesasampayuttâ?

Dvâdasa akusalacittuppâdâ—ime dhammâ kilesasampayuttâ.

1555. Katame dhammâ kilesavippayuttâ?

Catûsu bhummîsu kusalaṃ catûsu bhummîsu vipâko tîsu bhummîsu kiriyâvyâkataṃ rûpañ ca nibbânañ ca — ime dhammâ kilesavippayuttâ.

1556. Katame dhammâ kilesâ ceva saṅkilesikâ ca?

Teva kilesâ kilesâ ceva saṅkilesikâ ca.

1557. Katame dhammâ saṅkilesikâ ceva no ca kilesâ?

Ṭhapetvâ kilese avasesaṃ akusalaṃ tîsu bhummîsu kusalaṃ tîsu bhummîsu vipâko tîsu bhummîsu kiriyâvyâkataṃ sabbañ ca rûpaṃ—ime dhammâ saṅkilesikâ ceva no ca kilesâ. Asaṅkilesikâ dhammâ na vattabbâ—kilesâ ceva saṅkilesikâ ti pi—saṅkilesikâ ceva no ca kilesâ ti pi.

1558. Katame dhammâ kilesâ ceva saṅkiliṭṭhâ ca?

Teva kilesâ kilesâ ceva saṅkiliṭṭhâ ca.

1559. Katame dhammâ saṅkiliṭṭhâ ceva no ca kilesâ?

Ṭhapetvâ kilese avasesaṃ akusalaṃ—ime dhammâ saṅkiliṭṭhâ ceva no ca kilesâ. Asaṅkiliṭṭhâ dhammâ na vattabbâ kilesâ ceva saṅkiliṭṭhâ ti pi, saṅkiliṭṭhâ ceva no ca kilesâ ti pi.

1560. Katame dhammâ kilesâ ceva kilesasampayuttâ ca?

Yattha dve tayo kilesâ ekato uppajjanti—ime dhammâ kilesâ ceva kilesasampayuttâ ca.

1561. Katame dhammâ kilesasampayuttâ ceva no ca kilesâ?

Ṭhapetvâ kilese avasesaṃ akusalaṃ—ime dhammâ kilesasampayuttâ ceva no ca kilesâ. Kilesavippayuttâ dhammâ na vattabbâ kilesâ ceva kilesasampayuttâ ti pi—kilesasampayuttâ ceva no ca kilesâ ti pi.

1562. Katame dhammâ kilesavippayuttâ saṅkilesikâ?

Tîsu bhummîsu kusalaṃ tîsu bhummîsu vipâko tîsu bhummîsu kiriyâvyâkataṃ sabbañ ca rûpaṃ—ime dhammâ kilesavippayuttâ saṅkilesikâ.

1563. Katame dhammâ kilesavippayuttâ asaṅkilesikâ?

Cattâro maggâ apariyâpannâ cattâri ca sâmaññaphalâni nibbânañ ca—ime dhammâ kilesavippayuttâ asaṅkilesikâ.

Kilesasampayuttâ dhammâ na vattabbâ kilesavippayuttâ saṅkilesikâ ti pi, kilesavippayuttâ asaṅkilesikâ ti pi.

1564. Katame dhammâ dassanena pahâtabbâ?

Cattâro diṭṭhigatasampayuttâ vicikicchâsahagatâ cittuppâdâ, ime dhammâ dassanena pahâtabbâ, cattâro diṭṭhigatavippayuttâ lobhasahagatâ cittuppâdâ, dve domanassasahagatâ cittuppâdâ—ime dhammâ siyâ dassanena pahâtabbâ, siyâ na dassanena pahâtabbâ.

1565. Katame dhammâ na dassanena pahâtabbâ?

Uddhaccasahagato cittuppâdo catûsu bhummîsu kusalaṃ catûsu bhummîsu vipâko tîsu bhummîsu kiriyâvyâkataṃ rûpañ ca nibbânañ ca—ime dhammâ na dassanena pahâtabbâ.

1566. Katame dhammâ bhâvanâya pahâtabbâ?

Uddhaccasahagato cittuppâdo—ime dhammâ bhâvanâya pahâtabbâ.

Cattâro diṭṭhigatavippayuttâ lobhasahagatâ cittuppâdâ, dve domanassasahagatâ cittuppâdâ—ime dhammâ siyâ bhâvanâya pahâtabbâ, siyâ na bhâvanâya pahâtabbâ.

1567. Katame dhammâ na bhâvanâya pahâtabbâ?

Cattâro diṭṭhigatasampayuttâ cittuppâdâ, vicikicchâsahagato cittuppâdo catûsu bhummîsu kusalaṃ catûsu bhummîsu vipâko tîsu bhummîsu kiriyâvyâkataṃ rûpañ ca nibbânañ ca—ime dhammâ na bhâvanâya pahâtabbâ.

1568. Katame dhammâ dassanena pahâtabbahetukâ?

Cattâro diṭṭhigatasampayuttâ cittuppâdâ vicikicchâsahagato cittuppâdo, etth' uppannaṃ mohaṃ ṭhapetvâ—ime dhammâ dassanena pahâtabbahetukâ.

Cattâro diṭṭhigatavippayuttâ lobhasahagatâ cittuppâdâ dve domanassasahagatacittuppâdâ—ime dhammâ siyâ dassanena pahâtabbahetukâ, siyâ na dassanena pahâtabbahetukâ.

1569. Katame dhammâ na dassanena pahâtabbahetukâ?

Vicikicchâsahagato moho uddhaccasahagato cittuppâdo catûsu bhummîsu kusalaṃ catûsu bhummîsu vipâko tîsu bhummîsu kiriyâvyâkataṃ rûpañ ca nibbânañ ca—ime dhammâ na dassanena pahâtabbahetukâ.

1570. Katame dhammâ bhâvanâya pahâtabbahetukâ?

Uddhaccasahagato cittuppâdo etth' uppannaṃ mohaṃ ṭhapetvâ—ime dhammâ bhâvanâya pahâtabbahetukâ. Cattâro diṭṭhigatavippayuttâ lobhasahagatacittuppâdâ dve domanassasahagatâ cittuppâdâ—ime dhammâ siyâ bhâvanâya pahâtabbahetukâ, siyâ na bhâvanâya pahâtabbahetukâ.

1571. Katame dhammâ na bhâvanâya pahâtabbahetukâ?

Cattâro diṭṭhigatasampayuttâ cittuppâdâ vicikicchâsahagato cittuppâdo uddhaccasahagato moho catûsu bhummîsu kusalaṃ catûsu bhummîsu vipâko tîsu bhummîsu kiriyâvyâkataṃ rûpañ ca nibbânañ ca—ime dhammâ na bhâvanâya pahâtabbahetukâ.

1572. Katame dhammâ savitakkâ?

Kâmâvacarakusalaṃ akusalaṃ kâmâvacarassa kusalassa vipâkato ekâdasa cittuppâdâ akusalassa vipâkato dve, kiriyato ekâdasa, rûpâvacarapaṭhamaṃ jhânaṃ kusalato ca vipâkato ca kiriyato ca, lokuttarapaṭhamaṃ jhânaṃ kusalato ca vipâkato ca, etth' uppannaṃ vitakkaṃ ṭhapetvâ—ime dhammâ savitakkâ.

1573. Katame dhammâ avitakkâ?

Dve pañca viññâṇâni rûpâvacaratikacatukkajjhânâ kusalato ca vipâkato ca kiriyato ca, cattâro âruppâ kusalato ca vipâkato ca kiriyato ca lokuttaratikacatukkajjhânâ kusalato ca vipâkato ca vitakko ca rûpañ ca nibbânañ ca—ime dhammâ avitakkâ.

1574. Katame dhammâ savicârâ?

Kâmâvacarakusalaṃ akusalaṃ kâmâvacarakusalassa vipâkato ekâdasa cittuppâdâ akusalassa vipâkato dve, kiriyato ekâdasa, rûpâvacaraekakadukajjhânâ kusalato ca vipâkato ca, kiriyato ca, lokuttaraekakadukajhânâ kusalato ca vipâkato ca, etth' uppannaṃ vicâraṃ ṭhapetvâ—ime dhammâ savicârâ.

1575. Katame dhammâ avicârâ?

Dve pañca viññâṇâni rûpâvacaratikatikajhânâ kusalato ca vipâkato ca kiriyato ca, cattâro âruppâ kusalato ca vipâkato ca kiriyato ca, lokuttaratikatikajhânâ kusalato ca vipâkato ca vicâro ca rûpañ ca nibbânañ ca—ime dhammâ avicârâ.

1576. Katame dhammâ sappîtikâ?

Kâmâvacarakusalato cattâro somanassasahagatâ cittuppâdâ akusalato cattâro, kâmâvacarakusalassa vipâkato pañca, kiriyato pañca, rûpâvacaradukatikajhânâ kusalato ca vipâkato ca kiriyato ca, lokuttaradukatikajhânâ kusalato ca vipâkato ca, etth' uppannaṃ pîtiṃ ṭhapetvâ—ime dhammâ sappîtikâ.

1577. Katame dhammâ appîtikâ?

Kâmâvacarakusalato cattâro upekkhâsahagatâ cittuppâdâ, akusalâ aṭṭha, kâmâvacarakusalassa vipâkato ekâdasa, akusalassa vipâkato satta, kiriyato cha, rûpâvacaradukadukajhânâ kusalato ca vipâkato ca kiriyato ca, cattâro âruppâ kusalato ca vipâkato ca kiriyato ca lokuttaradukadukajhânâ kusalato ca vipâkato ca, pîti ca rûpañ ca nibbânañ ca—ime dhammâ appîtikâ.

1578. Katame dhammâ pîtisahagatâ?

Kâmâvacarakusalato cattâro somanassasahagatâ cittuppâdâ, akusalato cattâro, kâmâvacarakusalassa vipâkato pañca, kiriyato pañca, rûpâvacaradukatikajhânâ kusalato ca vipâkato ca kiriyato ca, lokuttaradukatikajhânâ kusalato ca vipâkato ca, etth' uppannaṃ pîtiṃ ṭhapetvâ—ime dhammâ pîtisahagatâ.

1579. Katame dhammâ na pîtisahagatâ?

Kâmâvacarakusalato cattâro upekkhâsahagatacittuppâdâ akusalato aṭṭha kâmâvacarakusalassa vipâkato ekâdasa, akusalassa vipâkato satta, kiriyato cha, rûpâvacaradukadukajhânâ kusalato ca vipâkato ca kiriyato ca, cattâro âruppâ kusalato ca vipâkato ca kiriyato ca, lokuttaradukadukajhânâ kusalato ca vipâkato ca, pîti ca rûpañ ca nibbânañ ca—ime dhammâ na pîtisahagatâ.

1580. Katame dhammâ sukhasahagatâ?

Kâmâvacarakusalato cattâro somanassasahagatacittuppâdâ, akusalato cattâro, kâmâvacarakusalassa vipâkato cha, kiriyato pañca, rûpâvacaratikacatukkajhânâ kusalato ca vipâkato ca kiriyato ca, lokuttaratikacatukkajhânâ kusalato ca vipâkato ca, etth' uppannaṃ sukhaṃ ṭhapetvâ—ime dhammâ sukhasahagatâ.

1581. Katame dhammâ na sukhasahagatâ?

Kâmâvacarakusalato cattâro upekkhâsahagatâ cittuppâdâ, akusalato aṭṭha, kâmâvacarakusalassa vipâkato dasa, akusalassa vipâkato satta, kiriyato cha, rûpâvacaracatutthaṃ jhânaṃ kusalato ca vipâkato ca kiriyato ca, cattâro âruppâ kusalato ca vipâkato ca kiriyato ca, lokuttaracatutthaṃ jhânaṃ kusalato ca vipâkato ca, sukhañ ca rûpañ ca nibbânañ ca—ime dhammâ na sukhasahagatâ.

1582. Katame dhammâ upekkhâsahagatâ?

Kâmâvacarakusalato cattâro, upekkhâsahagatacittuppâdâ, akusalato cha, kâmâvacarakusalassa vipâkato dasa, akusalassa vipâkato cha, kiriyato cha, rûpâvacaracatutthaṃ jhânaṃ kusalato ca vipâkato ca kiriyato ca, cattâro âruppâ kusalato ca vipâkato ca kiriyato ca, lokuttaracatutthaṃ jhânaṃ kusalato ca vipâkato ca, etth' uppannaṃ upekkhaṃ ṭhapetvâ—ime dhammâ upekkhâsahagatâ.

1583. Katame dhammâ na upekkhâsahagatâ?

Kâmâvacarakusalato cattâro somanassasahagatacittuppâdâ, akusalato cha, kâmâvacarakusalassa vipâkato cha, akusalassa vipâkato eko, kiriyato pañca, rûpâvacaratikacatukkajhânâ kusalato ca vipâkato ca kiriyato ca, lokuttaratikacatukkajhânâ kusalato ca vipâkato ca upekkhâ ca rûpañ ca nibbânañ ca—ime dhammâ na upekkhâsahagatâ.

1584. Katame dhammâ kâmâvacarâ?

Kusalaṃ akusalaṃ sabbo kâmâvacarassa vipâko kâmâvacarakiriyâvyâkataṃ—sabbañ ca rûpaṃ—ime dhammâ kâmâvacarâ.

1585. Katame dhammâ na kâmâvacarâ?

Rûpâvacarâ arûpâvacarâ apariyâpannâ—ime dhammâ na kâmâvacarâ.

1586. Katame dhammâ rûpâvacarâ?

Rûpâvacaracatukkapañcakajhânâ kusalato ca vipâkato ca kiriyato ca—ime dhammâ rûpâvacarâ.

1587. Katame dhammâ na rûpâvacarâ?

Kâmâvacarâ arûpâvacarâ apariyâpannâ—ime dhammâ na rûpâvacarâ.

1588. Katame dhammâ arûpâvacarâ?

Cattâro âruppâ kusalato ca vipâkato ca kiriyato ca—ime dhammâ arûpâvacarâ.

1589. Katame dhammâ na arûpâvacarâ?

Kâmâvacarâ rûpâvacarâ apariyâpannâ—ime dhammâ na arûpâvacarâ.

1590. Katame dhammâ pariyâpannâ?

Tîsu bhummîsu kusalaṃ akusalaṃ tîsu bhummîsu vipâkato tîsu bhummîsu kiriyâvyâkataṃ sabbañ ca rûpaṃ—ime dhammâ pariyâpannâ.

1591. Katame dhammâ apariyâpannâ?

Cattâro maggâ apariyâpannâ cattâri ca sâmaññaphalâni nibbânañ ca—ime dhammâ apariyâpannâ.

1592. Katame dhammâ niyyânikâ?

Cattâro maggâ apariyâpannâ—ime dhammâ niyyânikâ.

1593. Katame dhammâ aniyyânikâ?

Tîsu bhummîsu kusalaṃ akusalaṃ catûsu bhummîsu vipâko tîsu bhummîsu kiriyâvyâkataṃ rûpañ ca nibbânañ ca—ime dhammâ aniyyânikâ.

1594. Katame dhammâ niyatâ?

Cattâro diṭṭhigatasampayuttacittuppâdâ dve domanassasahagatacittuppâdâ—ime dhammâ siyâ niyatâ, siyâ aniyatâ, cattâro maggâ apariyâpannâ—ime dhammâ niyatâ.

1595. Katame dhammâ aniyatâ?

Cattâro diṭṭhigatavippayuttalobhasahagatacittuppâdâ vicikicchâsahagato cittuppâdo uddhaccasahagato cittuppâdo tîsu bhummîsu kusalaṃ catûsu bhummîsu vipâko tîsu bhummîsu kiriyâvyâkataṃ rûpañ ca nibbânañ ca—ime dhammâ aniyatâ.

1596. Katame dhammâ sa-uttarâ?

Tîsu bhummîsu kusalaṃ akusalaṃ tîsu bhummîsu vipâko

tîsu bhummîsu kiriyâvyâkataṃ sabbañ ca rûpaṃ—ime dhammâ sa-uttarâ.

1597. Katame dhammâ anuttarâ?

Cattâro maggâ apariyâpannâ—cattâri ca jhânabalâni ca nibbânañ ca—ime dhammâ anuttarâ.

1598. Katame dhammâ saraṇâ?

Dvâdasa akusalacittuppâdâ—ime dhammâ saraṇâ.

1599. Katame dhammâ asaraṇâ?

Catûsu bhummîsu kusalaṃ catûsu bhummîsu vipâko tîsu bhummîsu kiriyâvyâkataṃ rûpañ ca nibbânañ ca—ime dhammâ asaraṇâ.

Dhammasaṅganippakaraṇî samattâ.

INDEX TO THE DHAMMA-SAṄGAṆI.

[The numbers refer to the paragraphs.]

www.ingramcontent.com/pod-product-compliance
Lightning Source LLC
Chambersburg PA
CBHW060600030726
47498CB00005B/1477
9783337396718